The yellowbacks... classics of popular fiction

The yellowjackets or yellowbacks were a great series of bestselling adventure and crime thrillers that had its origins in the mid to late 19th century following on from the 'penny dreadfuls'. They virtually began the mass market revolution of the early 20th century with a clear standard format and imprint/series livery (what would today be called branding). Hodder & Stoughton published the yellowjackets in two main series with series run dates of: 1923-1939 and later 1949-1957.

As the tagline ('where thrillers really began') on the back cover implies, the imprint and series focused on thrillers that were the bestsellers of their time. This current reissue or retro revival if you will, brings back many of these masterpieces, now classics in their own way and extends it further by including key titles from that period that were either great crime or thriller or even general commercial fiction (including sub-genres of noir, horror, gothic, romance, westerns, etc.) influences of their time. There are some perennial favourites and many rarities either lost or not easily available being revived in the current series. Writers and characters ranged from adventure heroes like Bulldog Drummond, Allan Quatermain, Richard Hannay or the Saint through thriller grandmasters Edgar Wallace and E. Phillips Oppenheim, crime and mystery maestros like Patricia Wentworth, GK Chesterton, Agatha Christie and the Detection club, to western and swashbucklers like Zane Grey, Max Brand, Captain Blood and even romance or general fiction classics like Hermina Black, Denise Robins, Marie Corelli or Stella Morton. These were books that had storytelling at their heart and always entertained.

The yellowbacks had both hardback (with varying design elements) and paperback (which built the series look) versions with the latter still carrying the imprint 'yellowjacket'. The current reissues pay tribute to both and use an amalgam of elements from both editions while retaining the complete yellow (or 'mustard-plaster') livery with the author's name in blue beveled type with a 'simulated emboss' effect and a white outer 'outline', and the book title in black. These reissues retain the distinctive size of the original mass market paperback and follow the three main category variations—the thrillers (crime, westerns, mystery, adventure) had blue lettering for the author's name, while Romance and softer general fiction had red; and other categories like humour had green.

For more detail and a full list of titles visit https://www.hachetteindia.com/home/yellowbacks

THE COMPLETE PROBLEMIST

The Complete Adventures of
Thornley Colton, Blind Detective

THE COMPLETE PROBLEMIST

Clinton H. Stagg was an American screenwriter, journalist, and author who was only 26 when he died (in 1916), but left behind a rich literary legacy in the form of a remarkable detective for mystery enthusiasts to enjoy. Stagg also was employed by a newspaper in Newark, New Jersey, wrote numerous short stories and magazine articles, and later became a screenwriter of 'photoplays' during Hollywood's early era. Stagg was killed along with his friend, writer Malcolm Strong, when the automobile he was driving overturned on a rural road in Santa Monica, California, near Los Angeles.

THE
COMPLETE
PROBLEMIST

The Complete Adventures of
Thornley Colton, Blind Detective

Clinton H. Stagg

The Complete Problemist
The short story collection *Thornley Colton, Blind Reader of Hearts* first published by Simpkin, Marshall, Hamilton, Kent & Company London in 1915. *Silver Sandals* first published by W. J. Watt & Company New York in 1916.

This Hodder Yellowback edition © Hachette India 2023
(Registered Name: Hachette Book Publishing India Pvt. Ltd.)
An Hachette UK Company www.hachetteindia.com

1

All rights reserved. No part of the publication may be reproduced, stored in a retrieval system (including but not limited to computers, disks, external drives, electronic or digital devices, e-readers, websites), or transmitted in any form or by any means (including but not limited to cyclostyling, photocopying, docutech or other reprographic reproductions, mechanical, recording, electronic, digital versions) without the prior written permission of the publisher, nor be otherwise circulated in any form of binding or cover other than that in which it is published and without a similar condition being imposed on the subsequent purchaser.

The texts in these editions in most cases have been reprinted as is, with minimal editorial changes and by and large no bowdlerizing for political correctness; though in some editions, a few words and phrases considered archaic, or those considered offensive now, along with archaic punctuation may have been modified in places to make the text more accessible to today's readers. The narratives, language, beliefs, social mores and/or cultural depictions, in these volumes are a reflection of their times and must be viewed as such. They may also contain certain cultural, racial and gender prejudices and stereotypes that may be outdated or clearly wrong then and wrong today; but their removal would be tantamount to claiming these prejudices never existed. The Publisher does not endorse or support those depictions or stereotypes; and these books have been made available for a discerning audience that will read it for entertainment value and a chronicle/record of popular fiction of past times.

Cover design by Priya Singh adapted from the original classic yellowjacket by Hodder & Stoughton.

Cover illustration by Ishan Trivedi.

Series note: Some of the books in the series (unless otherwise credited) may have cover or inside illustrations from the original yellowbacks or early editions, and while full restoration has been attempted, some images may be grainy or faded due to the condition of the original material. The end notes or bonus material or blurb details may have been sourced from the public domain or free use publications such as Wikipedia and attribution is hereby made also allowing similar free use reproduction from here. Sources requiring further specific attribution may write in and further detailing and/or corrections shall be made in subsequent printings/editions.

Reprint specifications may be subject to change including but not limited to finishes, paper, colour sections.

ISBN: 978-93-5731-126-7

Hachette Book Publishing India Pvt. Ltd.
4th & 5th Floors, Corporate Centre,
Plot No. 94, Sector 44, Gurugram – 122 003, India

Typeset in Electra LT STD 10/12.5 pt by Manipal Technologies Limited, Manipal

Printed and bound in India by Manipal Technologies Limited, Manipal

CONTENTS

THORNLEY COLTON: BLIND READER OF HEARTS

1. The Keyboard of Silence — 3
2. Unto the Third Generation — 46
3. The Money Machines — 80
4. The Flying Death — 113
5. The Thousand Facets of Fire — 148
6. The Gilded Glove — 186
7. The Ringing Goblets — 230
8. The Eye of the Seven Devils — 269

SILVER SANDALS — 309

1. The Amazing Entrance — 315
2. The Problemist — 324
3. Evidence — 332
4. The Trail — 342
5. The House of Mystery — 351
6. Another Victim — 361

7.	The Panhandler	371
8.	Question and Answer	381
9.	A Smoking Trail	394
10.	Preparations for Murder	405
11.	Clews Not for Eyes	416
12.	A Brain for a Battle Ground	431
13.	The Lure of the Feather	440
14.	A Revelation	448
15.	Face to Face	460
16.	The Cryptogram	470
17.	Confessions	482
18.	The Summons	489
19.	Assassin	497
20.	Carl's Story	507
21.	No Human Hand	516

Thornley Colton: Blind Reader of Hearts

1

The First Problem:

THE KEYBOARD OF SILENCE

I.

Not often did mere man attract attention in the famous dining room of the "Regal," but men and women alike, who were seated near the East Archway, raised their eyes to stare at the man who stood in the doorway, calmly surveying them. The smoke-glass, tortoise-shell library spectacles, which made of his eyes two great circles of dull brown, brought out the whiteness of the face strikingly. The nose, with its delicately sensitive nostrils, was thin and straight; the lips, now curved in a smile, somehow gave one the impression that, released by the mind, they would suddenly spring back to their accustomed thin, straight line. For a smile seemed out of place on that pale, masterful face, with its lean, cleft chin. The snow-white hair of silky fineness that curled away from the part to show the pink scalp underneath contrasted sharply with the sober black of the faultless dinner-coat that fell in just the proper folds from the broad shoulders and deep chest.

The eyes of the girl at the sixth table seemed to be held, fascinated. The elder woman, who was with her, toyed with her salad and conformed to convention by stealing covert glances at the man in the archway, and the square-chinned, clean-looking young man who made the third of the party stared openly, unashamed; but his eyes held not the other diners' rude questioning, nor yet the girl's frank fascination.

"You are staring, Rhoda," rebuked the elder woman mildly.

The girl turned her eyes with a little sigh. "What wonderful character there is in his face!" she murmured.

"He *is* a wonderful character," asserted the man, his face lighting up boyishly, his tone one of admiration.

"You know him?" Both asked it in a breath, eyes eager.

"Yes. He is Thornley Colton, man about town, club member, musician, whose recreation is the solving of problems that baffle other men. It was he who found the murderer of President Parkins of the uptown National, and, when the crash came, secured me my position in the Berkley Trust."

"A detective?" The elder woman asked it the girl's eyes were again on Colton.

"No." The man shook his head. "He jokingly calls himself a problemist, and accepts only those cases that he thinks will prove interesting, for the solving of them is merely his recreation. He takes no fees. The man with him is his secretary, Sydney Thames, whose name is pronounced like that of the river. He, too, is a remarkably handsome man, but he is never noticed when with Thornley Colton, except as his coal-black hair and eyes, and red cheeks, form a striking contrast to Colton."

"I had not even noticed him," confessed the elder woman, as she glanced for the first time at the slim young man of twenty-five or six, who stood at Colton's side, eyes apparently taking in every detail of the big dining room. Then she remembered her duty as mentor. "You *must* not stare so rudely, Rhoda!" she chided.

"I don't think Mr Colton minds the stare," the man said quietly. "He has been totally blind since birth, though many people refuse to believe it."

"Blind!" They both breathed it, in their voices the tender sympathy all women feel for the misfortunes of others.

"He is coming," warned the elder woman unnecessarily.

They had seen the head-waiter apparently apologize to Colton, and step aside. The secretary had whispered a few words, and Thornley Colton, his slim stick held lightly and idly in his fingers, started down the aisle between the rows of tables, shoulders swung back, chin up, followed by Sydney Thames. The woman and the girl watched his approach with parted lips, in their eyes mother fear for his safety as he hurried toward them, stepping aside at exactly the proper moment to avoid a hurrying waiter, walking around the very much overdressed, stout woman whose chair projected a foot over the unmarked aisle line. As he neared their table, they saw the thin lips frame a smile of friendly greeting.

"How do you do, Mr Norris?" His voice, rich, of wonderful musical timbre, seemed to thrill the girl with its kindliness and strength, as he stepped around her chair to shake hands with her escort. "Sydney saw you while we were waiting for our table."

"Will you meet Miss Richmond?" asked Norris, when he had answered the greeting in kind. Colton turned instantly to face the girl, his slim white hand, with its long, tapering fingers, outstretched.

"It is a concession we of the darkness ask of everyone," he apologized.

Their hands met, the girl felt the warm grip, and her sensitive wrist seemed to feel a touch, light as the touch of wind-blown thistle-down, but it was gone instantly, and she knew it was but the telepathic thrill of the meeting palms. She murmured a commonplace, and bit her lips in vexation, because it was a commonplace. The man before her seemed to call for more.

"Your singing is wonderful, Miss Richmond," he declared enthusiastically. "Sydney and I have had orchestra seats three nights this week. You know, to me music must give the combined pleasures of painting, sculpture, architecture, and other beautiful things the average person doesn't even appreciate."

Her eyes expressed their pity, but her lips said only: "My mother, Mr Colton." They shook hands across the table, Mrs Richmond with a heartiness that was not part of the artificial code New York has fixed, he with a few words that brought a flush of pleasure to her faded cheeks.

"Why didn't Mr Thames stay?" asked Norris curiously. "He hurried on as though he thought we were plague victims."

"He usually does," smiled Colton. "He has a very curious fear. I'll tell you about it some time."

"Why don't you drop into the bank and see me some day? You haven't been in my tomb-like office for months. Miss Richmond and her mother saw me at work for a few minutes this afternoon. It compares very favourably with the dressing-rooms given to opera-singers, they say."

"I should say so!" laughed the girl. "If you can compare Persian rugs and mahogany with our cracked walls, and box-propped dressing-tables, and plugged gas-jets!"

"Men always do take the best," conceded Colton smilingly. Then he addressed Norris directly. "How is Simpson attending to business nowadays?"

"He has been away for a week. He came in this afternoon to amaze us with the news that he had just been married. He didn't have much to say about his wife, however, except that he was going to turn over a new leaf."

"That's news!" whistled Colton. "He never struck me as the marrying kind."

"Nor anyone else," laughed Norris, with a tender, significant glance at the girl across the table.

"I'll have to look him up and congratulate him. Till we meet again, then." And with a pleasant nod of parting to each of them, a touch of a chair leg with his slim stick, Colton hurried down the aisle to the small table in the far corner, where Sydney Thames was giving his order to the waiter. The serving-man responded to a friendly nod from Colton, closed his order tablet, and hurried away. Thornley took a cigarette from his case, scratched a match on the bronze box, and leaned comfortably back in his chair.

"Some time, Sydney, your terrible fear of beautiful women is going to get me into a very embarrassing position." He said it half seriously, half smilingly. "Instead of seventeen steps, it was but sixteen and a short half. If it hadn't been for Norris's habit of nervously tapping his glass with his fingertips, my outstretched hand would have gone back of his neck."

"I thought I had figured it exactly!" There was earnest contrition in the tone; the sombre, black eyes showed the pain of the mistake.

"It is forgotten," dismissed Colton. Then: "But you should have stopped, Sydney. Miss Richmond's personality is as remarkable as her singing, and her mother is so proud and happy she forgets to be embarrassed at the difference between Keokuk and the Regal. Norris is lucky, for she loves him, and he—" The smiling lips needed no finishing words.

"But she is already commanding two hundred dollars a week at the very beginning of her career, and Norris cannot be earning more than five thousand a year," protested Thames.

"You poor boy!" smiled Colton. "You'll never know women; that susceptible heart of yours, which drives you away like a scared sheep whenever a beautiful woman approaches, will never be good for anything but pumping blood."

"Thorn, don't I know my weakness!" The tone was indescribably bitter. "I must keep away, though I'm starving for the society of good women. To meet one would be to fall in love, hopelessly, helplessly. I'd forget that I was a thing of shame, a brat picked up on the banks of the river that gave me the only name I know."

Colton was instantly serious. "Starvation seems a peculiar cure for hunger," he mused. "But we have argued that so many times—" Again the thin, expressive lips finished the sentence.

Then came the waiter with a club sandwich for Thames and Colton's invariable after-theatre supper that was always ready when he came, and which he never needed to order; two slices of graham bread covered with rich, red beef-blood gravy, and a bottle of mineral water. Colton's slim cane, hollow, and light as a feather, the slightest touch of which sent its warning to his supersensitive fingertips, rested between his knees as he ate.

Sydney Thames nibbled his sandwich absentmindedly, eyes roving around the dining room, now stopping at a gaudily-dressed dowager, now at an overpainted lady who smiled her fixed smile at the bull-necked man at her table, now at the circle-eyed girl who stabbed the cherry from her empty cocktail glass with a curved tine of her oyster fork but always coming back to the fresh, wholesomely beautiful face of Rhoda Richmond. Then the sombre eyes would light up; for a beautiful face, to Sydney Thames, was more intoxicating than wine, and, to his highly sensitive nature, more dangerous.

Colton pushed his plate aside as the other's eyes once more started their round of the dining room.

"The gods give gaudiness in recompense for the eye-sparkle they have taken, and the wrinkles they have given," Thornley Colton murmured quietly. "One must come to a New York restaurant to realize the true pathos of beauty." Colton's mood had been curiously serious since those few words at Norris's table.

Thames did not answer, for no answer was needed. His wandering eyes had rested on a table to the left.

"One often wonders," continued Colton, in that same musing, low-pitched voice, "why a stout woman, like that one two tables to our left, for instance, will suffer the tortures of her hereafter for the sake of drinking high balls in a tight, purple gown."

Sydney had turned his eyes to stare at Colton, as he always did when the man who had picked him up as a bundle of baby-clothes on the banks of the Thames, twenty-five years before, made an observation of this kind. Many such had he heard, but never did they fail to startle him.

"How, in Heaven's name, did you know what I was doing, or that she was dressed in purple?" he demanded.

"You should keep both feet flat on the floor if you want to keep your staring a secret," laughed Colton quietly. "You forget that crossed knees make your suspended foot tell my cane each time you turn your head ever so slightly. See that my fingers are not on my stick when you covertly watch the women you fear to meet."

"But the purple gown?" demanded Sydney, repressing the inclination to uncross his knees, and flushing at the amused smile the involuntary first motion of the foot had brought to the lips of Colton.

"All stout women who breathe asthmatically wear purple," declared Colton emphatically. "It is the only unfailing rule of femininity. And to one who has practised the locating of sounds that come to doubly sharp ears the breathing part was easy. There is no one at the next table on the left, you'll observe. Now you can resume your overt watching of Miss Richmond; see"—he laid both hands on the white table-cloth before him—"I won't look."

The head-waiter stopped at the table.

"Mr Simpson would like to have you come to his table, Mr Colton. He wants you to meet his wife."

"His wife!" put in Thames quickly.

"She is, sir." It was said with a positiveness there was no gainsaying.

"Where is Mr Simpson?" asked Colton. "We had not seen him."

"In the east wing, sir, where the palms are."

"We will go to him immediately."

"I'll tell him, sir." His beckoning finger brought the waiter who had served them with the check.

Sydney Thames spoke. "Someone of his cheap actress friends has roped him at last," he said scornfully. "He's a pretty specimen of man to be first vice-president of the conservative Berkley Trust Company."

"I'll wager you're wrong," declared Colton quietly, as he handed the waiter a two-dollar bill from his fold. "If it were one of the women for whom he has been buying wine suppers for the past two years, she wouldn't be 'where the palms are,' nor would the waiter be so positive of the marriage relation."

"I'm not going," protested Thames quickly.

"Surely, Sydney, you are not afraid a married woman will kidnap you?" smiled Colton, as he took the stick between his fingers and prepared to rise. "How many?"

Sydney, who had turned half around in his chair to gaze toward the entrance to the east wing, faced him. "I'll go," he said shortly; another hasty glance, and he rose with Colton. "Thirty-seven straight, eighteen left, nine right. We will stop at the door of the east wing. I can't see it."

"There are no pretty women to disturb the distance judgment you have been so many years acquiring?" queried Colton mildly.

Without answering, Thames turned on his heel, and made his way rapidly between the tables toward the east wing. Colton laughed silently, picked up his change, and hurried after, his perfectly trained brain counting the steps automatically, his thoughts busy elsewhere. He was thinking of Simpson, who had gained such an unenviable reputation as a spender along the gay White Way during the past two years.

Simpson had always interested him, student of human nature that he was, as the one man who had never lived up to the impression Colton's unerring instinct had told him was the right one the first time they had met. The problemist had expected things of Simpson, and Simpson had done nothing but idle as much time as possible in the position as first vice-president of one of the most conservative banks in the city, and spend money on women.

Colton stopped for an instant beside Thames in the archway, apparently gazing idly at the crowd of men and women at the palm-shaded tables.

"Two left, nineteen straight, half in," directed Thames, stepping aside to follow.

The heavy-lidded, thickset man, with the faint lines of blue vein traceries in his cheeks, rose to meet them.

"This is a pleasure, Mr Colton," he exclaimed, in heavy-voiced heartiness. "You are the one man I wanted to see; though I hardly believed it would be my luck to catch you this night of all nights. You knew the pace I was going, and I want you to meet the little girl I went back to the old town to marry. We've been friends since we were tots. Thank God, I waked up in time to know what a good woman means! When next you see us it will be in our own home. One moment, please"—his voice sank to an almost reverent whisper—"my wife is deaf and dumb, Mr Colton."

Thames had heard; had seen, with curiously mixed feelings, the little woman with the small, boyish face around which the tendrils of brown hair curled from under the close-fitting toque, and had appraised the slim, quietly dressed figure, the half smile as she stared inquiringly at them. The girl seemed but a child, but he saw that her face was heavily daubed with powder and rouge, as though its application had neither been taught nor practised. Until those last explaining words he had stood back with a halfpitying light in his eyes, for he knew Simpson's reputation with women. But at the quietly spoken sentence he had undergone an instant change of feeling, such as only highly-strung, hypersensitive men like him are capable of, toward the man who had gone away from his women of wine to marry a simple country girl who could neither speak nor hear.

Simpson's fingers had been moving rapidly; he bowed toward Thornley Colton. The girl smiled, and put out her small hand, the movement throwing back from her wrist the filmy lace of the long sleeve. For a moment they clasped hands; then the girl's fingers worked again.

Simpson laughed. "She does not believe you are blind, Mr Colton; she says you have eyes like everyone else."

Thornley Colton smiled. "If you tell her that I've got to wear these large-lensed, smoked glasses to prevent the light giving me a headache you will probably never convince her," he observed, as he refused the chair the waiter had drawn up.

Sydney Thames acknowledged his introduction with a bow and the usual meaningless words, but his eyes were soft and tender as a woman's as they met those of the girl in the instant's glance she gave him before the lashes were lowered. A woman's face never failed to stir him.

"Won't you sit down?" pleaded Simpson. "It will probably be the last time you will ever find me in one of these gilded palaces. A man who has been my kind of a fool *can* appreciate his own fireside, and Gertie, who was all aflutter to visit one of the famous Broadway restaurants, recognized in ten minutes the crass artificiality it took me years to discover." He was holding her hand openly and unashamed as he said it.

Thornley Colton shook his head. "It is past my time for going home, and you know my habits. A glass of Célestin's at one-fifteen, the beauties of the Moonlight Sonata on my piano for fifteen minutes, and then to bed. If I may visit you at your home, Mrs Simpson?" his outstretched hand met that of the girl. "Ah, you read the lips? A wonderful accomplishment to us who have never had eyes." His lips framed a smile of pleasure; he turned to Thames. "The same, Sydney?" he asked.

The secretary's eyes travelled up the aisle. "The man nine steps up, is gesticulating quite freely."

"Lots of room." Colton's slim stick touched a chair-leg, he bowed, and hurried away, the hearty goodnight of Simpson following. Thornley Colton never needed any direction for going back over the same route, for his mind, trained to the figures of steps, neither hesitated nor made mistakes in following them backward. He stepped aside to avoid the swinging arm of the loud-voiced man who was punctuating his liquor-born blatancy with violent gestures, and paused at the archway of the main dining room for Thames.

"Is Norris still at his table?" he asked.

"It is empty."

"Um!" Colton's high forehead wrinkled a frown, his slim stick tapped his leg. "Time enough tomorrow," he announced finally, and started through the maze of tables towards the entrance.

They received their hats and overcoats and left the big hotel to enter the long, black car that awaited them at the north entrance at one o'clock each morning. They were well on their way to the big, old-fashioned brownstone house where Thornley Colton had been born, before the silence was broken. Then Sydney Thames spoke:

"There must be a lot of latent goodness in a man who could take a woman like that to love, and cherish, and protect," he said slowly.

"You mean Miss Richmond?" The darkness concealed the whimsical smile on Colton's lips.

"No!" The negative was short. "Norris will marry Miss Richmond just because she is beautiful and accomplished; because his man's vanity will be tickled to exhibit her before men as his possession. I mean Simpson, who took a simple country girl whom God had handicapped, just because he loved her. That means something."

"But, Sydney"—Colton's thin fingers rested lightly on the other's sleeve; there was just the faintest trace of laughter in the words—"don't you think she was a bit too heavily rouged?"

He felt the highly-strung man jump under his hand.

"Good heavens, Thorn!" Sydney burst out. "Sometimes I wonder if you *are* blind!"

"God gives fingers to the sightless, Sydney," Colton's voice was quietly serious. "In the darkness the keyboard of my piano gives me the soul secrets of dead men gone to dust. In the lights of a Broadway restaurant the keyboard of silence gives me the secrets of living hearts. And they cannot lie."

"What do you mean? What have I missed?" Thames asked the questions eagerly, tensely, for he knew the moods of this man who had been the only father he had ever known; he understood that something of grave portent had given its significance to the man who could not see, while he with five perfect senses, had seen nothing, suspected nothing.

Colton pulled his crystalless watch from his pocket, and touched it with a fingertip. "One-thirty; we are fifteen minutes late." He put his hand on the door catch as the big machine slowed up before his home. And it was not until they were ascending the broad brownstone steps that he answered the question.

"You have missed the first act of what promises to be a very remarkable crime, Sydney," he said quietly.

II.

Colton scowled when the red jack failed to turn up, but the mouth corners smiled when the ace of diamonds slid between the sensitive fingers to take its place in the top row of Mr Canfield's famous game. The deuce followed, the red jack immediately after; then the problemist looked up toward the doorway of the library.

"Well, Shrimp?" he smiled.

"They's the theatrical papers yuh wanted." The red-headed, freckle-faced boy with the slightly-twisted nose came forward with an armful of big magazines and newspapers, the front pages of which were adorned with full-length portraits of stage celebrities. Before he quite reached the table he stopped short, eyes crackling their excitement. "Snakes! You're gettin' it, Mr Colton! They's the four of hearts and the five of spades. Don't stop now."

Colton laughed. "All right, Shrimp. Do you want to do a little detective work for me?"

"Do I?" The eyes danced with eagerness. "Ain't I been studyin'? Nineteen steps from the kitchen t' the first chair in the dinin' room. Six—"

"I know," assured Colton hastily. "But you take those papers to your room and write down the names of all the vaudeville actors—men, you know—who have quit the stage within the last two months; where they have gone, and why, if possible."

"Snakes!" The boy's face showed his disappointment. "Nick Carter never had t' do that."

"He never had to count steps for a blind man, either," smiled Thornley Colton. "You do that and there'll probably be some real detective work—shadowing, disguises, and the rest of it."

There was no answer. The boy had taken a firmer grip on the papers, and was already out of the room.

The four of hearts and the five of spades had been placed when Sydney, face broad in a smile, entered.

"What's the matter with 'The Fee'?" he demanded. "He ran past me as though he were on his way to a fire." Thames always referred to Shrimp as The Fee, because the red-headed, freckle-faced boy had become part of the Colton household after a particularly baffling case, at the conclusion of which the joy of capturing the murderer had been overshadowed by the blind man's sorrow for the broken-nosed boy who had jumped between him and a vicious blackjack. And Shrimp had been his fee for the case. As the boy's mother was the murdered one, and his father the murderer, there had been no one to object.

Before Colton had a chance to voice his laughing explanation, the tinkling telephone-bell on the desk demanded attention. At the first words the thin lips tautened to a straight line, the voice became pistol-like in its crispness, the muscles under the pale skin of the face became tense.

The problemist had a problem.

"When? Last night. All right. Still that two-wire burglar connection on the safe? Never mind further details. We'll be right down."

As his hand dropped the receiver on the hook a finger pressed the garage bell button that would bring his machine instantly at any hour of the day or night.

"Get your hat and coat, Sydney," he ordered curtly. "We're going to the Berkley Trust Company. Somebody's gotten away with half a million in negotiable bonds'."

"Half a million?" gasped Thames.

"So they said. Didn't wait for details." Colton grabbed his private phone-book of often-needed numbers, and ran his fingers down the backs of the thin pages on which the names and numbers had been heavily written with a hard pencil. As Sydney hurried out he heard the curt voice give a number over the phone. And it was fully five minutes before Colton took his place in the car.

In the smooth-running machine, with the wooden-faced Irish chauffeur at the wheel, Sydney Thames voiced the question:

"Last night, you said?"

"Yes, the second act came sooner than I expected," broke in Thornley Colton. "I underrated the man." And the expression on the pale face augured ill for someone.

The funereal atmosphere of the Berkley Trust Company could be *felt* as they entered. In the office of the third secretary, the white-haired president of the institution stopped his nervous pacing to mumble a greeting in tremulous accents. First Vice-President Simpson's grave face broke into a smile of welcome. Norris raised his bowed head from his hands, and came forward joyfully, pleadingly. The red-faced man who had been standing over him kept a step away, but always near enough to touch him with an outstretched hand.

"My God, Mr Colton! They think I'm guilty!" There was agony unutterable in Norris's voice.

"Ridiculous!" snapped Simpson, his heavy-lidded eyes half closed. "Mr Colton will soon put this detective right."

The problemist nodded a grim acquiescence, and took the outstretched hand of Norris. "I know better," he said kindly. The red-faced man gave voice to a grunt, and Colton instantly swung around to face him. "So you've cleaned it up already, Jamison?" he asked mildly.

"Nobody said he was guilty," growled the red-faced central office man significantly. "I just been questionin' him, that's all."

"And accusing him with every question!" snapped Colton. "Like the rest of your kind, you haven't the intelligence to suit your methods to the crime. Every crime must be worked according to the old Mulberry Street formula. That didn't change with the modern Centre Street building."

"But we know enough not to make any cracks till we get all the information," sneered Jamison. "We don't hand out that know-it-all stuff till we know *something!*"

"True," smiled the problemist with his lips, but there was no smile in his tone. Two hectic spots glowed in his cheeks, the muscles worked under the pale skin. "What do you think, President Montrose?" The white-haired president halted his pacing once more, and stroked his Vandyke.

"The first stain on the unsullied escutcheon of the Berkley Trust Company," he groaned. "In all of the half century—"

"I know all that!" broke in Colton impatiently. "What happened? Why are the police here instead of the protective-agency men?"

"I was excited," moaned the president. "It was the first thing that occurred to me. In all the half century of—"

"I guess we were all excited," interjected Simpson, his lips twisted in a wry smile. "I know I was up in the air. I came down here, happier than I ever was before in my life, to arrange for a short vacation to take a wedding trip. Now this comes up. When I came to my senses I telephoned for you, because I want the robbery solved as soon as possible. The little girl has banked so much on our little time."

"Too bad," murmured Colton. "Tell me the story, Norris." Before he could get an answer he turned to Thames, who always stayed discreetly in the background when Colton was on a case. "See that no one goes near that safe, Sydney; I may want to examine it."

"Kind of dropped that bluff of bein' blind, ain't you?" sneered Jamison, who was one of the hundreds of persons in New York who would not believe that Thornley Colton was really sightless. And the problemist did not deign to explain that once he had been in a room and touched its objects with his cane his trained brain held the correct mental picture forever.

"The bonds were fifty in number, ten thousand each, government fours, negotiable anywhere," began Norris, licking his dry lips to make the words come easier. "They were the bulk of the Stillson estate, on which I was working. We are settling it up. As third secretary my work is with trusts and estates. It was necessary to have everything finished by tonight. I worked late yesterday, so late that the bonds and other papers could not go into the time-locked vaults, and I had to be at work on them this morning before the clock-release time."

"Is it customary to keep valuable bonds in the small safe in this office?" interrupted Colton.

"It is not unusual. The safe is practically as strong as the big vaults, and only lacks the clocks. This office is really part of the vault itself, the walls are windowless, and of four-foot concrete reinforced by interlocked steel rails. The sheet-steel door, the only entrance to the room, opens into a small cage that is occupied during the day by Thompson, head of the trust and estate routine clerks, and at night by one of our two watchmen. The watchmen never leave it, because it often happens that valuable papers and bonds are left out of the big vaults so that we can work on them before nine o'clock, the hour set on the vault's clocks. To get to the steel door of this office one would have to enter the outer and inner steel cages, the steel-barred door of the small ante-room, besides setting off burglar-alarms on all, disturbing the watchman, and ringing the bells in the burglar-alarm department of the Bankers' Protective Association, of which we are a member. And there was no sign of a break, the safe was opened with the combination that only Mr Montrose and Mr Simpson and myself know."

"The watchman could get to this door without any trouble?"

"Both have been in the employ of the bank for forty years. They are absolutely above suspicion. Both are illiterate. Even though they could enter the office, they could not open the safe, and even if they did that they would not know enough to steal all the notes I had made regarding the estate, or the bonds that have so utterly vanished. They have been sent for, however, and should be here any minute."

"Were the notes you made stolen, too?"

"All of them."

"Any of the other employees of the bank know the bonds were in this safe?"

"Several, probably."

"All have access to this room, at any time?"

"Only Thomas, the head of the T. and E. clerks."

"Trustworthy?"

"He grew up with the bank."

"You require other clerical assistance at times?"

"Thomas takes the papers from this office, and the clerks get them from him outside. All must be returned to me before closing time. I carefully checked over everyone last night before any of them went away."

"Anyone in here yesterday while you were at work on the papers; anyone who could have seen the bonds?"

For a moment there was no answer; then it came, almost in a whisper: "Miss Richmond and her mother were in for a few moments—"

"And I was, too, by Jove!" The interruption came from Simpson. "And I remember asking you how you were getting on with the Stillson estate. I just finished my part when I went away. I guess I really held them up longer than I should."

"Has Miss Richmond been sent for?" Colton paid absolutely no heed to the first vice-president.

A grunting laugh from the detective. "She sure has, bo. After I found out this guy's stage lady had been in here with a tailor's suitbox after closin' time, my partner went right up to her hotel."

"By Heaven! You—" Norris rose to his feet, face black with fury. Colton's hand on his shoulder forced him back into the chair. Sydney Thames, to whom all women were angels, clenched his fists.

"Is that true?" There was a new tone to Colton's voice.

Norris seemed to recognize the menace. "She isn't guilty, I tell you! She can't be. She's—Listen, man! She's my wife!"

"Your wife!" They all echoed it. The detective with laughing triumph; President Montrose with horror; Sydney Thames in dazed surprise; Simpson with a half-suppressed, significant gasp.

"We were married two days ago; but it was to be a secret until the end of her season."

"How long ago was she sent for?"

The detective answered: "My sidekick ought to be back now. We was on the job there, all right, all right."

Voices outside came to their ears—the harsh, commanding voice of a man, the half-subdued sobbing of a woman. The door was thrown open, and Rhoda Richmond, opera singer, and wife of Norris, was half pushed, half carried into the small room.

"Good work, Jim!" grinned Jamison. "Did she put up a howl at the hotel?"

"Hotel?" growled the other scornfully. "No hotel for hers. I had a lot of luck or I'd never've got her. She was boardin' a boat fer South America that sails in an hour."

"It's a lie!" Norris screamed the words as he leaped toward the man whose rough hand was clenched around the slim arm of the girl. Sydney Thames, obeying Colton's silent signal, forced him back, his own hands trembling. The problemist without a word untwisted the central office man's fingers, and gently seated the girl in a chair at the long table.

"Who the—" The blustering detective was cut off suddenly.

"We've had enough of your strong-arm methods!" Colton's voice was hard as flint. "We'll get some facts now." The hardness vanished; in its place came gentle sympathy. "When did you get the message, Miss Richmond?" he asked.

The voice seemed to have the reassuring effect of a pat on the head of a hurt child. With an effort the girl controlled her sobs, and answered as though it had been the most natural question in the world: "An hour ago—over the telephone—I thought I recognized How—Mr Norris's voice. He wanted me to meet him at the Buenos Aires dock. He had to go to South America secretly, he said, and I must tell no one. I hurried to the dock without even telling mother. I waited for an hour, but he did not come; then I decided to go aboard and see if he had missed me and gone to his state room. This man—said Howard had—robbed—I thought—" She broke down again.

"I guess that's bad!" grinned Jamison gloatingly. "In another hour there'd of been a clean getaway."

"The whereabouts of the bonds doesn't seem to worry you!" snapped Colton sarcastically.

"The stuff ain't never far away from the guy that took it," growled Jamison. "When you get through your know-it-all talk we'll sweat that out, all right."

"Did you have a tailor's suit-box with you yesterday?" asked Colton abruptly of the girl.

"Yes. I called to see if my new walking-suit was finished. It was all ready to be sent to my home, but when I saw the poor, tired little boy who would have to carry it I took it myself. The tailor is just around the corner, on the avenue; that is why mother and I dropped in here."

"Of course," nodded Colton, his teeth snapping together as he seemed to sense the derisive grins on the faces of the detectives. "Did you recognize the bonds among the papers on which Mr Norris was working?"

"Oh, he showed them to me, and we laughingly spoke of what we could do with half a million dollars. Then, when he took mother out to show her around the bank—I was too tired—I picked one up and read it."

"Rhoda!" cried Norris. He could realize the present significance of yesterday's innocent words.

"That'll be about all from you!" scowled Jamison. "If this guy wants to third-degree her, and cinch it for us, let him."

"An' if he don't cinch it this will." The other detective pulled a paper from his pocket. "Here's the *Buenos Aires*'s passenger list, and here's Mr and Mrs Frank Morris, who booked yesterday, added in pencil. Morris for Norris! Slick enough to be almost good."

Everyone in the room but Colton seemed to be shocked into a state of stupefied rigidity.

"Now—" Jamison said that word in the tone one uses to introduce some especially clever thing, and accompanied it with a sarcastic glance toward the blind man, who tapped his trouser leg with his cane in thoughtful silence. "If you ain't got no objection we'll take these two to headquarters, and get a line on where they got the stuff cached." He paused suggestively, mockingly.

The permission came, with a deprecatory wave of the cane, and a smile that was menacing in its very suaveness. "Go as far as you like, Jamison. Don't be too gentle with them."

"My God, Mr Colton! You don't think—" The words choked in Norris's throat.

"I think you had better go." The problemist's tone was peculiarly quiet. "Jamison and his partner have the reputation of being the two wealthiest detectives in the department. No one knows how they got it, but they've enough to give you and your wife a twenty-thousand-dollar nest egg each on a false-arrest suit. Isn't that worth a few hours' discomfort? I can prove your innocence when they have gone. They worry me here."

Simpson whistled, and turned it into a jerky laugh. "Gad, that was clever!" he exclaimed.

"Oh, is that so?" The detectives chorused it, in their voices sarcasm—and just a tinge of something else, too. Colton knew the one thing that would make them stop and think.

"Are you going?" snapped Colton.

"We'll see them two watchmen first," growled Jamison.

"Good!" The problemist laughed at the sudden change. "I think you'll have quite a crowd to take down to headquarters if you hang around long enough. Before I started I telephoned to the burglar-alarm telegraph department of the protective agency to get hold of the men who answered the alarm that rang in from this office early this morning."

"What burglar-alarm?" snarled Jamison. He whirled on the white-haired president. "Why didn't you tell us there was an alarm rung in?"

"Really"—the Vandyke received several severe yanks—"I didn't know it. We do not receive the clock reports and emergency alarm sheets until about noon. Er—Mr Colton, might I ask where you got this information?"

"I telephoned for it," answered Colton curtly. "If these policemen hadn't been so anxious to make arrests, and the robbery hadn't been too obvious for their thick heads, they might have investigated. But they are just headquarters men; the obvious arrest is the one they always make. Feet make good central office men, not heads. Ah, here are the men, all together."

They came in slowly, two old men first; one with straggly, white whiskers that concealed the weak chin and grew up around the faded, watery eyes; the other's parchment-like face a network of wrinkles. Honesty shone from every part of them; the weak, helpless honesty of their kind.

As Colton took each man's hand with a murmured greeting he felt it tremble in his. The aged watchmen knew that something had happened; something that concerned them and the bank they had guarded so long. The two men from the burglar-alarm company nodded to the two detectives, and their eyes narrowed as they shook the hand of the problemist. Both knew him, and both knew this had been no common summons. Thornley Colton never bothered with common things. Sydney Thames had pulled two chairs up to the table, and the old men sat down. Colton lighted a cigarette thoughtfully, then he spoke:

"This morning, gentlemen, that small safe was robbed of five hundred thousand dollars' worth of government bonds." His slim cane, apparently held idly between his fingers, touching the chair of the man nearest him, felt the watchman's involuntary jump. The others saw the old jaws drop, saw the watchmen glance helplessly at each other, their trembling fingers picking at worn trouser-knees. Colton heard the gasp of the two protective-agency men.

"I knowed it!" quavered the white-whiskered watchman. "I knowed something'd happen when Mary took sick."

"Who's Mary?" queried Colton interestedly. The others crowded forward.

"She's Mary, my wife. She's been scrubbin' the bank floors fer thirty years, an' nobody ever said a word against her." He glanced at them all with pathetic belligerence. "She even picked up the pins she found on the floor, and put 'em in a box on the cashier's desk."

"That's true," laughed Simpson. "It's the joke of the bank."

"And she was taken sick last night?" Thornley asked gently.

"A week ago." The other watchman answered, while the first brushed his dry lips with his work-gnarled hand. "Mrs Bowden, she's got the consumption, and lives across the hall from us and—"

"Where do you live?" interrupted Colton.

"Sixteen hundred Third Avenue. I been boardin' with him an' his wife fer thirty years. Mrs Bowden's been doin' Mary's work. We didn't say nothin' about Mary bein' sick, 'cause she might get laid off. An' Mrs Bowden's awful poor." His voice was a childish, quavering treble.

"Last night, after Mrs Bowden had gained your confidence, you allowed her to scrub Mr Norris's office?" encouraged Colton.

Norris started. "I'd forgotten that!" he ejaculated. A motion from Colton commanded silence.

"Yes," trembled Mary's husband. "John opened the door, an' started to punch his clocks, an' I stayed in the ante-room, like I all us do, to watch Mrs Bowden. Then somehow the door got closed. An' Mrs Bowden got scared there in the dark. She screamed an' cried till it was real sad. But John had the key, an' he had to punch his clocks on the minute, er Mr Montrose'd be mad when he got the records next day. An' I couldn't leave my place in the ante-room. So I encouraged her, sayin' that

John'ld be back in half an hour an' let her out. She quieted after a while, an' didn't scream so loud, but I could hear her stumblin' around. Then John had to run to the front door to see who was knockin', an' he let these gentlemen in. The burglar-alarm on the safe had rung, they said, an'—"

"Never mind that part," halted Colton. "One of these men will tell me that part."

"We was called at seven-eighteen," began the taller of the two Bankers' Protective Agency men, "by the safe bell. The safe is connected with one wire, and under the carpet, running all around the safe, is a thin steel plate connected with the other. A man standing near enough to touch the safe forms a connection that rings our gong. In the daytime, of course, we pull the switch. We got here, and found the door locked, an' we could hear moaning. This guy"—he indicated the one with the straggly beard—"unlocked the door, and behind it was a woman, her skirt pinned up around her, laying on the floor, frightened to death. When she seen us she jumped to her feet with a little screech, and muttered something about thanking God."

"You were satisfied that she was frightened?"

"Sure! But we didn't let it go at that. We snapped on every light, and examined the room. Nothing had been touched. We frisked the woman, gentle, of course, but enough to know that she hadn't a thing on her. We finally got it out of her that she'd fell against the safe trying to find the door in the dark. She didn't know enough to snap on a light."

"She couldn't have had fifty ten-thousand-dollar bonds on her person?"

Both men laughed. "Gee, Mr Colton," laughed the short one. "She was so frail you could almost see through her. She couldn't hardly have hid a cigarette paper without making a hump."

"What happened then?"

"She picked up the pail she had—it was full of dirty scrub water, and the yellow bar of soap was bobbing around in it—and John, here, took her into the cashier's cage. We hung around, talking, an' watching her scrub and weep into the pail until it was time fer her to go home. She was so all in I put her on a car."

"Um!" Colton puffed his cigarette in silence; then he turned to Jamison and his partner. "Looks mighty suspicious, doesn't it, Jamison? I'd advise you to arrest these four men and get the woman. Five hundred thousand is likely to make any honest man a crook."

"Some kidder, ain't you?" sneered Jamison. "I know Pete, there, an' if he says it was all right, it was. We got the guilty parties first off, an' we'll get the stuff, too!"

The smile went from Colton's lips instantly.

"You arrest them, and we'll start false-arrest proceedings in an hour!" he warned. "You leave Norris and Miss Richmond here! Anyone but a fool detective would know they weren't guilty."

As he said the last word he jumped toward the safe, ran his highly sensitive fingers over the steel surface, knelt down, brushed the heavy carpet lightly with his fingertips. The two hectic spots on his cheeks glowed redder; the nostrils quivered like those of a hound on the scent, even the eyes, behind the great, round, smoked glass lenses seemed to shine. Silently they watched him. He lowered his face almost to the floor, the cane was laid down, and his hand gave the carpet a resounding slap. They crowded closer. One hand went to his hip-pocket, a handkerchief brushed the hardwood floor under the safe, between the edge of the rug and the wall. He rose, touched the burning end of his cigarette ever so lightly to the linen handkerchief that was now covered with a fine yellow powder.

"See it! See it!" he snapped. "You couldn't before because it was the same colour as the hardwood floor."

"It's wood-polish powder, used for cleaning the varnished wood," sneered Jamison, stepping forward. "We don't want—"

"Smell it, then!" The blind man thrust the handkerchief under the central office man's nose. "Do you recognize it now? It's sulphur. Ordinary powdered sulphur. The thing that would tell any man how the bonds were taken out of the office. Go to a drug store and find out what sulphur is used for."

He thrust the handkerchief into his coat-pocket, brushed off the knees of his trousers, and picked up his stick.

"Come, Sydney," he said quietly. "We've finished."

Before the astonished men could make move or protest he hurried from the office, automatically counting the steps. He jumped into the waiting machine, Sydney Thames followed, and as Simpson and Jamison ran to the door, he snapped "Home, John!" to the Irish chauffeur, and the machine sped away.

Around the first corner he leaned forward. "Sixteen hundred Third Avenue—quick!" he ordered.

"You don't think those two old watchmen guilty?" asked Thames, in surprise.

"No!" The tone was almost brusque. "Merely an unimportant detail I want to clear up."

"You certainly left that crowd in the office at sixes and sevens." Thames laughed at the recollection.

"I intended to. That's why I went into all those details. I wanted to leave everyone up in the air, especially the two detectives. They'll begin to think now. And they won't let anyone get away before we have made this call. I want to think, now."

Sydney Thames knew the moods of the blind man; knew he could expect no explanations, or even replies, until Colton was ready to give them; so they sped in silence to the upper East Side.

Soon they were on upper Third Avenue. Overhead the clanking "L" trains pounded their din into the two men's ears. The streets were crowded with their heterogeneous mass of men, women, and children. The rusty fire-escapes staggered drunkenly across the dirty, red tenement-fronts.

The look of tense concentration left Colton's face. "A far cry from the luxurious, staidly conservative Berkley Trust, eh, Sydney?" He smiled, leaning back in the cushions, puffing his cigarette as though untroubled by a serious thought; his eyes, behind the smoked library glasses, seemingly fixed on the narrow strip of blue sky overhead.

The car came to a stop.

"Is this it, John?"

"Th' saloon on th' corner is fifteen-ninety-four, sorr."

"Lead the way, Sydney." Again the twin red spots glowed in Colton's white cheeks, he jumped to the sidewalk, his slim stick tapping his trouser-leg eagerly.

Thames stepped along beside him, close enough for his coat sleeve to touch that of Thornley Colton. And with that slight touch to guide him the problemist followed; for Thornley Colton was a trifle sensitive over his blindness, and nothing made him angrier than an attempt to lead him. Sydney found the entrance, between a second-hand-clothing store and a pawnbroker's shop. As he stopped to make sure of the weather-dimmed, painted number the clothing-store proprietor popped out, rubbing his dirty palms together, and coughing apologetically.

"On which floor does Mrs Bowden live?" asked Colton sharply.

"Der fourt', front. You maybe like some clo'es?"

"Is her husband watchman at the Berkley Trust Company?"

"He's dead. You means Mrs Schneider, across the hall. Her man watches. Dere boarder also. You like a elegant skirt for der poor vimens. Such a—"

Thames opened the door, and they left the clothing man in the middle of his sentence. In the dark hall Sydney made his way cautiously. Colton, cane lightly touching the heels of the man ahead, followed unhesitatingly. The journey up the rickety steps was torture to Colton. To his doubly acute ears and sense of smell the odours, the squalling of half-starved babies were terrible, but his brain automatically counted the steps so that he would have not the slightest difficulty in finding his way back to the automobile.

"Schneider first," whispered Colton, as Thames stopped in the fourth-floor hall.

In the dim light Thames saw that they were standing between two doors.

"I don't know which it is, but I'll take a chance." He knocked on the one at his left.

The one behind immediately popped open. "Mrs Bowden's gone away," shrilly proclaimed a tottery old woman, bobbing her head.

"Could you give us her address?" asked Colton, doffing his hat and bowing politely.

"Laws!" The woman's fluttering hand set her spectacles farther askew, in a hurried effort to straighten them. "She's gone to spend the day with her sister in Brooklyn. Them boys of mine pestered her till she's near sick. And she bein' so delicat' an' out late last night washin' dishes at the church sociable."

"Are you Mrs Schneider?"

The darkness hid the smile the reference to the "boys" had caused.

"I'm her. Be you the Associated Charities? Mis' Bowden said she'd asked fer help. She came here two weeks ago, after losin' her job in the department store on account of her weak lungs. She had to take in odd day's work. Asthma, she calls it, but I ain't fooled on consumption. Two of my—"

"And you helped her by pretending you were ill?" interrupted Colton.

"I was sick fer two days." The woman hastened to set him right. "But she was so powerful glad to earn a few cents fer her asthma snuff, not that it is asthma. My sister's brother—"

"Of course she left the key with you until her return?" Colton left the sister's brother in mid-air.

"Yes; but—" There was just a shade of suspicion in the voice.

"As agents of the Associated Charities we must make an examination of the room, to prove that she is really in need of financial help," assured Colton gravely. "We can wait until she returns, of course, but this is the last application day for this month."

"Laws! I'll get it right away." She darted back into the room with surprising agility, and returned a moment later with an iron key tied to a broken-tined fork.

"There's no need of bothering you, Mrs Schneider," declared Colton earnestly, as Thames took the key.

"Laws! Soon's I get these pataters on I'll be right with you. My boys had to go down to their bank—" The rest of the sentence was lost, for as she turned to the stove Colton had jerked Thames from the door.

"Quick!" he whispered. In an instant the key was in the lock, and the door was open. Colton pushed his way in, his cane touching the scarred, tumbled bed and the one broken chair. "Where's the trunk?" he queried, cane feeling around.

"No sign of one, nor a case."

"Damn!" snapped Colton. "The bureau drawers! See what your eyes find."

Thames had the top drawer open almost before he had finished. He whistled in amazement. "Nothing but an empty pill-box, with no druggist's label, three quills with the feathers cut off, and a tuft of cotton. What the—"

"Those are what I want! Put them in your pocket!" The tenseness went out of his voice; it became politely ingratiating, for his keen ears had heard the woman coming. "There is no doubt that Mrs Bowden is in need of our assistance, Mrs Schneider," he said smoothly. "Er—is that some of her asthma snuff in the top bureau-drawer?

She ran past him, and bobbed her head over the open drawer. "Yes, sir; there is a little sprinkled over the bottom. You got mighty powerful eyes, mister." She nodded vigorously at the blind man. He had not been within five feet of the bureau. "She's dead set on it bein' asthma, but my sister's brother was—"

"Do you know anything against Mrs Bowden's character?" Again the sister's brother was left dangling.

"Laws, no. She's that frightened she's afraid of her own shadow. I'm the on'y one in the house she took to, an' even me she kept at a distance." Another vigorous nod. "An' so modest Laws, she wouldn't ha' come into the halls half dressed, like some of the other women does. An' clean! Laws! She lugged all her clo'es over to her sister's in Brooklyn today, to be washed in their Thirtieth Century Washer; not that I—"

"Ah, thank you, but we have four other calls to make." And, bowing gravely, Colton backed from the room, and hurried toward the head of the stairs, followed by Thames and the shrill-voiced encomiums of the woman.

They took their places in the car silently, and it was not until they had left the noise of the avenue for the quiet of the side-streets that Colton spoke.

"What do you think of it, Sydney?" asked the problemist gravely.

"I'm completely at sea," confessed Thames, with a shake of his head. "It looked awfully bad for Norris when we arrived at the bank. Then that South American boat business. How did you know she had received a message?" he asked suddenly.

"Didn't. But I knew Miss Richmond, or rather Mrs Norris. Common sense would have told anyone that could be the only reason for her presence at the dock. Jamison and his kind don't use common sense. They use the old policeman's formula; arrest the logical suspect and then convict him. With persons like Norris and his wife, each half doubting, half suspecting, either would have confessed to save the other. It was an ideal arrest, from the police viewpoint."

"Then you seemed to involve the two watchmen and the two men from the protective agency. Jamison will have a whole waggonload."

"He'll take no one," answered Colton. "I know him. He'll spend the rest of the day trying to find out what I was talking about. Then he'll telephone to headquarters, and they'll send men to find out who sent the message to Miss Richmond, and to locate Mrs Bowden."

"There's the woman, Thorn!" Thames spoke nervously, excitedly. "She took a dress-suit case, presumably full of clothes, to her 'sister' in Brooklyn. The bonds—"

"You forget that the agency men saw her come out of the room empty-handed; they even searched her, and one put her on the trolley." Colton smiled curiously. "This was wholly a man's job, Sydney. The work of the rarest kind of criminal; a detailist. This crime, while perfectly simple, is, I think, unique in its attention to details. That's why it interests me."

"Simple!" ejaculated Thames. "Simple? You speak as though you knew the guilty man."

"I do. Perfectly. I knew last night."

"Last night? The—"

The robbery was committed early today. Exactly."

"Why—why—" Helpless amazement was in Sydney Thames's voice. "Why don't you arrest him? Why all this—"

"Simply because I would be laughed at. I haven't the proof—yet. The usual criminal stumbles on his opportunity, and seizes it in a haphazard fashion. The rare criminal, the detailist, attends to every detail; works his problem out with the shrewdness and forethought of a captain of finance, plans a coup months ahead. Then he creates the opportunity. You must understand, Sydney, that half a million is worth a few months' work."

"But suspicion points only to Miss Richmond, Norris, and this Mrs Bowden."

"Suspicion points to everyone," corrected the problemist. "Doesn't it seem suspicious that President Montrose should call in the police when he would naturally take all steps in his power to avoid publicity? Doesn't the very eagerness of the central office men to arrest Norris and his wife seem queer? Isn't there a bit of suspicion in Simpson's confession that he delayed the Stillson estate until Norris was compelled to work after hours on them? Doesn't Miss Richmond's story that she was carrying her suit home to save work for a delivery boy seem highly improbable and unwomanlike? How about Norris telling his wife of the bonds? An unbusinesslike proceeding in the case of half a million's worth of negotiable bonds, truly. Didn't the two men who answered the early-morning alarm seem a bit too sure that nothing was wrong? Weren't the two watchmen in the conspiracy to pretend that Mrs Schneider was ill, so that a woman whom they had known but two weeks could gain access to the bank? Doesn't the finding of an unlabelled pill-box, three featherless quills, and surgeon's cotton in the otherwise empty room of a woman dying with tuberculosis strike you as strange? As a further detail in this crime of details, doesn't my confession that I knew the criminal before the crime was committed seem a trifle like guilty knowledge?" He smiled broadly.

"Great Scott, Thorn!" Sydney Thames's voice trailed off in a whistle of pure bewilderment. "You've involved everyone."

"Oh, no." Colton snapped his cigarette into the street. "Not everyone. An unfortunate vaudeville actor will appear on the scene as soon as I get the list on which I left Shrimp busily at work."

III.

In the absolute darkness of the shade-drawn library Thornley Colton softly whistled a syncopated version of Mendelssohn's "Spring Song" as his deft fingers filled an empty goose-quill with a fine white powder from an improvised paper funnel. He plugged the open end with a small wad of cotton; then his wonderfully sharp ears caught the rustle of the double portiéres.

"Oh, Sydney," he called, "have you heard anything from the bank this morning?"

Thames entered the darkness unhesitatingly, for his constant practice of judging distance and figuring steps for Colton had made him almost as much at home in the darkness as the blind man himself.

"No," he answered shortly. Then, with the frank criticism of long friendship: "It's a crime, Thorn, for you to be idle while that girl is being dogged, and harassed, and—"

"I thought she sang remarkably well last night for a person under such a strain," interrupted Colton musingly.

"It was wonderful, wonderful!" Sydney Thames spoke with the breathless enthusiasm a beautiful girl always aroused in his woman-hungry heart.

"Here, here!" protested the problemist laughingly. "Remember that she is another man's wife!"

"Great heavens, Thorn! How can you laugh?" cried Thames resentfully. "Think of those two dogs of detectives, questioning, bulldozing, shadowing! Why, they didn't let Miss Richmond get away from the bank until late in the afternoon, then Jamison insisted on going with her. His partner hung around the bank till it closed—"

"Trying to discover the use of powdered sulphur," smiled Colton. "I thought he would. Anyone but a central office man would have gone to a drug store, as I suggested."

"Two other headquarters men hauled that frail old Mrs Schneider and the two watchmen to police headquarters, and put them through the third degree."

"And a half-dozen more were on the trail of Mrs Bowden, while we were enjoying the opera and an alleged cabaret show afterward, for which this dark room is the penalty. Too much light yesterday gave me a frightful headache."

The sudden ringing of the telephone in the darkness made Thames jump, and Colton's cane, which was never away from him, felt the movement.

"Answer it, Sydney," he requested.

The secretary's hands had not the sureness of his feet, and he had to fumble a moment. When he had given the customary salutation and had listened a moment he gasped:

"It's Simpson, Thorn. His wife is missing! He wants you." He extended the phone in the darkness, but Thornley Colton made no move to take it.

"Tell him I'll be down to the bank in an hour or so. I'll see him then." Colton spoke idly.

Sydney repeated the message. Followed a silence. "He's frantic, Thorn!" Thames's voice shook with excitement. "When he got home last night she was gone. The doorman at his apartment house said that she had gone out in the morning, for a short walk, he supposed. Simpson was so excited about the robbery he did not telephone her during the day, as he had promised. He spent half the night searching, and tried a dozen times to get you. She is deaf and dumb, Thorn. Think of it! Deaf and dumb, and lost!" It only needed a woman in trouble to shatter Sydney Thames's nerves.

"Tell him that I'm trying to figure out that robbery. Tell him also that I never let one case interfere with another. I'm not a detective. There's nothing interesting about a missing woman. Hundreds of 'em every day. I find my pleasure in interesting problems, not in police work." Colton's voice was sharp, curt, utterly devoid of sympathy.

Sydney knew that tone, as he knew the man who used it. He repeated part of the message, added gentle-voiced apologies, and hung up the receiver with a sigh.

"That was heartless, Thorn! Think of that woman, deaf and dumb, lost in this—"

"Sometimes, Sydney, that susceptible heart of yours becomes wearisome." Colton spoke a bit sharply. "A moment ago you were protesting because I was here instead of running around after the man who stole the half-million in bonds from the Berkley Trust Company."

"But Mrs Norris is not helpless—" And for fifteen minutes he argued, while Colton smiled imperturbably in the darkness, and filled two other quills with the white powder, and plugged the ends with tufts of cotton.

Suddenly Thames stopped, for Colton had picked up the telephone and was giving a number.

"Hello, Shrimp!" he called, when the connection had been made. "Everything all right? Fine business. Three hours, eh? Good! Be on time, and obey orders. Goodbye!"

"Where's The Fee?" demanded Sydney. "I haven't seen him since yesterday."

"Emulating the example of his worthy hero, Nick Carter. Shrimp is a real detective now." Colton returned the crystalless watch to his pocket, picked up the three quills, and arose. "Come on, Sydney. We'll walk over to the bank."

"Walk?" ejaculated Thames, for he knew the blind man's aversion to walking when he could ride. "Where's the machine?"

"John and the machine are helping Shrimp in his detective work," explained Colton. And in the twenty minutes' walk to the Berkley Trust Company he absolutely refused to answer questions, but kept up a continuous conversation on trivial topics, that was maddening to the nervous secretary.

The effect of the previous day's badgering, questioning, and threats of the central office men could be seen as one entered the bank. The aged cashier's hands trembled as he tried to count a sheaf of new bills. Book-keepers in the rear wrote figures and erased them. Thompson, head of the trust and estate clerks, in his little ante-room cage, was in a pitiable state of nerves. The typewriter's chair by President Montrose's desk was vacant, because the lady stenographer was at home under the care of a doctor. The fifty years of staid, conservative calm that had characterized the Berkley Trust Company during its long and useful life had been hit by a five-hundred-thousand-dollar storm.

The group in the vault-like office of Second Secretary Norris was little better. President Montrose could hardly control his trembling hand to stroke his Vandyke; Norris's eyes showed the sleeplessness of the night before; Miss Richmond was calm with the calmness that means coming nervous collapse; her mother was crying softly Simpson seemed positively haggard, and Sydney Thames murmured words of sympathy for the man who had two troubles. Jamison and the other central office man could not make their sneers wholly sceptical. The protective-agency men were plainly puzzled.

"I see you are all on hand." There was no smile in Colton's voice now, or on his lips; he was deadly calm, coldly earnest. "You didn't think it necessary to send for the two watchmen?"

"We got men watchin' them," put in the surly Jamison.

"Thanks!" came curtly from Colton. "Sit down at this table, all of you. I want to tell you a story."

"We didn't come to hear—"

Simpson interrupted the detective: "For God's sake, make it short, Mr Colton! My wife—"

"I'll look into that later." Colton's cane assured him that the chairs were around the long table, and his fingertips felt the face of his watch in his pocket.

"Will you?" Simpson's voice was almost sarcastically eager, his heavy-lidded eyes narrowed. Thames could not blame the man's natural resentment for Colton's offhandedness.

Silently they took seats. Colton sat facing the closed door; across the table was Simpson and Norris. Miss Richmond and her mother were at the end. The four detectives were on either side of the problemist.

"This is a story of a criminal who was born a criminal; who couldn't be honest if he tried," began Colton, in his quietly expressive voice. One hand lay idly on the table before him, the other on his knees, fingers holding the slim, hollow cane. "He wasn't just born crooked. He started petty thieving before he was out of short trousers. He was the rare criminal that works years as an honest man to pave the way for criminality. He had brains. He could have been a wonderful success as an honest man. But he couldn't be straight. The criminal instinct was there. He was waiting for the proper time. But the coarser side of his nature refused to be held in leash. He needed money. And with the inherent craft of his kind he began to plan the robbery of the Berkley Trust Company. It wasn't so hard, because, being an old, conservative institution, in which men had grown gray, the personal side entered as it cannot in the modern, up-to-date institutions where men come and go. Instead of elaborate safeguards the simple protection of proven honesty entered largely into the protection of the bank's valuables. And where there is simple honesty there is always vulnerability.

"This criminal had found the vulnerable spot years before the robbery was actually planned; when the time came for its consummation luck came to his aid, as it often does." He paused. On the outside door came a knock, so faint that only his wonderfully sharp ears heard it. "There was no possibility of suspicion attaching itself to him, for he had planned an elaborate programme to foist suspicion on others. And this robbery was but one of a series, for the method his shrewd brain had devised was capable of endless combinations. In a few years the Berkley Trust losses would have mounted to millions!"

His fist crashed down on the heavy table. The door opened. Between the sober-faced Shrimp and the expressionless Irish chauffeur was a sunken-eyed, tottering creature, unshaven—

"*There's your wife, Simpson!*" In the silence Colton's voice came like the crack of a pistol.

"My God, Thorn, it's a *man!*" In Sydney Thames's tone was agony that the sensitive blind man whom he loved could have made such a mistake.

"Yes, a man! *Sit still, Simpson!*" With a movement as quick as light itself Colton's fingers had dropped the slim cane that had given its warning, and held a blue-steel automatic. "Or rather what was once a man." His tone rang with deadly menace. "Charlie de Roque, vaudeville actor, the youngest and best female impersonator on the stage; Mrs Bowden, the consumptive who played so well on the sympathies of the three simple-minded souls at sixteen-hundred Third Avenue; Mrs Simpson, the deaf-and-dumb little girl who was going to make Simpson lead a better life."

"You lie!" The shambling shadow of a man screamed it as he tried to jerk away from the chauffeur. "They told me they were going to take me to a sanatorium. I don't know what you're talking about. They've kept me—" His whole body racked with sobs.

"Would you tell the truth for these?" The automatic did not waver a fraction of an inch as Colton's unoccupied hand threw down on the table three cotton-plugged quills.

"Merciful God! *Yes!*" With insane strength he broke away from the big Irishman and darted to the table. His twitching fingers snatched a quill, pulled the cotton from the end, threw his head back—

"Enough of these damn' theatrics!" Simpson snarled it viciously, but he did not move. "By Heaven, Colton, you can't railroad me to save Norris and his wife with the fool ravings of a cocaine snuffler!" His face was purple, the veins in his forehead seemed ready to burst. "Mrs Bowden!" He scoffed. "How did she get the bonds? Where are they? Find 'em!" he laughed triumphantly at Colton across the table, and the two central office men who now stood over him.

"Here yuh are, Mr Colton." It was Shrimp, staggering under the weight of a big bucket of dirty water. He set it down beside the problemist's chair.

"The bonds are here, Simpson!" Colton's hand plunged into the water, and came up with a dripping, shiny black object. "There's the first package, in an all-rubber ice bag!"

"You devil!" Simpson's rage made his voice a scream.

"Take your prisoner, policemen." Colton could not refrain from adding that last scornful word to the two detectives who had not seen until a blind man had shown them.

IV.

"Of course, De Roque, who was merely the drug-crazed tool of the real criminal, would have told where the bonds were," declared Thornley Colton, when they were once more in the shade-drawn library of the big, old-fashioned house. "But Simpson would have had time to be on his guard. The finding of the bonds, as I did, before he had time to recover his nerve, drew from him those last betraying words. The police can establish his connection with the telephone message to Miss Richmond, the booking of the two passages under the name of Morris, and the place where he and De Roque met while the fake Mrs Bowden was supposed to be out at day's work. Those details were not even worth bothering with, for me, because the keyboard of silence told me the guilty persons before the robbery was committed."

"I am as much at sea as ever," confessed Sydney Thames.

"In the Regal we saw the first act. Simpson, with the daredevilishness that characterizes the type, introduced me to the accomplice. It was not wholly dare-devilishness, however, for it was to prepare the getaway. He wanted, before the time came for her to disappear, to arouse your sympathy and my interest in the deaf-and-dumb woman, whom he had married to accomplish his reformation. After a fruitless search he would need a long vacation in Europe, with the bonds, of course, to recover from the shock. There could be no suspicion attached to him. No sane man would look for a deaf-and-dumb wife in the person of a vaudeville actor dying of tuberculosis and cocaine who had drug dreams of money coming his way. Once Simpson had gotten out of the country, De Roque could have raved and stormed, even confessed, and his confession would have been accepted as nothing but cocaine dementia. Simpson never intended to play fair; it isn't his nature. From the first time I ever shook his hand I have known him to be a born criminal, for I can read hands as the physiognomist reads faces. And I have the advantage, because men like Simpson, with the aid of their strong wills, can mask their emotions behind eyes and faces so that no man can read their minds. But they have never given a thought to their hands."

"Do you mean to say you could tell what Simpson was planning by shaking his hands there in the Regal?" demanded Thames incredulously.

"Not quite," protested Colton laughingly. "But you know how I shake hands. My long index finger always rests lightly on the keyboard of silence — the wrist. With a touch like mine, so light that I can read handwriting by feeling the ridges left on the blank side of the paper, not one person in a million could feel it. I think Miss Richmond did, when I shook hands with her, because I felt a responsive thrill. In the case of Simpson his heart was working like a steam-engine, though his face and eyes were a mask that neither you nor any man with eyes could read; my fingertip on his pulse told me that he was labouring under some strong excitement. When I shook hands with his 'wife,' I discovered why."

"Why?" echoed Thames blankly.

"Because the wife was a man, and a drug-fiend."

"Your hand told you that, and my eyes were deceived!"

"My knowledge of anatomy told me the man part. Don't you know that over the muscles of a woman is a layer of fat that gives the beautiful feminine curves? The man's muscles play directly under the skin, and the curves of female impersonators are due to flabby muscles, and not the feminine fat layer. Besides the cocaine pulse of the 'wife,' my fingertip immediately felt the play of the muscles as the hand gripped mine. Knowing Simpson, the impersonation could mean nothing else but a contemplated crime. I further proved it by getting her to put out her hand before she could have had any knowledge, by signs, of my intention to say goodbye. Remember my reference to lip-reading? Simpson was taking no chance of letting her talk. The cocaine gave her the brightness of eye, and the heavily-daubed rouge I knew would have to be there to convince you that she was really a country girl who didn't know the use of cosmetics, and also to cover any trace of man's beard and cocaine pastiness of skin. It would have deceived anyone who had eyes, where an artistic make-up would immediately have aroused suspicion. Simpson was a wonderful detailist.

"Commonsense told me that Simpson could not risk working with an amateur. Therefore I set Shrimp to looking up actors who had been forced to leave the stage on account of ill health within the last two months. The whole thing must have been rehearsed many times, for the detailist would overlook no detail. In Shrimp's list was De Roque. A few telephone inquiries proved that he was really a cocaine fiend of the worst kind, also that he had returned, yesterday morning, from a sanitarium, no better, to his old boarding-house. It was Simpson's scheme to let him do that, for it eliminated him. As soon as I found out that Simpson would not risk visiting him, Shrimp and John got him on the pretence that they were from Simpson. Cocaine snufflers as far gone as he need the drug every hour. For three hours before the time arranged for Shrimp to bring him to the bank De Roque hadn't had a pinch; he was insane with craving. The visit to Third Avenue, and the finding of the quills which cocaine snufflers use to hide the stuff on their bodies and conceal it in their palms so that no one can see them snuff it gave me the things I needed to make him talk. You saw how they worked."

"But the detectives who helped him out of the room? How did you ever figure the possibility of the bonds being in the scrub water?"

"The protective-agency men told me. Their eyes saw what my lack of eyes understood. The yellow bar of soap bobbing on top of the water, I think one of them expressed it. An instant's intelligent thought would tell anyone that the yellow soap used for scrubbing floors never floats. The finding of the powdered sulphur showed me the clever ice-bag trick, for powdered sulphur is always used by druggists to keep the thin rubber from sticking together when the bags are in the boxes. Of course, De Roque carried it with him every night waiting for his opportunity, and in pulling it out the powder scattered on the carpet. The natural thing was to brush it under the safe, where my handkerchief found it after my slapping hand had raised the scattered grains he had missed.

"The ringing of the burglar-alarm was a masterstroke. It was the link necessary to establish the innocence of Mrs Bowden. Simpson, of course, knew of the connection. De Roque probably removed his shoes and stood on the rubber ice-bags while he opened the safe and took out the bonds and papers Simpson had so accurately described. Then, when they had all been packed and the safe closed, a natural stumbling against the safe would bring the protective-agency men to swear that nothing could have been taken from the room. When the time came to leave the building, the pail, still full of water, was carefully put in a far, dark corner of the cellar closet, where the scrub pails and mops are kept. It would have been safe until Simpson was ready to take the bonds away. That was why I worked to keep Jamison and his partner around the bank; I didn't want Simpson to have any opportunity to get the loot out.

"Of course, it was he who suggested the calling of the regular police to the flustered President Montrose. Because, while he was sure that he could deceive me, he wasn't taking any foolish risks. He wanted the central office men to muddle the thing as much as possible, and he was shrewd enough not to overdo the casting of suspicion on Norris and his wife; the way he put in a word here and there, and looks, of course, was quite in keeping with the other details. This morning, I think, he had begun to realize what I was doing, but there was nothing he could do but count on a bluff. I took him off his guard."

For several minutes the two men smoked in silence.

"But why didn't you warn someone instead of letting the robbery go on?" Sydney asked finally.

Colton's expressive lips framed a wry smile.

"You will insist on showing the fly in the ointment, Sydney. The truth is, I was caught napping. But I guess it's just as well I didn't. Jails are built for the protection of society, and Simpson is the one man in a thousand against whom society needs protection."

2

The Second Problem:

UNTO THE THIRD GENERATION

I.

For weeks the five-hundred-thousand-dollar reception of the Jimmy Raeltons had been heralded as the greatest event of the New York social season. The news columns had been filled with accounts of the costly preparations, the wonderful gowns, the millions in jewels that would grace the first appearance of the Raeltons in society since the Carlton-Browne reception of thirteen months before. The newspapers had retold, lest their readers should forget, the tragic story of the mysterious suicide of Mrs Jimmy Raelton's sister, Mrs Donald Wreye, on the night following the Carlton-Browne affair. The consequent retirement of the Raeltons had been reviewed; the report of the ill health of Mrs Raelton had been substantiated; and the two months' cruise on the palatial Raelton yacht was said to have brought back the bloom to faded cheeks. And tonight the Jimmy Raeltons were formally to reenter New York's social scheme of things; again to fill the niche that had been vacant for thirteen months.

The small army of police herded the curious crowd from the sidewalk as a black limousine drove up silently and came to a stop at the canopied curb. The door swung open, and men and women, who would stand patiently for hours to catch a mere glimpse of the notables they worshipped from afar, saw the first man alight. The electric globe under the awning brought out the striking whiteness of the face and hair; the contrast of the great blue circles of the smoked-glass, tortoise-rimmed library spectacles that rested lightly on the thin nose; the broad shoulders, and deep chest under the Inverness. The first arrival rapped the pavement lightly with the slim stick he carried as the apple-cheeked, black-haired man who accompanied him spoke a word to the driver and stepped beside him.

A policeman touched his hat. "Early, ain't you, Mr Colton?" he greeted the other.

"These things never interest me, Peters," returned Thornley Colton, in his deep, musical voice. "A quiet chat with Jimmy and my goddaughter before the crowd arrives, then home and quiet."

He started briskly toward the wide steps, the red-cheeked man so close that his coat-sleeve touched that of the other. The policeman turned to his partner.

"A great guy, Tom," he observed, in a hoarse whisper. "He says he's blind, an' everybody else says he's blind, but if he is, then I wish I was! That's all."

The two men had ascended the steps. A man of impassive face opened the door, two others took their coats and sticks. Silent-footed servants were everywhere, deftly arranging the last details before the guests should arrive. On every hand was evidence of the lavishness that would mark the reception; but it was the lavishness of good taste, not the garishness of mere money. Through the great, high hall they were conducted to the Moorish room, where Jimmy Raelton greeted them with characteristic enthusiasm. But the super keen ears of Thornley Colton caught an undercurrent of seriousness in the host's voice.

"Robbery?" he asked quietly, as the slim, hollow stick he always carried found a chair.

"Scott, yes!" laughed Raelton; then, seriously: "That mind-reading stunt of yours is positively uncanny at times, Colton."

"Simple elimination," explained the blind problemist. "Something more serious would have been given publicity before this; something less serious would not have caused you to ask us here an hour before guests should arrive."

"It's more puzzling than really serious," declared Raelton. "You know I'm so foolishly happy tonight because Dorothy is herself again that nothing else could really matter." His face lighted up boyishly. The Jimmy Raeltons had been married five years, and society still called them the Newlyweds.

He took a small leather case from the inlaid taboret beside him, and snapped open the lid. Sydney Thames, the blind man's secretary and constant companion, could not repress a gasp of admiration as the wonderful diamond necklace sent its thousand flashing fires toward the shaded lights above.

"This is the thing I wanted to see you about," quizzically smiled Jimmy Raelton, as he extended the open case toward the blind man. A question would be needed here, at least.

Colton took the case, weighed it on his open palm an instant, brushed the stones ever so lightly with the tip of his forefinger, and snapped shut the lid.

"Worth fifty thousand—if it wasn't paste," he announced.

"Good Lord!" Raelton sank weakly into a big morris chair, the one anachronism his comfort-loving body demanded.

"To a person with highly sensitive fingertips there can be no such thing as a fake diamond; because no crystal less hard will hold a sharply-defined facet edge. When, and how, was the substitution made?"

"That is just the point. Since the morning following the Carlton-Browne reception they have been in the safe-deposit vault to which only Dorothy and I have access. You know she has never used them since; she hasn't been herself for six months or so." A troubled light came to his eyes. "It wasn't her sister's death so much—it seemed to be something else. Sometimes I almost feared that she was discontented; that she didn't want to stay at home with the kiddies any more. Her father was always a wanderer, and her grandfather died in China—you know how. But, thank God, that's over. The two months' cruise on the *Sea Mew* have made her the same old Dorothy."

He paused an instant, then came back to the point. "I'm quite an expert in an amateur way, and I recognized the substitution instantly tonight. The discovery seemed to agitate Dorothy terribly. She always set great store by the necklace—it was my wedding-present. The thing has upset her so that she will be positively ill, unless you discover how the substitution was made, and by whom. She wouldn't let me call the police."

"Where is Dorothy?" asked Colton anxiously.

"She is lying down. I'm afraid this thing is going to spoil the whole evening." Again came the troubled note. He touched a small silver bell. "I'll call her. I want you to convince her that it isn't worth worrying about. You can do it, because she has always looked upon you as a father."

A servant entered, bowed at the order, withdrew.

They waited in silence for the coming of Dorothy Raelton. Thornley Colton's mind went back to the death of Colonel Calvin, the promise given by the blind man that he would be a father to the two parentless girls. A look of sadness came to the thin expressive lips. He was thinking of the other beautiful daughter; the suicide that had never been explained.

The servant returned. His ruddy English face had lost a bit of its colour; his voice trembled slightly.

"Mrs Raelton is sleeping. The door's locked—and Dora can't wake her."

In three minds leaped a single, horrible thought. Jimmy Raelton leaped to his feet, dry-lipped.

"My God, Thornley!" He ran toward the door, and into the hall. Thornley Colton was at his heels, supersensitive ears following each footfall unerringly. Sydney Thames hurried after them; the servant brought up the rear. They raced up the marble stairs. In the upper hall a maid leaned against the wall, wringing her hands.

"Mr Raelton!" she sobbed. "Oh, I can't bear it!"

Thornley Colton had not paused; his slim stick found the closed door. He turned to face them, on his countenance an expression Sydney Thames had never seen before. He spoke to the white-faced servant.

"The guests will begin to arrive any moment, now," he said, and his tone was as strange as the look on his face. "Tell them that Mrs Raelton has been taken suddenly ill. The reception is postponed—indefinitely. Let no one in." He waited a moment till the man had gone; then his hand fell on Jimmy Raelton's shoulder. "Sydney and I will go," he said huskily.

"She isn't—" Raelton could not finish.

Colton shook his head sadly. "She isn't dead, Jimmy," he said, and stopped, with a world of suggestion in his tone.

"Then I want you to stay," pleaded the husband hysterically. "Nothing else matters—if she is alive."

He thrust his shoulder against the door. The lock gave way. He staggered in; stopped short with a gasp of horror. On the wide bed lay Dorothy Raelton, unconscious, hair disarranged, priceless gown dishevelled. From one limp hand dangled a long, black opium pipe. On a low table beside the bed a sweet-oil lamp burned flickeringly. A small can of opium was overturned beside it. The needle that had cooked the drug over the flame stained the white coverlet of the bed. The pungent smell of opium smoke was in the air.

Jimmy Raelton darted across the room, flung himself on his knees beside the bed.

"My God!" he moaned in agony. "My God!" Thornley Colton's hand fumbled for the knob, found it.

"Come, Sydney," he murmured softly. Mechanically Thames obeyed. The door closed softly behind them. The Jimmy Raeltons were alone.

II.

Black headlines in the morning papers told of the strange postponement of the Raelton reception. Black type told eager readers of the scene in front of the Raelton home when arriving guests were met at the door with a startling announcement: "Mrs Raelton is ill. The reception has been postponed indefinitely." And the door had been closed in their faces.

Eager readers learned of the silent line of servants that had filed from the rear entrance of the darkened house; the fifty thousand dollars' worth of flowers left to wilt unseen; the caterers' elaborate preparations—estimated to have cost thousands—left to spoil untasted. Much was made of the fact that Jimmy Raelton refused even to see a reporter, and all the papers, yellow and conservative alike, hinted at a sinister something that would explain a thing so unprecedented in the annals of New York society. Two of the most progressive sheets learned that Doctor Henry, the young physician who had made such rapid strides in his practice among the social leaders, had not been called, and knew nothing of Mrs Raelton's reported illness until told by the reporters.

In the library of his old-fashioned uptown house Thornley Colton sat with bowed head. At his feet were the crumpled papers Sydney had read to him.

"This is the saddest day of my life, Sydney," the blind man said slowly. "I promised Colonel Calvin that I would watch over his daughters. His father died an opium fiend."

Sydney's eyes widened. "I never knew that!"

"Few did. I have zealously guarded the secret all my life. Not even the girls knew it, though I told Jimmy when he married Dorothy. Colonel Calvin was always afraid of the stain being in the blood. He had fought the craving, but he feared for his daughters. I laughed at him, for atavism, to me, has always seemed merely a cloak for weakness. Now I am reaping my whirlwind. One is dead by her own hand, the other an opium fiend. I can never forget my feelings when I caught the unmistakable smell of opium smoke before we opened that door."

Silence came again, to be broken by The Fee, a red-haired, freckle-faced blue-eyed boy, who had become a part of the Colton household at the conclusion of a particularly baffling murder case.

"Dere's a feller an' goil downstairs wants to see yuh. Looks like solvents, and says dere name's Rayton."

Only for an instant was the expression of surprise on the blind man's face. "Send them up," he said quietly, and he rose to meet Jimmy Raelton and his wife.

A cry of pity came to Sydney Thames's lips as the man and woman entered. Jimmy Raelton, in an ill-fitting suit of blue, a plaid cap pulled down over his eyes, had grown an old man in a night. Mrs Raelton, in a tawdry dress, leaned heavily on the arm of her husband, as she had leaned when their disguises took them safely past the cordon of newspaper men.

Silently Thornley Colton took a hand in each of his, the mobile face telling them what his tongue could not; silently he lead them to chairs. Not until they were seated did Jimmy Raelton speak.

"We are going away," he said, and his tone was dead, hopeless. "We are going to fight the fight together. Dorothy wanted to say goodbye—and tell you."

"I couldn't go without seeing you," Dorothy Raelton sobbed chokingly. "It will make it easier—to know that you understand. I'm glad—that Jimmy knows at last." Her voice steadied, and she went on simply, bravely "If it hadn't been for little Jimmy and Dorothy, I would have done as Marjorie did—ended it all. Marjorie, too, had the curse, though I didn't know it until that hideous morning I waked with a terrible headache and the opium pipe on the floor beside me. I screamed for my maid. Then she told me why Marjorie had written that pitiful, pleading note, begging me to take Dora because she could be trusted if anything happened. Dora was the only one who even suspected that my sister was an opium fiend, just as my grandfather was. Marjorie had told her that. Dora said that she had heard me going downstairs in the night, and in a dream I seem to remember going to the Chinese room and taking the opium set and small glass jar of the drug we kept as curiosities; but it seems hazy, unreal.

"I hid the set in my room; I didn't dare risk getting it out. Every week the longing would come. I'd go blind, insane with craving, and in the morning I would wake, with the opium pipe beside me, and the little lamp still burning. Time after time I tried to hide the things, but in my blind delirium I always found them. One day I gave them to Dora for her to destroy, and that night I went and choked her until she gave them back. She had not had time to carry out my orders. I don't remember going to her at all, but in the morning I waked with the pipe beside me, and on Dora's throat were the marks of my fingers."

She stopped, sobs racking her slender frame. Beside her Jimmy Raelton's head was in his hands, his body quivering. She went on: "Jimmy thought it was nervous break-down. He insisted on a long cruise in the yacht. For two whole months I never once felt the craving! I thought it was gone! I romped and played with the children; I laughed and joked with my husband. Then we planned last night's reception. My God! The discovery by Jimmy of the substitute diamonds in my necklace overwrought me. I went upstairs, took a headache powder, and I waked—"

She broke down utterly. Jimmy Raelton raised his bowed head. "Now you know the whole pitiful story. Will you keep our secret till we win the fight?"

"Always," assured Thornley Colton softly. He laid a gentle hand on Dorothy's shoulder. "You may need help, little goddaughter; will you call on me?"

A nod answered him; she could not speak.

"The fight will be short; such faith cannot help but win quickly," he added. His voice brought a look that was almost hopeful into the woman's eyes, so full of assurance was it. Some subtle special sense seemed to tell him, for his thin lips curved in one of their rare smiles of encouragement. "I know you will win," he repeated. Then, to change the subject: "I will investigate the necklace substitution while you are gone. We've forgotten it completely."

Only the silent Sydney Thames saw the startled look leap to the eyes of the man and woman. Dorothy Raelton found her voice first. "Don't!" she cried brokenly. "I took the stones. They—were all—I had—to pay someone."

"What!" The tone of Colton's voice startled them. In it was amazement; under it was anguish, the anguish of a man who has made a horrible mistake. "You have been paying blackmail?" His voice was almost harsh.

"Yes." She scarcely breathed it.

"How long? To whom?" He was standing over her now; his attitude half menacing. His voice compelled an answer.

"For six months," she whispered, "the letters have been coming. They said I must pay, or the world would be told of the curse. I could do nothing else. I burned the letters as fast as they came, and I've sent fifty thousand dollars to a lock-box in Philadelphia. I had to sell my diamonds, and have them replaced by imitations to make the last payment."

"My God, what a fool I've been!" There was only anguish in the blind man's voice now. He paced the floor with tigerish strides.

"Do you ever remember cooking the opium pill?" It came like a pistol-shot.

"Cooking—" He gave her no chance to finish.

"Where did you get the headache powders you take?"

"Doctor Grayton gave me the prescription, just before he died. I have never taken any others."

"How often do you take them?

"Several times a week. They quiet my nerves. I have been taking them for years, renewing the prescription when necessary."

"Did you take any on the cruise?"

"Perhaps a dozen. They prevent sea-sickness."

"You never felt the craving for that two months?"

"Never."

"They put you to sleep?"

"A light sleep that comes of quieted nerves." She was answering the questions automatically, staring at him. Her husband listened, lips parted, breath coming fast. Sydney Thames was leaning forward, tense, expectant.

The blind problemist whirled from her and continued his pacing. Twice he made the length of the room.

"The inhuman devils!" they heard him mutter. "God, what devils there are!"

Jimmy Raelton could stand it no longer. "What do you mean?" he cried.

The blind man stopped before him, sightless eyes behind the round, dark glasses apparently staring deep into his. "I mean that my neglect is responsible for this." There was terrible bitterness in his voice. *"Not a breath of opium smoke has ever passed Dorothy Raelton's lips!"*

Dumb, stupefied, they could only stare; then, as though moved by hidden springs, the man and woman leaped to their feet. But as quickly as it came the look of hope died in Dorothy Raelton's eyes. She fell back into the chair.

"Don't!" she sobbed. "I can't bear it! I've used the horrible stuff a hundred times. I couldn't fight against it!"

The man still stood, swaying ever so slightly, fingernails biting into his palms, as his hands clenched convulsively.

Gently the blind man forced him down into his chair. "It is true, Jimmy," he said, and his voice was normal once more. "I should have known it last night when the whole game was in my hands. Now I must start at the beginning. The mind I have trained for years to be purely eliminative, that I have thought impervious to outside influences, is only human, after all. Last night I believed the evidence of my four senses and did not use my brain."

Only Sydney Thames realized what this confession cost the man who had so prided himself on his infallibility.

"I don't understand," came dully from Jimmy Raelton.

The blind man resumed his pacing of the room. "Dorothy doesn't even know that the opium pill must be 'cooked' over the sweet-oil lamp! She doesn't know the first thing about opium smoking! And last night there was no key on the inside of the door. *It was locked from the outside!* I remember distinctly that my fumbling fingers felt no key as I went out. I know—now—that none fell. Someone wanted you"—his finger pointed at Jimmy Raelton—"to see your wife!" He paused for an instant, then continued, rapidly, crisply: "The whole thing is the most devilish blackmail I have ever heard of. It is based on the one thing that all the past dead centuries have taught us to fear—atavism. When Dorothy's money had gone, and the selling of the necklace stones told the blackmailers so, the husband must be the next victim of the vampire. The scene of last night was arranged so that only a touch would be needed to explode the powder-magazine the reception postponement had started if Jimmy refused to pay. The fiendish simplicity of it!"

"But who—" began Dorothy Raelton, and there was almost eagerness in her voice. Then the hopelessness came back. "But it is impossible. I know—"

"You know nothing! Where is your maid?"

A terrible expression came to Raelton's face.

"The maid! She—" The words came like curses before the problemist stopped him.

"The maid is absolutely innocent! Absolutely! Remember that above all things!" cried Colton. "Where is she?"

"I sent her to mail a letter so that she would be out of the way when we started. I wouldn't even trust her," Jimmy Raelton answered slowly.

"To whom was the letter addressed?"

"To you. I didn't want to come here, but Dorothy insisted."

"Did you get a letter from the blackmailer this morning?"

Silently Jimmy Raelton took a letter from his pocket and extended it. Colton received it eagerly, jerked out the inclosure, laid it face down on the desk. His hypersensitive fingertips brushed lightly the reversed, raised words the typewriter keys had driven through the paper as he read aloud slowly:

"Mr Raelton.

"Sir,—May be you don't know it, but your wife smokes hop. If you don't want the wurld to get wise, send 25 one-thousand-dollar bills to lock-box 117, Philadelphia. Don't register. We'll take a chance they land safe. If you're too up in the air today give you till tomorrow, but put a personal in the *Telegram* saying when. And do it, too!"

The blind man paused an instant, then continued: "The fact that they want the money in thousand-dollar bills proves that the blackmailers are persons who can pass them without question, despite the childish attempt at illiteracy. They also know that the money would arrive safely without registry, which would necessitate signing a receipt. The fact that they want the money sent to a place so easily watched as a public lock-box proves that they have some means of getting their hands on it before it gets there!"

He grasped the telephone. "Six thousand Greeley. *Telegram?* Take a personal for the next edition. Ready? 'Lock-box 117. Not even twenty-five cents.—J. R.' That's all. On the street in an hour? Charge it to Thornley Colton. Right."

They listened, white-faced; he shot a question at Dorothy before a protest could be voiced:

"Have you ever called in Doctor Henry?"

"There are things one can't tell even one's physician," she said simply. "Jimmy called him, once, when he thought I was suffering from nervous breakdown. Doctor Henry never suspected, couldn't suspect. He told Jimmy that his plans for a two months' cruise were excellent. That is the only time I have seen him during this awful six months. He has dropped in several times to see the children, but I have been out."

"A curious coincidence," mused Colton idly; then his questions took a new turn. "You had no suspicion that your sister was an opium fiend?"

"No—I wouldn't have believed—if—" The words choked in her throat.

"Didn't you drift apart after her marriage?"

"Donald Wreye turned out a cad!" blurted Raelton. "You know that as well as I! He spent every cent of Marjorie's money. There wasn't a penny of the hundred thousand her father left when she died. Wreye tried to borrow ten thousand from me five months ago, and I ordered him from the house!"

"Five months ago?" murmured Colton. "He must have got it from someone. I know he was on the ragged edge about that time." He turned away from them and jabbed two desk-buttons. "You are going back home now. I want you to slip in the way you came. Shrimp will go with you."

He turned to face The Fee, who had answered one button. "The reporters will probably hold you up, thinking you servants. Let Mr and Mrs Raelton slip past, then let the newspaper men get the information that Mrs Raelton had a serious heart attack, also that Doctor Henry was asked not to divulge the fact that he had been called. I've rung for the machine. It will take you within two or three blocks of your home. Walk the rest of the way, and stay indoors until you hear from me. Now this is important: I want you to give Shrimp two of the headache powders you have been taking, without the knowledge of the maid or any one else. Can you?"

Mrs Raelton nodded dumbly.

"No one is to know that you have seen me. No one!"

He sat down at the desk and wrote rapidly for a moment.

"Send this telegram on your way back, Shrimp, and tell Michael not to wait for you. Sydney and I want to use the machine."

He held out his hands to the man and woman. "Goodbye, for a little while," he said. Silently he watched them out, then he turned toward Sydney.

"Tell John to serve us a cold lunch immediately."

For the first time in an hour Sydney Thames spoke. "Where are we going?" he asked curiously.

"To see Donald Wreye."

III.

Society had never called the marriage of Marjorie Calvin and Donald Wreye a brilliant one. Seven years before Marjorie had entered New York society, and society had knelt at her feet. She had many offers of marriage; all were laughed aside. Then came Donald Wreye, big, blond, masterful. He carried the little black-haired girl off her feet, swept the other suitors aside like chaff. He had neither money nor family. By sheer doggedness he had fought his way to a ten-thousand-dollar position in the Street. Society had pleaded with Marjorie Calvin. Thornley Colton had pleaded. But she loved with the love that only women of the Southland feel. They eloped.

For five years the marriage had seemed ideal. Then came the last year. Marjorie's sunny nature changed completely. Wreye was constantly at his club, drinking, gambling. Thornley Colton was received almost coldly by the girl he loved as a daughter. Then she was found in her room, the pistol she had used beside her.

Wreye cast restraint to the winds then. His position was lost because of dissipation. He had opened an office of his own, and although he was known to do comparatively little business, for the past few months he had seemed to have plenty of money. But to the men and women he had known in the old days he became a pariah.

And it was to his office that Colton and Sydney Thames started in the big machine an hour later. The blind man's lips were a thin, straight line the bloodless face sinister in its grimness. What his thoughts were none could tell. Sydney's were a maze of conflict. The astounding assertion of Colton's that Dorothy Raelton had never smoked opium had carried him off his feet, mentally, when it was made, but now, with sober afterthought, came the utter absurdity of it. Dorothy had known — *known* — that the blind craving could only be satisfied by the drug, and she had used it. It was not within the range of human possibility that she could be mistaken. And *they* had seen.

The car came to a stop before a tall office-building near Wall Street. Colton, cane in hand, stepped to the side-walk, and, with only the touch of Sydney's sleeve against his to guide him, made his way to the elevator. On an upper floor they halted before the door with its plain announcement:

"Donald Wreye, Broker. Odd Lots."

Following Thornley Colton's knock came the slam of a hastily-shut drawer, and a gruff invitation to enter. The smile of welcome faded as the heavy-featured man with the tawny hair saw his visitors.

"Well?" he snapped ungraciously, slumping into the swivel chair without even inviting them to be seated.

Thornley Colton's slim stick located a chair before he answered. "You won't be well very long unless you keep away from that black bottle in the drawer," be said grimly.

Wreye jumped to his feet with an oath. "That bottle's my own affair," he snarled. "I'll drink when I damn' please! I'm not in your bootlicking set anymore. I got—" He stopped suddenly. "Get down to cases! This is my busy day."

The blind man picked up the chair and placed it directly before the big man, not two feet from him. "I want you to answer a few questions." He said it simply, quietly, but some indefinable timbre of his voice made it a command.

"I'll answer if I see fit!" blustered Wreye.

"You'll answer whether you want to or not." Still that quiet voice; the velvet covering for the will of steel beneath it. Sydney Thames held his breath as he watched the two men. One, a veritable giant, clumsy in his very bigness, face flushed with anger and liquor; the other, half a head shorter, with the chest and shoulders of an athlete, belied by the well-tailored slimness the faultless clothes gave him; face and hair white, accentuated by the big circles of the smoked library-glasses, his cane, held idly between the slim, supersensitive fingers, touching the floor a few inches from Donald Wreye's foot.

"I'll see about that!" blustered Wreye, and the words seemed foolishly puerile.

"When did you first discover that your wife was an opium fiend?" It was put so unexpectedly, so baldly, that even Sydney Thames gasped.

The livid fury mounted to the face of Wreye.

"By God! You—" His voice trembled with unleashed passion.

Knife-like Thornley Colton's voice cut in: "Answer me!"

And, like lightning, the answer came—a vicious, smashing right fist straight at the face of the seated blind man!

The exact sequence of ensuing events could never be told by Sydney, for the simple reason that his eyes were incapable of following the moves of the man who was sightless. He remembered leaping to his feet with a cry of horror as the blind man's chair toppled over. Then he saw a purple-faced, cursing man straining and tugging to release the arms that were being slowly doubled behind him. A crash of a great body hurled downward in the heavy swivel chair, and Thornley Colton, unruffled, breathing accelerated but a trifle, straightened the tortoise-rimmed glasses and smiled down at the man he had so easily mastered.

Mechanically Sydney righted the chair and picked up the blind man's cane.

"Thanks," murmured Colton absently, and Sydney Thames gasped in amazement at the smile he saw on the thin lips of the problemist. It was a smile of pure joy; the joy of a man who has learned something more easily than he had expected.

"Don't you know that a seated man can't leap to his feet without a warning move of the foot on the floor?" Thornley Colton asked quietly. "My cane told me what you were going to do the instant you knew yourself. Do you want to proceed conversationally or physically?" he finished grimly.

"I could kill you for that!" The big man's voice was like a sob.

"It was raw," apologized Colton, but both knew he was referring to the question he had asked, and not the vicious blow, or the struggle. Then the menace came again to his voice. "Where did you get that ten thousand you needed so badly five months ago?"

The effect of this question was fully as startling, in a totally different way, to Sydney Thames as the other had been. The red rage receded from Wreye's face, the snarl went from the lips; a sneering smile came.

"So you come from my lily-fingered brother-in-law, eh? Hasn't got the nerve to come himself, I suppose?"

"Where did you get it?" repeated Colton.

"Oh, I'll tell you quick enough. *I got it from Jimmy Raelton!*"

If this reply was unexpected, it did not cause the slightest change of expression on the face of Thornley Colton.

"Quite strange that he should have given you the money after he had so emphatically refused it once before, wasn't it?" he observed quietly.

The black scowl came back to Donald Wreye's face. "The letter that came with the money was devilish plain. The ten thousand was to keep me away from him and his wife. I was told that I'd get something worse than mere loss of position if I even told where it came from. Now I suppose he wants it back."

"Oh, no," assured Colton, as he rose. "He doesn't even know I'm here."

"What do you want, then?" There was snarling suspicion in the voice now.

"Information — which I got." The blind man smiled down curiously at the scowling man; then the smile went as quickly as it came. "What became of Marjorie's hundred thousand dollars?" he jerked out.

"She—" Wreye's jaws snapped together, the big shoulders hunched aggressively. "If you're so damn' clever, find out!" he challenged sullenly.

Sydney Thames could see the man's huge muscles tighten under the coat, as if he expected force once more, and was prepared to meet it. But Colton only nodded and turned toward the door.

"I will," he promised grimly. "And I'm going to have you on hand when I make the discovery."

It was not until they were on the side-walk outside that a word was spoken.

"A man like that makes my blood boil!" ejaculated Sydney Thames.

"Yes?" replied the blind man seriously, but the rising inflection made it enigmatical. His beckoning finger brought a leather-lunged newsboy.

"Latest *Telegram*?"

It was thrust into his hand.

"Did Shrimp see the reporters, Sydney?" he asked, as he handed the paper to Thames and stepped into the car.

"The heart-stroke story is on the first page."

"Good! Then the advertisement I telephoned must be in. Take us to Doctor Henry's home, Michael."

IV.

With plenty of money, a distinguished appearance, and the manners of a courtier, Doctor Charles V. Henry had entered New York society three years before, with letters of introduction from prominent men and women in Paris. He soon opened an office in the fashionable uptown residential district. He had an independent fortune—his bachelor apartments cost him fifteen thousand a year—but it pleased him to follow his profession, and when Doctor Grayton died he fell natural heir to his society practice.

"Do not tell me that you are ill, Mr Colton!" he laughed, as he ushered the blind man and Sydney into his quietly luxurious office half an hour after they had left Donald Wreye.

"Old Hippocrates and I are sworn enemies," smiled the problemist. "I came to get a little professional information."

"Yes?" politely from the physician, as he accepted a proffered cigarette.

"It is this." Colton spoke seriously; all trace of the smile had gone. "Is there any medicinal cure for opium craving?"

The heavy lashes of the doctor veiled his eyes as he looked down thoughtfully at the floor. "There are several reputed cures," he said finally. "The most effective, and simple, probably, is rice powder and morphia. The morphia satisfies the violent craving at first, then the drug is diminished gradually, until the patient is satisfied with the harmless rice powder. This is effective, however, only in the first stages."

"I am speaking of atavistic craving. The opium craving, having skipped one generation, appears doubly strong in the next."

"You mention a rare case," said Doctor Henry slowly; "and an incurable one. The effect of opium smoking, primarily, is a sensation of the nerves, or, rather, lack of sensation. The nerves feel the craving first. When that craving finds lodgment in the brain, the case is hopeless. With the inherited craving the process is absolutely reversed. The seat of the trouble is in the brain before the nerves know the drug, and when the nerves once feel the satisfied craving, it becomes a monomania. There is no cure."

For a full minute there was silence in the office. Thornley Colton blew thoughtful smoke-rings toward the ceiling. Sydney Thames was conscious of a strange, new feeling toward the man he loved; the man who had picked him up as a bundle of baby-clothes on the banks of the English river that had given him the only name he had ever known. The feeling was almost bitter. He could not keep his mind from the man and woman that Colton had sent back to their home but a short time before, full of hope, of joy. Now he realized that the words had been but empty encouragement. And there was no hope!

Thornley Colton spoke again. "I disagree with you, doctor. There is a cure!" He had risen to his feet; his voice trembled with vehemence.

The physician, startled from his usual professional calmness, was on his feet, staring. Colton took a step forward, stumbled blindly against a chair, his hands thrust out gropingly. Before Sydney Thames could reach him, Doctor Henry was again the cool physician. He extended a hand, and led the blind man back to his seat.

"I forgot myself," apologized the blind man huskily. "This thing has unnerved me." He swallowed hard, his voice became normal. "The time for equivocation is past, doctor; I'm going to be frank. Dorothy Raelton is an opium fiend!"

The physician half rose again from his chair in amazement. "Why—why—such a thing is incredible!" he gasped.

Briefly, dispassionately, Colton told him of the night before. "Now," he continued, "for the cure." Again there was excitement in his voice. "Early tomorrow morning the Raeltons start for a year's cruise on their yacht. I am making all the arrangements. They will go to the South Pacific, and keep wholly out of touch with the world, Mrs Raelton will not take her maid, Jimmy will not even have his man. They will be absolutely alone, except for the crew. What do you think of that?"

Doctor Henry's fingers ceased their nervous drumming on the chair-arm, his lowered eyes raised. "It may be effective," he admitted, in his deepest professional tones. "At what time—do they start?"

"With the seven-o'clock tide. Tonight Mrs Raelton is going to receive a few intimate friends, and explain last night's postponement. By the way"—he took the newspaper he had purchased from his pocket—"I used your name in explaining to the reporters the cause of last night's affair. I knew you wouldn't object." The physician took the paper eagerly.

The problemist was almost to the door before he remembered another question. "Did you ever suspect that Mrs Donald Wreye was an opium fiend?" he asked.

The unexpectedness of the question made Doctor Henry forget his usual suave manner for an instant, and his voice was almost sharp as he replied "She was not! Her death was—" He stopped suddenly; then, in a different tone, "I am going to meet your frankness with frankness," he said slowly. "I have always thought Mrs Wreye's suicide was a natural result of an utter breaking of her hypersensitive nervous system."

"Her husband?" put in Colton.

"Yes!" emphatically.

"Marjorie Wreye's death was not a suicide!" Colton spoke quietly, but in his tone was that ominous menace Sydney Thames had noticed so many times that day. "It was deliberate murder! Good day, doctor."

He extended his hand. It was taken by the serious-faced physician. Thornley Colton nodded a jerky farewell, and hurried from the office, his brain automatically counting the steps it had registered when he entered.

In the car, speeding homeward, Sydney Thames drew a long breath.

"Great Scott!" he murmured. "What a villain he is!"

"Doctor Henry?" There was mild surprise in the blind man's voice.

"Donald Wreye," corrected Sydney shortly. "Hanging is too good for him!"

"Did you notice the almost curious resemblance between the deep professional tones of Doctor Henry and the ordinary voice of Wreye?" asked the problemist seriously.

Without giving Thames a chance to reply he leaned forward to speak to the driver. "Take us to the nearest drugstore telephone pay-station, Michael," he ordered. And as the car turned in toward the curb he explained to Sydney: "I must tell the Raeltons of my plans; also get twenty grains of trional and a heavy rubber band. Trional is one of the few harmless narcotics. The rubber band is *highly* important. It is going to trap the most inhuman criminal I have ever known!"

V.

Sydney Thames paced the library floor impatiently. Where was Thornley Colton? For three hours he had asked himself that question. The blind problemist had spent fully half an hour in the closed telephone booth at the drug-store after he had purchased two morphia powders and half a dozen strong rubber bands. Then, when Michael had driven them home, Sydney had been curtly ordered from the machine, and the eager-eyed Shrimp had taken his place as guide.

As he walked he tried to piece together the events of the day; to discover some loose end in the snarl of circumstances. But his mind refused to find logic in the tangle of statements, of events that apparently led nowhere. Donald Wreye was a villain. He had driven his wife to suicide after squandering her fortune. That was certain. But what part had he in the life of Dorothy Raelton? Why had Jimmy Raelton secretly sent him ten thousand dollars after openly refusing it? Why had Raelton pretended such bitterness against his brother-in-law that morning? Why had Colton made the astounding statement that Dorothy Raelton had never smoked opium, and then sought a physician's advice for a possible cure? Why had the blind man remarked the similarity of Donald Wreye's voice to that of Doctor Henry? These, and a hundred more, raced back and forth through his brain like a flying shuttle. He took out his watch for the fiftieth time; then turned eagerly as the blind man hurried into the room.

With a sigh of weariness Thornley Colton dropped into a chair and lighted a cigarette; when he spoke there was weariness in his voice.

"A strange case, Sydney," he said slowly, as though he had accepted this first quiet opportunity for retrospection. "The strangest I have ever known. A crime so damnably ingenious that even I—who have made a study of crime and criminals for years—did not recognize it. A crime so infernally clever that even the victim refuses to believe that it is a crime. A criminal who could confess this minute, and be laughed to scorn by any jury in the land. It is a crime unique in the annals of crime."

He took a telegram from his pocket. "Here is the answer to a query I sent regarding the lock-box in Philadelphia."

Sydney took it and read:

"Lock-box 117 one of six rented to Philadelphia Insurance Co. for past five years."

"That means an accomplice there!" ejaculated Sydney.

"It proves my former statement that the blackmailer never allowed the money to get to that box. And there could be only one method of interception in this case. It was never mailed!"

"But Mrs Raelton said—" began Sydney dazedly.

"She also said she was an opium fiend," interrupted Colton brusquely. Again his hand went to his pocket; on his palm as he extended it were two white, folded papers. "These are the powders Shrimp brought. The papers have been changed by me, but these powders have been used to mask the weapon of a fiend. Get me a glass of water."

Mechanically Sydney obeyed. He returned in a moment with the water and a question.

"But Mrs Raelton declared that Doctor Grayton had given her those powders?" he objected.

"Yes." Thornley Colton carefully unfolded one.

"And Doctor Grayton has been dead two years." He held the paper, opened, between his thumb and forefinger. "These powders were used to cause the suicide of Marjorie Wreye and make Dorothy Raelton, to all intents and purposes, an opium fiend!" He raised the powder to his lips, dropped it on his tongue. Sydney could not repress a gasp of horror. The blind man took a sip of the water, and stood up, fingers feeling the crystalless watch in his pocket. "It is seven o'clock, Sydney, time we were starting for the Raelton home. The machine is waiting."

Thames licked his dry lips. "My God, Thorn!" he choked. "It isn't—poison?"

"No." The blind man's smile held no humour. "These powders are perfectly harmless. Doctor Grayton was a careful practitioner, and his prescriptions have helped my headaches before."

"But what—how—" gulped Sydney, amazed into incoherence by this new convolution.

"I'll tell you later," promised Thornley Colton. "I can't now. There is too much at stake to spoil with premature explanations."

He took his hat and coat from the tree, and hurried down the stairs, Sydney following. In the automobile the blind man lay back in the deep seat, only rousing when the machine came to a stop before the Raelton home. The awning canopy was gone now; there was no waiting crowd. Another machine came to a stop behind them; where it had come from Sydney did not know. Then came a feminine greeting; the blind man lifted his hat, and hurried to the other car unerringly.

"How are you, Mrs Neilton, and you, Mrs Bracken, also your husbands?" The assumed cheeriness in the voice seemed perfect to the listening Sydney Thames. As the blind man assisted the women to alight, Thames was surprised to note that they were all strangers to him. As Colton's constant companion and guide he knew most of the blind man's friends, though his memory of faces was not to be compared with the blind problemist's wonderful memory of voices.

Sydney was introduced to the men and women as Thornley Colton's secretary; they were presented to him as friends of the Jimmy Raeltons, who had come to see them on the eve of the departure for the South Pacific.

Together they mounted the steps. Thornley Colton rang the bell. And the door was opened by the red-haired Shrimp!

"The servants is all gone," explained the boy, as he closed the door after them. "All but Mrs Raelton's maid. Mr Raelton's in the Moorish room."

But at the first sound of their voices Jimmy Raelton had hurried out to meet them; his face was still haggard, and in the eyes was a piteous expression of pleading.

"Where is Mrs Raelton?" asked Thornley Colton quietly.

"She is lying down. I'll call her." Raelton had not even nodded to the two men and the women who were quietly watching.

"Wait!" Thornley Colton grasped his arm. Someone was coming up the steps outside. The door-bell rang. Shrimp opened it, and into the hall stumbled Donald Wreye! His bloodshot eyes blinked in the bright light as he glared at them, his hands twitched at his sides. He hunched his great shoulders, and clenched his fists to get a grip on himself.

"Where's—" he began, in the deep, hoarse voice so like that of the physician.

From above them came a frightened scream—a woman's scream.

"Mr Raelton! Mr Raelton!" It was the maid.

He bounded toward the stairs, the others at his heels. At the top was the maid, weeping and wringing her hands.

"She told me to get myself something to eat, and I wasn't downstairs twenty minutes," she cried hysterically. "And I found her—"

Jimmy Raelton dashed past her. Sydney felt Colton brush past him, and realized that somehow he had gotten behind the others when they started.

At the door of the room where they had stopped the night before they halted again. The door was not even closed this time, and once more their eyes took in the same scene. But the electrics were out now, only the flickering rays of the sweet-oil lamp shone on the sleeping woman and the opium-pipe at her side.

"My God! Again!" The words came in sobs from Jimmy Raelton.

He tried to leap forward, but the outstretched hand of Thornley Colton stopped him. Then the others saw the blind man dart across the room to the bed without a false move; saw him pick up a white, dangling arm, brush his fingers up the whole length of it, under the flowing sleeve of the loose kimono, then stop at the wrist. They were all around him now. He straightened up to face them.

"It's something more, this time," he said huskily. "Mrs Raelton is dead!"

"Dead!" the terror-stricken word came from the maid. The others seemed suddenly turned to stone.

Silently Colton held the arm for her to feel the pulse. Her fingers found the artery, her face went dead white. They could hear the fluttering gasp of her breath as she dropped the arm.

Raelton brushed past her; his trembling fingers searched for a single faint heart-beat. A cry of agony burst from him. Colton gently drew him away.

"Phone Doctor Henry, Dora!" he ordered sharply. Then he seemed to sense that the maid was staring at Donald Wreye, who stood in the centre of the room, swaying back and forth, hands clenching and unclenching at his sides.

"*You*, Wreye!"

The blind man's voice seemed to galvanize Donald Wreye into action. He whipped a revolver from his pocket.

"Like Marjorie, eh?" His laugh seemed insane. "Get out of here, all of you!"

He stood beside the doorway, the revolver threateningly sweeping the silent men and women. Jimmy Raelton tensed his body for a spring, but Thornley Colton's hand viced his arm.

"We can do nothing," he whispered.

Like sheep they filed past the menacing pistol, the two men and women who had met them outside going first. In the hallway they stopped.

"Straight ahead!" ordered Wreye. He spoke over his shoulder to the maid. "Call Doctor Henry," he sneered. "Go downstairs and call him."

The girl's limbs seemed hardly able to support her as she walked past him to the head of the stairs. He turned his attention again to the driven men and women. Sydney's eyes caught a glimpse of a portiered doorway at their left, but Colton's grip on his arm held him. Down the hall they went. A door was open at the extreme end, the key in the outside of the lock.

"In there, all of you!" ordered Wreye.

The women stumbled in. The men followed. The door slammed behind them. The key turned. Outside they heard running footsteps.

"He's gone down the backstairs," muttered one of the men.

The dot of light at the keyhole disappeared. "He's put out the lights," hoarsely whispered the other.

Thornley Colton took something from his pocket. He inserted it in the keyhole; they heard the bolt slip back.

"He'll return," he whispered. "You four stay here and kick at the door. The darkness means nothing to me. I'm going to take Sydney and Raelton outside to watch. Give us a minute, and then begin your noise."

He opened the door without a sound. His hands on the two men's arms drew them out. The blackness of the unlighted hall was impenetrable, but the blind man pulled them forward almost on a run. Sydney's feet mechanically obeyed the pulling arm; Raelton, still in a daze, was merely an automaton obeying the will of a master. The blind man thrust them through the portieres Sydney had noticed before.

"Not a sound!" he warned, as he dragged them down to the floor, his fingers biting deep into their arms.

The house echoed with the blows of feet and fists on the door of the room they had just left. A door slammed downstairs. They heard the voice of The Fee, shrill with fright.

"Dere all locked in back!"

Hurried footsteps sounded on the stairs. They heard a woman's voice whisper; a man's deep, hoarse voice in answer. Sydney's muscles grew tense. It was the heavy voice of Donald Wreye!

"She's dead, I tell you!" trembled the maid. They were passing the door now.

The man's answering whisper sounded like the growling of an animal. "You little fool!" he hissed. "You let the other get away from us, and this one was worth a million—"

The words ended in a woman's scream. They heard the sound of a falling body. A man's curse. A short struggle. Then the dull impact of fist against flesh. Thornley Colton's gripping hands relaxed. He jumped through the sheltering portieres. His voice cut the darkness:

"Stop, Wreye, stop! Doctor Henry is unconcious! Shrimp!"

The incandescents leaped to light.

On the floor was the maid, senseless. Near her was Doctor Henry, limp, torn, his face bruised and beaten. Standing over him was Donald Wreye, panting, trembling.

The two men who had stayed in the locked room came running forward, shining handcuffs in their hands.

"Handcuff Mrs Henry," ordered Colton. "She has only fainted." He turned to face the still-dazed Jimmy Raelton and Sydney. "There is the atavistic vampire!" He touched the limp body of the physician as though it was a snake. "God knows how many lives he has ruined with his devilish schemes. He blackmailed Marjorie Wreye out of a hundred thousand dollars, and murdered her as surely as though his finger had pulled the trigger that sent the bullet crashing into her brain. He made Donald Wreye a pariah. And he almost succeeded in ruining the lives of you and Dorothy."

The name aroused Jimmy Raelton.

"Dorothy!" he cried brokenly. "He killed Dorothy!"

The blind man's hand fell gently on his shoulder.

"It was necessary that she should sleep through it all," he said quietly. "I didn't think she could stand another dose of the doctor's morphia, so the powder she took was trional powder. She will wake in an hour, suffering no ill effects. If you'll remove the tight rubber band I put on her arm under the kimono sleeve the blood will flow back through the pulse."

VI.

Sydney and Thornley Colton were back in the library of the old-fashioned house. The blind man had removed the tortoise-rimmed glasses, and around his head and over his eyes was an alcohol-soaked bandage to relieve the splitting headache the loss of his usual four hours of darkness in the afternoon had produced.

"Yes, it was melodrama, Sydney," he admitted. "But it was necessary. It was carefully staged to shatter the nerves of the cool Dora, and arouse the doctor's anger at what he thought was a mistake of his accomplice. That last resulted in the angry confession we overheard. I knew his temper would give way under certain conditions, and I made those conditions. Shrimp was stationed downstairs to let him in at the proper moment, and also to keep the maid and the doctor from confidences until they were upstairs, where they could hear the door-pounding, and would suppose we were all together. Of course, the quartet of men and women were private detectives posing as guests to deceive the maid. They were stationed around the corner with orders to follow right behind us. Wreye was across the street from the Raelton house, so that he could run over and ring the bell a moment after we entered."

"But how did Doctor Henry happen to be there?" demanded the puzzled Sydney.

"Shrimp, mimicking the maid's voice, called him up the minute our machine appeared, and told him that Mrs Raelton was dead. He rang off before the doctor could get in a word. But that gave Henry all the time he needed to get there. Shrimp says the physician fumed and fretted in the vestibule fully three minutes before the boy heard the door-pounding that was the signal to admit him."

"But I thought Donald Wreye—" began Sydney helplessly.

"It was Doctor Henry and the maid from the first. Pure elimination and the headache powders told me that."

"But you said the powders were harmless, that Doctor Grayton was careful," objected Sydney.

"Their harmlessness was the crux. It put them above suspicion, but when it became necessary to impress Dorothy Raelton with the fact that she was a hopeless opium fiend the powder the maid gave her was a heavy dose of morphia, which is the base of opium, and produces almost the same after-effects. Of course, as soon as Dorothy became unconscious the outfit was arranged for her awakening. Dorothy's highly-strung nervous system, like that of her sister, made it easy for a strong mind like that of the maid to make her know—*know*—that she had smoked the drug in a blind delirium of craving. And the wonderful suggestive stories of the maid, and the fake finger-marks on her throat, made the thing complete. I understood them all when I heard of the blackmail, but it was necessary to impress the Raeltons with Dora's innocence so that she would be unsuspicious until the time came for the dénouement.

"The ten thousand I knew Wreye must have got puzzled me at first, though it didn't seem possible that he could be in the plot. The interview in the morning proved his utter incapability of such a thing. The game required a cool, iron-nerved man. His actions during our talk proved conclusively that he was neither. Five minutes' conversation with Doctor Henry gave me all I wanted to know. His coolness, his nerve, the fact that he had called at the Raelton home several times when Mrs Raelton was out, ostensibly to see the children, but really to see the maid, the clever way he blamed Wreye for Marjorie's suicide, his eager desire to know at what time the Raeltons sailed in the morning, the manner in which he took the paper he knew should contain the personal, were all guideposts on the right track. His beautifully clever explanation why the opium craving I described could not be alleviated was intended to show me my helplessness. But it gave me what I wanted. Pretending to stumble, I got his hand in mine; my finger was on his pulse—the Keyboard of Silence. He knew I was going to tell him of Dorothy! Though his face was a mask, his heart-beats showed the nervousness underneath; the nervousness no eye could have detected. That was the final proof.

"Then I realized his real cleverness. *He* had sent the money to Wreye with a forged note, apparently from Raelton. The maid had undoubtedly told him of Wreye's need and attempt to borrow from his brother-in-law, and the doctor was afraid that Wreye, in a hot-headed rage at continued refusals, would blurt out Marjorie's trouble, and cause a premature confession from Dorothy before the blackmailer had gotten her firmly in his clutches. Henry was overlooking no possibility, and the ten thousand was a paltry amount, beside what he expected to get. Of course, you see how he really got the money into his hands? The envelopes containing the bills, given to a trusted maid to mail to the fake lock-box, were merely handed over to the real vampire. There was no chance of detection.

"This afternoon Shrimp and I went to Wreye's office and explained the whole game to him. He refused to believe, at first, because Marjorie had confessed five months before her death that she was an opium fiend. Wreye was more of a man than we ever thought. He hid the fact from the world. He let her go her own way. He didn't suspect the blackmailing, because Marjorie probably feared to tell him, lest his temper should lead him to expose the secret in his efforts to seek out the blackmailer. And when she died, penniless, he supposed she had lost her money gambling, the usual passion that follows opium smoking. He kept quiet, but naturally he was bitter against the whole world.

"But I finally persuaded him to do his part in trapping the vampire. Remember the similarity of the two voices? That was my trump card. I knew that my story of the Raeltons' early departure and the curt advertisement would rouse the doctor to drastic action, and force him to call up Dora, and give new instructions. That was what I wanted—it would make her unsuspicious when the second call I planned came. It worked like a charm. She never suspected the voice. It was then, by the way, that we learned Dora was really Mrs Henry, and that she was getting tired of her part. We learned, also, that Mrs Raelton was to be given an extra heavy dose of morphia, so that it would be impossible for her to get away in the morning. Doctor Henry needed time, you see.

"Wreye, impersonating the doctor over the phone, gave her new instructions. The same plan was to be followed, but the doctor would send her two new powders—they were my trional powders I wouldn't take a chance on morphia again—and she was to arrange the opium set as usual, and scream for Jimmy as soon as Donald Wreye arrived. Then, if anything went wrong, she was to foist suspicion upon Wreye, who, she was told, was on the verge of delirium tremens, and would be sent by the doctor on some pretext.

"Donald, as you saw, could hardly control himself, but that made him perfect in her eyes, though I had to stay behind a second after you started upstairs to warn him, and I also had to give him his cue in the room before he acted. My little trick with the rubber band utterly unnerved the maid, who supposed that her husband had really sent poison. So, when the doctor got there, they were at cross-purposes, and the angry betrayal we heard was the logical result."

For a minute there was silence; then Sydney Thames spoke. "But Wreye, why did you let him—" There was no need to finish.

"It was pure brutishness, Sydney," confessed Thornley Colton slowly. "The brutishness that makes us think of physical revenge before we think of the law. There are crimes so foul that we want to pound, to tear their perpetrators. The driving to death of one innocent girl and the nearly successful attempt to make a mental wreck of Dorothy Raelton, who had never known the taste of opium smoke in her life, is one of them. My fingers itched for Doctor Henry's throat. But Donald Wreye's right came first. He took it. I am glad."

3

The Third Problem:

THE MONEY MACHINES

I.

The man in the long blue car was a person of consequence. The big traffic policeman had stopped all north and south traffic, but the chauffeur of the blue machine darted in front of a stopped Bowling Green car without the slightest slackening of speed, and shot between an eastbound slot car and a westbound delivery truck. Traffic cop 7389 saluted gravely and silenced with a warning scowl the snarling driver of a held-up van, who had to reach the ten-thirty boat.

The lone occupant of the roomy tonneau, rigidly straight on the cushions, answered the salute with a barely perceptible nod of his head, and a half smile of the thin, almost bloodless lips. But there was no change of expression in the granite-hard gray eyes, nor a movement of the straight back. One lean hand gripped the tonneau door, the fingers resting just above the small silvered monogram on the blue enamel; the other dropped lightly on the seat beside his knee. John T. Villers, the power behind the throne of Money, was on his way to his office.

It was characteristic of the man that he did not lounge back in his seat; that his pose was one of tense rigidity. No one had ever seen John T. Villers relax; none of the hundreds who knew him thought that he could relax. Alert, watchful, a machine for the massing of millions; a machine that never required rest; that never needed the lubrication of pleasure to insure its smooth running; a human mechanism that never deviated a hair's breadth from its schedule. Such was the king of the kings of finance.

At ten-fifteen he would be at his office in Wall Street. Elsewhere, a monarch of half a million fighting men paced the floor of his castle room, impatiently awaiting the word that a simple touch of a desk button in that Wall Street office would bring. Ten thousand yellow coolies, half a world away, idled in bamboo-thatched construction huts for a stroke of John T. Villers's pen. And he answered the salute of a traffic policeman!

Men and women on Broadway halted in their hurrying to stare at the big blue car, and the silent, straight-backed occupant; for the face and the pose of the financier were as familiar to the reading public as Broadway itself. Weak-chinned men of the unemployed ranks cursed the "luck" that gave him money and them hunger. Clerks, from high office windows, bemoaned the fate that compelled them to commence work at eight and allowed him to begin at ten. There was no sign in the hard gray eyes of the man who answered the traffic men's salutes that the money machine had been working until daylight over the inch-thick packet of papers now buttoned tightly beneath his coat. The machine never showed signs of its running.

At Murray Street a deeper inclination of the head was the honour paid a business friend in a passing automobile. At Park Place the blue machine skirted ahead of the traffic block where the huge Woolworth Building mounted skyward. A taxi darted in front of it, tried to cut in ahead; then stopped. Villers's chauffeur cursed under his breath as he swerved toward the curb. The wheels of the smooth-running car struck the thin end of a building girder, ran over it with a great jolt that jarred the car body down on its springs. A fat traffic cop hurried across the street just as the stalled taxi came to life and scurried down Broadway. The blue car had never even paused; the incident was closed.

The chauffeur bent lower over his wheel so that his muttered oaths would not reach the silent man behind him, for he knew that his job hung on the hair of his employer's morning humour. John T. Villers's one rule, whether it be for trusted clerks or chauffeurs, was smoothness; he did not like jolts.

The next traffic cop, who had sworn sympathetically when he saw that jar, let his jaw drop and his salute become a gesture of surprise. The lone man in the tonneau was lying back in the cushions, his eyes closed, the fingers of the hand that had been on the door relaxed.

"'Tis a tired man he is this mornin'," muttered the traffic man in sympathy.

The car swung into Wall Street, stopped before the world-known banking house of Villers. Instantly the chauffeur was down, his hand pulled open the door. But the machine that never relaxed was sleeping. Wonderment came to the face of the driver; then fear. He laid a hand lightly on the shoulder of his employer. The breathing man did not stir. The fear on the chauffeur's face deepened. Mr Villers must be sick!

He obeyed the first instinct, and looked wildly around. Relief chased some of the fear away when he saw the approaching private watchman, who had been stationed before the Villers's house for years.

"Mr Villers is sick!" he cried.

The watchman brushed him aside, and stared at the bloodless face with the closed, blue-veined lids.

"He must 'a' fainted!" gasped the watchman; and he, too, looked wildly around for help.

"Can I be of any assistance?" Both jumped nervously as the stout, full-bearded man with the black satchel spoke. "I am a doctair." He enunciated the words slowly, distinctly, with a pause after each.

"Mr Villers has fainted." They chorused it, huge relief in their voices, and stepped back instantly.

The bearded man stepped to the car, ripped open the unconscious man's coat and vest, and placed his hand over the beating heart professionally.

"Heart trouble. Seerious," he told them slowly, as if the words caused him trouble. "Tell them inside." Both started. He called the watchman back. "Spread the robe on the sidewalk." The watchman's clumsy fingers fumbled with the robe as the physician put his ear to the financier's chest, muttered an angry ejaculation, and fumbled with the black bag at his feet.

"It's ready, sir." Then the watchman swore under his breath at the crowding men and boys who had apparently sprung from the very sidewalk.

The big man paid not the slightest attention. He lifted the slight form of the man of millions and laid it gently on the robe-covered stones. "He must go to a hospital," he announced with precise distinctness. "I will call the ambulance."

The crowd parted, he hurried through.

Inside the banker's office the chauffeur blurted the news to the multi-millionaire's private secretary, utterly unmindful of the two strangers who were with him.

"Fainted?" echoed the secretary blankly.

"Fainted?" repeated the red-cheeked, black-haired stranger.

"Men like Villers don't faint. Where is he?" The chauffeur stared at the deep-chested, striking-looking man with the wavy white hair, fine as silk, and the strong, lean face, whose extreme paleness was accentuated by the great blue circles of the smoked tortoise-shell library glasses that rested lightly on the nose with its delicate, sensitive nostrils. "Show me where he is, Sydney." The cleft chin was set at an ominous angle, his slim stick, apparently of heavy ebony, dangled idly between the tapering fingers of his right hand.

"Can't you see the crowd running?" The shock had made the chauffeur forget that he was only a chauffeur; he jerked his head toward the door he had opened so unceremoniously.

"I am blind." The white-haired man said, it simply, quietly.

"Come, Thorn." His apple-cheeked secretary led the way from the office, the blind man at his heels. Villers's private secretary and the chauffeur followed dumbly after.

There were now two policemen to keep the surging crowd from the still body of the master of millions on the cold sidewalk. The outer ranks parted for the apple-cheeked man, the blind one followed him to the centre. One of the policemen mopped his brow in relief as they entered the small circle.

"It looks like heart trouble, Mr Colton," he murmured nervously.

"Think so, Thompson?" The end of the slim stick touched a knee of the prostrate man lightly. Thornley Colton knelt and picked up a lax arm. His fingers felt the pulse.

"That's what the doctor said it was." The watchman licked his dry lips. "He ought to be back by now."

"Doctor?" snapped the kneeling man, without looking up.

"He laid him there t' call th' ambulance." Once more the watchman wet his lips.

"Who is Mr Villers's physician?" The blind man's fingertips were lightly brushing the coat-lining.

"Doctor Clayton." The private secretary answered.

"Get him. Quick!" The tone of the voice sent a bareheaded clerk who had followed them on the jump to obey.

"Is it a serious heart attack?" stammered the still-dazed private secretary.

"Heart attack? *No!*" The blind man spoke sharply, crisply. "This is a morphine stupor!"

"Morphine?" gasped the dazed secretary incredulously.

"Yes!" The word was jerked out, a slim forefinger and thumb raised an eyelid of the prostrate man. "See the contracted pupils? Pin-points!"

"But how—Thank Heaven, Mr MacLaren!" The secretary's voice changed from helpless amazement to joyous relief as the square-shouldered, square-chinned man with the iron-gray hair pushed his way through the crowd.

"My God! What does this mean?" cried the newcomer.

The blind man rose, picked up his stick, and brushed his trousers knees.

"It means robbery—now," he said grimly. "It will probably mean murder in a few hours!"

Dreyfus MacLaren, the one man in all the world who enjoyed the full confidence of John T. Villers, paced the floor of his office with nervous strides, halting at every turn, ears strained to catch the faintest sounds from the inner room, where the doctor worked over the unconscious money machine. On the street outside, stretching from the sub-treasury steps to the dingy buildings where the sugar brokers buy and sell, the crowd still waited, whispered. In the outer room of the financier's office came the low-voiced hum of half a hundred newspaper men, tensely waiting a word from that inner room. At the end of his small office MacLaren swung around to face the blind problemist, who rolled the thin, hollow stick he always carried between his tapering white fingers.

"My God, Mr Colton!" he broke out. "It couldn't have happened!"

"It did," answered the blind man mildly.

"But he was in an open automobile; a thousand persons saw him; he answered the salutes of, perhaps, fifty policemen along Broadway. No one was near him; no one could have got near enough to render him unconscious with morphine."

"The fact that he is still in a morphine stupor is the best answer to that." Thornley Colton's voice was still mild, even gentle.

"You say that the man who lifted him out of the car did not inject the stuff?"

"Yes. The bounding pulse my fingers felt told me immediately that it had been in the system at least ten minutes. The bounding pulse, as it is called, is peculiar to morphia. I have made a special study of pulse beats." The blind man did not add that the pulse, to him, was the Keyboard of Silence that told many secrets of the heart to the supersensitive fingertips that always rested on the wrist when he shook hands.

"Then that puts it right up to the chauffeur, whom the police arrested," admitted MacLaren. "But I can't see how he did it," he added.

Sydney Thames, silent in a corner chair, also shook his head.

"He didn't!" snapped Colton. "If the police were forced to use brains instead of feet to hold their jobs, there wouldn't be so many fool mistakes made. They should have arrested the automobile," he finished seriously.

Before the surprised expression on MacLaren's face could be put into words the inner door opened, and the grave-faced doctor stood before them.

"Has Mr Villers's family been notified?" he asked.

"He won't die!" There was utter disbelief in MacLaren's tone.

"He will die," amended the physician quietly.

"His nerve has been keeping his worn-out body going for years; such an overdose of morphine could not but be fatal. I have tried to arouse him, but heroic methods would only result in an instant stopping of his heart. He will sleep for, perhaps, an hour more; then he will quietly stop breathing."

"My God, doctor! That is murder!" MacLaren's great body dropped limply into a chair, his face was white. He had refused to believe, before, that the master of millions could die. It was impossible. The wonderful machine could not stop. Now it was silent, useless.

The doctor was speaking: "There is no doubt that a heavy dose of morphia is responsible; every symptom points to it unmistakably, but"—the physician stroked his Vandyke perplexedly—"I have been unable to find the spot on his body where the hypodermic needle entered. I have minutely examined the chest, the abdomen, the arms, thighs, even the face. It is puzzling, very."

"Mr Villers is still lying on his back?" The question was put casually by the blind man, whom the physician had not even noticed.

"Certainly!" The doctor answered as one answers a foolish question.

"If you will turn him gently on his side for a moment you will probably find the broken point of the hypodermic needle under his shoulder-blade."

"His back—why—" The physician darted through the inner door.

The doctor's going left them silent. MacLaren's square shoulders were hunched forward, his eyes fixed steadily on the closed door. Sydney Thames, in the big leather chair in the corner, was tense, rigid. A hundred times he had heard the blind man, whom he loved, make a statement of this kind. Never had he known him to be wrong; but always did he fear that Thornley Colton would make some terrible mistake in his sureness of himself. And the sightless problemist smoked his cigarette calmly, the great, blue circles of eyes fixed on the ceiling above him. The door opened; the doctor faced them.

"The needle had broken under the right shoulder-blade—as you said." Doctor Clayton's keen eyes bored the blind man with a look of half-suspicion.

The words seemed to arouse MacLaren; he realized their significance. "How—did—you—know—that?" Each separate word was a gasp. "And blind!" The tone of his voice was a demand for explanation.

"I knew it because of my blindness," explained the problemist quietly. "We of the darkness must learn to visualize, mentally, what your eyes accept unconsciously. We learn to see with our brains, you see without them. My whole life has been spent in this development of mental visualization. I can instantly picture, in my brain, a scene that has been given me in pieces by my four other senses. And that mental picture often goes back to events that lead up to, and make, the scene."

"Do you mean that you can *imagine* who administered the morphine?" asked MacLaren incredulously.

"Not at all!" There was just a shade of impatience in the tone. "I have no clairvoyant powers. I haven't the remotest idea of the guilty persons' identity—yet. But I knew Mr Villers; I knew his habits, just as every man in New York, and Europe, too, who reads the papers, knows them. He has probably been given more columns of newspaper space than any other man who ever lived. Everything he did was machine-like, never changing; as sure as the sun and moon. I know how he sits in an automobile; I know the attention he attracts. You do, too, but you accepted them merely as something too obvious for the brain—as merely a routine report of the eyes. So, when I felt the unmistakable morphia pulse, an instant's thought told me the only possible way it could have been administered. The trained mind doesn't have to take up time with the consideration of innumerable possibilities; it is trained to the instant elimination of impossibilities. The back was the only place it could have been injected."

"How? By whom?" They chorused it eagerly. "By the innocent tool of a mastermind: Mr Villers's automobile."

"The automobile! What do you mean?" Incredulity, amazement were in the voices of the excited men.

"During the excitement attending the carrying of Mr Villers to his office my fingers were examining the cushions of the tonneau. The upholstery had been cut in the crease formed by the two tuft buttons, about where a man's back would come. A specially made hypodermic was inserted, and the cut sewed. Of course, the crease concealed the stitches. No one ever used the car but Villers, and everyone knows how he sits in the machine. You heard the statement of the chauffeur before the police arrested him. The jolt caused by the girder and the stalled taxi in front of the Woolworth Building were all that was needed. If that had not succeeded, the taxi would have swung in front and caused a collision. Then the 'doctor' would have gotten right on the job there, as he did here, when the taxi hurried on ahead to be on hand here. The breaking of the hypo needle was almost a certainty. It only required the barest fraction of an instant for the stuff to enter the body, and the broken needle would at once destroy the instrument and make its presence for some time unsuspected by anyone sitting in the car."

"How fiendish," murmured Doctor Clayton, and the words seemed puerile.

MacLaren shook his head, as if to clear the cobwebs from his usually alert brain; then he leaped to his feet, totally unmindful of the dying man in the next room.

"Colton, he *can't* die! The quarter-billion Chinese loan must be put through today. The new German bond bid is being held open for us till midnight. Another twenty-four hours' delay means that we lose both. He had all the data, the papers! They were—"

"Stolen," finished Thornley Colton quietly. "That was the object of the game—as I told you outside."

"I never thought of them!" In MacLaren's voice was the strong man's contrition for an unpardonable oversight. His teeth snapped together with the squaring of his jaw as he paced the room before the silent blind man and the red-cheeked, black-haired Sydney Thames. Behind the closed door they could hear the hum of the doctor's voice, as he tried vainly to call up the Villers's uptown house; though a hundred thousand black-typed extras were on the street telling of the racing special train that was bringing the family to the city and the dying man.

MacLaren made a circuit of the office before he stopped in front of the blind man, who idly twirled his cane. The sudden stopping of the machine that he had thought could not stop had unnerved him completely, driven every other thought from his mind. But theft was something he understood. It meant money. MacLaren, too, was a money machine.

"The loss of those papers means millions!" He was calm now, with the calm of deadly earnestness. "More than that! The stealing of those data Mr Villers had means that the United States will be frozen out of both the Chinese and German loans. You know how we had to fight for the chance! Ours is the only American banking house that could handle them. All the figures were prepared by Mr Villers, and you know his invariable rule to hold things like this until his last minute of grace. Those papers must be recovered before midnight! Even the murder—there seems to be no doubt that it will be murder—pales into insignificance beside this, and"—there was a curious catch in his voice—"God knows I loved John T. Villers. But the loss of that Chinese loan means that the United States won't have a say in the new republic; that American interests will be crowded out by the powers who control China financially. Every last detail was in those papers he was to have ready today. Think of the German loan!" He was pacing the floor again, talking as he walked. One money machine had stopped; another must take its place. "The loss of those papers means a loss of at least ten millions to us, and American interests in China and Germany will lose a hundred millions in the next ten years!"

"Midnight," murmured Thornley Colton, as a sensitive fingertip touched the crystalless watch in his pocket. "And it's now one-fifteen."

"Less than eleven hours!" MacLaren fairly jumped to the telephone on his desk. "The police must have inducements to hustle!" One hand lifted the receiver; then he swung round. *"You!"* It was almost an accusation as he hurled it at the blind problemist. "You solved that code-book theft for us a year ago. I'd forgotten! There isn't a minute to lose!"

"A man is dying in the next room," reminded Thornley Colton quietly.

MacLaren wet his dry lips. "I know." His voice was lower, calmer. "But think what it means. The hugeness of it! A theft of a hundred millions!" It wasn't lack of human feeling in MacLaren. He was a money machine, doing what the man in the next room would wish done.

The blind man nodded understandingly. "I came in this morning to see Mr Villers regarding his cheque for our Home for Blind Children. We haven't received it this year."

"If you can recover those papers I will give you my personal cheque for a hundred thousand!"

"I never accept fees," corrected Colton. "The solving of mysteries is my recreation. But if you will continue Mr Villers's contributions to the home—" His expressive lips finished the sentence without words.

"Yes! Ten times the amount." MacLaren was half out of his chair, staring at the blind man.

"Thank you. That home means a lot to me." The blind man spoke reverently. "Sydney and I will look into the case after lunch; I am hungry."

"Hungry? My God!" MacLaren fell back weakly into the chair. "Don't you realize that you have less than eleven hours? Don't you understand that every minute of delay may be fatal?"

"Oh, no," replied the problemist easily. "It will be at least several hours before the man who has the papers finishes his elaborate precautions for putting the police off his trail. There is no sense in hurrying after a man who is dodging and doubling to avoid possible pursuit. When he is convinced that his trail has been covered he will resume his normal way. The chased hare can wear out a hundred dogs that follow his devious windings, and when they are worn out he returns to the bosom of his family, contented and serene. That's where the ferret gets him."

For a full minute MacLaren stared, as if the blind man had presented a problem in Euclid which he could not understand. Then he brushed his sweat-beaded forehead with a trembling hand. "But the police didn't waste an instant," he protested. "There are two hundred detectives working now. They've got a minute description of the man." He stopped suddenly. "You weren't even present when they questioned the chauffeur and the watchman!"

"The senseless bulldozing of the police always makes me lose my temper," confessed Thornley Colton. "I spoke to the chauffeur for ten minutes before the detectives arrived. Afterward I preferred to sit here, where I could smoke a cigarette and use the telephone."

"But the police learned that the man who lifted Mr Villers from the car was stout, with a full brown beard, and dressed in light gray," persisted MacLaren.

"And in this office, alone with my cigarette, I learned that he was slim and smooth-shaven," smiled Thornley Colton, as he rose. "But those are minor details. He had the nail of his right index finger broken, and wore a curious thumb ring. Also, he did not actually place the hypodermic in the tonneau cushions. That was done by a small, slightly built man, and a very beautiful woman who is left-handed."

"Without eyes—" began MacLaren gaspingly.

"With my ten eyes." Thornley Colton held out his two hands, with their tapering hypersensitive fingers.

Broadway was a pandemonium of newsboys' shouts; Wall Street a murmur of low-voiced speculation; newspaper offices a buzz of humming activity. John T. Villers was dead—murdered. London whispered it solemnly, Paris gesticulated over it, Berlin gutturaled the news phlegmatically, Tokyo took it with characteristic lack of characteristics. Men in tin-roofed cable offices on the coast of Africa caught the telegraph clicks with news eagerness instead of curses. The wireless aerials of a thousand ships filched the story from the air. The man who had built the American empire of money was dead. Would the empire crumble? Would the worldpower of money return to the seats of the mighty on the other side of the ocean, where it had been before the money machine had demanded a hand-grasp on the golden sceptre the, jealous hands of Europe had wielded so long? The money machines of Paris, London, Berlin awaited the answer that would be in the Chinese loan, the German loan—the answer that was in the pocket of a murderer!

And in the quiet dining-room of the old Astor House Thornley Colton complained to the waiter of the lack of crust shortening in the apple-pie he was eating. It was three o'clock.

Across the table Sydney Thames chewed his cigar nervously and tried to keep his mind on the "latest" extra he held in his hands. He had read the life story of John T. Villers, printed under the great black word: "DEAD!" It was the story of the poor boy who came to the city, the story of machine-like habits, of putting through vast deals only when he had taken the last possible hour to consider every point, until he became known in Europe and America as "Last-Minute" Villers.

He read of Johnson, Villers's personal chauffeur, who slept alone with his wife and three small children in the big private garage that was now empty because the dozen other Villers machines and their drivers had gone to Bar Harbour with Mrs Villers and the two sons. He read of Johnson's five years of service, of his exemplary habits, his nights spent at home with his family; even of his taking his wife and two larger children to the theatre the night before, while the baby was cared for by a neighbour. Even the police admitted that he was innocent, but police-like, they still held him.

The story of finding the curious hypodermic, surrounded by a strong spring to hold it in place, caused Sydney to laugh nervously. The police had not discovered it until reporters, who had interviewed MacLaren after Thornley Colton had left, told them of it. Now the search was on for the taxi which had caused the Villers machine to run over the girder. And there was no clue! The three traffic policemen who had seen the whole thing had neither number nor idea of the machine. It was red; so were a thousand others. An expert had said that the hypodermic of death had been made abroad, possibly in Germany. And that was all.

But the papers revelled in the details; they gave inch-typed prominence to the announcement that MacLaren had offered a huge reward for certain papers stolen from the unconscious Villers. It was a big story; the biggest story of the most daring crime New York had ever known.

Yes, Sydney read, and re-read, until the inch paragraph in the lower left-hand corner regarding the activities of a band of international smugglers was a relief. On any other day that story would have been given prominence, today it was only a filler. He glanced up at the clock on the wall, then his eyes turned toward the blind man, in them a look of appeal for hurry.

"Nervous, Sydney?" smiled Thornley Colton over the top of his glass of milk.

Thames flushed, as he usually did when this man, who had picked him up as a bundle of baby-clothes on the banks of the English river that had given him the only surname he had ever known, read his thoughts.

"It is five minutes past three," he murmured apologetically.

"And we haven't done a thing," finished Colton, the smile still on his thin, expressive lips.

"But this is so big; the consequences—"

"Do you expect the success of this murder to pave the way for others?" interjected Thornley Colton mildly.

"I wasn't thinking—" Sydney stopped suddenly.

"Of the murder." The problemist again finished the sentence for him. "You were thinking of the stolen data. So are a million others." The smile was cynical, now. "What a pitiful thing a human life is, compared to a few millions. No one thinks of Villers's death as the death of a man. It is merely the stopping of a machine with its work unfinished." He took a bill from his fold and laid it beside his plate. "Come, then; I'll get busy."

"To the Villers garage?" asked Thames eagerly. "There should be countless clues, for you, leading to the persons who placed the hypodermic."

"All superfluous," declared Thornley Colton, with a slight wave of the thin, hollow stick he always carried. "Following a multitude of unimportant clues is police work. We are going to the office of the Manhattan Tug and Lighterage Company; yesterday was quite foggy. Remember?"

"What—" began Sydney amazedly.

Thornley Colton interrupted. "The same?" he asked quietly.

Sydney Thames choked back the words and glanced over the dining-room. His brain, trained for years to count steps for the man who could not see, and who refused a guiding arm, calculated rapidly. "The waiter is serving the table twelve steps straight. Turn eleven, four right, and seven to the door, left."

A nod, and the blind man hurried forward confidently with long, swinging strides, the hollow cane dangling idly from his fingers. Sydney followed, and, at the door, he stepped beside Colton. The slight touch of his sleeve on the sightless man's arm guided him to a taxi-cab. It was not until the directions had been given, and they were on their way toward the Battery, that Thornley Colton spoke.

"The Manhattan Tug and Lighterage Company got a whole lot of free publicity a few weeks ago in connection with that rescue at sea of the Oldwell private yacht by one of their big sea-going tugs that happened to be near. Recollect?"

"Yes," admitted Thames, puzzled. "But what has that to do with it?"

"Nothing, except that the story went the rounds, and the name would naturally occur to anyone who needed a sea-going tug. I have an idea that the fog of yesterday caused several persons a whole lot of anxiety. Ah, here we are."

Dazedly Sydney Thames followed the blind man to the sidewalk. What had a sea-going tug to do with a robbery on Wall Street? What had the fog of yesterday to do with the murder of today? But Sydney knew the uselessness of the eager questions that were in his mind. The problemist would tell him, all in good time. So, silently, he fell in beside Thornley Colton, and guided him into the offices with the slight touch of his sleeve.

President M'Inness was the man Colton asked for, and they were shown into the private office immediately.

"Glad to see you, Mr Colton; glad to see you!" boomed the wide-shouldered, rugged-faced man, as he took the other's fingers in his vice-like grip. "What is it this time; smugglers again? They say a new gang's workin'. They're even watching my boats."

Thornley Colton shook his head, for answer to that last. Then he came right to the point.

"You got a wireless from the *Moravia*, early yesterday morning, to take a passenger off at Quarantine, and rush him to New York." It was not a question; it was a simple statement of a known fact.

"Sure," admitted M'Inness. "Then the Lord stepped in and brushed away the fog at midnight, and the *Moravia* docked at eight o'clock this morning."

"Can you give us the name that was on the wireless?"

"Sure. I guess you've heard it often enough. Percy Vanderpoole."

Sydney Thames could not repress a gasp of surprise; but Thornley Colton's tone was merely casual as he said:

"Dreyfus MacLaren's nephew?"

"That's him. He's got about nine million dollars, you know, and he's certainly been making it fly in the four years since he left college. Hasn't brains enough to get in out of the rain, either."

"Um!" Thornley rolled the hollow stick between his fingers absently. "Nothing else in the wireless, I suppose?"

"Nope. Just wanted a tug if the *Moravia* was held up after two o'clock. Wasn't. The fog lifted, she docked, and we lost two hundred dollars." The sentence ended in a wry smile.

"From what I've heard of Vanderpoole, and from what I know of him, I should think he'd have taken that tug anyway, and hang the expense." The blind man rose. "He must have been taking someone's advice," he finished.

"Be the first time he ever did, then, according to the papers," grunted M'Inness. "Accordin' to them I've seen, he has a bug for giving fool dinners."

"So I've heard," murmured Colton, backing toward the door.

"Ain't any use asking your game, I guess!" grinned the amiable Mr M'Inness.

"You'll probably read about it in the morning papers," smiled Colton. Then he hurried out, his brain automatically counting the steps it had registered as he entered.

On the sidewalk outside, Sydney allowed his thoughts to find expression in two words:

"Great Scott!"

"It was a surprise," admitted the problemist. "It means a total change of plans. Take me to a telephone."

There was one at hand in the corridor of a big office building. For nearly half an hour Colton telephoned, while Sydney waited outside the closed booth vainly trying to understand this new complication. What connection had the nephew of the man who had offered them a hundred thousand dollars for the recovery of the papers with their theft, and with the murder of John T. Villers?

Colton emerged from the booth, a smile of triumph on his thin lips.

"Now a jewellery store, Sydney," he said crisply. "I want to buy a cheap, unset diamond."

"A diamond?" echoed Thames blankly.

"Exactly. I've just accepted an invitation for you and me and MacLaren to a little dinner aboard Percy Vanderpoole's yacht this evening. I'm going to see if a diamond really has the wonderful power of suggestion so often attributed to it."

II.

The Fee's eyes sparkled with delight as he listened. When Thornley Colton had finished, queer gurgling noises of joy issued from the boy's throat before the words came:

"Jumpin' Jimmy, Mr Colton! A motor boat at night an' a disguise. That's real detective work!"

The blind man's lips framed a whimsical smile as he gazed down at the red-haired, freckled-faced youth, with the slightly twisted nose, who had become a member of the Colton household as the result of a particularly baffling murder case, for which he had been the only fee.

"A whole lot depends on you, Shrimp," said Thornley Colton seriously. "Michael will go with you, but your part will have to be done all alone. I don't think you will be in any personal danger; if I did I wouldn't let you go."

Some of the joyous light went from the boy's eyes. "Chee! I wisht there was goin't' be some real gun play," he sighed.

"You have a long life before you," laughed Colton. "Hurry now; here comes Sydney."

As his secretary entered he turned to face him.

"Your foolish fear of women is not going to spoil it, Sydney?" he asked amusedly.

"No!" Sydney answered with the gruffness that was always in his voice when this subject was brought up. Sydney's fear of woman was really adoration. All women, to him, were angels; his fear was that he would fall in love with one—and he was nameless, a bundle of rags, abandoned on the banks of the Thames in London. This was constantly in Sydney Thames's mind.

"Here comes MacLaren," the blind man said suddenly; a moment later the big, square-jawed man burst into the room.

"Where are they? Have you got them?" he gasped, the topcoat, flung over his arm, dragging on the floor.

"Your coat will need the services of a dozen brushers in a short while," murmured Colton.

"Damn the coat!" flared MacLaren, flinging it on to the library desk. "I've walked forty miles, in that office of mine, this afternoon. Every reporter in the world has baited me. I've had a very devil of a time getting here without them on my trail. Our code messages from Europe say the financiers are grinning up their sleeves at us. They know! And all the word I get from you is to be here at seven o'clock, and you'd show me where the papers were."

"I said I'd get the papers, and show you where the murderers were," corrected Colton mildly. "I have an old-fashioned idea of the value of human life."

"Yes. Certainly," choked MacLaren. The hours of inaction had done their work.

"We have a dinner engagement at eight," went on Colton smoothly.

"Dinner!" exploded the square-jawed man. "My God, man! You—"

"Exactly." The voice of the blind man held a new tone now; a steel-like timbre that Sydney Thames instantly recognized. "I am taking you to that dinner to get your mind off the terrible events of this afternoon. Nothing else!"

"Where is the dinner?" The meekness of the big man was almost ludicrous.

"On the yacht of your nephew, Percy Vanderpoole."

"That fool!" There was acridity in the voice this time.

"He has that reputation." Sydney Thames thought the tone dry. "He is giving what he calls a wireless dinner on his yacht, anchored off the Metropolis Yacht Club. All the arrangements were made, and the invitations sent out from the *Moravia*, by wireless. You know Percy has quite a reputation for unique affairs of this kind. I called him up this afternoon regarding some other matter, and he insisted that I come. I sought an invitation for you, and I got it. Several men who were friends on the way over are included."

"All right," agreed MacLaren gloweringly.

"We'll go to the club in your car," was all Thornley Colton said, as he led the way from the room.

Vanderpoole's guests were all awaiting their appearance, and introductions were hurried through. There was a gushy, blackhaired Miss Clements, who was paired with an anaemic, slightly-built American; a tall, stout German, who answered the name of Von Wagnen, with pale cheeks, and chin that contrasted strangely with his ruddy forehead; a dissipated-looking Englishman named Brookes; several feminine nonentities, and one or two of Percy's male society friends. It was a mixed party, characteristic of the money-flinging Percy Vanderpoole.

The hurry was in honour of the military-looking Count d'Auboi whom Percy had met in Europe two years before, with his charming wife, the countess. The count had been aboard the *Moravia*. So had the countess, though Percy chaffed her for taking her cabin before he even knew she was aboard, and staying there the whole time. Her cheeks were colourless, but her eyes shone, despite the fearful ordeal of seasickness she now laughed over. And there was the great joke of the count, who confessed that he had never been in America, losing Percy on the pier, and wandering around the city for several hours, with his nervous wife, until they succeeded in locating Percy by telephone.

"They finally got to the Waldorf, Lord knows how," laughed Percy, as he led the way to the dining-cabin. "And now they're going on the midnight train to Frisco, so we'll have to hustle this little affair through."

"My seestair, she is married there," smiled the count, in his broken English. Then, with entire disregard of connection: "An' I even mees my brother-in-law, Mr Clauson"—he indicated the anaemic-looking American—"who come to meet us."

Sydney took his seat, almost tremulously between the Countess d'Auboi and the vivacious Miss Clements, at the table in the mahogany-finished cabin. But in a few minutes he was surprised and delighted to find that his foolish fear of the sex was being driven away like mist before the sunshine of the charming countess's conversation. Miss Clements, at his left, chattered away at a mad rate to Clauson, and did not bother him. But the countess, her wonderful voice surcharged with sympathy and the intuitive understanding of women, drew him from his shell immediately.

Across the table the blind man chatted with Count d'Auboi, who was even more charming, if possible, than his wife. At the head of the table Percy laughed uproariously at the dissipated-looking Englishman's account of his first pigsticking in India. At the foot, MacLaren glowered in silence, utterly ignoring the sullen-looking German and the yellow-haired woman who was his partner. The dissipated Englishman and the German were cabin friends Percy had met on the *Moravia*. They had both been interesting, and that was all Percy ever asked.

During a lull in the conversation Percy happened to glance at the face of the German, who had relapsed into sullen silence after repeated attempts to get a word from MacLaren.

"Anyone would think you'd committed a crime, Von Wagnen," he laughed.

The blind man was the only one who did not see the blood mount to the strangely pale cheeks of the Teuton; but MacLaren was the only one who caught the lighting eye signal from the Englishman. His own eyes narrowed cunningly. This was no mere dinner engagement!

"But what a horrible crime the murder of Mr Villers was!" gushed Miss Clements, with a shiver.

"By Jove!" The ejaculation came from Percy Vanderpoole. "You used to be quite clever at solving mysteries, Mr Colton. Why don't you get on this one?"

MacLaren cursed under his breath. Sydney Thames could not keep the startled look from his eyes.

"You are a detective, Mr Colton?" The countess asked it almost accusingly, the charming touch of accent in her voice giving it a subtle undercurrent of laughter.

Thornley Colton's thin lips smiled back at her. "I do a little in that line," he admitted.

"Tell us about eet." It was the count at his side, eyes eager with interest.

"My cases are only simple little affairs, naturally," deprecated the blind man. He thrust two fingers into his waistcoat pocket. "Here is something that I expect to solve a mystery for me."

He held a small, glittering diamond on his outstretched palm. MacLaren's keen ears caught the sharp intake of breath of the German at his side. "Yes," continued the problemist. "That came from the thumb ring of a pickpocket, torn from the prongs by the lining of his victim's coat."

"An' he deed not know eet—what a joke!" laughed the count, picking up the diamond from the extended palm, more closely to examine the stone. The light from the shaded incandescents above reflected in the four small rubies that formed the eyes of the twisted snake ring he wore on his thumb.

The sullen-looking German had apparently recovered his nerve. MacLaren looked puzzled.

"Let's see it; I know a bit about the bally things." The Englishman took the stone from the count. "There's a flaw in it as big as a shilling!" he announced, with the disgust of an expert. Again MacLaren caught the signal of eyes to the German beside him.

"Dere iss few goot stones," announced the Teuton ponderously.

"Ple-ese tell us about it?" pleaded the countess.

"Oh, do, please do," pouted Miss Clements, as if to forestall a refusal. The request was chorused by the others.

"It really isn't worth it," protested Colton; then he seemed to know, for the first time, that the Englishman held the stone for him to take back. "Thank you," he smiled, as he replaced it carefully in his pocket. "I was afraid someone would switch off the lights and steal it in the darkness and confusion. By the way, Percy, is that deck-light switch still where it used to be when your father was alive?

"The same place," nodded Vanderpoole. "Right beside the cabin-door, on the after-deck."

"See!" Colton's laugh was loud, but somehow it did not seem to ring true. "Anyone could steal the stone in the darkness, and get away with it."

MacLaren scowled. His quick mind understood that Colton wanted the location of that switch for some purpose of his own. And, without eyes, he must take this method of learning its location. But he knew that the other guests, too, had recognized some sinister motive under the palpable affectation of banter the blind man had assumed. There came a tenseness there had not been before. And everyone knew the location of the switch that could plunge the decks into instant darkness.

"Let's have the coffee and cigarettes under the awnings on the after-deck," suggested Percy, to cover the break.

"Let's," acquiesced Colton eagerly, then he paused impressively for an instant. "If you'll hurry I'll tell you something about the Villers murder. I am working on that case!"

Instantly chairs were pushed back as the guests crowded to the door.

As Sydney rose, the countess found time to whisper in his ear:

"He speaks strangely, your Mr Colton." There was feminine nervousness in her voice. Sydney nodded dumbly, sick at heart. The blind man he loved had made a mistake.

MacLaren kept close to the sullen German, utterly ignoring his yellow-haired dinner partner. The money machine's hands were clenched in his pockets, his shoulders braced for some attack. "A big, stout man, with a full beard," was the description he remembered. The Teuton answered that description perfectly; the pale cheeks showed where the beard had been recently shaven. He passed out to the awninged, dimly-lighted deck, brushing the coat of the blind man, who stood beside the door, almost over the small wicker table where the countess and Sydney had taken their seats with the brother-in-law of the count and the chatty Miss Clements.

For several seconds the blind man stood there, apparently calmly eyeing them. The light of the switch incandescent shone on his wavy, white hair, his broad shoulders, his deep chest. The German moved uneasily. The dissipated-looking Englishman, who had manœuvred to a seat beside him, gripped his arm. Every muscle in MacLaren's body was tense. The yellow-haired woman and the three other feminine nonentities bit their lips nervously.

Sydney Thames could not repress his own nervousness. Was the blind man going to accuse desperate men who had murdered a man and robbed him of papers worth a hundred millions No help was near. The sky was cloudy, the anchorage was deserted, except for an empty speed boat that rode at anchor in the silent darkness two hundred yards away.

Then Thornley Colton spoke quietly, smoothly.

"The story of the diamond is the story of the Villers murder." One hand drew out the crystalless watch. "It is now ten-thirty; at ten-forty-five the police will search this boat for the papers stolen from the unconscious man in front of his office!" Men and women jumped to their feet. "Sit still!" His hand went above his head. The switch snapped out. They were in darkness.

A chair toppled over. They heard him fumble with the switch lever. Then, shrill, frightened, came the voice of a boy:

"Let go! Let go! I'm workin' fer Mister Colton!"

The lights came. Startled men and women saw a small boy squirming in the grasp of a brawny man. Sydney Thames knocked over the empty chair at his right as he leaped to his feet. It was The Fee, caught, and in his hand was a black bag.

"It's the papers!" yelled The Fee.

Thames knew instantly the reason for that sudden darkness. It was Colton's plan—and an ignorant deck hand had ruined it!

But almost in a bound Thornley Colton was at the boy's side. He tore the man's hands from his arm, with fingers like steel.

"It's all right, Mike; start 'er!" screamed the freckle-faced boy.

Under their very feet, seemingly, came the bark of a gasoline engine.

"Stand back!" ordered Colton.

Dumbly, as if dazed, they obeyed. The boy stood alone at the rail. Below him the motor boat coughed.

Dreyfus MacLaren jumped forward to take the bag. A clenched fist sent him sprawling. A hand tore the bag from the boy's hand. A black automatic swept before the circle of white faces. Behind it was Count d'Auboi, lips drawn back in a snarl.

"I take it!" The snarling smoothness went out of the voice; it rose to a yell "Jean!"

At the signal the darkness again shut down on them. They stood huddled together before the menacing automatic they could not see.

"A move, I shoot into ze crowd, a woman, maybe," came the flint-like voice of the count before them. Somewhere behind them came the sounds of a short scuffle, a snarled oath. A man leaped to the rail. A splash sounded below; then a hoarse order in French.

"'Nette!" snapped the count. There was no response. Again came that hoarse voice from the water. A scrambling shadow over the rail. The motor boat leaped away from the side.

Out of the darkness came the piercing call of a police whistle. Across the black waters a broad beam of dazzling white shot out—picked up the boat—held it. Men were running on the decks of the speed craft two hundred yards away. It fairly leaped in pursuit of the smaller boat.

The white searchlight brought out the escaping boat with startling vividness. The two men crouched over the wheel. The black bag was on the seat beside them. A line of fire shot from the pursuing boat. Another. The small engine went dead. The space was closing now—fifty yards—twenty—the searchlight still held like a calcium.

The stupefied watchers on the yacht saw the count stand up in the boat; saw him look wildly around. He stooped, picked up the black satchel, and flung it far out into the water. In the bright glare they could see his very teeth bared in a snarling smile as he waited. The ripples gleamed in an ever-widening circle where the satchel had sunk.

"Nervy devil, isn't he?" It was the cool voice of Thornley Colton. For the first time the watchers realized that the lights were on again; that they had been actors in reality, not wraiths in a dream.

Dreyfus MacLaren was first to recover, and as he raised his voice it had in it the strong man's sob: "My God! The data!"

"The charming Countess Annette is sitting on them," smiled Thornley Colton. "I couldn't bear exposing her to police shots. She is handcuffed to her chair."

III.

"Yes, Sydney, the police can't be beaten when it comes to making arrests. Find the guilty ones, label them, lead them up to the police, and the cops'll get them every time. And the police dearly love a plant, that's why they worked so well tonight. You see, I made all the arrangements this afternoon when you had left me in disgust to walk off your nervousness. The telephone is a mighty handy thing for the blind." He took a sip of the vichy at his elbow, and touched the crystalless watch lying on the old-fashioned library table before him. It was twelve-thirty.

"But how—where?" Sydney Thames changed it to a confession. "I am still dazed."

"I suppose you'll have to have it all," smiled Colton. "All right. Ten minutes' intelligent conversation with the chauffeur before the fool detectives arrived save me practically all of the information I needed. He told me of the theatre party with his wife and two eldest children. I was interested because they went to a famous Broadway children's show, where the seat prices are high. The tickets had been given his wife by a rich woman who devoted her time to showing mothers how to care for their babies, and had taken an interest in his own. Of course, that told me immediately how the chauffeur had been gotten away while the car was fixed. Through his wife and tots was the only way he could be reached.

"Then I wanted to know if there was a good, quiet hotel nearby. The woman must have taken quarters near his home to be on the watch for the opportunity to get acquainted with his wife and children. They are fairly well-to-do, and would resent the professional interference of a settlement worker. There was a telephone call from MacLaren's office while you and the others were outside with the police—with the description the chauffeur had given me—fixed her as a Mrs Allen, a widow, who was spending her money and time on poor babies. She had been there two weeks. She wasn't in when I called, but would be in the morning. See how clever. Not a breath of suspicion by telling them that she was going to leave. Did she have a habit of calling a special taxi? She did, from the Nelson House. It was easy to get a description of the chauffeur from the starter there. The calls had been made without any attempt at concealment; for who would connect a settlement worker in New York with the wife of a French count? The chauffeur had been employed a week. He was undoubtedly an American. The woman was French, though she spoke English perfectly. See how simple the possibilities are when the foolish impossibilities the police delight in are eliminated?

"Then the chauffeur's recollection of the bearded man who had lifted Villers out of the car; his stilted way of speaking. I knew then that he, too, was a Frenchman, trying to hide it by repeating, slowly and carefully, without his usual accent, words he had learned by rote. Where had he been while the other two were making the arrangements? A man with the brains and knowledge to plan a crime like that couldn't be common enough, even in appearance, to hide successfully for two weeks. I remembered the *Moravia*, due from Havre last night. What could be a greater alibi than that of a man who had been in the city but a few hours? But the fog must have caused him considerable anxiety. That's why I went to see M'Inness. I knew the name of the Manhattan Tug and Lighterage Company would still be in everybody's mind. You know that Percy stepped in and sent that message on his own hook — at a hint from the count, of course, who was quick to see that that would cover his last possible connection. When I got him on the phone I learned of the count and his wife for the first time. Then I realized how infernally clever they were, and knew I'd have to act accordingly. The Englishman and the German also entered to complicate affairs. I didn't know whether they were in it or not."

"But the description you gave in MacLaren's office," interrupted Sydney. "It was wholly at variance with that of everyone who had seen him. And the left-handed woman who placed the hypodermic?"

Colton laughed. "The first came from knowledge of human nature. If he was stout and full-bearded when he exposed himself before the eyes of several hundred persons, it was a moral certainty that he was neither, with the disguise off. He'd absolutely reverse it when he stepped into the taxi that was waiting around the corner after it had let him off in time to get the papers. The stitches in the cushions told me the other. They were too fine to have been made by a man. My fingers showed me that the needle had been thrust upward, instead of downward, as would have been the case with a right-handed person."

"But the actual robbery?" insisted Sydney. "The man with the broken fingernail? I paid particular attention at the dinner. All seemed perfect."

"You are learning to observe," smiled the blind man. "When my fingers brushed the coat-lining of the unconscious man they felt the torn threads of the caught fingernail as it swept upward when he thrust his hand under the coat for the thick packet of papers. But the packet was evidently wedged, in some way, for it was necessary for him to thrust his whole hand down into the pocket. His thumb ring tore the lining slightly at the corner. These things could not be seen with the naked eye, but they could be felt with fingers trained to read handwriting by touching the reverse side of the paper, and feeling the indentations of the pencil."

Sydney nodded understandingly. "Now if you'll explain the diamond, and The Fee's entrance?" he asked.

"Suggestion. Psychology," declared Thornley Colton seriously. "The diamond held on my palm was primarily intended to find the man whose broken fingernail had pulled the threads from the coat lining. Held on my palm, the man who picked it up must touch my flesh with his fingernail. The count's was cut to the quick; that of his thumb was long and tapering. Then the Englishman wanted to see it. I knew he wasn't the man, therefore I caused the stampede to the after-deck with the promise of telling about the Villers murder to find out what he and his German friend really were. A quick touch in the crowd, as they came through the door, felt the heavy belt around the German's waist. Smugglers!

"That was easy, merely an incident in the case. But the police seemed glad to get them. They were part of the long-sought band. So we'll dismiss them. But their presence shows further cleverness on the part of the wily count in including them to divert suspicion if it became necessary. He probably knew their game, and would have used it to cover his, if he had to.

"My talk of the thumb-ringed pickpocket was intended to make the count suspicious of me. My reference to the light switch and the darkness were for the sole purpose of showing him how he could escape if it came to a showdown. My idiotic attempt to cover up what he, and others, supposed to be the only means I had of locating that switch was not intended to deceive them; it was intended to make them understand that I thought I was deceiving them. I knew the papers must be somewhere near; they planned to get away at midnight. But I couldn't take a chance of arresting them, and then searching; for men clever enough to steal those papers would be clever enough to put them where no one could get them. Therefore the talk of the police search and the pulling of the switch to put out the lights.

"By that time they understood that the only thing they could do was get away. I'd stood watching them in silence long enough to let them see that the anchorage was deserted, and that they had a pretty fair chance of escaping. When the darkness came I knew one of them would take instant advantage of it, and get the papers if they weren't already on his person. You didn't give a thought to Clauson's being absent when you toppled over his empty chair, as you saw The Fee with that fake bag bait. I did, and I knew the count would look at that bag as I intended he should. He wasn't given an opportunity to see that Clauson had gone. He was told of the ready boat, given an opportunity to grab the bag from the boy's hand. He called 'Jean' as a signal for Clauson to put out the lights. Jean wasn't there, but the quick-witted countess was. Jean, of course, heard that call, and came running. I met him at the cabin-door, held him long enough to get the packet from his inside pocket. It was easy, for"—a whimsical smile came to the thin lips—"I am quite at home in the darkness. It was done so quickly that the frightened Jean hardly knew it, I guess, and, of course, the count supposed the boy had gotten the data for me. Then the police stepped in, and we saw the spectacular play of the greatest crook I ever had the pleasure of meeting, while the countess struggled on the chair to escape. I'd put the papers under her for safekeeping, and also because they wouldn't go in my dinner-coat pocket."

"Then," puzzled Sydney, "the doctor who first attended Villers was—this count. But I can't see why—he needed his bag—"

"Because he was a mighty clever man. He knew it would be easy to take a thick packet of papers from Villers's pocket without being seen, but he also knew that it would be almost impossible to slip them into his own unobserved. Therefore the open doctor's bag at his feet, where they could be dropped in an instant."

"Papers worth a hundred million," murmured Sydney Thames, almost in awe.

"And costing a single, human life," digressed Thornley Colton wearily.

4

The Fourth Problem:

THE FLYING DEATH

I.

The last sobbing notes of the violin died away. Slowly, reverently, the girl lowered the bow and lifted her chin; the throat-filling hush wrought by the conjuring of her music became wild, unrestrained applause as the spell broke. The beating surges of sound from the gallery, the balcony, the floor seemed to frighten her a little; the frail body in its simple white frock shrank before it; but the girlish lips smiled bravely as she bowed her way to the wings.

Clamorous, insistent, the applause continued. She reappeared; silence came as she lifted the violin to her chin. The lilting fantasy of a folksong rollicked from under the dancing bow. Once more came the enthusiastic outburst when she finished. She gestured her thanks, smiled an instant at the upper right-hand box, laughed and kissed her hand to the lone occupant of lower left and ran from the stage.

"Sheer genius, Sydney!" murmured Thornley Colton, in expression of the reverence good music always aroused in him; for music, to the blind man, held all the pleasures that painting, sculpture, and beautiful architecture hold for those whom God has given sight. Now his whole face, from the high forehead to the lean, cleft chin, was alight even the sightless eyes seemed to shine behind the great blue circles of the smoked-glass, tortoise-shell-rimmed library spectacles that accentuated the striking whiteness of his face and hair.

"Wonderful!" breathlessly agreed the red-cheeked, black-haired Sydney Thames, secretary and constant companion of the blind man.

"It makes my woids muss up when I try to talk," gulped The Fee, freckle-faced, red-haired, blue-eyed boy, who had become a member of the Colton household at the conclusion of a particularly baffling murder case. Thornley Colton laughed softly and pushed back his chair. Then real alarm came to the boy's voice. "Gee, yuh ain't goin' now?" he pleaded. "They's a coupla comedy acr'bats an' a wop knife t'rower yet!"

"We'll wait," promised Colton, as he made room for a pale-faced young man who had just risen to hurry past him and out of the box.

The problemist moved his chair farther back, and whispered to Sydney. "Our friend who just left seems to be troubled with a mighty bad case of nerves," he observed. "My cane could feel his chair trembling under him the whole time the girl was playing. He seemed to jump a foot when she left the stage that last time, and he's been muttering under his breath ever since. What happened?"

"I'd say he was wildly in love with her, and madly jealous of someone else," accounted Sydney. "She smiled up at him an instant after that last encore, but she immediately turned and kissed her hand to the man in the lower left-hand box. If ever black rage shone in a man's face it was on that of our neighbour. He isn't more than twenty-two or three, and he doesn't look as if he had ever learned to curb a nasty temper."

"He left as if he were going in search of someone's heart blood," smiled the blind man, leaning back in his chair.

One of the comedy acrobats had just succeeded in pushing the other from a high table, and was joyously dancing on his rubber stomach, to the great delight of The Fee, and some fourteen or fifteen hundred others.

"You don't happen to know the occupant of lower left?" asked Colton. Somehow the thought of sordid jealousy of two men, and a girl whose witchery could produce such music, seemed to jar.

Sydney gazed covertly down at the occupant of lower left. He was a big-bodied man, and fat. There were fleshy pouches of good living and bad drinking under his eyes; but no dissipation could hide the iron will, the dominant arrogance the heavy chin showed. He sat back in the deep box, the black of his evening clothes verging into the black of the heavy velvet hangings that covered the wall behind him. The white expanse of shirt front contrasted strikingly with the sombre background; one white fist rested on the back of a gold chair.

"It's James P. Cartwright, the theatrical manager!" returned Sydney suddenly. "Her manager!" he supplemented in sudden anger as he compared the innocent girlishness of the violinist and the coarse grossness of the recognized man in the box. Sydney Thames deified all women from afar, for he had forbidden himself the joys of propinquity, because he could never forget that he had no name but that of the English river on the banks of which Thornley Colton had found him, a bundle of dirty baby-clothes, years before.

"Cartwright has an unenviable reputation among his women of the stage," muttered Colton. The smile was gone from the thin, expressive lips now. The rocking notes of the fantastic folk-song still haunted him; the sobbing cadence of the piece she had played before was in his mind: an omen of tragedy. A soul that could conjure music like that—and a Cartwright who, gossip said, demanded his price for others' success.

The two comedy acrobats had disinterred themselves from an avalanche of chairs and a table; the first to his feet had been promptly knocked down by the other, and dragged off the stage by his heels, while The Fee and a few hundred others shouted and clapped their approval. A card announced Signor Delvetoi and his marvellous whirling knives.

Sydney, watching the occupant of the lower left, saw him take out a big watch impatiently, lean ponderously back in a chair, and summon an usher. The uniformed man came, listened a moment, nodded, and opened the door at the stage end of the box, to reappear a moment later and whisper his message, or news. Cartwright nodded, and turned his attention idly toward the stage, where the signor sent a whirling knife toward the high boards before which his yellow-haired partner had set a red apple swinging on a long string. The knife point thudded into the wood; the cut string parted, and the apple rolled to the stage floor.

"Gee, that's some stunt!" ecstatically exclaimed The Fee, as he enthusiastically described the feat of the black-bearded signor to Colton.

A handful of playing cards flurried before the wooden stop. Three whirling knives shot across the whole length of the stage; three cards were pinned fast, and the assistant held them up triumphantly to show the pierced ace spots.

Cartwright inclined his head in a nod of grudging approval, then turned quickly as he heard the door that led back to the stage open. Sydney saw the girl who had played appear in her street clothes, a simple white shirt waist and dark skirt, her coat thrown over her arm. He gritted his teeth at the greeting she gave the theatrical manager, and as he saw the flush of happiness on the winsome face, while the thick lips of the man grinned as he took her coat. Cartwright jerked his thumb toward the stage where the dexterous signor had just succeeded in planting five knives in a black spot not bigger than a half dollar.

He pulled his chair close to that of the girl, and they sat talking; the girl with many pretty, unconscious gestures, the man listening, with a jerky nod now and then. They were in the rear of the box, not three feet from the heavy velvet hangings that covered the wall back of them. They could not be seen from the body of the theatre, but from the upper box opposite, where Sydney sat, everything in their box was visible.

Sydney interrupted The Fee's excited description of the signor's act long enough to tell the news to Colton; and he made no excuse for his spying. The blind man nodded grimly, and continued his patient listening to The Fee, who was having the time of his young life. The signor, in his suit of black silk and his black, pointed beard, had performed miracles with the whirling knives. Now the boy waited breathlessly for this last feat, because the soft music of the orchestra told him it would be the best of all. A huge frame was being lowered from the flies. The blond assistant stepped to the small shelf, thrust her hands through the leather loops, and stood against the golden back, arms spread wide, feet apart. The signor brought his table of glittering knives to the footlights; the frame and the assistant swung aloft. The lights went out. Darkness for a few brief seconds, then the calcium from the balcony outlined the suspended woman and the gold background.

"Ah!" The Fee's gasp swelled a thousand others, as the knife shot into the calcium beam from the darkness below, whirled with a thousand silver fires, and buried its point in the wood, blade grazing the cheek of the woman. A few seconds of breathless suspense, and another followed, to graze the ear. Even Sydney forgot the man and girl in the box as he watched the whirling blades. The weirdness of the thing held him fascinated; the knives, hurled from the hands of the man who was invisible in the darkness below the single light beam, pinwheeled through the light to find their place unerringly.

Then something caused Sydney Thames to turn his eyes again to the lower box. At the instant a flash of lurid light leaped from the darkness, silhouetting with startling vividness the seated man and girl. The roar of a pistol came to his ears and while the light cut the darkness he saw behind the seated man and girl the face of the youth who had been in the box with them; the man whose jealousy had been shown so plainly.

Pandemonium followed instantly. A chair crashed over in the darkness across the theatre clear above the cries of the panic-stricken men and women came the scream of a man:

"My God! I didn't do it! I didn't! I didn't!" The scream stopped. "Lights!" frenziedly called someone from the darkness.

They came in the box opposite, Sydney Thames saw Cartwright struggling with the man whose face he had seen so distinctly in the pistol's flash. On the floor of the box, face downward, was the girl of the violin. Between her shoulders, on the white shirt waist, was a widening splotch of crimson.

II.

The girl was dead. The white-coated ambulance surgeon who examined her had shaken his head, and refused to take her in the ambulance. The morgue waggon had taken the body but a short time after the police reserves had beaten their way through a mob of thousands to arrest the white-faced, hysterical prisoner, who cried his innocence through lips battered by the fist of Cartwright.

In the precinct station the prisoner had collapsed, and Cartwright told his story. He had heard a slight noise, and swung around in his chair. At that instant came the flash of the pistol behind him. He heard the man drop it, and he leaped to grapple with him. Yes, he knew the prisoner; name was Nelson, a half-baked kid, who had bothered Miss Reynolds for months. Yes, this was Miss Reynolds's first engagement; her first appearance on any stage. He was her manager. No, nothing else. Emphatically!

The prisoner, brought around roughly, swore that he was innocent. He had known Miss Reynolds for months, they had been friends in Europe. She had asked him to be present at her first appearance, and at the end of her act he had gone to meet her at the stage entrance. It was there that he was told that she had an engagement with Cartwright. That this made him wild with jealousy he admitted; he knew Cartwright by reputation, and Miss Reynolds was but a girl, innocent, unsophisticated.

He had walked around outside the theatre for about fifteen minutes, then he had decided to go to the box and demand an explanation. The theatre was in darkness for the knife-throwing act, but he knew his way. His hand had been on the black velvet hangings when he stopped. And the revolver flash had come *from the air* not a foot ahead of him. No, he could not explain how the shot had been fired. No one could have moved from the spot where the pistol had been, *because the weapon dropped on his toe!*

He was taken away to a cell on a charge of murder.

Cartwright, leaving the station when the last of the curious crowd had drifted away, seemed to have aged ten years since the tragedy. He was haggard, the grim, hard smile that had been characteristic was gone, his big hands trembled. He tried in vain to get permission to remove the girl's body from the morgue immediately. But the law demanded that the coroner see it first; and the official was out of town.

Cartwright remembered his political friends. He tried to locate a dozen over the telephone and failed. Then, by chance, he met the one man in the city who could help him; the one man among the four millions whom he could trust: Theodore Rogers, the theatrical lawyer, a friend for thirty years.

He tried to tell Rogers what he wanted, but his nervousness made his words a jumble.

"What is it, Jim? What's the trouble?" Rogers shook him, and he looked into his eyes anxiously.

Cartwright told him of the shooting. "And, by God, Ted!" he finished passionately. "I won't rest a minute till I see that devil in the electric chair! God! To kill a girl like that!"

The lawyer looked at him curiously. This was not the cool, suave Cartwright he had known so long.

Cartwright read the look on the lawyer's face, and the thoughts behind it. "Not that! I swear it's not that, Ted!" he choked.

"Come, have a drink," pleaded Rogers, pulling him toward the lighted entrance of a rathskeller.

"With that girl on a slab in the morgue?"

"One drink," insisted Rogers. "You are worse than useless this way. Come!"

He dragged Cartwright down the steps. The clock over the bar said half-past two, and the leather-seated booths were in darkness. But drinks could be had. The barman dozed, and the lone waiter yawned as he carried a tray toward the booths in the rear. Rogers led the theatrical man to a seat at the side of the room in front of the bar, ordered whisky, and waited patiently until Cartwright had gulped down the liquor.

"Now tell me about it, Jim," demanded Rogers.

Cartwright, as near the end of the leather seat as he could get, glanced at the dark booths in the back, then turned and surveyed the front of the place. The rathskeller was empty, except for the dozing barman and the waiter, who had gone into one of the front booths to figure his day's checks.

"Don't think—what you've been thinking about me and that girl, Ted." There was almost pathetic pleading in the manager's voice; it was pitched so low that even the lawyer at the other side of the narrow table could scarcely hear. "She was—a daughter to me—the daughter of the only woman I ever loved."

Rogers stared. This from the man Broadway thought it knew!

"Remember twenty years ago?" continued Cartwright, in that same low, pleading voice. "The girl I took away from Kelly, that drunken burlesque magician?"

The lawyer nodded, a look of understanding in his eyes.

"You know we loved each other, and we ran away; she, and I, and the six months' old kid," he went on. "You know how she died: killed in the C. & O. wreck two hours out of Chicago, two hours after we started—and the kid under her body, alive! I guess that's what woke me up. All I thought about after that was making money for the kid. I put her with good people, and I didn't tell them who she was, or who I was. When she got old enough to understand, I adopted her legally. But she never knew who her father and mother were. I couldn't tell her about the drunken sot that died in the Chicago alcoholic ward. A thing like that would have spoiled her.

"She was born with music in her. I kept her away from me and the people that knew me. I sent her abroad. And tonight was her try-out! I wanted to see if she could face the lights, because I wouldn't have her laughed at by the highbrows if she couldn't make good. And she did! God, how they went wild! I wouldn't tell a soul that she was my adopted daughter— until tomorrow. Now—" He fingered his whisky glass with twitching hands.

Theodore Rogers, whose heart was reputed to be of stone, felt a lump in his throat. He pushed his gloves from the table, so in bending he would get the needed instant to hide his feelings. Something made him jerk up his head! He saw—

The roar of the pistol in his ears deafened him. He cried out as the long-barrelled gun recoiled across the table and struck him, butt foremost, on the chest. His glass was crashed to a hundred pieces as the pistol fell on the table before him. The white shirt front of Cartwright was black, a small circle of fire glowed in the linen; on his face was an awful look of horror as his head pitched forward on his arms.

And then Rogers understood what his eyes had first seen; the picture that had lasted but the hundredth part of a second, perhaps, but which would be graven on his mind for a lifetime.

He had seen the pistol against Cartwright's heart, *with nothing to hold it there*; the recoil of the explosion had driven it across the table before it fell, *because no human hand had grasped it*; *no finger had pulled the trigger!*

III.

In the darkness of his library Thornley Colton paced back and forth. The cigarette-end glowed and died as he puffed thoughtfully. Each detail of the girl's murder at the theatre, described to him by the excited Sydney, while panic had raged above them and below them in the playhouse the night before, was being visualized by the wonderful brain that so unerringly found logic in seeming absurdity; explanation in apparent impossibility—because that brain had never been tricked by seeing eyes.

The murder of the girl had moved him mightily; the stilling forever of that wonderful music seemed more a crime against the world than against an individual. And as he paced the curtained room the mosaics of detail became a complete picture, and he knew—*knew*—that the man who had left their box so hurriedly the night before; the man whom Sydney had *seen* fire the shot, was guiltless of the murder!

He turned to face the door as hurried footsteps proclaimed to his trained, supersensitive ears that Sydney Thames was approaching.

"Cartwright has been murdered!" cried the red-cheeked secretary breathlessly. "It happened too late for the morning papers, but The Fee got some early extras of the evening editions with full details."

"Where? How?" asked Colton.

"In an uptown rathskeller. He was shot by Theodore Rogers, the lawyer."

"He was not," corrected the blind man quietly.

"How did you hear of it?" demanded Sydney, in surprise.

"This is the first intimation I had of such a thing, but your statement was just a little too positive; your voice told me that *you* believe Rogers guilty because of the utter impossibility of the story he must have given the police."

Sydney flushed. "But his story is crazy, insane!" he insisted.

"Perhaps if I heard it—" suggested Colton.

Excitedly, with utter disbelief in his voice, Sydney Thames told of the unheld pistol Rogers swore he saw; of its firing with no finger near the trigger; of its recoil, and fall.

"Of course the police arrested him," continued Sydney. "Cartwright held a lot of Rogers's paper. That's the motive. They've got a clear case, as clear as the one against the love-crazed kid who shot the violinist."

"Just as clear," echoed Colton slowly. Then:

"But haven't you withheld the fact that the pistols used in both murders are exactly alike?"

"How—did you know—that?" gasped Sydney. Many times he had heard the blind man make such amazing statements, but they always startled him.

"Because both crimes were committed by the same man in the same way!"

"But Nelson, the kid who shot the girl, was locked up in a cell," protested Thames.

"Exactly," admitted the blind man. "But he killed Cartwright as surely as he murdered the girl."

It was several seconds before the meaning of that sentence struck Sydney. "He shot that girl in the back!" rebelled Thames.

"I saw his face over the flash of the pistol. Even he admits that no one else could have fired it, because it fell on his toe!"

"Rogers swears that no one did fire the bullet which killed Cartwright," reminded Colton. "And the pistol fell on the table in front of him."

"That's impossible," asserted Thames emphatically. "Someone must have held the gun. Someone must have pulled the trigger. There can be no explanation of what he says he saw. The days of ghosts and black magic have passed."

"But not the days of black murder," retorted Colton. "There is no black art, ghosts, or hypnotism in the murders of last night. The method is unique, that's all."

He picked up the slim, hollow stick he always carried. "I'm going to find that murderer," he said. "A man who could kill a girl like that is either a fiend or a hideous blunderer. I think it's the latter. Will you call the machine?"

The big automobile was always ready for instant service, day or night, and ten minutes later they were on their way down town. Beside the driver, eager-eyed, joyful, was The Fee. Colton had promised to let him help on the case, and the boy's cup of happiness was full. The Fee had but two heroes: Thornley Colton in real life; Nick Carter in his favourite fiction.

"We'll go to police headquarters first," decided Colton. "The prisoners will be there this morning, and I'd like to question Rogers." Then he got from Sydney all the details the papers had given of Cartwright's murder.

The Fee found a friendly doorman when they reached police headquarters and prepared to have the time of his life. Colton's card secured them grudging admittance to the office of the chief of detectives. The chief, like his men, had all the professional's scorn for the amateur, but he knew the blind man, with his wide acquaintance with influential people, was not a person to antagonize. And the police had found Rogers a different proposition from the youth whose infatuation had led him to the dark box and the murder charge. The lawyer was well known, and his story demanded respect despite the utter impossibility of the thing he described. Of course, the barman and the waiter had been arrested as witnesses, but they had not seen the actual shooting. The barman had been dozing, and the waiter had been busy in a front booth. The shot had aroused them.

"Going to give us some more pointers?" asked the chief tolerantly, when he had shaken hands with Colton and nodded curtly to Sydney.

"I'd like to look into that double-murder case a bit," confessed the problemist, paying no attention to the tone.

"You mean the two murders committed last night," corrected the chief gruntingly. "Nothing to 'em. We've got the goods on young Nelson. Twenty people in the three front rows saw him do it. And Rogers's fool story is enough to hang any man." The real detective's scorn for the criminal whose methods are crude came to his voice. "He might have got away with a suicide story—Cartwright was all broken up about the girl—but Rogers swears it wasn't suicide, because the manager's hands were not near the pistol when it was fired. He says Cartwright's look was one of horror, as if he'd seen his end coming, and couldn't get away from it."

"He did see his death coming," put in Colton quietly; "and I think that during the last instant he lived he realized at whose hand it came."

"You think he got wise to Rogers at the end, eh?" guessed the chief.

"No!" The negative was sharp. "Rogers had no more to do with the murder than you or I. Cartwright was killed by a man who had been planning the murder for years; the death of the girl was a terrible mistake."

The chief jumped from his chair. "What do you know?" he demanded.

"Nothing—definitely. With a little help from you I think I can show you the real murderer."

"You can't show me any murderer but Rogers and Nelson," snapped the chief, with an air of finality. "Because you can't convince me or anybody else that a man could see what Rogers says he saw. A pistol with no hand near it. It's impossible! It's dam' foolishness!" He snorted.

Unconsciously Sydney Thames found himself nodding confirmation. That was the whole thing: an impossibility. No one had been near Cartwright but Rogers. The girl had been shot in the back, and no one could have been behind her but Nelson. This last Sydney knew, and had seen.

"Let me see the pistols which killed Cartwright and the girl, and I'll convince you that the same man murdered both," offered Colton.

"Duplicate guns aren't so rare," instantly resented the chief. This man was practically telling him that he didn't know his business!

"Those two pistols—and others that may be in the possession of the murderer—are the only ones of their kind in the world!"

"Look at 'em, then." The chief grabbed them from his desk. "They're a standard German make, single-shot target pistols, blued steel, with barrels six inches long, numbered and sold all over Europe."

Colton took the two pistols, and Sydney drew his chair closer to see.

"In the first place," began the blind man, as his thin, supersensitive fingers examined one gun, while the other lay on his knees, "murderers don't usually have this kind of pistol. They can't be carried in any ordinary pocket, and"—his forefingertip rested over the shallow slot near the muzzle—"you never before saw target pistols without front sights!"

"Took 'em off so they wouldn't catch in the pocket," grunted the chief knowingly.

Colton's lips curved in a smile. "An ingenious theory," he grunted. "Have you one to fit the banged-up appearance of these butts?" He held out the pistol and indicated the nicks and scratches.

"Been used to hammer nails," declared the chief, exaggerated weariness in his voice. "Gun owners use 'em that way sometimes, like a woman uses a hairbrush. Nothing to that."

"Yes there is! No gun owner in the world ever drove a nail by holding a gun vertically, hand on the barrel, and pounding it up and down like a pile driver! See, the hard usage doesn't show on the bottom of the butt, as it would have done had the pistol been swung as a hammer. The dents and scratches are all on the outside edge!"

The chief took the extended gun. The sarcastic smile on his lips faded as he tried the two ways of holding it. The blind man was right! No driving of nails could have made nicks and scratches where they were on this pistol! "What's that got to do with the murder?" he growled.

"Everything," answered the problemist shortly. He took the other pistol on his palm. "Didn't it strike you that these were two finely balanced pistols, even for target use?" Before the chief could reply Colton shot another inquiry: "Didn't you wonder at the fact that both triggers had been filed to a hair so that the slightest jar would cause the hammer to fall? See!" He cocked the pistol and jammed the muzzle against the chief's desk. The hammer clicked down sharply. He tried it again, this time jamming the butt down on a chair arm. Once more the hammer snapped on the empty chamber.

The chief's jaw dropped. "That's how those nicks were made!" he ejaculated, shocked from his supercilious attitude. The lightning-like questions, the proving of fact after fact by Colton, had disconcerted him. In ten minutes the man who was sightless had shown him details that neither his keen eyes nor the eyes of his hundred men had seen, and Colton had made of those details startling, vivid possibilities.

"May I speak to Mr Rogers?" Colton asked the question quietly, simply, but under his voice was a subtle note that was dominantly compelling; a note that had made bigger and stronger men than the chief of the New York detective bureau bow to his wishes.

"That's all very interesting stuff," began the chief pompously, "but Rogers is the man who shot Cartwright, and we know that Cartwright held a dozen thousand dollars's worth of his paper."

The door opened to admit an attaché, and Sydney hid a grin with his hand. He had seen the chief press the call button even before he began to speak.

"Bring Rogers here," grunted the head of the detective bureau.

The lawyer came in a moment later, and the two men who accompanied him were curtly ordered out.

The strong face of the prisoner was marred by lines indicating loss of sleep; his lips were shut grimly, a scowl creased his forehead, his eyes, sharp and piercing, were fixed on the chief.

"This is Mr Colton, Rogers," introduced the detective shortly. "He's got a sort of a theory on the Cartwright murder."

"If it's the right one he'll save you a lot of trouble," snapped the lawyer ungraciously. He turned to Colton. "I've heard of your work on the Villers case." His tone was almost amiable; then into it came dull wonder. "But that was simplicity itself beside this. I saw that revolver before the shot was fired, unsupported by human hands, against Jim Cartwright's shirt front. It must have flown there on invisible wings!"

The chief grunted sarcastically, as he had grunted at each repetition of that unvarying statement.

Thornley Colton, tapping his foot lightly with his thin stick, looked up. "That is just what it did do!" he said. The three men stared blankly. The blind man continued: "According to the newspapers, Mr Rogers, you said that something caused you to jerk up your head in time to see that picture. Do you know what it was?"

"I do not." Rogers shook his head. "I can only describe it as some inner impulse."

"Wasn't it"—Thornley Colton's tone was impressive—"wasn't it a shadow, a swift-passing shadow, your eyes saw on the floor?"

Rogers leaped to his feet. "By Heaven, it was!" he shouted. "I remember now!" His voice trembled with excitement. "I had lowered my head, and across the streak of light between the seat edge and table flew a shadow—like a bird passing overhead." He stopped suddenly, the bewildered look on his face telling the sudden realization of his words. "How could you know that!" he burst out.

"The human brain is a curious thing," explained the blind man slowly. "It unconsciously records impressions the eyes give, but they are instantly forgotten—because the giving is so automatic—until something recalls them. Without sight I have been compelled to figure all things in my brain. Even the steps that you take without seeing must be mentally visualized by me. I knew it *must* have been a shadow that caused you to look up. To you it was merely one of the thousand unconscious-conscious things your eyes see during the day which are locked up in the brain until some outside influence brings them back."

"You can solve this thing!" Rogers shot out the words as if he had just made a wonderful discovery. The blind man's conscious power in himself had won the confidence of the lawyer; made him realize that there was some logical explanation for the thing which his eyes had seen, and which his reason refused to accept. He forgot that he was a prisoner formally charged with murder, he paced the room nervously. And the chief, scowling down at his desk, was silent. "If you can find the man who killed Jim Cartwright!" The excitement died from Roger's voice, a new tone came. "I knew him for thirty years, yet I never knew him until last night!"

"I want to bring to justice the man that could kill a girl whose soul held the music of Miss Reynolds's." There was unconscious rebuke in the problemist's voice. All his powers he had brought to avenge the innocent girl; but he knew his efforts must be concentrated on the Cartwright murder because that was the key, the only key that would lead to the murderer.

"The love-crazed kid did that! He—" Rogers stopped, his eyes saw the two pistols side by side on the commissioner's desk. Instantly his keen brain recognised the significance. "They're the same!" he exclaimed.

"'What were Cartwright's relations with Miss Reynolds?" It was a command, as Colton put it. Rogers lifted his eyes from the two pistols.

"You wrong Jim Cartwright," he said quietly. "You've accepted the general opinion of him; the opinion he never cared enough about to refute. He wasn't an angel, but he wasn't the devil a thousand jealousies have painted him. I'm going to tell you the story he told me last night." And he did, with all the deep feeling of his friendship, splendidly, simply.

As the men listened they understood the tragedy of Cartwright's love for the woman who had been killed in the first moments of her newfound happiness—and his; of the little girl he had taken from her dead mother's arms to work for, to protect, to give the happiness the mother had been denied—only to see her foully murdered when her cup of joy had but just been filled. The fiendishness of it held them spellbound. The two beings that Cartwright had loved had been snatched from him, and he had been killed, knowing in the last instant of his life that the real murderer of the girl was not even suspected, could not be suspected, because of the devilish ingenuity of his crime.

"Kelly, the drunken magician, is the man who killed Cartwright!" ejaculated the chief.

Rogers was startled for a moment, but Colton, with an inscrutable smile on his thin lips, put a question:

"The father of the girl is dead, isn't he?"

Rogers glanced at the blind man in surprise.

"Yes," he admitted. "He died in the alcoholic ward of a Chicago hospital three months after his wife was killed. He was buried in the potters' field."

"Where did you find that out?" scowlingly demanded the chief.

"That I didn't proves the fact," answered the blind man crisply. "If Cartwright hadn't known he was dead you'd have heard of him before. Do you want me to go on?" he asked.

"Might as well," granted the chief. "Maybe this is your lucky day."

"Then I'd like to ask a few questions of the boy who was arrested as Miss Reynolds's murderer."

The chief gave the order, but there was a light of triumphant anticipation in his eyes as he waited. Unlike the murderer of Cartwright, there was nothing mysterious in the killing of the girl, despite the clever efforts of the blind man to prove differently. A score of persons had seen the flash of the pistol from the rear of the box. His men had examined the velvet-hung wall toward which the girl's back had been, and there was not a break in it, not a crack.

When the boy—he was little more—was led in by two detectives there came a look of pity to the faces of Sydney and Rogers. He staggered to a chair when the men released his arms. His lips were purple and torn where Cartwright had beaten him to the floor the night before. A haunting look of terror was in his eyes; his face was pasty white.

"I didn't do it! I didn't! I didn't!" he whispered hoarsely, when he had wet his dry lips to make even the whisper possible.

Colton put his hand on the boy's shoulder. "I know you didn't," he said, and there was a world of sympathy in his voice. A new look came to the boy's eyes, a trembling hand sought that of the blind man.

"I loved her and she loved me," he said chokingly. "We were going to be married—but that Cartwright—" Shrill vehemence came to the tone, and he stopped.

Colton's hand quieted him. "Listen closely now, Mr Nelson, and tell me if this is what happened: You groped your way to the box with your right hand on the wall. You felt the black velvet hangings, stopped, and the pistol went off while your right hand was stretched above you, on the hangings, and you were facing the door that led back off the stage."

"I remember that!" interjected Sydney. "His left side was towards Cartwright and the girl!"

"Yet you said that the pistol flash crossed his body."

"It did!" broke in the boy. "It was not twelve inches ahead of me! My right foot was extended to take another step, and the pistol fell on my toe!"

Colton turned to the three listening men. "To have fired that shot he would have had to double his left arm behind him and have shot around his body—a physical impossibility, even with a longbarrelled pistol." He placed his hand gently on the boy's shoulder once more. "Go outside to the men who brought you in," he said. "You will be free in a few hours."

Silently the boy obeyed. When Colton faced them again there was a curious expression on his face; the expression of a man who has seen a thoughtless boy destroy a priceless work of art by his clumsiness.

"He killed that girl as surely as if he had placed the pistol at her back," he said sadly. "Yet he is as innocent of her murder as a child unborn!"

Eager questions, demands for an explanation of that cryptic remark, were fairly hurled at the blind man by the excited

Rogers. What did he mean? How could the boy have killed Miss Reynolds and not be guilty of her murder? How had she been killed? By whom? Sydney Thames forbore the questions he knew would not be answered. The chief scowled down at the two pistols, silent thoughtful. Colton's statement regarding the firing of the pistol across the boy's body had struck him like a dash of cold water. It was true! The boy could not have fired the shot that killed the girl! Once more the blind man's unerring instinct for truth had torn down the case he and his men had been building for hours. In less than five minutes the sightless problemist had proved a fact that twenty pairs of eyes had failed to see.

"Where are the two men who were arrested in the rathskeller?" asked Colton curtly, utterly ignoring the questions.

"Bailed by their boss," answered the chief. "They can only establish details anyway."

"I want to interview at least one of them," declared Colton. "I also want to visit the rathskeller. Can Mr Rogers go, in your company, of course?"

"Yes." The chief took the responsibility unhesitatingly. He realized that he must see the thing through now.

"Is your machine down here? I want to send my boy on an errand with mine."

"Outside, waiting." The chief took his hat and coat from the tree. "I'll go with Rogers while he gets his," he added, as he opened the door.

The blind man hurried out, feet unerringly retracing the steps his brain had registered when they entered. The red-haired boy ran from the group of detectives he had been entertaining.

"Shrimp!" The blind man used the name he always called the boy, and took him aside. He whispered instructions, thrust two or three bills into the other's hand. The youngster darted for the machine, and jumped up beside the driver as the chief and Rogers came from the front door.

In silence the quartet climbed into the car; in silence they made the journey to the rathskeller, where James Cartwright had been shot a few hours before. The waiter who had been on duty early in the morning was again on hand, heavy-eyed. The barman was at his home.

"Where's the booth you occupied?" asked Colton of Rogers, when the chief had established their identity with the nervous proprietor.

The lawyer went to it, stopped at the table, and stared down at the dark stain that could not be removed.

"This is where we were," he said huskily.

Colton stepped in between the table and the seat edge, and sat down, facing the rear of the rathskeller. "Cartwright was seated at the end of the seat, like this?" He illustrated.

Rogers nodded. "He was on the extreme end, so he could assure himself that no one would hear."

Colton rose, and with only the slim stick to guide him, made his way to a booth that faced the front of the rathskeller, at right angles to the one where the watching men still stood.

"Who was in this booth when Cartwright was shot?" It was snapped out like the crack of a whip to the waiter.

"Nobody," faltered the serving man, wincing under the battery of eyes.

"There was!" The voice held accusation. "A man was in this booth, and he entered a moment or so before Mr Rogers and Mr Cartwright!"

The waiter brushed his dry lips with the back of his hand. "He couldn't have had nothin' to do with it," he mumbled, fingers twisting and untwisting the napkin in his hands.

"No one said he did!" said the blind man sharply. "You've been a witness in a murder case before, haven't you?"

The watching men saw a look of alarm come to the man's eyes. The chief stepped toward him menacingly. "Yes, sir," muttered the waiter, shrinking. "I saw a man shot while I was at the Royal. The police kept me in the detention for three months, and I lost my job."

There was a grim smile on Colton's lips as he nodded understandingly. "You weren't going to take a chance on that again, were you?" His tone was less brusque. "I'll assure you that you won't be held a minute if you give me a description of the man."

The chief opened his mouth, then closed it with a snap.

"Then I'll tell you," consented the waiter eagerly. "He was a good-sized guy, with a yellow, old-lookin' face, bald-headed, with a scar on the top, and he had eyes that was like slits. He came in that door." He pointed to one that opened at the rear corner of the rathskeller, apparently on a side street. "He was so drunk he couldn't hardly walk, and he almost fell into the seat. I was goin' to put him out, we closed in half an hour, an' I didn't want to have to throw no drunks in the street. But he wanted a whisky and—" The waiter flushed and stopped.

"Go on," prodded Colton.

The waiter looked at the proprietor and gulped nervously. "He gave me a five-spot, an' told me to keep the change. I was bringin' the drink when the other two came in. I got theirs, and went up front to figger my checks. Then I heard the shot. When I thought of the drunk again he was gone. But he couldn't 'a' done nothin'. He had a horrible bun, an' we seen the gun layin' in front of this guy." He indicated Rogers. "Me an' the bartender figgered we wouldn't say nothin' about him. If we did the police 'id put us in the detention till they found him. His gettin' out like that would 'a' looked suspicious to them if it didn't to nobody else. He was scared sober an' beat it quick. That's my idear."

"Probably he'd had an experience in the house of detention, too," declared the blind man dryly; then: "You never saw him before?"

"No, sir."

"That's all. Let's go, chief. There's a detail I want to clear up at the theatre. I've got to prove that girl's murder." Again there was the ominous ring in the problemist's voice.

The chief glowered at the waiter. "You stay right here till I want you," he warned. "If you try to beat it you go up the river." He turned to Colton. "Wait a minute, until I call up headquarters. I'll give 'em the description of that drunk, and have every man in the city on his trail."

"And spend a week following up clues," snapped the blind man impatiently. "I'll show you where he is in less than an hour!"

He paid no further attention to the gaping chief of detectives, but made his way out of the place, the silent Sydney Thames at his elbow, the latter's coat sleeve lightly touching that of Thornley Colton. And the chief followed meekly.

The blind man climbed into the front seat with the driver, and Sydney realized that he wanted to avoid interrogation; to figure out the last steps alone. But in the tonneau the men could not resist voicing the questions that filled their minds. Who had killed Miss Reynolds, and what could have been the object of the murder? What connection could a drunken man have with the murder of Cartwright; with a pistol that had been fired without the aid of human hands.

They were at the theatre. The box-office had just been opened for the day, and the manager took them into the darkened house. The big interior, dim and tomblike, sent a shudder through Sydney Thames. Last night there had been brilliant lights, happy men, laughing women—and the girl of the violin. Today the great stage gaped before them, huge, untenanted; the seats were covered with their white dust cloths; voices sounded eerie in the barnlike emptiness. The velvet hangings at the rear of the box, which had looked so striking with their sleek blackness the night before, now appeared worn and dusty. The overturned chairs had been righted, the bloodstained carpet had been replaced.

Thornley Colton's thin stick located the chairs. His right hand groped along the wall, so that the velvet moved under it. He thrust his slim cane under his arm, and the wonderful fingers went over the velvet inch by inch, sometimes so strongly that the thick stuff moved under them, then the pressure was so light that not a quiver of the loose velvet betrayed their presence. Inch by inch the feeling fingers made their way, as the men watched breathlessly. Rogers could stand it no longer.

"Was the murderer concealed behind those hangings?" he asked excitedly.

"No," Colton answered him, without moving. "The pistol flash came from this side of the velvet."

Silence came again. The slow-moving fingers stopped. The blind man looked up; then his doubly keen ears caught the sound of hurrying footsteps coming toward them down the aisle.

"A telephone message for me?" he asked, as the attaché stopped.

"Mr Colton?"

"Yes." He turned to the others. "Come! I think this is the last detail."

They were at his heels as he entered the boxlike office. Tense, expectant, though they knew not for what, they listened to the one-sided conversation.

"Yes. Good. Did you see him? No, that's all right. Stay there until we come." He spoke an aside to the ticket-seller: "Will you please take this address for me?" The man picked up his pencil and drew a small pad toward him. "Nine hundred and ninety-seven West Forty-fourth." The blind man hung up the receiver.

"What is it?" The question was chorused by the excited men.

"The address of the man who murdered Cartwright and Miss Reynolds!"

IV.

Before the gasps of amazement, the ejaculations of incredulity could become coherent questions, Thornley Colton had turned and made his way from the office, light stick dangling idly from his fingers. Dazedly they followed him from the theatre and into the waiting automobile. He had located the murderer of Cartwright and the girl! They were dumb with the wonder of it. Swiftly, unerringly, the blind man had found the murderer whose very being they had not suspected a short time before. To the men who had followed every step of the problemist, who had seen things that he could not see, the finding seemed magic comparable only to the magic of the pistol that had apparently flown from the air to deal its death. There was a new expression on the face of the chief of detectives now. The scowl was gone; the sarcastic curve of lips had vanished. In their place had come wonder, tinged with awe toward the man who had builded a wonderful structure of truth from the pieces he and his hundred men had either discarded or had not seen.

The car turned into Forty-fourth, passed the brownstone houses where every door bore its sign: "Table Board. Furnished Rooms." A red-headed boy ran out into the street, and the chauffeur slowed up.

"It's t'ree houses down, Mr Colton." The Fee's voice fairly trembled with excitement. "He's on the top floor. Kin I go with yuh?"

Colton nodded and stepped down from the machine. "We'll walk the rest of the way," he told them. He started, the bright-eyed boy at his elbow.

They mounted the steps of a brownstone house, and Colton rang the bell. A frowsy-haired lady in a grease-spotted kimono opened the door. The smell of cooking onions assailed their nostrils; somewhere within a piano banged out a ragtime tune; a raucous voice screeched: "I call her Little Hy'cinth, but her name's M'Swigg;" from the depths of the house a squeaky clarinet piped off-key opera.

"Profesh'n?" snapped the lady of the kimono suspiciously before any one had a chance to speak.

"We want to see Signor Delvetoi," said the blind man quietly.

Sydney Thames never remembered the short colloquy that followed; never recollected just how they entered the house. Signor Delvetoi! That name drove everything else from his mind. Once more he saw the black-clothed, black-bearded man at the theatre; again he saw the whirling knives flashing from the darkness into the beam of the calcium to bury their points beside the woman of the golden frame; once more came to his mind the wonderful skill that had directed those keen-pointed knives toward their target of living flesh — to brush a cheek and not even scratch it.

Then he found himself following the others up the narrow stairs. In the second floor hallway a fat, greasy-faced woman murmured husky endearments to a monkey in her arms, while a goose waddled at her side. A dozen discordant tunes came from the closed rooms. This was the place they had come to arrest a murderer!

On the third floor Thornley Colton stopped and knocked on a door panel. Thomas could feel the tenseness of the men's bodies as they crowded up close to the door as it slowly opened. Standing before them, framed in the light that came into the hallway from the room, stood a big man in a stained red bath-robe that trailed the floor behind the worn carpet-slippers. His head was bald, and across the skull ran a livid scar; his face was a deep-lined, jaundiced yellow.

"We want you for the murder of Cartwright and the girl at the theatre." That was all Colton said, and his voice was low.

For an instant the face of the man went a fish-belly white; then murderous red rage leaped to the cheeks, and darted from the slit eyes.

"You devils!" he shrieked.

The red robe was flung back; but with a movement as quick as light itself Colton's hand darted out, closed with a grip of steel on a wrist, and the red robe whirled as the man spun to his knees.

"Better handcuff him," advised the blind man quietly, as he pushed aside the fallen knife with the thin cane that had warned him of the murderous movement. The handcuffs clicked on the knife-thrower's wrists as the chief dragged him to a chair.

"So you're the one, eh?" The detective chief tried to make his tone casual, but he could not keep the wonder from his eyes, or voice.

"Oh, you got me right," sneered the knife-thrower.

"How did you do it?" put in Rogers dazedly. The picture he had seen the night before was still in his mind.

A cunning light leaped to the half-closed eyes of the red-robed man. "D'you want to hear the whole thing?" he asked. "You might as well," he boasted. "I'll never swing for it."

"Go ahead," growled the chief, drawing his chair up closer and placing his revolver on his knees. The knife-thrower grinned sneeringly.

"Well," he began, and his evil eyes seemed to gloat at them. "I'm the only man in the world that could have pulled the trick. It took years of practice to get it down pat, but there's Indian blood in me, mixed with the Irish. They don't know much about me in this country, and I didn't want them to, till I got Jim Cartwright. But in Europe I'm the best in the business, and I'm the only one that could ever plant five knives in a spot the size of a half dollar at thirty feet, and do it on the level."

There was boasting in the tone, but to Sydney Thames, who had seen his amazing work of the night before, it was not idle boasting.

"The story of why I killed Cartwright is the same old game: I had a woman and he took her. She wasn't much good, only a dollfaced fool, and there was a squalling kid that got on my nerves; but she was mine, body and soul." The listening men gritted their teeth at the tone, and he sneered at them for it. "Cartwright took her, and I went after them both. I had a little money, I was headin' the olio in a burlesque. Before I started I went in a place along the river front in Chicago, where I was. I musta showed my roll, because—now I don't expect you to believe what's comin', and I don't give a damn whether you do or not!" There was sullen defiance in the voice. "But I woke up in a hospital I never saw before, and the nurse talked German! It was in Berlin, and it was ten years after! Oh, it wasn't anything new, the doctors, told me. One of the Windy City thugs had lead-piped me for my roll; you can see the scar I got. Something cracked in my head then, and when I woke I'd just been in a German train smashup. The doctors said the bump I got there straightened me out.

"I remembered everything after a while. I was doin' a knife-throwin' act. Some wop had picked me up when I didn't know my own name, and brought me to Europe with him. Somehow the kink had kept me off the booze, and I was even better than him, and he was the best in the world, bar none. He died a few months after I got out, and I copped his layout. We'd been rehearsin' a stunt that was going to make 'em all sit up. The Flyin' Death, we called it, and we threw pistols instead of knives. We had a blank board at one end of the stage, and a target at the other. We'd stand in the centre, let it fly at the blank board, duck, and the butt striking would jar down the trigger, and the bullet'd go over our heads and hit the bull's-eye three times out of five. It was big stuff! But I wasn't satisfied, because

I wanted to hit the bull's-eye every time. I was goin' to play that act fer one man; the one that stole my wife and ten years out of my life. So I put in two more years on the Continent, still practisin'. If you looked at the nicks in the pistol-butts you can see how many times they'd been used.

"When I got so I couldn't go wrong I came to the States. I learned I was dead—one of the thugs that got my coin and papers, I guess. But that suited me right down to the ground. I found Cartwright was the big cheese in the business, but I couldn't find the wife, or the kid. I wanted to get them, too; ten years don't make no difference to me." Again came the sneer to the evil, yellow face, as his eyes caught their looks of horror and disgust. "I spent a year touring here before I could book Cartwright's house. I wanted to get him right before everybody's eyes. That's why I had that dark act. He was up to the rehearsal in the mornin' with a kid that looked something like the woman he stole, but it wasn't my kid, because he made it plain he was only her manager. You can bet he'd a showed it if he had claims. I heard him make a date for the box after her act, and that looked good to me, because I'd get him right beside her.

"Under the knives for the spotlight act was the pistol with a real cartridge, of course. I only used minichure ones with a pinch of powder for the act. The guns was balanced special in Germany, and the front sights was off the barrels so they could slide out of my hand. I could see the white of the girl's waist and his shirt between every knife-throw, because I waited a few seconds each time to get 'em right. Then, when I knew I couldn't make a mistake, I let the gun fly. I was goin' to have the butt hit the wall in back of him, and bullet catch him between the shoulders. It was easy, because I was above him on the stage, and I thought there couldn't be any suspicion because I was in front of him, and he'd be shot in the back. But that darn' fool kid," he spat out snarlingly, "had to have his hands on the hanging just when the gun hit, and throw it off enough to kill the girl."

Sydney Thames gasped audibly.

"It wasn't my fault she was in the way, but a little thing like that wasn't going to keep me from gettin' the man I wanted. I got another of the guns out of my prop trunk and went after him. I couldn't get him right until I heard the other feller arguin' with him in front of the rathskeller. I ducked around to the side-door. I'd been in there before, but I'd had my black stage-whiskers and wig on, and the waiter didn't know me. I played drunk, and gave the waiter a five-spot for a drink, and told him not to turn on the booth-light.

"Cartwright faced my booth, but I was in the dark. They started to whisper. The waiter was out of sight, and the bartender was sleepin'. I had the gun ready for five minutes. This man bent down—and I let her fly. There wasn't going to be any mistake this time, because I was going to put another half turn on the gun and make it jam its muzzle against his heart. No chance of missin' that way! And he saw the gun comin' when it was too late to dodge! And he knew me then! And the last thing he ever saw was me grinnin' at him! It was a cinch to slope out in the excitement after."

There was silence in the room when he had finished. From beyond the closed door came the discordant medley of the tinny piano, the screeching clarinet, the hoarse-voiced singers. Before them a manacled man, with sneers in his voice, and boasts, and snarls, had just told them of the man whose death he had accomplished with such fiendish cunning; of the innocent girl whose life he had destroyed.

"Do you mean to say that you could fling those pistols as accurately as all that?" demanded the chief, who was a policeman, first, last, and all the time. The case, to him, had ceased to be one of human emotions, of sorrow and tragedy; it was a matter of proof, of conviction. Such is the policeman's philosophy of life—and death.

"Do you want me to prove it?" taunted the murderer. "There's the other pistol for the act on the bureau. It ain't loaded. Get it and I'll show you."

"Better take his word," suggested Colton warningly.

"I'll see that he plays no tricks," boasted the chief. It was his case now. He got the pistol from the bureau. "I'll take one cuff off, and I'll have this gun on you every second!" he snapped.

The knife-thrower leered at him with his bloodless lips, and the slit eyes shone with an exultant gleam. He took a stubby pencil from his bath-robe pocket and drew a small circle on the blank wall. He walked to the other end of the room, the chief watching him like a hawk. The pistol dangled from the man's hand as he turned. A snap of the arm, and it became a flying whirl of blue. The muzzle struck the exact centre of the small circle, the hammer snapped down, and for an instant the gun seemed suspended against the wall before it jangled to the floor.

"God! That's what I saw last night!" choked Rogers.

The knife-thrower picked up the pistol. "It's just as easy to make the butt strike first, with the muzzle pointed at me, as it should have pointed at Cartwright's back last night."

The commissioner watched every move as he walked to the end of the room.

Suddenly Colton's voice rang out:

"Don't let him throw that pistol!"

The chief jumped from his chair as the red arm swung.

A line of fire leaped from the blank wall toward the scarlet-robed figure across the room. The explosion echoed and re-echoed in the room. The pistol clattered on the bare boards under the small circle it had struck so unerringly. On the butt were flakes of the white plaster where it had been driven into the wall. The red robe seemed slowly to crumple as the knife-thrower sank to the floor; and as they ran to where he lay, the lips twisted in an evil leer of triumph, the slit eyes gleamed their gloating.

"I told you I'd never swing for it!" he sneered up at them. "Palming that cartridge was easy. I used to be a magician — when my name was — Kelly!"

V.

"Yes, Sydney, he paid the price the State puts on murder, and I guess it is just as well." A fleeting smile crossed Colton's thin lips for an instant. "But the chief is naturally angry that such a spectacular murderer should escape his clutches so easily. My keen ears caught the click of the breech as he put in the cartridge. But I was too late; he had waited until the last second."

The two men were in the library of the old-fashioned house, where the blind man had come to spend his regular afternoon four hours in darkness that meant insurance against the splitting headaches too-long-continued light on his sensitive, sightless eyes always caused. The knife-thrower had lived but a few minutes, for his skill had not failed him, and the bullet had pierced one of his lungs. Rogers had gone to arrange for the funerals of Cartwright and the daughter he had loved. They were to be side by side in death, and the story would go to their graves. On that the men had agreed in the big bare room where the last act of the tragedy had been played.

"How did you ever connect the knife-thrower with the murders?" asked Sydney finally.

"Your story of the shooting in the box, as you told it to me while we were waiting for the panic to cease in the theatre, gave me the first clue," explained the blind man thoughtfully. "The fact that you saw the face of Nelson so plainly told me that the flash must have crossed his body, and, in groping his way in the darkness, his right hand must have been on the hangings. Shrimp's enthusiastic description of the knife-thrower's act told me how wonderful it was, and—he was the possibility.

"Then the murder of Cartwright was the proof needed. There could be no explanation but that of a thrown pistol for the thing Rogers saw. And the two pistols being identical was the last link. But no one would believe the theory without irrefutable proof. That I got, first by the nicked-up butts of the guns, showing how long they had been used in practice. Then Rogers's story of Cartwright told me the guilty person. But then came the necessity of explaining where he had been all the years. I sent Shrimp to the stage entrance to get the knife-thrower's address and locate him. He did, and, being a boy, he aroused not the slightest suspicion when he made an inquiry at the house. I knew also that at least one of the two employees of the rathskeller must have known another man had been on hand when the murder was committed. I had to go there to see why they had withheld the information from the police. The explanation was logical enough, but the police would never have seen it. Then I had to go to the theatre and find the place where the butt of the gun had struck on the wall. The finding was more of a job than I thought. In his excitement the boy must have moved the hangings a foot, for the scar in the velvet was a foot lower than I should have found it. And you must remember that it was a scar that no eye could have seen, one that could only be found with a microscope, or supersensitive fingertips like mine. Then came the message from Shrimp, whom I had told to call me up either at the rathskeller or the theatre."

Silence came in the darkened room. When Thornley Colton spoke again his voice was low, solemn, its tone one of reverent wonder. "The death of that girl is one of the higher mysteries, Sydney. Was she murdered because of a terrible mistake, or did a merciful Providence send a thoughtless, foolish boy to grope in the darkness at just the right instant to deflect that pistol, and send the bullet into her back? She died in the happiest moment of her life; joy was in her heart and on her lips. If the pistol had not been turned by the moving velvet, Cartwright would have died. Her whole story would have had to come out then; she would have heard it bandied by unclean lips on the street-corners; to know that her father, the father who did not even recognize her, was a murderer. A merciful Providence? I'll always wonder, Sydney."

5

The Fifth Problem:

THE THOUSAND FACETS OF FIRE

I.

Outside was the hurry and bustle of the busy avenue; inside was the quietness and calm that characterised the house of Osmuhn & Son, jewellers and dealers in articles of vertu. The Heppelwhite chairs were carefully placed before each velvet square on the crystal cases that extended the length of the shop on both sides. In rows of expert array on the shelves and in the cabinets on the velvet-carpeted floor were rich European and Oriental porcelains: Faience and cloisonné; rare pieces of Limoges, Satsuma, Arita, and Ninsei; lacquer ware of Kajikawa, Ritsuo, and Korin. The salesmen, soft-footed, soft-voiced, appeared merely indolent to the casual observer, but to one who could look beneath the surface of things, they gave the impression of being alertly on guard against a hidden something.

A limousine stopped before the door. The woman who alighted was beautiful; the girl who followed her was wonderful—the type that makes men putty and women envious. The uniformed attendant opened the door, they stepped inside.

If those two women had crossed the threshold of any other shop on the avenue, there would have been a noticeable flurry of excitement instantly. But not a clerk in the shop showed more than courteous readiness. Osmuhn's customers were all of the same type: the richest, the most cultured, the most exclusive persons in New York. A diamond ceased to be merely a diamond when it had been sold by Osmuhn. It became a gem with the reputation of the seller behind it; a flawless, matchless carbon. So it was with anything else one bought from Osmuhn & Son.

But if the clerks showed no particular interest, the same could not be said of the light-haired, blue-eyed young man who had been talking with two others at the end of a long glass case. A smile of welcome came to his lips as he hurried forward, hand outstretched.

"Mrs Marie!" he exclaimed. "And Helen!"

His two hands met theirs in more than friendly clasp; the left to the woman, the right to the girl. Only one man in the shop could not see the light in the man's eyes as he looked at the girl; but that one had recognised love in the man's voice.

"You knew I'd be here, didn't you, Mr Osmuhn!" laughed the woman ripplingly.

"The ruby." It was not a question, just a smiling statement.

"Could mother ever resist a wonderful jewel!" put in the girl.

"It hasn't been taken out of the private safe since you saw it before, three months ago," said the younger Osmuhn. "Five-hundred-thousand-dollar rubies aren't the playthings of the average gembuyer."

"Respect my weakness, please," pouted the woman in mock pleading; then her eyes saw for the first time one of the men young Osmuhn had just left, and they lighted with pleasure.

"I must speak to Mr Colton," she said, and she hurried to where he was standing. The girl and the man followed slowly, talking in earnest undertones.

Thornley Colton's pale face lighted with pleasure as he took, her hand, and his thin, expressive lips smiled their glad welcome. Only the eyes behind the great, round lenses of the smoked, tortoise-rimmed library glasses did not change. His slim stick, apparently of ebony, hung lightly from the tapering fingers of his left hand, as did the hat which a moment before had covered the snow-white hair that curled from the pink scalp.

"Now tell me where you've been keeping yourself!" the woman demanded severely. "No evasion! We haven't seen you since that wonderful thing you did for the Jimmy Raeltons. It *was* wonderful!" she added earnestly.

"Thank you," Colton said simply. There was no mock modesty; only quiet sincerity in his rich deep voice.

"But you didn't answer my questions," she smiled. She turned to the apple-cheeked, black-haired man who had stood silent. "Can you answer them for him, Mr Thames?"

The black-haired man started nervously as she spoke, for he had been paying attention only to the beautiful girl with Osmuhn. Mrs Marle repeated the question before he had time to stammer the apology she saw trembling on his lips.

"I am merely Mr Colton's secretary." He said it a trifle stiffly, and she understood that his hypersensitive nature resented her intuitive understanding.

"I don't like gaiety," put in Colton quickly. "A quiet chat is my greatest pleasure. Crowds confuse me, and make my eyes nervous." He laid his hand fondly on the other man's shoulder, and to her eyes came womanly sympathy. She knew what Thornley Colton meant. He was blind, and the red-cheeked man beside him furnished the only eyes he knew.

"But you'll come to my reception tomorrow night?" she asked earnestly. "Only for a few minutes, but *do* come."

"I had intended to," he smiled.

"That's settled," she nodded. "Now," she added, with mock pleading in her voice, "who is to be the happy recipient of your favour this time?" One gloved hand made a small gesture toward the trays of jewels under the glass. The blind man, whose years of practice had made him reader of every inflection, understood instantly, but young Osmuhn came up in time to answer.

"Mr Colton has kindly consented to investigate a small matter for us," he said nervously.

"The necklace robbery you were telling me about?" asked the girl, eyes shining.

"Here comes father." Young Osmuhn's face was red, his tone guilty.

Mrs Marle repressed a smile with difficulty. She had never heard a whisper of a necklace robbery in the house of Osmuhn & Son. She understood how carefully the secret must have been guarded, and she understood also the lack of caution that was part of youth and love. But she was a wonderfully bright woman, and apparently she had not even heard her daughter's remark. All her attention was on the stout little man with the shiny bald head and the bright eyes that gleamed from under bushy brows.

"A great pleasure, Mrs Marle," said the elder Osmuhn, as he bowed gravely. "You have come to see the Thousand Facets of Fire."

"To buy it, I think," she smiled, extending her hand.

"Ah," murmured the gem-dealer, in a tone of quiet satisfaction. "I will show it to you at once. It is in the vault." Then a troubled light came to his eyes, as they rested on Thornley Colton and Sydney Thames. Some subtle fifth sense seemed to tell the blind man the cause instantly.

"Sydney and I will wait in your office, if you don't mind," he put in quickly.

Osmuhn's voice showed his relief. Experience had taught him that there was much more appreciation when the customer was alone. "My son will tell you everything," he said. He looked around to where the other member of the firm had been standing a moment before; then shrugged his shoulders in parental helplessness. Osmuhn, junior, was leading Miss Helen Marle toward the rear of the shop.

Mrs Marle laughed. "You would have done the same thing at his age," she accused.

The jeweller shook his head. "I suppose so." Then, to the blind man: "A minute only, Mr Colton," he apologised.

"Make it ten," smiled Colton. "Your son told me practically everything, and I'd like to have ten minutes or so to think over the facts."

Osmuhn turned toward the small, glass-enclosed office at the rear of the shop, from which he could see everything that went on. The blind man followed unhesitatingly, super keen ears noting each footfall of the man who preceded him.

"Only a minute," repeated the seller of jewels again, when the two men had been made comfortable in the two big chairs by the desk. "Come, Mrs Marle." He seemed to take an unnecessary step or two as he said it, and only the blind man heard the click of some secret electric connection releasing the steel door that Osmuhn opened a minute later by a curious pressure of his fingers on the knob, and a peculiar-looking key.

Mrs Cornelius Marle, probably the richest woman in New York, lover of jewels because they were jewels, and not merely as ornaments, owner of what was reputed to be the finest collection of rare gems, entered the innermost citadel of the house of Osmuhn. The steel door shut softly behind her, and she knew that she was as far removed from the world outside as though she were a thousand feet underground. She knew that the tapestry-covered walls of the twelve-foot room were of eighteen-inch concrete, interlaced with steel rails; that the

Winton-carpeted floor and the panelled ceiling were the same. The steel door behind her was the only opening in the walls of man-made stone.

She needed no direction to take a seat at the small Sheraton table against the wall at the far side of the vault. She had been there before; each time when Osmuhn had picked up some rare and costly jewel. The jeweller, with a soft-voiced apology, leaned over her shoulder to press the pearl-centred black button in the brass wall-plate a foot from the woman's elbow. The table light shed its brilliance on the white velvet table-pad.

"The Thousand Facets of Fire is the most wonderful ruby I have ever seen or handled," declared Osmuhn enthusiastically, as he stepped behind her to twirl the two combination knobs on the door of the steel safe that was imbedded in the concrete wall. "Mr Norvel heard of it when he was in Europe last year. He negotiated for months, and sent it to me just ten days before his horrible accident in France."

"The accident left him a hopeless cripple, did it not?" she asked politely, turning in her chair so that she could see the deft fingers at work with the combination.

"Yes." Osmuhn's voice was sad. "He must walk with canes always." Then a note of pride came to his voice. "But he refuses to give up. He is here every day, and I need him. In the twenty-eight years he has been with me he has learned everything I know about stones, and today he is probably the greatest living expert on diamonds."

The round safe-door swung open, and, with a wholly unconscious flourish, he placed the big jewel-case before her and snapped back the lid.

A thousand blood-red flashes of living fire seemed to leap upward, battling with their myriad sword points against the soft glow of the electric—then the whole room seemed lighted only by the wonderful ruby in its velvet case.

As great music hypnotises, intoxicates to sense-numbing silence, so the refraction of the ruby's million rays held the woman spellbound. She could not speak, nor move; her eyes were held by the lights that danced and flashed from the thousand facets—now invitingly, now mockingly, but always sure of their victory.

Osmuhn's eyes, under their bushy brows, gleamed brighter—they understood. At his first sight of the jewel he, too, had known why men had risked their lives and why women had bartered their souls and bodies for the Thousand Facets of Fire.

"Is it not well named?" he asked.

His words seemed to break the spell that bound her. She nodded as one in a dream, and put forth her fingers almost timidly to touch the flashing stone.

"Take it in your hand, feel the weight of it." He turned away, walked the length of the room. When he came back she was holding the ruby on her palm. The velvet box had been thrust aside, and in her eyes was almost childish wonder that a thing so full of fire could be so cold.

With a quiet nod of satisfaction Osmuhn turned away again—it was no time for words. Mrs Marle would want to speak in a moment; until then—. He went behind her, and bent down to the safe, his hands idly rearranging the small boxes that held the most valuable jewels in his possession; jewels that were never allowed to go from the specially-constructed safe in the specially-constructed room, unless his hands removed them.

The woman still gazed at the jewel. A wavering streamer of mist seemed to hover over it for an instant—or was it a picture the jewel had conjured in her brain? As she watched, immovable, it spread over her hand, then over the whole table—an impenetrable veil of filmy nothing. She lifted her unoccupied hand to brush her eyes.

A gasping noise came from her throat. The man behind her seemed to sense something wrong in the very sound. He wheeled, the hand that had been on the safe-door clanged it shut.

"It's gone!" she choked. "*Gone!*"

The mist had vanished as it had come. The hand that never moved; the hand that had held the ruby was empty!

II.

As the steel door closed behind Osmuhn and Mrs Marle, Thornley Colton leaned back in his chair and thoughtfully puffed a cigarette. But Sydney Thames, the secretary the blind man had picked up twenty-five years before as a bundle of baby-clothes on the bank of the English river that had given him his name, could not remain silent. The story young Osmuhn had been telling them when the Marles had interrupted was not one calculated to keep the ever-doubting Sydney still.

"What do you think of that necklace disappearance Osmuhn asked you to investigate?" he demanded.

"One of the most interesting problems I've been called to solve in a long time," answered Colton. A smile of joy curved the thin lips, for a problem, to the blind man who solved crime-puzzles as his recreation, was the greatest pleasure he knew.

"But the thing is utterly impossible!" protested Sydney. "Such a thing couldn't have happened in broad daylight and in New York."

"As I've told you once or twice before, Sydney, the fact remains that it did happen. And there must be some explanation."

Sydney shook his head. "The statement that a man in full possession of his senses could stare blankly at a two-hundred-thousand-dollar diamond necklace while it disappeared into a thin mist before his very eyes is a trifle too strong for me," he averred stoutly.

"Do you think young Osmuhn is lying?" smiled Colton.

"He seems to be absolutely straight," hesitated Sydney. "But his story—" The rest was obvious.

The smile on the blind man's face broadened.

"But consider his frankness in telling of it, Sydney. If he'd been lying I imagine he'd have concocted a better story than that. Consider how every detail of the disappearance is firmly impressed in his mind. The robbery, for that's what it was, occurred after closing hours, when all the clerks and other employees had gone. Only the younger Osmuhn and the diamond-expert for the firm were on the premises. Norvel, the expert, seeing young Osmuhn behind the long case in the shop, wanted to show him the completed diamond necklace that was to be delivered at the Nevin home next day. He laid it before Osmuhn, and together they examined it for possible flaws. Norvel placed his cane on the case while he took a cigarette from his pocket. Finding he had no matches, he limped with the aid of his other cane to his overcoat, which he had thrown over the back of a chair five feet or so away. A gasp from Osmuhn caused him to turn, with the overcoat still on his arm. He saw the other man staring wildly at the place where, a few minutes before, the diamond necklace had been. Osmuhn swears that, while Norvel was walking toward his overcoat, a thick mist, which he describes as not unlike steam, appeared over the necklace, completely hiding it from his eyes. He confesses that the thing was so remarkable that for an instant he could do nothing but stare. Then the mist began to dissolve, and he saw that the necklace had vanished utterly. His gasp caused Norvel to turn. Norvel hadn't seen the mist, for it had entirely disappeared when he had hobbled back to the case. Together they searched for the missing diamonds without finding a trace. Also, without leaving one another's sight for an instant, they telephoned to the elder Osmuhn, and sat watching one another for their mutual protection, until he and a private detective came. They submitted to a thorough search, and took part in the all-night hunt for the jewels that covered every part of the store and building. Why, the very impossibility of the story stamps it with truth!"

"But Norvel was there," reminded Sydney.

"He had no possible chance of touching the necklace. He had turned away, and his back was toward Osmuhn."

"But the mist!" persisted Sydney. "That is the impossible part of the whole thing. How, in Heaven's name, could there be a mist such as he describes in a New York jewellery shop? It's absurd!"

"Not absurd, Sydney," corrected the problemist mildly. "Merely the solution; the solution of the whole thing."

The smile went from his face, he leaned forward with a sudden tenseness of face and body; the delicate nostrils quivered like those of a hound scenting a new trail.

"Something's wrong inside, Sydney!" His sightless eyes were fixed on the closed, soundproof door, his head was bent forward expectantly. Then he straightened back in his chair, and was quietly puffing his cigarette when the door opened, and the elder Osmuhn, white-faced, trembling, staggered out of the vault-room.

"It's gone!" He choked the words just as the woman had choked them a few minutes before. "The Thousand Facets of Fire has vanished!"

The blind man had risen at the first word, and before the gem dealer had finished speaking he had brushed past him, the thin, hollow stick that gave its messages to the hypersensitive fingertips locating the steps unerringly.

The sobbing, hysterical woman at the small table did not even look up as he laid his hand gently on her shoulder, but he felt her body shudder under the touch, as though her overwrought mind had already pictured visions of the police. "Tell me how it happened, Mrs Marle." The words were soft-spoken, kindly.

"There is nothing to tell," she sobbed. "The ruby just—went."

"Dissolved into mist?"

She looked up, sudden, wild hope showing behind the tears in her eyes. "Would you believe that?" she asked breathlessly. "It seems so—impossible—I was afraid—."

"I know that is how it disappeared," Thornley Colton said quietly. "Mr Osmuhn will tell you that a diamond necklace vanished in the same way nearly ten days ago."

The white-faced jeweller brushed his sweat-beaded forehead with a shaking hand. "Yes," he groaned, "that, and this ruby, will bring the loss to nearly three-quarters of a million. But it couldn't have happened!" he declared, almost fiercely. "Mrs Marle was holding it in her hand! I wasn't two feet away. The walls are solid concrete! There isn't a crack in them!" Each staccato sentence was jerked out almost passionately. Osmuhn seemed to be trying to convince himself, as well as his hearers, that the thing he knew had happened was utterly impossible.

Colton paid no attention. He spoke to the woman, still quietly, gently, smoothing his questions so that they became merely statements for which he wanted confirmation.

"You knew the ruby was gone, even before your eyes saw the empty hand?"

Osmuhn and Sydney Thames came closer to the little table.

"Yes." She spoke more calmly. "I raised my other hand to brush my eyes—I thought it was an optical illusion of some kind—then I felt the stone—go."

"How?"

"I don't know," she faltered, looking from one to the other in bewilderment. "I could see nothing but the thick mist that seemed to cover the whole table. Then—I suddenly felt my outstretched hand relieved of the weight. It—seemed to just fly away!"

"A ruby weighing nearly two hundred carats would make a very good flyer," observed the blind man smilingly. Then: "But the mist, wasn't it a trick of the lights?"

She shook her head. "Mist is the only word that describes it. When my eyes first noticed it, it was a ribbon that widened almost instantly to hide the whole table, though the light shone above it perfectly. I know that last unconsciously, for I think the jewel had hypnotised me—I couldn't take my eyes away, even when the mist hid it from sight."

"Where is the switch for the table-light? Snap it off, Mr Osmuhn."

The jeweller leaned across the table to obey. Colton examined every inch of the table-light with his fingers.

"Absolutely nothing there," he murmured. Then his fingers felt the two buttons in the brass plate that he had made the jeweller locate for him. He snapped the light on again, then off, and back.

"It wasn't a trick of the light," he declared emphatically. "Nor of your eyes, Mrs Marle." He stood erect. "Tell your son to come here, Mr Osmuhn," he said quietly.

The white-faced jeweller almost tottered from the small room. The instant that Osmuhn's footsteps told the blind man that he had gone through the door, Thornley Colton spoke.

"Mrs Marle." His voice was crisp, imperative. "At the instant you first saw the mist, was it as wide as a ribbon?"

She answered steadily enough, despite the sudden change in the blind man's tone: "Yes, it seemed to stretch over the table lengthways, waving slightly, as a ribbon would do in a breath of air, but almost instantly it widened and widened, until it covered the whole table." There was only a slight tremor in her voice, but in her eyes was awe, as she spoke of the inexplicable thing her eyes had seen.

"Mr Osmuhn had his back toward you?"

"Yes."

"How do you know that?"

She smiled wanly up at him, forgetting, as people usually did when Colton was speaking, that he could see nothing. "I don't know it because I saw him," she replied, "but I do know it because he always turns toward the small safe back of this chair, and idly arranges the jewel-cases on the shelves when a customer is examining one of the rare gems he keeps in this room. He knows the value of silence when a lover of jewels is looking at a wonderful stone like the Thousand Facets of Fire."

Colton smiled understandingly; then wheeled to face the door as Osmuhn entered, followed by his son. Following them, unnoticed, came Helen Marle. She took her place behind her mother without a word.

"Father says the ruby has vanished!" cried the younger Osmuhn, and his voice, and eyes, and very manner seemed a wild plea for denial.

Colton merely nodded. "Utterly," he confirmed. "Just as the necklace disappeared—into a mist. Now tell me, Mr Osmuhn," he continued quietly, "what was the appearance of the mist when you first saw it over the necklace on the glass case outside?"

"Why, it was just a mist," stammered the son. "Just a cloud that spread instantly."

"You never lifted your eyes from the stones?"

"I don't think so—though I may have looked up for an instant as Mr Norvel started toward his coat."

"Cloud—ribbon," murmured the blind man, apparently to himself, tapping his trouser-leg with his slim stick.

"That wonderful ruby—gone!" muttered the elder Osmuhn, sinking, almost inertly, into a chair at the other side of the small table.

"My God!" They all turned, as the cry burst from the man who had entered the vault-room unnoticed. The newcomer was a cripple who hobbled along with the aid of two heavy black canes. But it was the lean, intelligent face, with the coal-black eyes and the thin nose, that held Sydney's gaze. Mentality was stamped in every deep-graven line, but now there seemed a pitiful helplessness in the tremulous lips of the man as he advanced toward them.

"Mr Norvel!" Colton stepped to meet the man with outstretched hand. Then he answered the surprised looks some inner consciousness told him was on the faces of the other persons in the room: "Mr Osmuhn told me of you when we were talking outside, and the tap of your canes as you entered was all the identification I needed."

"Yes, I am Mr Norvel." The words came almost gaspingly, and Colton felt the man's hand tremble in his. "I was in my office when I saw Mr Osmuhn speak to Henry. I knew there was something wrong with the Thousand Facets of Fire, and—."

He gasped chokingly, and staggered. Osmuhn jumped from his chair with a cry of concern, the sight of the man before him momentarily driving from his mind even the loss of the great ruby. "Sit down, Philip," he commanded, leading the crippled man to a chair.

"These things—are taking the life out of me," gasped the diamond expert of the firm. "The necklace—then this!"

"Mr Norvel is on the verge of collapse," whispered young Osmuhn. "He has had valvular heart trouble for years. The loss of the diamond necklace he had worked on upset him terribly—and he worked for months to get the Thousand Facets of Fire."

Colton nodded sympathetically. "He should take a long rest," murmured the blind man.

Norvel heard him. "I'll get it soon," he said helplessly, "in the grave."

"You have years before you yet," smiled Colton encouragingly. "Disappearances like these are calculated to frazzle the best of nerves." Then, in the same gentle tone he had used in questioning Mrs Marle, he went on: "Mr Osmuhn told me of the terrible auto accident you had in France last summer, Mr Norvel. Your driver and the occupant of the other car were killed, weren't they?"

"Yes," the cripple shuddered. "And it made an old man of me, that and my rotten heart."

Again Thornley Colton nodded sympathetically.

"You hovered between life and death for several months, I understand?"

"Practically dead," Norvel answered.

"Um!" The blind man rolled the thin stick between his slender fingers, and puzzled lines appeared on his forehead.

"What is the object of those questions?" demanded the elder Osmuhn, and he could not keep the impatience from his voice.

"A long chance, nothing more," Colton assured him quietly. "A chance that Mr Norvel, in his delirium, might have told secrets that gave the criminal information necessary to commit these robberies."

The diamond expert half rose from his chair, his hands clutching his heavy canes. "That may be true—I may be responsible!"

"Ridiculous!" snapped Osmuhn, and he made no attempt to keep the impatience from his tone now.

"We can't afford to overlook even the remotest possibility in a case like this," said Thornley Colton evenly.

Norvel lowered the hand that had been clutching at his heart. "Why don't you search?" he cried. "The stone couldn't have gotten out of the room! The walls are of solid concrete, impregnable. The ruby must be here!"

The elder Osmuhn looked around nervously, eyes travelling from one face to the other, seeking vainly for some way out. Mrs Marle rose and slipped her arm around the waist of her daughter.

"I will submit to a search," she said quietly.

"Thank you! Thank you!" Osmuhn fairly choked his relief. "I will get Miss—"

"Do you want to search Sydney and me?" asked Thornley Colton, with a half smile on his expressive lips.

"I don't think it is necessary; you weren't—." Osmuhn stopped, understanding that he had practically admitted that Mrs Marle was the only one on whom suspicion rested. His son opened his mouth to protest, but the woman forestalled him.

"I understand," she said steadily.

"Then we will go; it is long past my lunch-hour." The blind man's fingers touched the crystalless watch in his pocket.

"Don't you want to know the result of the search?" Osmuhn asked blankly.

"I know it now," said the blind man, with that same curious smile on his lips. "Goodbye, Mr Osmuhn." He shook hand heartily with the jeweller, and held the woman's hand in his for an instant.

"I shall be at your reception tomorrow night," he reminded, and she murmured a steady-voiced "Thank you."

The blind man touched the fingers of the daughter, clasped the palm of the younger Osmuhn and that of Norvel, and hurried out, leaving them staring after him.

It was not until he and Sydney were in the big car on their way to the old-fashioned up-town house and luncheon that Thornley Colton spoke.

"One of the most remarkable crimes I've ever had the good fortune to work on, Sydney. And a remarkable thief—a criminal with an imagination."

"But how did they vanish; where did the ruby and the necklace go?" asked Sydney Thames helplessly.

"Regarding the first part of your double-barrelled question: Is it possible, after all you have heard, that you don't know *how* they vanish?" The smile on the thin lips was inscrutable. "Where they go, Sydney, is not half so important as where they are. That's where the work comes in. I am sure that I know where the Thousand Facets of Fire is, but I don't know where the necklace is. I never half complete a case. By waiting I can get both the necklace and the ruby. By jumping recklessly I can arrest the criminal and recover the ruby; but I'm not a detective, Sydney; problems are merely my recreation. So I'll recover both."

"The ruby!" exclaimed Sydney. "You know where that is?"

"Certainly," nodded Colton, snapping his smoked cigarette into the street. "The thief has been safe because he has worked against men who have imaginations that are handicapped by eyes. My imagination is unhampered. As I told Osmuhn, the search will reveal nothing, despite the fact that the ruby is just about three feet from the place where it disappeared!"

III.

The red-haired boy with the slightly twisted nose who had become a member of the Colton household as the only fee to a particularly baffling murder case, shifted from one foot to the other in an ecstasy of joy, listening intently and eagerly as the blind man talked. When Thornley Colton had finished, he could contain himself no longer.

"Gee! I'm gettin' to be a reg'ler detective. Yuh reelly want me to trail him?" He asked the last anxiously, fearful lest he had heard wrong.

"Yes," smiled the problemist. "Shadow him."

"B'lieve me, Mr Colton." The boy's eyes were round and serious. "If I locate that nigger, I'll show him Nick Carter ain't got nothin' on me. An' I'll find him, too!" he boasted.

"There's a Hindu somewhere around," nodded Colton. "He doesn't amount to much, except as a trail to the real criminal, but I expect him to do a certain thing, and I want to make sure of it. That's all."

"I'll get him," chirped the boy, and, pulling his cap down over his ears, he darted from the room.

Colton snapped out the light and sat puffing his cigarette in the darkness. For half an hour he did not move, except to light a new cigarette. Sydney Thames entered with a slip of paper in his hand, and Colton switched on the light again.

"Three boats leave this week," announced Sydney. "The Bordeaux tomorrow, the *Trevoila* Thursday, and the *Paris* Saturday."

"I think that last is about it," mused Colton, his thin fingers beating a devil's tattoo on the arm of his chair.

"What?"

"The date of the thief's departure for Europe."

"The date of—," gasped Sydney.

Thornley Colton nodded. "He'll have time for that one after he finds out that the next trick he's going to play hasn't thrown me off the track. He doesn't realise—yet—the possibilities of blindness; he doesn't understand that the things which deceive the ordinary man only make facts clearer to me." Colton pushed the desk-button that would summon the automobile at any hour of the twenty-four. "Let's take in a matinée, Sydney," he said, rising.

That afternoon, and that night, not a word was said regarding the remarkable thefts at the shop of Osmuhn & Son. Thornley Colton had apparently forgotten all about it. Early the next morning he answered an anxious query from Osmuhn by saying that he was hard at work, and immediately after he idled away two hours in his music-room. At ten o'clock the telephone rang, and the puzzled Sydney heard the following one-sided conversation.

"Hello, Shrimp. English valet, eh? Funny! What! Invalid who has a Hindu servant that wheels him out every afternoon at four o'clock? Hindu went away alone at ten o'clock this morning? Where? Good! Good! That's all now. Go to one of your moving picture shows for the rest of the day."

There was a broad smile on his lips as he hung up the receiver.

"What is it?" asked Sydney.

"Just another example of how a clever man will accomplish his object in a clever way. Look up Irotette's number, will you? I haven't got it on my list."

"The caterer?"

"Yes." When Colton got the connection, and gave his name, there was no doubt of his standing with New York society's biggest caterer. "I want a favour," he said, when the head of the firm was at the other end of the wire. "An exceptionally intelligent-looking coloured man just applied for a night's work at Mrs Marle's reception tonight. You took him? I thought you would, for I know the difficulty of getting good men for a big affair like that. Now for the favour. Can you fix it so that his work will allow him the freedom of the rooms? Thanks!"

Sydney started to ask a question, but the blind man forestalled him. "Tomorrow you'll know all about it," he promised.

Sydney realised that Colton would not say a word till the time came, and, under protest, he accompanied the problemist to the Marle reception that night. Colton apparently enjoyed every minute of the time, but Sydney, as usual, was on edge continuously, for his fear of pretty women amounted almost to an obsession. Even the wonderful personality of Mrs Marle, who went from one guest to another, as though she had not a care in the world, and as though the disappearance of the ruby had never occurred, was not able to put him at his ease.

Promptly at eleven o'clock next morning Colton summoned his car. "We're going to make a party call on Mrs Marle," was the way he answered Sydney's question.

"Didn't you get enough last night?" groaned Thames.

"Quite," nodded the blind man, "but did you notice that bright-looking serving man with the coal-black eyes? Mrs Marle pointed him out to me. He is the Hindu whom I spoke to Irotette about."

"Hindu?" ejaculated Sydney. "Why should a Hindu be serving ices at a fool reception?"

"Because he had a little job to do. I'm going to call on Mrs Marle this morning, and see how he did it," replied Colton, as he pulled on his gloves.

When Mrs Marle appeared, Sydney Thames had hard work to repress a gasp of astonishment. Last night she had been happy, cheerful. Now she was haggard, there were circles under her eyes, and her hand trembled as she held it out.

"An unexpected pleasure, Mr Colton." She tried to say it graciously, but her voice shook, and there was a piteous look in her eyes.

Thornley Colton spoke quietly, evenly. "The ruby, please." The words struck the astounded Sydney like a pistol-shot.

The woman choked a sob in her throat, and swayed slightly. Thornley Colton led her gently to a chair.

"I didn't take it!" she cried brokenly. "I didn't! I'm not a thief! I found it in my jewel-case last night. I don't know how it got there—and Helen saw it, too!" The last words came in a sobbing gasp.

"Of course you didn't take it!" declared Colton. "You haven't even got it!" She looked up, searching his eyes to find the truth she had prayed for during the long hours of the night.

"You mean it! You know!" Her hand was on his arm; pleading, joy unutterable was in her voice.

"I didn't think that you would find it until this morning," Colton said contritely. "It was placed there last night by an accomplice of the real thief. I knew it would be. The thief realised that he must throw some dust in the eyes of all of us. He failed to understand that dust wouldn't affect my eyes. The ruby you have is only an imitation, but it would have served its purpose. Let me have it."

"Yes! Yes! Take it!" The hysteria of reaction was in her voice; she held out her left hand, and the red stone gleamed as the folds of the covering handkerchief fell away from it. "I must tell Helen—I asked her to call up Mr Osmuhn."

"I'm going to see him now," Colton told her, and he hurried out, followed by her tremulous thanks.

The elder Osmuhn seemed on the verge of nervous prostration when they arrived at the shop. He jumped from the chair in his glass-enclosed office, and fairly ran to meet them.

"I've been trying to get you for fifteen minutes!" he said hoarsely. "Mrs Marle has the ruby. Henry has just gone there. I never thought—."

"I have seen Mrs Marle," said Colton sharply. "You should know her better than that. The ruby she had was a mere imitation. Here it is."

Osmuhn snatched it eagerly, glanced at it, and groaned. "But how did she get this stone?" he demanded. "It is exactly the same weight and cut as the Thousand Facets of Fire. She saw the ruby three months ago!" There was suspicion in his voice now. "She is the only one in New York who did see it! No one could have made an imitation so exactly in the few hours since the original was stolen. And her story of the disappearance was so impossible!" Hours of brooding over the loss of the stone had apparently done their work.

"Don't you believe your son's story of the necklace disappearance?" asked Colton impatiently.

"But *she* has a passion for jewels. The ruby must have destroyed—."

"If she had stolen it, she would have had more sense than bring this new suspicion against herself. I'll get the thief, also the ruby and necklace. But I'll get him in my own way and my own time. You'd better wait. Good day!"

Leaving the head of the house of Osmuhn & Son staring, mouth agape, he left the shop. Thornley Colton never had patience with men who couldn't see through a ladder when God had given them eyes.

"Telephone-booth, Sydney," the blind man said, when they were out of the shop. "I'm going to put joy into the heart of Shrimp. Then we'll kill a few hours before the next act. This is a show with long intermissions."

The next three hours seemed the longest Sydney Thames had ever spent. They went to an uptown restaurant, and Colton ate as though there was not another thing worth thinking about in the world. Sydney was a flutter of impatience. He couldn't enjoy his food; the music of the orchestra grated on his nerves; the waiter angered him by his continued hovering. But Sydney knew the futility of questioning the blind man. He knew that each apparently irrelevant thing the blind man had done would lead logically to the finish of the case. But what was the finish? Who was the thief? Where were the jewels that Thornley Colton expected to get by waiting?

At last the crystalless watch told the blind man that the time had come. "We'll take a little walk along Ninety-first Street," he said. "I expect to meet a white-haired invalid in a wheel-chair, with a Hindu servant. Watch for him."

They reached Ninety-first Street, and strolled along casually; two idlers out for an afternoon walk. Suddenly Sydney saw the invalid.

"A man in a wheelchair was just brought out of that brownstone house a block up the street. The man wheeling him is coloured."

"Don't notice him," warned Colton.

They walked slowly toward the oncoming wheelchair. Sydney tried his best to appear as calm as the blind man, but he could feel his heart pounding in his chest. What was going to happen? The street, for a block, was deserted, save for them, the two others, and a ragged street gamin, who was speeding along the smooth pavement on roller skates.

Sydney could see the man in the chair plainly now. His long, white hair almost touched his shoulders, the white beard swept his breast, and came up almost to his eyes. His legs were wrapped tight in a red blanket, and a shawl was thrown over his shoulders.

Only five feet separated them. As they stepped out to let the chair go past, the gamin, with a wild whoop, came speeding up in back of the chair, head down. He skated straight at the Hindu servant struck him, and bowled him over. With a shriek of joy he continued on his way after staggering Sydney Thames as he brushed past him.

Colton leaped forward with a cry of mingled anger and sympathy. His hand on the round iron handle of the chair kept it from going over, and he grasped one of the big knobs at the handle-ends to steady himself as he helped the muttering servant to his feet.

"Little devil!" snapped the invalid, in a high-pitched, querulous voice. Then, as Thornley Colton stepped in front of him: "Thank you, young man."

"He should be arrested," declared Colton emphatically. He held out his hand. "I am blind," he apologised. "Will you shake the hand of another of the afflicted? My secretary described you to me as you came along."

"Well, you're no worse off than I am," cackled the man in the chair. "I see too devilish much! Good day."

Colton bowed and stood aside. The impassive-faced servant pushed the chair down the side-walk.

"It's a crime the way those gamins carry on," muttered Sydney, when they had walked a hundred yards or so in silence.

Colton chuckled. "I'll have to tell Shrimp how good his disguise was," he laughed.

"Shrimp!" echoed Sydney in amazement.

"Certainly." Thornley Colton grinned broadly. "He was on hand to give our Hindu friend a bump when the proper time came."

"In Heaven's name why?"

"So that I could locate the probable hiding-place of the ruby and the necklace when the time came for hiding them there. Also, to give me a chance to shake the hand of the man who stole them. Davidson is the invalid's name. Quite a character, isn't he?"

IV.

In the darkened music-room Thornley Colton's fingers wandered idly over the keys, now improvising, now filling the room with the ever-living soul of Beethoven, now swinging crashingly into Wagner; then his fingers on the upper treble brought forth a strange discord of notes through which ran a weird minor melody. The last seemed to please him, for he repeated it, until Sydney Thames, who had been nervously pacing the room, stopped in his tracks.

"What the deuce do you call that?" he demanded, the discords still ringing in his ears. "It's horrible!"

"Because it doesn't agree with your orthodox ideas of music," declared Colton seriously. "That is one of the most beautiful pieces of music I know. It is a Hindustan adaptation of the 'Chinese Flute Song' of *Siao She*. It is a fitting accompaniment for this latest case of ours."

"And just as understandable," observed Sydney, walking up and down the room again. Colton turned again toward the keys, and Sydney broke out impatiently: "Why don't you do something, Thorn? Two whole days have passed since you found the man who stole the ruby, and you haven't done a thing! Osmuhn suspects Mrs Marle, and she is on the verge of collapse. You haven't made an attempt to clear up the mystery.

It isn't right! Osmuhn is rapidly losing his patience; his son must stand helplessly by and see the mother of the girl he loves suspected; and the thing is making a nervous wreck of Norvel. It is only a matter of days when he will have to leave the business for good."

"Osmuhn's patience became exhausted last night," Thornley Colton said. "He advised me that he had lost faith in my efforts, and that he was going to call in the police."

"Great Heaven!" exclaimed Sydney. "That means that they will arrest Mrs Marle!" It only needed a woman in trouble to put the susceptible Sydney Thames at sixes and sevens.

"I think even the police will hesitate before arresting a woman like Mrs Marle on mere suspicion," the blind man declared.

The electric bell at the front door sent out its announcement.

"See who it is, will you? Shrimp is out on a little job for me."

Sydney hurried out, and the problemist's sensitive fingertips felt the face of the crystalless watch in his pocket. A frown furrowed his forehead for a minute. He went into the library, and was sitting at the desk which held the telephone when Sydney came back, followed by Henry Osmuhn, junior.

"They are going to arrest Helen's mother!" burst out Osmuhn the instant he crossed the threshold.

Colton's mobile face expressed sympathy. "I don't think they will," he assured quietly.

"But they're going to!" cried Osmuhn fiercely.

"My father put the thing into the hands of the police yesterday afternoon. The days of brooding over the loss of the Thousand Facets of Fire have driven him half crazy. The finding of the imitation ruby in Mrs Marle's possession, and your refusal to explain what you are waiting for, have driven every bit of commonsense from him. Detectives badgered her for two hours last night. She is on the verge of hysteria. And Helen—." He paced up and down the room like a caged tiger, each word tumbling over the other as it came from his lips; his hands clenched and unclenched at his sides. The sensitive-nerved Sydney Thames caught the contagion.

"It's a crime to let those innocent women suffer, while you sit there, calmly smoking a cigarette!" charged the secretary bitterly. He turned away as the blind man's lips curved in a smile. "He has known the thief for two days!" he told Osmuhn, beside himself at the injustice of the problemist.

"He knows the thief!" Osmuhn stopped dead in his tracks, staring incredulously at Sydney. Then he whirled to face the blind man, who sat quietly back in his chair, blowing smoke-rings towards the ceiling. "Why don't you have him arrested?" he demanded, voice high with excitement.

"Because I want to get the jewels," answered the blind man.

"But a search, a confession, will—."

"Do you suppose that a man with the daring and cleverness necessary to accomplish those robberies would either confess or hide the stones where they could be found?" he asked, a trifle impatiently. "I'm waiting for the thief to hide the jewels in a place where I can find them. That will be when he is about to start away. To arrest him before would mean an endless search. You must understand that the thief who could commit robberies like those is a wonderfully clever man. I know that he is marvellous, for he is the only man I ever saw whose heartbeats failed to show any emotion whatever."

"Who is the thief?" asked Osmuhn soberly. All the excitement and incredulity had gone from his voice now.

"A man who calls himself Davidson; an invalid who is wheeled around by a Hindu servant for an hour or so each afternoon. He is never seen at other times. He lives next door to Mr Norvel, your diamond-expert."

"So that's how he knew!" cried Osmuhn, eye alight with understanding. "Was he in France when Mr Norvel's accident occurred?" The question Colton had put at the time of the ruby robbery flashed back in his mind.

The blind man nodded. "I am going to see him the minute my boy calls me up and tells me that he is getting ready to start to the steamer *Paris*, which sails at noon today."

The jangling telephone-bell came as a period to the sentence. Colton removed the receiver, listened a moment, said a single "All right, Shrimp," and rose. "The curtain is up for the last act," he said soberly. He pulled open a drawer of the desk and took out a wicked-looking blued-steel automatic and slipped it into his side coat-pocket.

"There won't be any need of that?" Osmuhn asked nervously.

"The man we are going after isn't the kind that holds his hands out for the steel bracelets," replied the problemist grimly.

"But you are blind!" cried Osmuhn. "You can't see!"

The blind man's smile was one of amusement as he answered: "If I had not been blind, I wouldn't have solved this case, and, if I'm not mistaken in my man, my lack of eyes is going to do more toward his actual capture than your keen ones. I have an idea you'll see another mysterious disappearance—of men this time."

He slipped on his overcoat and led them out of the house and into the waiting car, which had stood at the curb for the last half-hour. There was not a word spoken by the three men until the car turned into Ninety-first Street.

"Hadn't we better stop at the corner and walk?" asked Osmuhn, as the car continued on and swerved in toward the curb before the brownstone house.

Colton flicked his cigarette away and shook his head. "I guess Mr Davidson is expecting us. I've had Shrimp working pretty openly in the last day or two. I think the thief will want to pull off one last grand-stand play before he leaves."

The red-haired boy who had been leaning against a tree at the other side of the street ran over and hopped on the run-board.

"Kin I go in with yuh, Mr Colton?" he asked eagerly, eyes shining with excitement.

The blind man shook his head. "No, Shrimp," he denied. "You go over and telephone for the police. We'll need them in a few minutes."

The boy's face showed his disappointment, but he tried bravely to keep it out of his voice. "All right, sir," he said, with an assumed cheeriness that was pathetic.

Sydney opened the tonneau-door, and Colton alighted, his slim stick before him locating the way up the wide stone steps. His lips were a grim, straight line as he pushed the button, and Osmuhn saw him put his hand in his pocket to assure himself that the automatic was ready for instant use. The nerves of the junior Osmuhn were taut, and his muscles tensed as the door swung back and the grave-faced Hindu that the disguised Shrimp had bowled over two days before stood looking at them gravely.

"What wish the Sahibs?" His voice was deep and rich. He had only muttered when they had seen him last.

"Is Mr Davidson in?" asked Colton politely. Sydney thought he saw a gleam of fire in the Hindu's dark eyes for an instant.

"Sahib Davidson is busied. He starts for the German baths at noon on the boat."

"It is highly important." The blind man's voice was suave.

From somewhere in the rear of the house came the piping, querulous voice of the invalid: "Who the devil is it, Pinjur?"

"I know not, Sahib," called the Hindu, in reply.

"The blind man who spoke to him two days ago when the boy of the street nearly upset his chair," enlightened Thornley Colton, and the ears of the old man were keen, for they heard.

"Send him in!" snapped the squeaky voice. "And come in yourself. There's a very devil of a draft!"

The Hindu stood aside gravely as they entered, closed the door carefully behind them, and, with a bowed invitation to follow, led the way down the hall toward the library.

Osmuhn's tense muscles relaxed, and a gasp of amazement came to his lips as they stepped inside the semi-darkened room, and he saw the white-haired, white-bearded old man Thornley Colton had declared was the thief who had stolen the Thousand Facets of Fire and the diamond necklace. Could this be the man, who, by some infernal magic, had caused three-quarters of a million dollars' worth of jewels to disappear while people watched them?

The old man drew himself closer to the desk, with his white hands on the wheels of his steel-framed chair, and peered at them short-sightedly.

"What do you want, gentlemen?" he piped. "I haven't but a minute. Have I, Pinjur?" He darted a queer, bird-like glance toward the Indian servant, who stood, straight-backed, before the one window that broke the lines of high bookshelves surrounding the room. The Hindu bowed.

Colton advanced half a step toward the desk. "We want," he said, slowly and distinctly, "the Thousand Facets of Fire and the diamond necklace!"

The old man's cackling laugh came from the white beard even before the last word had been uttered. "You want the ruby, eh?" he squealed, his hand falling on the desk before him. "He wants the necklace, too, Pinjur."

Osmuhn's eyes turned toward the Hindu; he saw the Indian lift one hand—then a rising curtain of mist seemed to hide him! Another rose over the desk! In an instant the two had joined, and a solid wall of fog, dense, impenetrable, hid half of the room.

"The mist!" he cried, falling back a step, the fear of the supernatural in his eyes.

He saw Thornley Colton leap forward; saw him swallowed up—vanish utterly. He could not move, nor could Sydney Thames beside him. They both heard a weird, gurgling cry, an oath in a strange language. Then the report of a pistol echoed through the room; the flash showed yellow-pink through the mist.

Thornley Colton's voice rang out:—

"Fling open the door!" The words loosed the leaden muscles of Sydney Thames. He sprang to obey. The current of air seemed to tear the mist to shreds instantly. Osmuhn took a half-step forward—stopped. Horror showed on his face for an instant; then amazement.

On the floor beside the bookcase lay the Hindu. The blood from his wound was staining the carpet. Beside him was a curious-looking knife, with the point stained a dull green. But Thornley Colton and the invalid had vanished utterly!

The line of bookcases was still unbroken. The wheelchair was where it had been before, but the occupant and the blind man were gone!

Fascinated, horror-stricken, the two men gazed at the empty chair and the silent form of the Indian. A soft click sounded like a pistol-shot in the death stillness of the room. A section of the case swung outward, and Thornley Colton, his overcoat slashed from shoulder to waist, stood before them, smiling grimly.

"My God, Thorn!" gasped Sydney, his strictured heart beating once more.

"Is there any blood on that knife-point, Sydney?" asked the blind man quietly.

Thames picked up the knife to examine it.

"Careful," warned the problemist. "By the way he slashed at me I think there is one of the devilish Indian poisons on the point."

Osmuhn and Sydney looked at the green-stained point, the slashed coat of the man who stood before them, smiling calmly, as he awaited the verdict of life or death.

"No," choked Sydney. He staggered against the wall. "Thank God! Thank God!" he prayed, eyes on the man who had been the only father he had ever known.

Thornley Colton dismissed his escape with a nod and spoke to the white-faced Osmuhn. "I think I told you that eyes would be of very little use in the *dénouement*. I knew the man, and the chances he'd take. I expected the fog. The game was to spring open the secret door, wheel the man and the chair inside, and leave us gaping idiotically. Would you like to see the thief; the cleverest, most daring I have ever encountered?"

He stepped aside. Dazedly Osmuhn and Sydney followed, only to stop at the doorway.

Manacled on the floor was the thief. Beside him, in a little heap, was the white wig and beard.

The thief was Norvel, the diamond expert!

"No," said Thornley Colton, "it isn't Norvel. It is the man who has been impersonating him for months. The man who lay in a French hospital learning every secret of the real Norvel, as he raved in delirium following the accident. Where Norvel is—." He paused significantly.

"His carcass is feeding fishes in the Seine!" snarled the crippled man. Then he burst into a vicious, sneering laugh. "Find the jewels?" he taunted.

"Easily." Colton went through the door that Sydney and Osmuhn now knew connected Norvel's house with the one next door. He wrenched off one of the knobs at the end of the wheelchair handle. They saw the red flash of the ruby as he held it up to the light.

"The necklace and the dozen other jewels that haven't yet been missed are in the hollow handle," he said quietly.

V.

It was several hours later. In the ornately furnished vault at the shop of Osmuhn & Son were the younger Osmuhn and Helen Marle, seated side by side in two Heppelwhite chairs, their hands clasped, unashamed. At the small table was

Osmuhn, senior; across from him, where she had been when the wonderful ruby disappeared, was Mrs Marle.

Young Osmuhn jumped to his feet as footsteps sounded outside.

"Here he comes!" his voice rang out joyously, as Thornley Colton entered, a long, paper-wrapped bundle under his arm.

Osmuhn, senior, came forward and held out his hand. "I can never thank you enough," he said brokenly.

"Thank me?" smiled the blind man. "The thanks are all on my side. It was the most interesting problem I ever tackled."

He laid down the long bundle on the small table, and took Mrs Marle's extended hand. She did not say a word, but the expression on her face told volumes; and she understood that the man without eyes knew.

"Now tell us how it was all done," broke in Helen Marle eagerly. "Henry has just told us how wonderful you were at the house. Tell us how the ruby vanished."

The irrepressible curiosity of the girl brought a smile to the blind man's lips. "I'll start right at the beginning," he promised. "At the police station the false Norvel consented to talk—a little. The Hindu is in the hospital. The two of them followed the Thousand Facets of Fire all through Europe, trying to get their hands on it. The real Norvel bought it before they had a chance to steal it, and substitute the imitation they had had made. Not knowing that he had already sent it to America, they were following Norvel when their automobile crashed into his on the outskirts of an obscure French village. The drivers of both cars were killed. Norvel got a knock on the head that resulted in concussion of the brain.

"The thief, who refuses to tell his name, or anything of his history, had both hips broken, and was made a cripple for life. But he is a wonderful man. He had a cot next to Norvel, and for weeks he heard Norvel rave of his past life, the ruby, the business—things that are reiterated over and over in the raving of delirium. The thief realised what the knowledge was worth. The fake news of Norvel's death went out. When he had recovered sufficiently to leave the hospital, he was murdered, and the thief became Norvel. He returned here, a changed man, but there was never a chance for suspicion. He was a wonderful actor. He knew everything that Norvel had known, and he knew jewels even better than Norvel himself.

"His Hindu partner and an Englishman who merely played the role of Norvel's valet came with him. But the thief was a master. The crude stealing made possible by his position didn't appeal to him. He wanted excitement, to astound people. So he planned to make a million by the cleverest thefts ever committed in the world. The Hindu had learned secrets from the greatest yogi in India, and he was a wonderful worker in gold plate and other metals. For weeks he worked and produced these." Colton stripped the paper from the long bundle, and the two heavy canes Norvel had always carried were revealed.

"What—," began Osmuhn dazedly.

Colton took one of the canes and laid it on the table. "This is the cane Norvel put on the glass case when the diamond necklace disappeared. Let me have that one he stole for a minute, will you?"

Osmuhn swung open the door of the safe and laid it before the blind man.

"Your son was talking, while Norvel was fingering the necklace like this." Colton pretended to examine the string of stones with his eyes, placing them in a perfectly straight line with the end of the cane, not four inches from its feruled bottom. "Watch!" he commanded. "Don't take your eyes from the stones!" He turned away; not one of them saw the delicate pull he gave to the black thread that was attached to an almost invisible knob at the cane handle. But they did see the feruled bottom spring open. They saw a small claw dart out, swift as the fang of a snake, catch the first stone of the necklace, and in a fraction of an instant the necklace had been drawn into the hollow cane like a snake in its hole—swiftly, silently. The cap closed at the bottom, the cane was merely a cane once more.

He showed them the thread, like the one Norvel had pulled when he started toward his overcoat.

"But the mist I saw?" demanded Osmuhn, junior. "What was that?"

"That is the most wonderful thing the Hindu yogi have in their bag of tricks. I was present at a private exhibition of it twenty years ago in the hill country of India. The men who were with me said that they saw a man disappear in a cloud of mist, just as you saw it attempted today. Twenty years ago it was one of the most profound mysteries, of India. Today it isn't."

"Isn't?" echoed Osmuhn.

"No. The trick is done with a wonderful powder called *scurtii-scurtii*. The powder is so finely ground that when let free in absolutely still air it hangs in the shape of a mist until a breeze blows it away. But it doesn't billow out like mist, or fog. By some curious property it hangs in the form of a thin, impenetrable curtain, either vertically or horizontally, according to the way it has been shot into the air. The disappearance trick in India can be done only on an absolutely calm day. Just as it could be done only in a vault like this, or in the store outside, when everyone had gone, and there was no possibility of a door opening. The powder was released from the cane when the end opened."

"But the ruby?" asked Mrs Marle. "There is no break in the concrete walls; no way that Mr Norvel could have gotten access to this room."

Colton pointed toward the brass wall-plate, with its two light buttons, a foot from her elbow. "There is the explanation, and the thing that told me how the trick had been done."

They crowded around the table to gaze at the two innocent appearing buttons.

"When you snapped off the light for me," said the blind man to the jeweller, "my ear, trained for years to read every sound, immediately caught the false note in the snap of the button against the contact. When I snapped on the lights my fingers found something that no eye could ever have detected. Instead of being roughly ground mother-of-pearl, as the centre of those black buttons always is, my supersensitive fingertip knew instantly that it was highly polished glass; a lens, in fact."

"By Jove, you're right!" Osmuhn had been examining it with a powerful glass.

"Yes," nodded Colton, "and if you put the glass to the other plain button you'll see a narrow slot, not much thicker than a sheet of paper, through which the *scurtii-scurtii* was injected the minute Mr Osmuhn turned his back to follow his invariable rule of arranging the small boxes in the safe, while the customer looked at the jewel. The minute the mist had covered the ruby, Norvel, in his office on the other side of the wall, where there is a plate exactly opposite this, so that the electricians would only have to make one hole for both in the solid concrete, swung the plates back and stole the jewel like this."

He unscrewed the heavy knob from the other cane, and from the hollow interior took what looked like a slender cane that, they could see, was made like a telescope of wonderfully thin metal sections. At the small end was a shallow, heavy rubber cup, with the interior smeared with a thick, gummy substance. Colton's fingers found a curious trigger-like projection at the larger end.

"I don't need the ruby for this. When the wall plate, which he and the Hindu had fixed when Norvel was supposed to be working late, swung open—hidden, of course, from Mrs Marle by the mist—he thrust the cup end of the cane through the opening like this." He thrust the cane toward Mrs Marle's hand. Before she could jerk it away, his finger touched the trigger, and the cane shut up like a telescope, as swiftly and silently as a darting shaft of light. "The actual theft didn't take an instant," explained Colton, and he couldn't keep the admiration from his voice. "All he had to do was to touch the stone in your hand, which wasn't a foot from the wall plate, the partial vacuum of the cup and the gummy substance would make it stick, and the spring inside would bring it through the plate-hole instantly. Then the plate closed, and the thing was accomplished before you could move a muscle."

"But what made the mist disappear?" Osmuhn wanted to know. "There was no current of air here."

"When you turned you must have shut the safe door. Of course, that would blow it away instantly, and the powder is so fine that you'd never see a trace of it. In the robbery of the necklace Norvel swung around with his coat on his arm, so that it formed a fan."

"But how did you ever connect the man who had fooled us all; the man who had impersonated Norvel so successfully?" queried Osmuhn.

Colton's lips curved in a curious smile. "The impersonation was so perfect that it would have deceived anyone with eyes, just as his thefts did. And his acting of Davidson was a wonderful piece of work. He could impersonate everything but valvular heart disease."

"Valvular heart disease?" queried Osmuhn dumbly.

"Yes." Colton's lips and voice were serious. "He was the most wonderful criminal I have ever met. A criminal with imagination great enough to plan such crimes, and daring sufficient to execute them when a single move, or a breath of air, would have betrayed him. But his acting was too good. When he came in here after stealing the ruby there was not a fraction of a beat above normal in his heart. He was as cool as ice when the heart of ninety-nine men out of a hundred would have been pounding like a trip hammer. It was steady as a clock even when I left him in the chair apparently on the verge of collapse. Even then he was planning an unsuspicious getaway. Even when Shrimp, my boy, almost knocked his chair over, there wasn't a flutter. I shook hands with him, so that I could establish his identity absolutely. To me there is as much difference between hands and wrists as there is between faces to men who see. But the pulse beat of valvular heart disease is absolutely unmistakable. The heart of the man who played Norvel so successfully was as sound as my own.

"I spoke in here of the possibility of the thief having learned his facts by listening to Norvel in his delirium. The thief realised that a cable to France might give away his whole game. I was afraid that he had hidden the necklace so cunningly that we wouldn't find it, though I knew where the ruby was ten minutes after it was stolen."

Osmuhn half jumped from his chair.

"You—knew where—the ruby was!" he gasped.

"Yes. I took care to touch his cane handles as I shook hands with him. Your son's story of the necklace theft told me that one of the canes was responsible for that. While he was in here the ruby was in the big knob at the end of the cane, not three feet away from where it had been stolen. But with my own stick and wonderfully sensitive fingertips, I knew that the necklace had been put somewhere else. Therefore, I gave him the hint he needed about Mrs Marle's reception. I knew if he had an imitation—which was likely, because he must have been on the track of the ruby to meet Norvel on the other side—he would try to get it into Mrs Marle's possession for the purpose of confusing all of us. Then my boy found out about his dual role of Davidson and Norvel. Davidson appeared only after Norvel had arrived home, and Norvel was supposed to be in such physical condition that he couldn't be seen at home. I immediately told you that the jewel was an imitation, put in Mrs Marle's home by the real thief, because I knew Norvel would hear all about it, and understand that I wasn't fooled for a minute. It was time for him to go. The French boat sailed at noon today. I knew he would see me, because he wouldn't miss an opportunity to prove his superiority, and make a final grandstand play by disappearing before our very eyes as Davidson, and walk out of the next house a few minutes later as Norvel the diamond expert, whose twenty-eight years' service with Osmuhn & Son placed him above suspicion. You see, he was taking no chances; he always had two ways open. But he forgot that the mist he had appear in his library meant nothing to me. *My eyes can't be deceived!*"

6

The Sixth Problem:

THE GILDED GLOVE

I.

A hundred eyes turned as the woman entered the dining-room; a hundred ups parted in admiration as she made her way through the winding aisle of tables in the wake of the straight-backed headwaiter. There were many beautiful women in the room, but, among them all, she was wonderful. Under the soft glow of shaded lights the ivory tints of her skin, with the colour of rich warm blood under it, were accentuated by the burnished gold of her hair. Behind the full red lips the pearl of her teeth showed; the great brown eyes looked over the room calmly, with aloofness. There was nothing girlish about the new arrival. Every line, every curve, bespoke perfect maturity.

Then the lips that had been parted in admiration curved in a smile as the eyes saw the man who followed her. He was scarcely five feet tall; a caricature of a man. His small moustache and ragged Vandyke were so colourless that they could not be seen at a distance. And he walked behind the woman with a peculiar lifting of knees at each step that reminded everyone who saw of a helpless little coach-dog. To a hundred minds flashed the simile: the beauty and the beast of Madame Villeneuve's immortal story.

The waiter, conscious of the new attraction that was to make his dining-room picture perfect, stopped at a table in the corner and pulled back a chair with an unconscious flourish.

"Your table, madame!" Then real regret tinged his tone: "It was all we had."

A startled look leaped to the eyes of the woman died on the instant. Her tone was merely casual as she asked:

"You got the reservation—how long ago?"

"A scant ten minutes, madame."

She turned her great eyes on the little man, and in her voice as she spoke was the lilt of badinage. "And you were to telephone an hour ago, Pierre?" she censured. Her hand idly moved the napkin on the table.

But the man did not answer. He had slumped into the chair at the other side of the small table even before she had made a move toward taking her own seat. His teeth chewed his ragged moustache-ends. Under the table his fingers interlocked and twitchingly separated.

The woman's opera cloak slipped to the back of the chair, revealing the white purity of the skin of her shoulders, and the curves of the throat. She picked up the *carte du jour* languidly, and a little pout came to her lips, and a tracery of a scowl appeared on her forehead as she studied the items.

"Absinthe, Pierre, and a cup of bouillon?" she smiled.

The man nodded.

"Only the bouillon for me."

A slight inclination of her head dismissed the waiter, and he hurried away. The woman rested an elbow on the table-edge and leaned forward. The wonderful smile still curved her lips, but the voice was hard as flint as she whispered in sibilant Italian:—

"Stop it, you fool of a coward!"

His tongue touched his lips. "It has found us!" he muttered chokingly, and the language he used was Russian.

"Hasn't it always found us?" she demanded hissingly, but the expression on her face changed not a bit. "Hasn't it always been on our heels? But have I not laughed at it for years? Laugh!" The last word came like the lash of a whip through the smiling lips.

The man's throat twitched, his face contorted, and a tremulous parody of laughter came. "Hideous!" she snapped. "Pitiful ape of a man! Stop it!"

"We cannot all be creatures of steel and stone!" he muttered, in the curious patois of northern Hungary.

"We can all act! We can play our parts! Be a gay boulevardier of Paris with the false courage of the green poison in the water of your veins. She spoke vehemently, and her words were the words of the Gascony peasant.

She turned her gracious smile on the waiter as he appeared with the bouillon and the absinthe for the little man.

"We shall order again presently," she said, in her perfect English, and the serving-man backed away.

Without touching the folded napkin, she took a sip of the bouillon. Her eyes, pin-points of fire under the shade of the long lashes, watched the man take up the glass of dull-green liquor and drain it at a gulp. The fire died from her eyes as they saw the faint flush of colour come to the yellow skin of the man and the steadiness of the hand that put the empty glass on the cloth.

"Ah," she murmured, in liquid Spanish, her eyes fixed fondly on the face of the little man. "My Pierre is himself again. Sip of your bouillon, my dear."

The little man obeyed her meekly. "The gaming-table has played the devil with my nerves," he growled.

"But they are strong once more. See!" Her fingers lifted the folded napkin and laid it on her knee. The man leaned forward to stare at the white tablecloth it had covered. A gasping whistle of indrawn breath came from his lips. On the white linen beside the woman's bouillon cup were five smudges of gold; prints of the finger and thumb tips of a right hand.

"The sign of the Gilded Glove!" he choked, and the colour went from his face.

"Cease staring, owl of a man!" she commanded in Italian. "Have you not seen the sign before? Do the wrecked nerves of the *rouge et noir* table need another franc's worth of green heart? Summon the waiter."

With a doglike shake of his body the man threw off the fear that gripped him. He touched his empty glass. The woman gave another order, and the waiter hurried away. Then the man's eyes were drawn again to the five spots of gold.

"The fingerprints of warning, the crushed glove of sentence, the clutched glove of death!" He repeated it as though it were a lesson that, once learned, was never to be forgotten.

"But have they not always been at *my* side?" she asked quietly. "In Paris, in Constantinople, in Budapest, in St. Petersburg, have I not seen them always by my side? Yet I live! Should I fear in New York, when I have escaped in Europe, where the Long Arm sweeps everything?"

The waiter returned with the absinthe. The little man took the glass up slowly, sipped part of the liquor, and set it down. A glance from the eyes of the woman rewarded him.

"Does my Pierre see anyone who might wear the Gilded Glove?" she asked.

His small eyes roved around the dining-room, gazing intently at every face. He shook his head. "They are all Americans; men of wood and women of china. Assess all!" The heavy gutturals of the German he now used made even more incongruous the puniness of his body.

She nodded. "Those who so carefully reserved the table that we might see the sign have gone," she said, "and other ears cannot follow our talking."

The man caught a glimpse of someone his eyes had missed before; he moved a trifle to the left, to see behind a great pillar in a far corner of the room.

"Your blind friend is eating his midnight meal of bread and beef-gravy," he said.

"Mr Colton?" There was a new tone in the voice now, and the man instantly recognised it.

"A blind man?" There was a sneer in the words.

"I fear him!" she whispered. "He is the only man on earth I have ever feared. He is the only man on earth I know I cannot deceive. All the things I have—my beauty, my nerves of steel, my acting, are to him as nothing. They delude only men of keen eyes! The American secret agents who watch us are fools but he—."

"Bah! A blind pig of an American!" he sneered again. It was the man whose nerve was perfect now; it was the woman who was unstrung.

"His blindness makes me afraid!" She was talking passionately in French. "Minds that are closed to all the world are an open book to him. I know it!"

"You think he knows of the plans; of our going away tomorrow?" The voice was sarcastic, but the words came slowly, haltingly, droned in the dialect of the lower Yang-tse-Kiang River.

"I know not!" she whispered, in purest Japanese. "He may; he may not. But no mistake have I ever made in a man!"

"Then hide your fear," warned the man. "He has emptied his last glass of Westin, and is coming toward this table."

The woman's hand fluttered tremulously toward her throat; but in an instant she was her calm, collected self. As she ate, and talked French commonplaces to the little man, she watched the approach of Thornley Colton from the corner of her eyes. She saw the white hair that curled and waved from the pink scalp; the wonderful paleness of the face that was brought out strikingly by the great round lenses of the smoked-glass library spectacles with their tortoise-shell rims. She knew that the eyes behind them had been sightless from birth; yet the strides of the approaching man through the winding aisle of tables were long and confident. Not a false move did he make, stepping aside at just the proper moment to avoid hurrying waiters, halting a second to let a nimble omnibus pass; never once turning to ask a question of the black-haired, apple-cheeked man who followed at his heels.

At the table he stopped, a smile of pleasure lighting his pale, strong face, as he extended his hand. "A delightful surprise, Madame Gorski!" he said, with quiet enthusiasm. "Sydney told me that you were here, but I could scarcely credit my good fortune. When is the next of your marvellous recitals to be?"

The woman's smile of joy and surprise as she took his hand had been wonderful in its perfection, and as she answered his last question, no human ear could have detected the lie behind the words: "In a few days, M'seur Colton. You are an inspiration. One seldom finds so appreciative a person. My husband thinks them frightful affairs."

"But Monsieur Gorski is not blind," smiled Colton, as he took the hand of the little man. "Music is the only beautiful thing we of the darkness have, you know. Eyes can see God's wonderful creations and the beautiful things man's hands have wrought. We can only hear."

A tender look of genuine sympathy came to the eyes of Madame Gorski. "Won't you sit down and talk?" she invited.

She saw Thornley Colton's hand go to his vest-pocket, and she knew that the supersensitive fingertips were feeling the face of the crystalless watch he carried.

He shook his head. "It is twelve-forty," he apologised. "I make it my invariable rule to be in bed at one." He stepped back regretfully. "Pardon me," he said suddenly, "your napkin has fallen to the floor." He leaned over quickly, picked it up, and put it on the end of the table. "Au revoir." He smiled again, and with a nod to the silent Sydney Thames, who had merely bowed to the man and the woman, he started between the tables towards the entrance of the dining-room.

The woman's eyes followed him. When he had disappeared through the door she turned to her husband. "A wonderful man!" she murmured. "Wonderful!" She expected a sneer, but her husband was staring at the crumpled-up napkin Thornley Colton had picked up.

"You say he is blind!" he hissed in French.

She nodded, puzzled.

"Then how did he know your napkin had fallen? Can he hear the fall of linen on velvet? Can he?"

She reached toward the napkin, lifted a corner as she pulled it toward her; then withdrew her hand suddenly. In the crumpled-up folds of the linen both had seen the dull glint of gilt; both knew that concealed in the napery was a crushed, gilded glove!

"The sentence!" choked the man.

The woman lifted her eyes to the door through which Thornley Colton had passed a few minutes before. "Can he be one of the sinews of the Long Arm?" she murmured: "A man like that!"

Her fingers toyed with her fork a moment. "Pay the check, Pierre," she said finally, and there was a note of hopelessness in her voice. "We will go home. I am tired."

The admiring eyes that had watched the woman enter followed her as she left the room. The face, calm, patrician, was beautiful; and the long lashes hid the look in the deep, brown eyes. In the taxi seat she relaxed; the beautiful face held an expression of utter weariness. The little man's hand touched her shoulder reverently, caressingly.

"Do not falter now, *ma chère*," he murmured. "Tomorrow we will have the plans of the harbour mines and the hundred thousand dollars they will bring. We will go far away, then, out of reach of the Long Arm and its glove of gilt."

"Tomorrow," she breathed softly, and she touched his cheek with her lips. She was a woman, was Hedwig Gorski, strange, unreadable. Her heart was a woman's heart, and grim-lipped men in a hundred cities knew that she loved this little caricature of a man. A smile came to her lips. "Yes," she whispered, in low-voiced Russian, "tomorrow we will be through with it all."

At the big hotel where they stopped the woman commanded the same admiration; the man the same derisive smiles. But they did not see. In their apartment on the thirteenth floor, whose door was watched night and day by the floor clerks they had bribed to see that no one entered, the woman sank into a big chair beside the table. The man snapped on the lights in every room, and peered into every corner. "No one has entered," he announced, when he had seen that every window still held the screws he had driven through the frames the first hour they had occupied the apartments.

"Leave me a few minutes, *mon cher*," the woman said, and she pulled his head down to kiss him. "I must think—alone."

Obediently, doglike, he went out into the hall and turned the key in the lock behind him. The woman sighed. She rose and went to the small cabinet, took from it a bottle of wine and a glass. She started to pour the liquor; then shook her head.

"Poison," she whispered. "That would be their only chance. I can't risk it." She went into the bathroom and turned on the hot water, rinsing the glass under the stream until the water was almost boiling. Then she filled the glass to the brim under the cold-water tap, drained it. She walked slowly back to the room, switched off the lights, and seated herself again in the big chair.

The minutes passed. The woman never moved; her eyes stared unwaveringly into the darkness before her. And from out the dark a gilded hand came slowly, certainly. It touched the throat of the woman. Hedwig Gorski did not move. The fingers of gold tightened.

Outside the door came the voice of Gorski: "Do you wish anything, Hedwig, *ma chère?*"

And from the darkness came the voice of his wife "*Non, Pierre, mon cher.*"

But neither the eyes nor the lips of the woman, nor yet the gilded fingers, had moved.

Silence. The man's voice called again. There was no answer. Shaking, he unlocked the door and entered the room. A curtain that had been pulled to the bottom of the window was up now. A shaft of moonlight shone on the woman's face—a dead face. At her throat a golden hand seemed clutched. But he came nearer, and saw that it was an empty, gilded glove. And in the air of the room was the faint odour of crushed bananas.

II.

The little French clock had just chimed the hour of three when the tinkling telephone-bell waked Thornley Colton. He reached forth a hand to the crystalless watch on the small table at his bedside and whistled. The bell jingled again. He threw a bath robe over his shoulders and went into the library.

He answered the inquiring voice instantly: "Good morning, Mr Ames. Certainly. I will be ready in ten minutes."

For a minute after he had hung up the receiver he stood in the darkness, his sightless eyes fixed on the mouthpiece of the instrument. Then he went into Sydney Thames's room and touched him lightly on the shoulder. "Get dressed," he said quietly, but the apple-cheeked secretary saw the grim, ominous lines that were around the thin lips. "Ames, of the diplomatic secret service, will be here in fifteen minutes, Madame Gorski has been murdered."

"Murdered!" The emotional, highly-strung Thames echoed the word in horror.

"Yes." Still that tone of quiet certainty. "An hour or so ago, I should judge. We will probably go down to the hotel. Hustle!" he admonished again, as he hurried from the room.

In less than ten minutes Thornley Colton, fully dressed, and smoking a cigarette, was seated in the library awaiting the coming of the secret agent. The doorbell rang, and he rose to answer it.

He stopped in the hall, when his super keen ears caught the patter of bare feet on the carpet. "Go back to bed, Shrimp," he ordered.

"Gee, is it a case, Mister Colton?" The wide-eyed boy, with the fiery-red hair, the multitude of freckles, and the slightly-twisted nose, asked the question eagerly. His hands literally trembled with anticipation as they fumbled with the front of his purple pyjama coat.

"Yes." Thornley Colton's lip curved in a slight smile, and he patted the boy's shoulder fondly. "But you can do nothing tonight. Go back to bed, and tomorrow there may be some real detective work for you to do."

"Gosh, I hope so!" the boy exclaimed fervently; then his voice became almost wistful "Gee, Mister Colton. I wisht youh'd let me get in a case where there was real Nick Carter stuff; blackjacks, an' assaults, an' stuff like that."

"You've got a long life before you, Shrimp," smiled the blind man, as he started downstairs to answer the second ring of the bell.

The man who entered had his raincoat buttoned up to his chin, and the brim of his soft hat came down to the eyes that gleamed from under it.

Colton bowed gravely. "Rather an early-morning call, Mr Ames."

The gimlet eyes of the secret agent were fixed on his pale face, seeming to bore and probe into the very soul of the blind man. "Mind telling me how you knew my name?" he asked. "To my knowledge we have never met before."

"I think we never have." The grave smile still curved Thornley Colton's thin lips. "But I never forget a voice I have once heard. I heard yours, several years ago, when I was trying to solve the puzzle of the missing Villers code book. The diplomatic service was somewhat interested in that case, I believe."

"So you're that man!" There was new respect in the tone, and the eyes of the secret agent gleamed brighter.

"A lucky touch of the fingers found the solution of the case," explained Colton modestly. "If you will come up to my library we can talk more comfortably." He turned and ascended the stairs.

Sydney Thames was already in the library, and Thornley Colton introduced him. "My secretary, Mr Ames." He seemed to sense the other's desire for a private conversation, and added: "My eyes, also."

The secret agent accepted the presence of a third person, and took off his raincoat. Seated in a big chair, which a gesture of the blind man's arm had indicated, he asked his first question abruptly, curtly:—

"Mr Colton, what do you know about Hedwig Gorski?"

A thin ribbon of blue smoke rose from the blind man's lips. He seemed to watch the smoke waver ceiling ward before he answered: "I think she is one of the most remarkable women I have ever met. There is no subject she cannot discuss intelligently. She speaks all languages, apparently, and she is the only woman I ever met who can interpret Grieg properly. In fact, I would consider her the most accomplished and wonderful international spy I ever met."

Ames straightened in his chair as though he had been suddenly jabbed with a pin. "How did you know that?" he demanded.

"By a process of elimination made necessary by lack of eyes. I sought an introduction to Madame Gorski after I had heard her husband address her in the Cantonese dialect. I spent several years in China, and, naturally, I was interested. And her *musicales* have been wonderful affairs—wonderful, and food for considerable thought!" he finished musingly.

"You know that she is dead—murdered?"

"Your visit at this hour could mean nothing else. I have known for some time that Madame Gorski feared something. I have known also that she was constantly watched."

For a minute there was silence in the room. Ames took a cigarette from his case, lighted it, and became absorbed in the spiraling smoke. Sydney Thames, silent, as always, sat back to listen. The secret agent reached his decision and spoke:—

"Mr Colton, I came here with a different plan of procedure in my mind. I'm going to be frank. For months we have known that negotiations have been going on with a foreign government to obtain possession of the secret naval plans of the harbour mines in New York harbour. When you understand that those planted electrical mines are the only real safeguard against the invasion of the greatest city in America, you will know just what they are worth. We know Hedwig Gorski came to this country to get them—from whom we have never been able to discover. But we have watched every movement, opened every line of mail she has received, and have not been able to find a single clue. For a month my wife and I have occupied an apartment in the hotel directly opposite the Gorski rooms. We have been on guard day and night, as have the floor clerks we learned that she had bribed. This morning at one-twenty-five Hedwig Gorski and her husband returned to their apartment. They went in, lighted every light, and I know they were examining everything to see whether or not the rooms had been entered. In a few minutes Gorski came out, locked the door, and began pacing up and down before it. This was something new, and we watched him curiously. He called. His wife answered cheerily in French. Ten minutes later he called again. There was no answer. He unlocked the door and stumbled in. I was at his heels. Madame Gorski was dead in her chair. At her throat was an empty gilded glove—like a hand of gold that had strangled her."

"A gilded glove." Colton repeated it without incredulity or surprise in his voice; merely as the verification of a known fact.

"You know of the Gilded Glove?" asked the secret agent quickly.

"Yes. My world wanderings have taken me to Russia. The glove has always had a peculiar significance. In China two thousand years ago a glove was always given to make legal the transfer of land. The custom was also in vogue among the ancient Egyptians and Phoenicians. In the correct literal translations of the Bible the word 'glove' is found instead of 'shoe' in the fourth chapter of Ruth, and in the one hundred and eighth Psalm."

Ames nodded, and the blind man went on: "Twenty years ago a certain Russian order first used the gilded glove as a death sign for traitors to the government. With a love of the significant that only the true Oriental mind has—and the mind of the Russian is all Oriental—the gilded glove was left at the throat of persons who transferred their allegiance for gold."

"That is right," corroborated Ames. "Hedwig Gorski and her husband were the greatest spies Russia had. Then, for some unknown reason, they went into the service of another country. And for five years she has laughed at the Gilded Glove and its wearers, who have been constantly on her trail." Again he smoked in silence for a few minutes, his eyes fixed on the ceiling. "You seem to know a whole lot about this thing, Mr Colton," he said frankly. "I'd like you to come with me to the hotel. When I entered the room, Gorski, who is a little rat, and heaven only knows how a woman like Hedwig could love him, was absolutely insane. He moaned and cried without seeing me for several minutes. When he did, he accused *you* of the murder!"

"Accused—" Sydney Thames half rose in his chair and flopped back into it with a gasp of amazed horror.

Thornley Colton's face had not a flicker of expression. "Yes?" he said politely.

The gimlet eyes of the secret agent went ceilingward once more. "He muttered something about his wife having always feared you—which is the highest compliment that could possibly come from a woman like Hedwig Gorski. He also babbled something about your not being blind because you had seen his wife's napkin fall to the floor, and that, when you put it on the table, its folds concealed a crushed gilded glove— the sentence of death. He swears that you couldn't have heard the napkin fall on the velvet carpet."

"The napkin had not fallen," Colton said evenly. "I pulled it from Madame Gorski's knees as I leaned over to pick up the crushed gilt glove I knew was on the carpet by her chair." His fingers felt the crystalless watch in his pocket. "If you don't mind," he apologised, "I'd like to get down to the hotel as soon as possible. The most valuable clue, I think, will disappear shortly."

Ames opened his mouth, then closed it. "My taxi is waiting at the door," he said quietly, as he picked up his raincoat. "I warned the hotel manager that the police were not to be notified until I gave permission. Even the murder is of secondary importance to finding a clue to the damned traitor who is going to sell those harbour plans!"

"A human life, to me, is a wonderful thing," murmured Colton, as he slipped into his overcoat and took the thin cane that gave its messages to his supersensitive fingertips. There was unconscious rebuke in his tone.

It was not until they were in the taxi, well on their way down, that the silence was broken. Then Ames spoke again. "I'll frankly admit that the murder is a most wonderful piece of work. I went over every inch of the rooms while Gorski was gibbering. The door is absolutely the only entrance, and I know they looked over the apartment pretty thoroughly. Gorski could not have done it, even if he had the nerve. I heard his wife answer him. I couldn't see a thing!"

In the darkness Colton nodded. "I don't think this will be a case where eyes will be of much use," he said quietly.

The taxi stopped at the entrance of the big hotel, and they went through the lobby without exciting comment or receiving a single stare. The news of the murder had not been allowed to get downstairs. But a man lounging, half asleep, in a leather chair, made a slight signal that Ames understood. The secret-service agents had covered the hotel, and were working in a dozen different places.

As the three men entered the Gorski apartment, Monsieur Gorski rose from his chair with a half-suppressed scream of rage. "Murderer!" he hissed, in French. "Murderer!"

A heavy hand forced him back, and an apologetic voice came to the ears of Thornley Colton.

"He's been ravin' that way for an hour, Mister Colton," put in the red-faced man at Gorski's side.

"Good morning, Joe," Colton greeted the house detective.

The white-faced manager of the hotel, who had stood back, nervously biting his fingernails, came forward. "We must notify the police, Mr Ames," he protested. "I have obeyed your instructions, but if they ever know—" The manager left unspoken the horrible possibilities, but his whole manner cried them aloud.

"You can notify them in a very few minutes, Mr Jones," the blind man's voice cut in curtly. He went to the side of the dead woman unerringly. A faint flush seemed to mount to his pale cheeks; his thin nostrils quivered like those of a hound on the scent. Almost reverently he touched the cheek of Hedwig Gorski. His fingers, light as wind-blown thistledown, brushed the beautiful cold skin under the eyes, then down to the throat, stopping short before reaching the five finger-marks of gold that were deep in the flesh. The gilded glove was on the table, where it had fallen as soon as Gorski had touched it. The blind man seemed not even aware of its existence.

"Have you a glass, Mr Ames?" asked the problemist, and there was unintentional curtness in his tone. Thornley Colton's whole mind was on the case before him; nothing else existed.

The secret agent took a magnifying glass from his pocket.

Look at the gilt fingerprints'." ordered the blind man, as his two hands lifted the woman's arms. "Are the prints cleanly cut, sharp?"

"Not a single blur!" announced Ames, raising his eyes. "She never moved a muscle after those fingers clutched her throat."

"Ah!" Quiet triumph was in the blind man's voice. "Madame Gorski was poisoned!"

"Poisoned!" It seemed that everyone in the room echoed it. The clutched glove at the throat, the deep graven fingerprints of gilt had seemed to point to but one thing.

"Yes. No hand of that size could have sufficient strength to keep the woman from moving and blurring the gilt prints that were put there with another gilt glove worn on the hand of the murderer. The wearer of the gilt glove would not overlook a detail. He probably carried the other glove in a box so that its shape would not be lost, and fitted it to the prints after. It is the usual way."

"The bottle and the glass!" Ames took a step nearer, but Colton's hand picked up the glass beside the tall wine bottle. He stepped away from the table, and raised the glass to his lips; held it there for several seconds.

"Hedwig Gorski did not drink from this glass!"

"Why? How do you know that?" Ames gasped it.

"Because it was put there by the man whose gloved hand made those marks on Madame Gorski's throat after she was dead."

"Bah!" The expletive came in a snarling sneer from the dead woman's husband. "You think my wonderful Hedwig a fool? She would drink of no wine that had been unguarded all evening! I heard her in the bathroom washing the glass for one, two, three minutes. If she drank she drank fresh water."

"How long after you heard the water running did she answer you?" asked Colton; and even in his sightless eyes there seemed to come a light.

"Five, six, seven, ten minutes. Ten minutes," repeated the husband, with sullen positiveness.

"As long as that?"

"Yes."

"Where is the bathroom, Sydney?" snapped Colton. The muscles under the skin of his lean jaws played back and forth. He was tense as a hound in leash.

"Five steps to the right, half turn," Sydney answered mechanically, his eyes judging the distance instantly because of years of practice.

Colton darted inside. He turned on the hot water and bent down so that his face was not an inch away from the running stream. He did the same thing when he had turned the cold-water tap.

"The devilish ingenuity of it!" They heard him mutter as he straightened up.

"What is it?" Again Ames asked the question. Student of men as his work had made him, Ames had realised, minutes before, that he was in the presence of a man who would lead always; he understood that he was but a pupil before a master.

"They knew Madame Gorski was too clever to be poisoned in any ordinary way. They knew that she would even suspect the presence of poison in an empty glass, and would wash any glass, under the hot water tap, before she drank, because the heat would dissolve any poison. They knew, also, that if she wanted a drink it would be of cold water, fresh from the tap. The poison, a paste of peculiar odour that my keen sense of smell instantly detected, is smeared on the inside of the cold-water faucet. The minute it was turned, the stream that flowed was almost pure poison!"

"Good God!" came the horror-stricken voice of the hotel manager.

"But there must have been someone here to make those marks and leave the gilded glove," put in Ames.

"Where is the clothes-closet?" Colton asked.

The secret agent hurried into the bedroom that adjoined the room of death. Colton was at his heels, the slim, hollow cane locating every piece of furniture as he passed. Ames opened the door of a closet full of clothes, and stepped inside. Colton stood at the threshold, his head bent forward, apparently peering intently into the depths of the closet.

"Another?" he asked curtly.

In the other bedroom was a huge wardrobe. Ames opened it, and again the blind man seemed to look into every corner of it. "The murderer hid in there behind the clothes! Take some of them out and you'll find flecks of gilt from the glove he wore!"

The secret agent grabbed an armful and threw them on the bed, with no regard for their mussing. He pawed them over. His eyes found what they sought, and he uttered a shout of triumph. "Here they are! On the Inverness and this black evening gown!" Then awe came to his voice. "How did you know that?" he asked. "How could you know it—and blind?"

"Because I am blind. Because my other senses are abnormally developed to recompense the loss of sight. I knew the murderer had hidden in the closet; I knew the gilt from the glove he wore on his hand would come off on the clothes that concealed him, just as I knew the glass on the table was not the one Madame Gorski had used, and just as I knew the crushed glove was at her feet in the restaurant—because I have a sense of smell that is more than doubly acute. Wherever there is gilt there is banana oil. It is always used in gilding, and its odour is unmistakable. I knew of the men of the Gilded Glove, and I suspected that Madame Gorski feared it. When my nostrils caught the odour and located it at the floor beside her chair, I knew instantly what it meant. I covered it with the napkin so that people would not stare. I wanted her to see it so that she might be warned. The glass on the table has the banana oil odour because the murderer placed it there with the hand that still smelled of the oil with which the soft kid of the glove had become saturated. The smell was also in the wardrobe. Simple, isn't it?" A mirthless smile curved his thin is. Thornley Colton could not forget that in the next room was the body of the woman killed by the hand that left its trail so faintly that only his blindness enabled him to follow it.

"Where are the windows?" Colton asked sharply, before any one had a chance to say a word.

"In the next room, overlooking the street."

"Show them to me."

Ames hurried back to the sitting-room. The hotel manager still bit his fingernails. The husband of the woman who was dead had buried his face in his hands, and was sobbing. The eyes of the hotel detective were fixed on Colton, following his every movement, in them a look of wondering admiration.

The blind man's feeling fingers examined every inch of the casements that overlooked busy Broadway, thirteen storeys below. "Nothing here," he said, when he had finished. "There must be another window!"

"Only a small one, in the bathroom, that overlooks an air-shaft," the secret agent informed him.

Colton turned and darted into the bathroom. "This is the one!" Once more his exploring fingers went over every inch.

"But that hasn't been touched. Not a screw has been loosened," declared Ames positively.

"No, there hasn't been a screw touched. The murderer was too clever for that, but he wasn't clever enough to get the banana oil smell from his fingers. The entire pane was taken out by cutting away the putty, and probably put back with triangular tin tacks that would never be noticed through the frosted glass."

"That's a mighty small opening," Ames said slowly.

"The murderer must have been small, and as active as a cat. Also—" Colton did not finish; he stepped out of the bathroom. "Who has the rooms directly over this one?" he asked the manager.

"They have no occupants yet," hesitated the nervous Mr Jones.

"When were they coming? Who were they?" The questions came sharply, crisply.

"A couple from Philadelphia, who telegraphed to have them reserved. They had occupied them once before, and liked them."

"Clever," muttered the blind man. "They wouldn't take a chance of occupying them, but were going to see to it that they were empty when wanted. Let's look at them."

"But what am I going to do?" began the nerve-frayed manager. "The police—"

"Notify them."

Colton gave the permission grimly; then a look of compassion came to his face as he seemed aware of the presence of Monsieur Gorski for the first time. He took a step toward him; then halted. He could do nothing—now.

"Joe?" he said softly. The house detective glanced at the inert figure of the man, and came forward. "When the police come, let them arrest Gorski," Colton whispered. "He will be safe in their hands, and God knows he isn't safe from that band of gilt-handed devils anywhere else. It will only be a short time before the real murderer is found."

The house detective nodded. "It'll be best that way," he admitted.

"Show us the rooms!" ordered Colton; then, as the manager hesitated: "Let Joe telephone police headquarters from here," he advised shortly.

With Ames and Sydney at his heels, he followed the manager to the floor above. The minute the lights were snapped on in the apartment, Ames ran to the open bathroom window. In a heap on the floor under it was a thin, strong rope. Beside it were fragments of what had been a wine flask, and an empty pasteboard box, with the inside smeared with gilt—the one in which the gilt glove found at the woman's throat had been carried to prevent it handling. And under the bath-tub was thrown another glove of gilt, with most of the gold worn off the inside of the fingers.

"Good Lord!" gasped Ames eagerly. "There's clues enough here!"

"Too many!" declared Colton tersely. He turned to the manager. "Who has the apartments opposite this?"

"A German family," the head of the hotel answered, as a pupil to a teacher.

"How many?"

"Three. A big, bearded man and his wife, and a gawky boy. They've been here a week."

"The boy! Describe him!"

"Well," began the manager nervously. "He's about seventeen, I should judge, but small. He's awkward, and speaks the rottenest English I ever heard in the darndest, squeakiest voice.

Seems to like to listen to people, though, and he's always sitting around the lobby gaping at the guests."

"I want to see him!" Colton's voice had a new note, dominant, compelling.

"At this hour?" stammered the manager.

"Now!"

Ames, attracted by the tone and the words, came from the bathroom.

"What is it?" he asked eagerly.

"The man who murdered Madame Gorski."

"Where?"

"I don't know—now." Thornley Colton spoke the words over his shoulder, for he was following the manager out of the room. A knock at the door across the hall brought no response. Colton pushed the manager aside, and, with his horrified protest unheeded, opened the unlocked door. A snap of the lights under Ames' fingers, and the men saw that the rooms were empty. But in the air was a strong smell of banana oil.

"The floor clerk!" demanded Colton, and the manager went meekly to get him.

Ames was everywhere, rummaging, prying with practiced fingers into every drawer, every closet. Each piece of clothing he pulled out was examined with lightning-moving fingers. He picked the lock of the big trunk, and cursed when the opened lid revealed only cloth-wrapped stones. But in the bottom was an overturned bottle that had once held gilt.

"The glove had just been gilded," guessed the secret agent.

The floor clerk entered, visibly nervous.

"When did the German boy return here tonight?" asked Colton.

"About twelve-thirty."

"Alone?"

"Yes."

"Were his mother and father in the room?"

The floor clerk scratched his head. "I didn't see them come in, but I heard them giving the kid the very devil. They raised an awful row." He grinned at the recollection.

"Ah!" The blind man's tone held quiet satisfaction. "And an hour or so later the boy slipped out, saying that his mother and father were asleep, and he was going downstairs to watch the people for a while."

"Yes." There was amazement written all over the hotel clerk's face.

Colton turned to face Ames. "The bird has flown," he said quietly. "He is the one who entered Madame Gorski's rooms, put the poison in the tap and the glove at her throat. For a week the three have been waiting their opportunity. Tonight all was ready. The father and mother left early in the evening, and did not return. They, or another accomplice, dropped the glove at Madame Gorski's chair in passing, expecting her to look down and see it. The waiter probably kicked it so near her chair that she couldn't have noticed it if the smell of the banana oil hadn't made me find it."

"But the clerk heard the father and mother talking?" protested Ames. "He didn't see them go out, and," he added, "there are several of my men around who would have stopped them instantly."

"No one left that room but the boy!" There was no gainsaying the positiveness in the floor clerk's tone.

The grim smile came again to Thornley Colton's lips. "When I learned that Madame Gorski had answered her husband *ten minutes after* he had heard the water running, and she must have taken the poison, I began to suspect the true facts. A poison that left no signs of agony must have killed quickly and painlessly. It wasn't her voice monsieur heard at all! It was the voice of a wonderful mimic; the mimic who made the floor clerk believe that his mother and father were scolding him in this room. And who would stop a gawky German boy? You have his description. Put your men at work." He rose. "Come, Sydney, it is time for breakfast."

The secret agent took his hand and shook it fervently. "I can't tell you how I thank you," he said, and there was genuine feeling in his voice. "But I will see that Washington recognises this night's work of yours."

Once more the mirthless smile that had been in evidence so often that night came to his lips. "I want no recognition," he said slowly. "I merely want to avenge the death of the most wonderful woman I ever met. There is nothing half so precious as the life of a woman, or a child."

He bowed gravely. Silently he and Sydney walked to the elevator and into the lobby. Halfway out Thornley Colton stopped.

"I want to telephone the house, Sydney. There's a foolish fear in my mind that I can't throw off." He went into the telephone booth. When he emerged a minute later, there was a look on his face that Sydney Thames had never seen before; a look terrible in its earnestness.

"Do you believe in presentiments, Sydney?" The blind man's voice was calm, even. He gave his secretary no chance to answer. "I have just had one come true. John found five finger-smudges of gold on the white tablecloth in the dining-room, and Shrimp has disappeared absolutely!

III.

Thornley Colton paced the floor of his library with long, tigerish strides. His head was bowed, and over his eyes the lines of concentration had deepened in the hours of the long day. His fingers touched the face of the crystalless watch in his pocket.

"Three o'clock," he muttered. He turned to the desk and its telephone; stretched forth a hand, withdrew it, and shook his head. Again his strides covered the length of the room; across and back, across and back.

He lifted his head eagerly—lowered it. The steps his super keen ears had heard were only those of Sydney Thames, as he left his bedroom on the floor above.

"Any news yet, Thorn?" asked the apple-cheeked secretary as he entered. The blind man shook his head.

"Nothing," he said quietly. He took a half-turn around the room, then suddenly wheeled to face the silent Thames. "If anything happens to that boy, Sydney, I swear to God I'll punish those responsible!" The voice, always so calm, so unstirred by any inner feeling, now trembled with fierce passion. The blind man seemed to realise that the mask he had cultivated so carefully for years had dropped; for his tone was even as he continued: "I thought when I took him that I could give him the real life he had been denied. But I understand now that I was only bringing him to take the risks that have never caused me a second thought. I realise now the dozens of times I have sent him into places of danger, merely to satisfy my own conceit; to enable me to beat someone else on a baffling case. Now he is gone! All my vaunted powers are useless, and I'm as much at sea as the veriest tyro. A problemist? I!"

His voice vibrated with scorn and self-denunciation.

"You are in no way to blame!" defended Sydney Thames instantly.

Colton turned again on his heel. "I'm as guilty as hell!" he declared vehemently. "Why do you suppose John or the other servants heard no noise? Do you think it was because the man who murdered Madame Gorski, the man who made those glove prints downstairs, overcame Shrimp so easily and so quietly? No! It was because of the training I have given the boy; training to be instantly on the alert to follow, to shadow, to discover; training that no boy should have had. Shrimp, sent brusquely to bed by me, couldn't sleep. What boy could? But I didn't understand. I only looked at it from my side. He probably heard the man who entered. Instead of raising an alarm as a normal person would, he probably followed him outside. Then—" His hands spread wide before him in a gesture of helplessness.

This was a side of Thornley Colton that Sydney Thames had never seen before; a new side, a human side. He understood now the deep love for the undersized, red-haired boy with the twisted nose that was in the heart of the blind man. He hadn't understood the depths of Colton's feelings when the blind man had gone through the house calmly when they returned to search for clues. He hadn't suspected that there was anything but the cold, analytical love of a problem in the cool voice that had put ten thousand police in the big city on the trail of the missing boy. Nor had he understood the cool way Thornley Colton had directed Ames and his squad of underground diplomatic workers to rake the city with a fine-tooth comb for the murderer of Hedwig Gorski. No, he hadn't understood then. Through it all Colton had been the same dominant, emotionless machine, directing, suggesting, issuing curt orders.

But the hours of inaction had done their work. For the first time in his life the problemist was completely at sea. The signs he had read so unerringly a hundred times before; signs that were usually hidden from men of eyes, were missing in this new development of the Gorski case. The man who had left the fingerprints of the gilded glove had apparently entered with a key, for there was not a scratch on a window or door. He had touched nothing but the white tablecloth, for there was not a trace of the banana oil anywhere else. There was nothing, absolutely nothing, to tell a fact about the disappearance of The Fee. He was gone. That was all. And Thornley Colton could do nothing but wait. His blindness made him helpless now.

The telephone-bell rang, and Colton sprang to answer it. The eager expression died from his face as the voice of the secret agent came over the wire.

"No trace of the boy yet—Ah!—A bundle of manuscript music addressed to Madame Gorski at the post office?—No word?—Yes, bring it up to the house. I think it will fit a theory I have been constructing for some time. Goodbye."

He hung up the receiver wearily, and his voice was tired as he spoke to Sydney Thames. "Not a word," he said slowly. "Ames is wholly engrossed with the search for those harbour-mine plans. That is the big thing to him. The murder of Madame Gorski and the disappearance of Shrimp are only incidents." He resumed his pacing of the room. "It's another case like that of the Money Machines, Sydney. Human life and happiness are pushed aside as unimportant because of a few papers and figures in lifeless ink."

Sydney Thames silently withdrew. He knew that the man who had picked him up, as a bundle of dirty baby-clothes, on the banks of the English river that had given him the only name he ever knew, wanted to be alone. So he left him to his tireless pacing while the wonderful brain behind the high forehead figured each step in the problem; aligning motives; testing theories.

When the front-door bell announced the coming of Ames, Colton seated himself at the desk, and when the secret agent entered there was no inkling of the thoughts in the mind of the blind man.

"There's absolutely nothing in this," began Ames apologetically, as he laid the thick envelope on the desk. "It's just music, poor stuff, too. Probably written by some sentimental amateur who has read of Madame Gorski and her recitals, and wants a criticism."

"Such persons usually inclose a long letter of pleading," remarked Colton dryly, as he took the thin sheets from the big envelope and ran his supersensitive fingertips over the back of the paper to feel the indentations of the pen. "You have no trace of the boy, yet?" His tone was almost uninterested, and his fingertips still brushed the back of the music sheet.

"No." Ames shook his head. "The men are combing the city. Finding the boy means finding those harbour-mine plans, probably."

Colton's lips tightened. "No, it doesn't," he said quietly. "These are the plans of the location of every electrically-operated mine in the harbour and bay."

"*What!*" Ames fairly shouted the word as he leaped to his feet. He jumped to the desk and picked up one of the manuscript sheets Colton had examined and laid aside. As he stared, the expression of incredulity gave way to one of bewildered puzzlement. "What do you mean?" he demanded. "There is nothing concealed here. This is straight music."

"It would contain some horrible discords if you tried to play it, I imagine, though it was done by a man who has some knowledge of composing. But, as you said before, anyone with *eyes* would put that down as mere amateurishness. Eyes are the greatest handicap pure eliminative reasoning has. For weeks you have watched Madame Gorski. You have had men at her *musicales*, and have attended them yourself, no doubt. To you those wonderful affairs were merely a cloak the woman had assembled to hide her real purpose for being here. To me they were something else. They were part of a carefully thought-out plan. She knew that you were watching her. She knew that every person who approached her and every bit of her mail would be examined. But who would suspect a dozen sheets of music manuscript? Who but a blind man!" The faint colour of excitement was in his cheeks, the lean, cleft jaw was set. "See!" He turned over the sheet he had examined last. "Every sheet is written in five flats, yet in this page alone there are more than a dozen sharp accidentals. Three notes out of five must be played on the black keys. Every sharp and flat on every sheet denotes the placement of a blind mine! Look!" He snatched up a pencil from the desk, located the middle bar in the top staff with his fingertip, and drew down the paper a wide, curving line, following the course of his feeling finger, to a measure in the lower right-hand corner. "Notice," he observed quietly, "that not one of the measures the pencil has touched contains either a sharp or a flat."

"The secret naval lane through the outer harbour," whispered Ames, and in his voice was the awe that had been there once before.

"Yes." Thornley Colton leaned back in his chair. "You know that the harbour is laid out in half-mile squares, subdivided by smaller squares of two-hundred-and-eighty-yard mine placements. Take the sheets numerically, and draw perpendicular parallel lines. Each one of these will represent the two-hundred-and-eighty-yard square. The measures of the treble and bass clefs placed directly under each other will make the half-mile squares. The sheets lettered A, B, C should be laid from left to right, I imagine, to give the anchorage width. I think a line following the staccato notes will give the rough shore-line necessary." He lighted a cigarette, and his sightless eyes were apparently fixed on the ceiling, his thoughts far away.

Ames lifted his eyes from the papers to the impassive face of the blind man. "My God, Mr Colton!" he cried, and his voice shook with feeling. "Do you realise what you've done? Do you understand that in ten minutes you have accomplished a thing that has baulked every secret agent in the country for months? Do you know that you have kept in the hands of this country the greatest naval secret we possess"—his voice choked—"the secret I was about to let slip through my fingers? It means—"

A wave of the problemist's hand stopped him.

"It means that my boy is missing, perhaps dead," the blind man said dispassionately. "It means that the most wonderful woman I ever knew is dead. That is all."

A look of pity came to the face of the secret agent. "We will do all we can," he assured. "We will find the boy just as surely as we will find the traitor who is responsible for these." He picked up the precious sheets, and put them carefully in his pocket, and buttoned his coat.

"Finding the traitor should be comparatively easy," Colton told him. "Men who have the knowledge of music composition necessary to put that together are not common in the war department."

Ames picked up his hat and held out his hand. "Believe me, Mr Colton, Washington will not forget this work of yours. I will let you know the instant we hear anything. Good day!"

Colton sat quiet while the secret agent and Sydney Thames left the room. There was no hope in his heart. By his showing the government agent the secret of the music he had filled his mind with thoughts of finding the man who was responsible. Every effort of the secret agents would be in that direction now. What was a little, red-headed kid beside a traitor who would betray his country? Nothing—to the men who were paid to guard the secrets of state.

By silence Colton could have kept the trained government-men on the trail of the boy he loved. But he had given all that was in him to solve the puzzle of the music. The secret agents would go on that track now. The police could do nothing against men like those of the Gilded Glove. They had been content to arrest Monsieur Gorski; they had proclaimed in every morning-paper that he was the murderer. They were already lying back on their laurels, smug, complacent. No, there was no one but the blind man to find The Fee!

The long hours of the afternoon passed. Still Thornley Colton sat in the armchair, immovable. From time to time Sydney Thames came to the doorway, looked in, and went away. He knew that the problemist did not want to be disturbed. And the blind man's mind through the hours was the mind of the men who were behind the gilded glove. His mind worked as their minds would work; planning out each step they would take in their next move; leading off into tangents that made necessary the discarding of entire trains of thought. Patiently he would start again at the beginning. Finally his brow cleared; the rigid lip-lines softened.

"It is the only way," he murmured, and his hand went out to the button on the desk that would summon his automobile any hour of the day or night. Another button brought Sydney on the run.

Colton sensed the unasked question and shook his head. "No," he anticipated. "I am going out in the machine to get a breath of fresh air—alone."

"But—" Sydney started to protest.

"Alone," repeated the blind man. "I shall not be gone more than an hour."

Sydney Thames went with him to the waiting car, and watched with anxious eyes as the stolid Irish chauffeur whirled him away. It was less than an hour later that the blind man returned.

"Any news?" he asked of Thames, as he threw off his hat and coat.

"Headquarters report that they have gone through every house in the Russian sections."

"The one place where he would not be likely to be," sneered the blind man. Then weariness made his voice heavy. "I'm going to bed, Sydney. I don't want to be disturbed under any circumstances. Goodnight."

He went to the bedroom that adjoined the library, undressed, and in a few minutes was under the covers, sleeping peacefully. Sydney Thames shook his head and went to his own room. It was the first time in years he had known the blind man to miss an evening out.

When the little clock on the mantel chimed twelve, Thornley Colton waked immediately, got up noiselessly, and put on his clothes, all but his collar and tie, coat and vest. From his overcoat pocket he took the thing he had gone out for in the early evening. It was a small rubber bulb with a long rubber tube that had a curved end of hollow, red glass. He carefully placed the bulb in his right armpit, adjusted the tube down the length of his arm, so that the curved end of red glass was concealed in his half-shut right palm. He drew the coat of his pyjamas over his shirt, and, without even removing his shoes, crawled back under the covers.

The little clock chimed one—two. The calm, even breathing of the blind man came regularly. The super keen ears caught the faint sound of an opening door. But he did not move. Dead silence. He heard the library door open, and to his nostrils came the strong odour of banana oil. His regular breathing was the only sound that broke the stillness. The library door closed. Instantly, noiselessly, he was out of bed. Seemingly with one motion he was in his coat, and vest, and overcoat. His hand touched the loaded automatic in his outside pocket. He did not even wait to put on the smoked glasses his sensitive, sightless eyes needed to protect them from the burning light. He did not wait to pick up the thin, hollow stick that gave its message to his fingertips. Nor did he pause an instant in the library, where the smell of bananas told him that a crushed glove of gilt had been laid on the desk. Down the stairs he ran with steps that were as silent as the night itself. He flung wide the front door.

Down the street he heard an automobile door slam the engine barked.

"Was I mistaken? Was it all wrong?" ran the bitter thought through his mind. He had staked everything on his ability to anticipate a probable plan of action on the part of the murderers. Then an eager look came to his face.

"Gee, Mister Colton, I'm glad yuh come!" The piping boy's voice came from his side.

"What is it, Shrimp?" he asked tensely. "Where have you been?"

"I been watchin' them guys. I follered the one that got in the house, an' I know where dey hang out. Gee, Mister Colton, dere's a taxi."

"Hail it!"

The shrill voice brought the cab to the curb. The chauffeur nodded at the low-voiced instructions. In the darkness Thornley Colton lolled back in the cushions. On his face was a curious look of resolution, content, victory. His wonderfully-keen ears, trained for years to know every sound, every voice and inflection of voice, knew that the person at his side was not Shrimp! He had known from the first that the voice was that of the man whose marvellous mimicry of Hedwig Gorski's voice had deceived even her husband. He knew that the man beside him was Madame Gorski's murderer. Blind, helpless but for the automatic pistol in his pocket, he was allowing himself to be taken to the men who had left their death-sentence sign on the desk in his library; to the men who had taken the boy he loved!

One chance in a thousand there had been, and the blind man had grasped it eagerly. He knew that one false move would destroy even that chance. He had realized that hours before. He had not dared give an inkling of his plan to a soul; he had not dared ask for help in the one desperate chance, for he did not know how many keen eyes were watching. He did not know where he was going, and he could not risk having men who would come to his aid shadowing him. No, the one chance in a thousand could only be taken *alone*.

As they rode the voice chattered on, telling of trailing the man who had left the glove-prints to a little house in Harlem; of stealing a basement-door key from a servant. Thornley Colton complimented quietly and often, but his whole mind was fixed on the street-corners the cab turned, calculating distance, remembering directions. And he knew they were not going near Harlem; but were in the dark, winding side-streets of Greenwich Village.

The taxi came to a stop. "The house is three doors down, Mister Colton. We'll chase dis guy an' slide up soft."

Colton took a bill from his pocket, and the hand of the murderer snatched it to pay the driver. "Dis way," whispered the voice, when the chauffeur had gone. Colton felt a hand lightly touch his elbow to guide him.

Stealthily they went, keeping close to the dark shadows of the houses. With a hiss of warning the hand drew him against the wall of a house, seconds after the blind man had heard the sound of approaching footsteps. A policeman passed, swinging his stick and whistling softly.

"Come on!" The hand pulled him forward and down an areaway. He heard a handle turn and an iron-grille door open rustily. A key in the hand of his guide opened another door, and he felt the carpet of the basement-hall under his feet as the door closed behind him.

"Wait here a minute, Mister Colton," came the whisper at his side. "I want a scout 'round a little."

Obediently the blind man stood in the darkness. He heard the light, almost soundless footsteps retreating until they died away somewhere in the depths of the house. Like a flash he whirled to the door. His fingers found the catch, sprung it back. The way to escape was open! Then he crept forward into the darkness, every nerve strained to catch the slightest warning sound. From the floor above came the hoarse murmur of voices, but even his wonderful ears could not distinguish words. Then his lips tautened to a thin, straight line. A moan, faint, quavering, came from the darkness. He knew instantly that it was the voice of the boy he had come to find. He had heard it before, years go, when the boy had tossed on his bed and dreamed horrid dreams of his murdered mother and his murderer father, from whom Thornley Colton had taken him.

"Only a few minutes more, kiddie," he breathed, then he darted back to the place his guide had left him. His super keen ears had warned him.

"Dere upstairs playin' cards an' half drunk," whispered the piping voice so like that of Shrimp. "Got a gun?"

Thornley Colton knew that the man was leaning forward, watching him in the darkness, but his hand touched the pocket that contained the heavy pistol, and he nodded. The lips of the blind man set even grimmer as he heard the sharp breath-intake of satisfaction. So the thousandth chance demanded that he lose even the pistol! Well, he would play the game according to their own set rules.

Up the stairs he followed at the heels of his leader, his brain automatically counting the steps and turns, as it had been taught to do years before. The guide stopped. Colton could hear the faint murmur of voices.

"Dere's where dey are!" whispered the voice. "Get in before dey know where dey's at." The blind man's hand fumbled for the doorhandle. He flung the door wide.

The bright lights of the room stung his naked eyeballs like a million swords of living fire; his hands went involuntarily to shield them. Instantly he felt the fingers of the man who had guided him dive toward his pocket, snatch out the pistol.

"Welcome, Herr Colton!" The voice came from in front of him in heavy German, and each word was a sneer. "Fool!" grated the voice. "Into our hands like a baby you come. Three pistols are pointed at your heart! Sit down!"

Colton groped forward blindly, his hand found a chair, his fingers told him that it was set close to a heavy oak table.

"Goot!" grunted the man who had spoken. Colton knew that he was sitting directly in front of him, across the table. The blind man's ears also informed him that on either side of the voice was another man. Three against one! Three with loaded pistols against an unarmed man who was blind!

The door closed softly, and Colton knew that the man who had led him was gone.

"Where's my boy?" demanded the problemist suddenly, fiercely. "Where is he!" He leaned across the table, and the heavy voice commanded him to sit back. But Thornley Colton had learned the table's width; a powerful lift of his knee had told him of its weight. That table was his thousandth chance! He slumped back in his chair, his left hand protecting his burning eyes, his right hand half closed on the arm of his chair.

"You have offended the Gilded Glove," began the rumbling German voice.

"I understand Russian!" broke in the blind man curtly.

The man at the right drew in his breath sharply. Colton heard the man at the left tilt his chair until its back touched a wall.

"The Gilded Glove has always been sacred to traitors," the voice went on, and the language was Russian. "But you have learned things that men with eyes would never have learned. We have watched you with Hedwig Gorski, and we knew that you knew. We know that you discovered the secret written in the music. But for you, that secret would have been our secret. The clutching fingers of the Long Arm are always reaching for those who fight the Little Father. You fell into our trap. You are a brave man. Your hands do not shake, nor does your body tremble. Your death will be an easy death."

"Thanks." The word came laconically from the blind man, but every nerve, every sense was alert as he mentally pictured the room and its occupants. He knew that the heavy table must be less than three feet from the wall. The tilted chair had told him that. Even the quiet breathing of the men located them for the blind man, who was waiting the thousandth chance.

"This chamber is soundproof. Its secrets are always secrets," continued the voice. "We could riddle you with bullets, and the world would be none the wiser. But we will be merciful."

Colton heard the click of a bottle-neck on a glass, heard the gurgle of the flowing wine, then the glass was pushed across the table.

"Drink!" ordered the harsh voice. "It is the poison that killed Hedwig Gorski; swift, powerful, painless. Drink!"

Thornley Colton drew back, a look of horror on his face.

"That, or the bullets which do not kill painlessly!"

The problemist's right hand reached blindly for the glass. His palm almost tipped it as it covered the top for an instant; then his fingers lifted it.

"You will not harm my boy?" he asked, and there was a queer chokiness in his voice.

"Drink!"

"You will not harm my boy?" The voice was pleading.

"I shall count three!"

Slowly, his hands shaking so that it required both of them to keep the drink from spilling, Thornley Colton lifted the glass to his lips. Six eyes watched him, but the nervousness seemed to pass as the fire of the wine entered his veins. He set down the empty glass and wiped his lips with his handkerchief. Narrowly the men watched him. A hectic flush seemed to mount the pale cheeks; the lean, cleft jaw was set rigidly. Suddenly Thornley Colton bent forward across the table; his left hand gripping its edge. And his voice came to their ears like the snap of a steel cable.

"For every minute of pain you have caused the boy I will make you suffer hours of agony!" he swore passionately. The voice became dull, then, the words came slowly, haltingly. "Hours—hours—for my boy's—hours—hours—"

The half-closed right fist dropped to his chair arm; the left hand dropped limply to his side; his body convulsively turned in the chair so that his hip was at the table-edge; the eyes stared straight ahead.

"It has done its work—as always," whispered the man at the left.

"A pity we could not make of him another Boris!" said the man at the right.

"Put away the needless pistols!" commanded the heavy voice. "Darkness for the sign!" The hand that had held the pistol reached back of him. The fingers pulled a switch, and the lights went out. The door opened softly.

From the darkness a gilded hand came slowly, certainly. The fingers touched the throat of the blind man—

With every ounce of strength in his powerful body, Thornley Colton sent the table crashing on the three men, pinning them like rats in the narrow space their chairs had occupied, knocking the breath from them, half stunning them. So instantaneously that it seemed part of the same lightning movement the blind man's hand darted out to grasp the invisible arm that held the gilded glove. A snapping jerk, and Madame Gorski's murderer was on his knees. Colton's right fist went out; the curved glass tube in his palm that had sucked up the wine to the bulb in his armpit while his hands had concealed the wine glass, shattered with the impact, cutting his tender palm in a dozen places. A choking gurgle came from the torn lips of the murderer, and the problemist knew that the sudden movement of his right arm had sent a spurting stream of the poison down the throat of the mimic. He let the lax body slide to the floor. A groan came from one of the pinned-down men. It was only a matter of seconds now.

The steps of a running man sounded in the hallway. The super keen ears of the problemist located them in the direction of the basement-stairs, and he realised that the approaching man must have been on the lower floor guarding the boy. That would leave the coast clear! He darted across the room; crouched beside the door. The man who had groaned cursed jerkily, and one of the heavy chairs creaked as he tried to writhe from under the big table. A hoarse growl came from the doorway. Like a cat, crouching, Thornley Colton spun on the balls of his feet and caught the man around the knees. A wrestler's twist of his body, and the new comer went down. The problemist pulled the door closed with a slam and jumped into the hallway.

A shot sounded in the room, and the blind man's lips curved in a grim smile. The way to escape was clear! In the darkness of the closed room the men of the Gilded Glove would be for precious minutes wholly at sea; in the darkness of the halls, Colton was at home—himself. He knew that he had gained several minutes now, because in the dark and the confusion of returning senses the men would not realise that he had escaped; every suspicious sound made by one of them would mean, to the others' bewildered brains, the location of the enemy.

Colton ran down the hall noiselessly; every nerve, every faculty alert to warn him of danger before a man with eyes would ever suspect its presence. His brain counted the steps without conscious effort. At the top of the basement-stairs he paused a second. From the room came a crash, and he knew the crushing weight of the table had been lifted. Then another shot. They were fighting among themselves in the darkness! Down the basement-stairs he ran. His wonderful ears told him that no other guard was there.

His hand brushing the wall, as he hurried back into the dark lower hall-way, located the door. He found the bolt and slid it back. From the corner came a faint moan. In a single stride he was across the floor. He leaned over a pile of blankets in the corner, and his hand brushed the face of the boy; his fingers felt the warm stickiness of the hair, and he cursed the men upstairs.

"Shrimp!" he called softly. The boy stirred, and his eyes opened as Thornley Colton picked him up tenderly in his strong arms.

"I fought 'em like—the very dickens!" Shrimp's voice was scarcely a whisper, but it took every bit of the gameness in the small body to make it even that. "They blackjacked me." His body went limp.

Colton ran with his burden down the dark hall to the front door. The confusion upstairs had ceased. He heard a door slam; a rumbling Russian curse; running footsteps. The minutes he had counted on had become seconds again! He jerked open the door he had unlatched, swung back the iron grille, and took a great gulp of the cool night air; let the wind fan his still-burning eyeballs. Running footsteps sounded; a dozen of them.

"Colton! My God, Colton!" It was the voice of Ames; and there were men with him.

"In the house with the open basement-door!" gasped Colton, and in his voice was a prayer of thankfulness for the thousandth chance. "The whole crowd!" he finished.

The running footsteps sounded once more. Ames lingered.

"The taxi-driver put us wise," he jerked out. "He knew the boy, and realised there was something wrong when the man with you imitated his voice. Reported it to the police. I got the tip instantly. Called up your house, and Thames found you gone. I got half a dozen of my men here in taxis."

"Where are the cabs?" snapped Colton, "I want one. My boy is hurt!"

"Around the corner." Ames whistled shrilly. "Here comes one. I've got to be with my men!" He was gone.

Colton laid the boy gently on the cushions, and, as the taxi started uptown, Shrimp's eyes fluttered open. "Gee!" he murmured faintly. "I got m' real detective work—that—time— assaults—blackjacks—" The voice died as unconsciousness came again.

IV.

The afternoon sun came slantingly through the great glass windows, lighting the happy face of the blind man and the pale, smiling face of The Fee, as he lay in bed, his head swathed in bandages, one arm in a sling.

"I was goin' round, 'cause I couldn't sleep, an' I heard somebody open the front door"—Shrimp scowled as his voice became weak, and set his teeth for a moment. "I thought it was you. Then I seen his whole head was covered with a black thing, an' there was black gloves on his hands, an' he didn't wear no shoes."

Colton nodded. "So that he could not be seen, nor heard, in the darkness. The hood covered everything but his eyes and lips; the latter were left free so that he could mimic a voice."

"I watched him sneak into the library an' come out. Then I beat it down the backstairs, an' when he got in his automobile I was hangin' on the back. He musta knew I was there all the time, but he never let on. I was scoutin' 'round the house when three of 'em jumped me. I guess they knocked me out good, for it was a long time 'fore I come round. Then a guy I couldn't see came in the dark room where I was an' started knockin' you. I told him where he stood, all right."

"It was the mimic," Colton explained. "He wanted to learn every tone of your voice."

"The government agents got everyone of them," put in Sydney unnecessarily.

"Yes, and the house has been the scene of many crimes. Ames and his men found a lot of valuable papers, together with the ringleaders of the Gilded Glove. Jones, of the hotel, identified the bearded man who did all the talking as the German husband who had the rooms. The chair arms didn't protect him very much from the falling table, and his three broken ribs will keep him quiet for awhile. The one who posed as his wife, and the third man at the table, have bruises and contusions enough to last them a lifetime. The murderer of Hedwig Gorski"—Thornley Colton paused a minute and went on—"was brought around all right by the ambulance surgeon; only a little of the poison went down his throat; but he told his story. He was a wonderful boy mimic fifteen years ago. Any sound, any voice was as easy for him to learn as names would be to you and me. Then the Gilded Glove got him. What devilish method they used I don't know, but they made him their tool. Boris Strevelski forgot that he had ever been anything but a dealer of death to traitors; that he was the Hammer of God was the only idea left in his mind. But they taught him all languages, and he picked them up as the average man would remember names.

"He worked for half an hour to get the pane of glass from the window of the Gorski bathroom, and, in a skintight suit of black silk that covered everything but his mouth and eyes, he hid behind the coat and dress in the closet after putting the poison in the tap. He had on the same suit at the house. My hands told me that."

"But how did you know he would come here?" asked Sydney breathlessly.

"I risked everything on my mental ability to follow the workings of the Oriental mind," Colton said slowly. "The Caucasian mind is always content with mere killing. But the Oriental mind must have the significant! Think of the risk of staying in the Gorski rooms when they knew the poison would do its work. But to them the mere death was only part; their whole course of thought demanded that the sign be left.

"I knew it would be the same in my case. So I gave them no chance to leave the crushed glove anywhere but here; and I knew they would come. I didn't know that they had been watching me for weeks because of my friendship with Madame Gorski, nor that they had gotten a duplicate key. But I was almost at the heels of the stranger. When he saw me I knew he would instantly think of luring me to my death. The sign had been left, and death was next. I knew, also, that he would never overlook the opportunity to mimic Shrimp's voice, because in the years mimicry has become a mania with him. He slammed the door of the car in which he came so that I would think he had escaped. Then his playing Shrimp's part seemed easy and logical. What was there to do but take me to the New York headquarters of the Gilded Glove? Following out their mind-processes further, I had no doubt that they would give me a chance to drink the poison, for that, too, is a peculiar kink of the Oriental mind. Hence my precaution. The rest was simple."

"Simple!" gasped Sydney Thames, and there was sweat on his brow. "My God, Thorn, think of you, *blind*, risking yourself alone with those men."

"My blindness was my greatest ally there," smiled Colton faintly. "The instant darkness came they were helpless, while I was my normal self, which I couldn't be in the burning light, but"—he touched the alcohol-soaked bandage that covered his head and eyes—"the tortures of the Inquisition were mild beside that light on my unprotected eyeballs."

He patted the hand of the boy gently. "And it was Shrimp who led the secret agents, after all," he said quietly. "If the taxi-driver hadn't been one of the hundred friends he has made around the city, there might have been another story to tell. The men of the Gilded Glove weren't far behind me."

The doorbell rang downstairs. "Ames again," commented Colton, a trifle wearily, and in a few minutes the government agent was ushered into the room by John, the butler.

"We got everything, Mr Colton!" he cried.

"The whole gang is cleaned up. Gorski was released from jail today, and is going back to Paris. Without his wife he will never bother anyone. Even the Gilded Glove didn't think him worthy of their attention. And those harbour-mine plans! A wonderful piece of work! Placed in order under an onion-skin paper map of the harbour, with the staccato note marks at certain points on the shore line, every sharp and flat traced on the map gave, as you said, the exact locations of the mines."

"Have you found the traitor?" asked Colton.

"Yes." Ames's voice was sober. "His body was found this morning in his office. The pistol he had used was beside him. A closed incident." Then enthusiasm came to his tone once more. "What you have done on this case will never be forgotten, Mr Colton," he said earnestly. "It will not be made public, of course, but the secretary of state will write you a personal letter offering you any reward you may ask. The president himself will tender you a position that—"

Thornley Colton's upraised hand stopped him. The blind man turned his sightless eyes toward the closed eyes of The Fee, and gently withdrew his fingers from the clasp of the small hand. "Hush," he said softly. "The boy is sleeping."

7

The Seventh Problem:

THE RINGING GOBLETS

I.

His chin resting on his chest, his hands gripping the widespread leather arms of the chair, the man stared at the log fire—fixedly, intently; as though the ceaseless war the flames waged against the darkness held him enthralled by its hopelessness. The wind, whistling encouragement down the wide chimney, caused the fire to leap upward and drive the shadows in retreat to the farthest corner of the library. For an instant the flames crackled their triumph; then died down. The shadows rushed forward, swiftly and silently, to recover the territory they had lost. The fire sputtered its chagrin.

The man in the chair shivered, though his hands felt the warmth of the leather arms. For an instant the hopeless look went from his eyes; his chin lifted. Then the eyes resumed their staring at the flames. "I won't!" he muttered. "I won't! I'll—" The thin right fist doubled; he raised it to smite the arm of the chair. In the air it unclenched and dropped lifelessly.

"There must be some way!" Hope again shone in his eyes. The flames, apparently encouraged by his spirit, again leaped to their fight with the shadows. "There is!" His voice, low, passionate, died suddenly. He jerked his head around the side of the high chair, and darted a fearful glance at a dark corner. A trembling chill shook his body, and his lips formed the silent words: "I mustn't forget *that* devilish thing!"

The door opened softly, and the man in the chair heard, but he did not move. The impassive-faced servant came forward with soundless footsteps.

"You wish anything, sir?" he asked humbly.

"Nothing, Paul."

"A bit more wood on the fire, sir?"

The seated man turned his eyes back to the glowing logs that had given up their fight with the darkness, and whose flames no longer leaped their defiance, but spluttered their defeat.

"I think not," came finally.

"Your wine, sir?"

"At eight, Paul."

"Yes, sir. I'll remember, sir." The servant bowed himself back a step, then stopped. "Miss Nadine says as 'ow she 'opes you are quite fit this evenin', sir."

A sudden draft of cold air seemed to strike the man, for his body shook and his hands gripped tighter on the leather arms.

"Tell her I feel much better," he lied pitifully, moistening his dry lips with his tongue.

"I will, sir." The man bowed gravely and withdrew, closing the door quietly behind him.

Silence came again to the room, broken only by the crackle of the dying fire that gave to the haggard, deep-lined face of the man a pink glow of health that belied the hunted look in his eyes, and the lines of utter hopelessness around the mouth. For minutes he sat, immovable, swallowed in the depths of the big leather chair.

The door opened again, and the sound of it brought a new expression to his face; a curious expression of mingled joy and dread. His thin hands clenched as if the very action were intended to brace his whole body. Then his lips formed a tremulous smile as the golden-haired, pink-cheeked girl ran across the room, and flung her arms around his neck. Her lips touched his cheek; she drew back and gazed deep into his eyes for an instant before he lowered them.

"Oh, daddy-father," she pleaded. "You *mustn't* worry so!" She seated herself on the chair arm, her small hand patted his shoulder. "It will all come out right," she whispered fondly.

"Hush!" he breathed, and she could feel his body tremble under her fingers.

"The curs!" she said passionately, lifting her head to look over the back of the high leather chair and gaze into the dark corner, as her father had done a few minutes before.

He lifted a hand and touched her lips warningly, but she shook her head away.

"It's killing you, daddy-father!" There was a sobbing catch in her voice. "You've grown old, old, in the past month. Won't you *please* let that wonderful blind man help you? Oh, daddy-father"—both hands were on his shoulders now; her eyes bright with held-back tears, looked into his—"think of what he did for Ned—and I love you so!"

"No, no!" he choked. "I—he—please don't make me talk." The last was a whisper, even the girl in the armchair barely heard it.

"I don't care!" she cried. "I'll—"

From the shadowed shelf over the fire-place came the mellow chime of a clock. The girl and the man started as though some sudden electric shock had passed through them. Her hand clutched at his shoulder; a sob came from her throat. The man's fingers picked at the leather chair-arms; his dry lips moved mechanically as he counted the eight strokes of the clock-bell. When the last note had died away the girl's hand fell lifelessly from his shoulder; she rose to her feet.

"You are going to the opera tonight, Nadine?" he asked, trying bravely to keep the quaver from his voice.

"Yes," she said steadily. She bent down to kiss him, her hand touched his thin white hair for a minute before she turned to go. Half-way across the room she stopped, and her little hands clenched at her sides as the door-handle turned softly; but she merely bowed bravely and hurried past the wooden-faced manservant who entered.

"Your wine, sir?"

The man rubbed his hands together, as though warming them in the glow of the logs; his face was hidden in the shadows above.

"Yes, Paul."

From the shadow beside the fire-place the servant brought a small, round tabouret, and set it beside the big chair.

"Turn me around a bit, Paul. The light hurts my eyes."

Obediently the servant placed the big chair so that its side was to the firelight. The little man was completely swallowed up in its depths. Only the tip of one slippered foot showed in the ruddy crimson that came under the chair. The tabouret was in the dark at the side away from the fire.

"The usual two goblets, sir?" asked the servant, as he swung back the door of the cellaret.

"Yes, Paul, and a cigar."

The man placed the two wine-filled goblets on the small table, and a few drops of the wine spilled as it swayed a trifle on its uneven legs.

"Table seems a trifle wabbly, sir. Shall I put something under the legs to steady it?"

The seated man merely shook his head and stretched forth a hand to lift one of the goblets to his lips. Slowly he sipped it while the servant stood patiently by with the box of cigars. In the flare of the match, held to light the cigar he had selected, the servant's eyes, invisible in the shadows above, studied every line of the haggard face. But there was no commiseration in the studying—only satisfaction and triumph.

"That is all; I won't need you again tonight, Paul."

"Very well, sir." The servant bowed and withdrew.

For several minutes the smoke from the unmoving cigar spiraled in the darkness. Then the seated man turned in the big chair, and the ashes dropped to his knee unheeded as he shuddered. His two hands on the small tabouret moved it an inch toward him. He shook his head, and moved it half an inch to the right. The wine in the full glass was spilling, and he poured half of it into the other goblet. Apparently the uneven legs that caused the tabouret to teeter back and forth bothered him, for he spent several minutes setting it to his satisfaction. Then he carefully placed the two goblets in the exact centre, so that the rims touched, and leaned back in the big leather chair.

One hand showed on the armchair nearest the fire; the other was in the shadow. Suddenly the two glasses clicked together with a musical, ringing sound, as though his hand had nervously fallen on the table and caused it to sway. Then his shaking fingers on the tabouret-edge caused a musical soothing jingle of the egg-shell rims. The sound seemed to please him, for the clink-click-tap-tap-clink kept up for minutes.

"I won't!" he cried suddenly, vehemently. His trembling fingers made the wine dance in the ringing goblets.

The hand holding the cigar rested on the chair-arm, the fingers clenched so that the wrapper almost crackled under their pressure.

"No, no! Nadine—" The moaning voice died; he bent forward in his chair. The slipper that showed in the light under the chair lifted, then dropped back to its original position. The cigar smoke curled upward from the chair-arm, an iridescent ribbon in the feeble glow of the darkness-defeated logs.

Clink! Clink-clink! Tap! Tap-tap! came the ring of the goblets on the tabouret. The clock on the mantel ticked off minute after minute.

Softly, silently the door opened—an inch, two inches. From the darkness of the hall outside two eyes stared into the darkness of the room.

The streamer of smoke rose steadily; the glasses still sang their song of nervousness. Suddenly the door opened a full half. The owner of the watching eyes had smelled burning leather. The servant stepped into the room, stumbled over a big chair near the door, and swore softly.

"Do you wish anythink, sir?" It was the respectful voice of the servant.

The smoke still ascended unwaveringly; the music of the goblets did not cease. But no answer came from the big chair.

The servant approached the chair on tiptoe. A sound made him turn toward the door. It was swinging open. He walked to it, and stopped it before it struck the heavy bookcase, and closed it noiselessly.

"Do you wish anythink, sir?" he whispered again.

The slipper still showed in the ribbon of light. The glasses were still ringing. The cigar still burned. The man sniffed again, then reached the side of the chair in a single bound.

A curse escaped him; a deep curse of bafflement, rage.

The chair was empty!

On the arm the cigar was burning the leather. The empty slipper was just where the foot had been. The wine still moved in the now-silent glasses. But the man he had left a few minutes before, the man whose nervous fingers had caused the glasses to ring but a second before, had vanished!

Two steps took the servant across the room. A snap, and the incandescents sprang to light. The big chair by the door, a counterpart of the one at the fireplace, was unmoved. Everything in the room was as he had left it. But the man was gone.

"Damn him!" muttered the fellow who had been a servant. But he wasn't a servant now. His shoulders were hunched aggressively. The wooden look had gone. In its place was tenseness, animal strength; the muscles played back and forth under the tightly-drawn skin of the cheek-bones.

"He's gone, chief!" he said, and his voice was low. "How the devil he did it is more than I can figure." He ran to the fireplace and knelt on the hearth, his sharp eyes studying every inch. And as he leaned over the fire he talked: "I watched the door every minute. His infernal nervousness gave me the willies. I heard the glasses clink till I got to the chair, chief—*to the chair!*"

He ran to the high window, and searched every inch of the sill and curtains, still speaking in that level, even tone: "Get the boys out and cover the house! Spread 'em around the block! He can't have been gone more than ten minutes. There's not a damn' crack in the wall. I know that!"

His fingers were running over the bookcases, his eyes seeming to bore into their very depths as he went on: "The girl's all ready for the opera—" His keen ears heard footsteps, and his voice changed to an agonised wail as the girl entered: "'E's gone, Miss Nadine, 'e's gone!"

"Gone!" she cried, staggering against the chair near the door. "Gone!" she repeated, and her voice was scarcely a whisper.

"I smelled 'is cigar burning the leather. I thought as 'ow 'e was asleep."

She forced her limbs to support her weight across the floor. She looked down into the chair where the untouched cigar still burned. The opera cloak slipped from her shoulders unheeded as she touched the tabouret-edge with her fingers for an instant. The glasses clinked mockingly.

"Gone!" she said again. "He has gone to them—at last!"

She swayed, fell, sending the tabouret and glasses crashing to the floor. The servant leaned over her for an instant; then ran to the corner of the room.

"Hear that, chief!" he whispered tensely. "Get it? Rip out the wires when I cut 'em. There'll be merry hell around here in a little while!"

A gleam of nickel showed in his hand as he thrust it behind a high bookcase. Came two sharp clicks, and as he turned toward the girl he put into his pocket a round, black disc. It was a dictograph.

II.

For two hours Nadine Nelson had sat, white-faced but steady voiced, as the three men questioned, cajoled, badgered, and threatened. At her right, his chair within a foot of that in which she sat, was the man who had posed as a servant. At her left was another, just as keen-eyed and alert. Before her sat a heavy-chinned, broad-shouldered man whose fingers crackled the typewritten sheets as he jerked out his questions. The girl's eyes met his fairly, unwaveringly. Yet she knew he was Chief Whittson, of the United States secret service.

"You know that, for months, hundreds of thousands of dollars have been passed through the agency of your father's bank?" he snapped.

"I know nothing," she said unemotionally.

"Then why did you say—" He referred to the typewritten sheets "'It will all come out right?'"

"Because it will," she replied steadily.

The men at her sides snorted impatiently.

"Did you know that your father was the head of the best-organised counterfeiting gang in the country?" jerked out the secret-service chief.

Her eyes did not flinch for an instant. "I knew nothing."

"Where is your father, Miss Nelson?"

"I do not know."

"Then why did you say"—his forefinger punched the typewritten page viciously, and in his voice was snarled impatience—"'he has gone to them at last.' Who did you mean?"

"I know nothing," came the unvarying answer she had given a hundred times before.

"Why didn't you call in the police when you knew that your father had disappeared?"

For the first time a shade of expression came to the girl's face; her lips curved in contempt. "Because I knew that the police could do no more than the secret-service men of the United States." There was more than a tinge of contempt in her voice.

Chief Whittson straightened back in his chair. "Did you know that your servant was not what he pretended to be?" he demanded.

"Yes," she said defiantly. "We knew from the first that he was a spy."

The former servant leaped to his feet, face red with rage. "So that's why you took it so cool, eh? That's why you didn't raise the fuss I expected?" he flared. "And you went to your own room and locked the door to cry. And I was *sorry* for you. Me! A wise guy! Some—clever—actress!"

She shrank back before the lashing sneer in the words.

"Then you knew of the dictograph?" demanded the chief, instantly alert to take advantage of the first signs of breakdown.

"Yes," she whispered tremulously. "We knew, and we—" she stopped, her breath catching suddenly.

"'We,'" repeated the chief sharply. "What? What?"

Her lips quivered piteously. The nerve that had forced her frail woman's body to bear the rack for hours was breaking.

"What did you do? Tell me!" he commanded viciously.

"Don't you think you've gone quite far enough on that line?" The quiet, even voice of the man in the doorway caused the two men at the girl's side to leap to their feet, and the chief to jerk his body erect. "If I were you, Miss Nelson," the man in the door-way spoke to the girl, and his voice was gentle, "I would answer only courteous questions."

His white face, with its lean, cleft chin, and thin, firm lips, lighted in a wonderful smile of encouragement; the hand that was not holding the slim stick brushed back from his high forehead the hair whose whiteness was accentuated by the great blue circles of the tortoise-rimmed library glasses.

"Who are you?" demanded the chief, but there was no bluster in his tone. The manner he had assumed for the girl had dropped like a mask. He was the calm, alert detective once more, and his keen judgment told him instantly that the new comer was not the type to bluff.

Before the man at the doorway could answer, a youth rushed past him to the girl's side.

"I found him, Nadine," he cried joyously. "Here's Mr Colton. He'll find uncle."

"Thank God!" breathed the girl, and her body relaxed.

Thornley Colton turned his head to speak over his shoulder. "A glass of water, Sydney. Quickly!"

"So you're Thornley Colton, eh?" The secret-service chief eyed him sharply. "I understand you've done some rather remarkable work—for a blind man."

Colton smiled, then stepped aside as his black-haired, apple cheeked secretary came in with a glass of water. The girl's eyes fluttered open, and the blind man realised that she needed time to regain her scattered senses.

"You have the average person's idea of the blind, chief," he said. "And the average person gets his notion from the blind beggar on the street-corners who hobbles along led by a small boy and a dog, and taps every inch of the sidewalk with a heavy cane. Very few realise that is mostly for effect. Fewer still know that in New York there are nearly two hundred sightless men and women who go to business every day without help or guidance. Some of the highest-paid private secretaries and stenographers in the country are blind. Several of the blind proofreaders are famous. And for many years the court of last resort in the dead-letter office at Washington was a blind man. He was the most expert ever employed by the government, and could read with his supersensitive fingertips addresses that had passed through the hands of the keenest-eyed readers of illegible writing in the world. So you see, the blind are not so helpless as one might imagine. Ah, Miss Nelson, do you feel better?"

"Yes." She looked up at him with a curious expression in her eyes. It was the look of a child who has sought a protector only to be a little frightened at the result. But she smiled bravely. "You did such a wonderful thing for Ned"—she rested her hand fondly on her cousin's arm—"when he was arrested for the murder of the girl in the theatre, and I thought—" Again came the look that was almost fear.

"I will do my best," promised the blind man. "Do you mind my hearing the story from Chief Whittson—his side of it?"

"No," she said, with only a bit of nervousness in her voice.

Whittson smiled quizzically. This blind man might be interesting. On his face and the faces of his men there was no doubt of the outcome. They were government men, trained, efficient; the interloper was an amateur—and blind.

"We know that Dryden F. Nelson was the biggest passer of counterfeit money in the country!" began the chief. "He is the cleverest of them all. Who would suspect the bank of a man like Nelson as a clearing house for the cleverest counterfeits ever made? The scheme was wonderful, the only organised gang in the country who could pass 'queer' at its face value was that of this girl's father. How long it's been going on we don't know. The bills have the 'feel,' something no other counterfeiter has ever been able to get. It was only within the past six months we traced the bills to their source. And that was Nelson's bank! For six months we have tried to locate the plant, and failed. For the past three weeks my man here has been in the house, and there has been a dictograph in the library."

"And you discovered nothing?"

"Nothing except to make morally certain his guilt. And he knew we were closing in. He was frightened stiff! Now we find out that the girl, here, was wise. She's fooled us right along. We never suspected that she was one of the gang."

The girl cowered in her chair. "I'm not," she faltered. "It isn't true."

"Now Nelson's slipped through our fingers," went on the chief relentlessly. "Just when we had him worked up to a confession. He got out of that room in some devilish way."

"I've got the facts of his disappearance," put in Colton.

"So have we!" snapped the chief. "Within ten minutes of the time he went, every inch of this block was covered, and today ten thousand police and two hundred secret-service men are scouring the city for him. He can't get out of it, and he can't stay in it—long."

"Why didn't you arrest him before if you were so certain of his guilt?"

"Because we wanted his pals! We wanted to locate the plant! And he went while Jim was watching the door every minute! While my ears were glued to the dictograph-receivers and my pencil taking every word down in shorthand."

"You heard nothing?"

"After Jim brought the wine there wasn't a sound but the infernal ringing of the two glass rims on the teetery tabouret he insisted on having beside his chair."

Colton looked up with sudden interest. "Did you ever hear those glasses ring before?"

"Every night at eight, when Jim here served his wine."

"What other time did he have wine served?"

The former servant answered: "He only had it at eight in the library, and he wanted it on the minute."

"Significance—somewhere," mused the problemist. For several seconds there was silence as his slim cane idly tapped his shoesole.

Suddenly the girl sat rigid in her chair. "I can't!" she cried. "Oh, please! Please! I can't!"

The expression on the blind man's face was the only one that did not change. The three secret-service men looked the amazement the sudden irrelevant words had caused. The youth who was kneeling at the girl's side gazed at her in wonder.

"The truth will help us all, Miss Nelson," said Colton gently.

But she paid no attention to the words. Her eyes, widened in fear, were fixed on the shoe of the problemist.

"Yes," she said, and her voice was barely a whisper. "Every night!"

The chief jumped to his feet. "What's that?" he demanded. "What's that?"

"The one thing you overlooked; the significance of two plus two," declared Thornley Colton. "If you will show me the library perhaps I can point out some other things that your eyes have missed."

The girl lifted her bowed head. "Oh, Mr Colton," she pleaded, "do not show them—you don't know what it means!"

The blind man went to her side, and put his hand gently on her shoulder. "It is necessary," he said, and his voice was tender. Then, to the chief: "If you will lead the way."

Chief Whittson rose, and jerked his thumb toward the girl as she buried her head in her arms. One of the men nodded. She was to be guarded every minute.

"I'll stay here," whispered Sydney Thames, as Colton passed him. The black-haired secretary, tender-hearted, deifier of all women, was going to guard the girl against further badgering.

The government man who had posed as the servant opened the door of the library. "This is the room," he growled. "There isn't a break in the walls. We've gone over every inch."

Colton's thin cane located the big chair near the door. He walked around it, touched its back, the walls behind it, and measured the distance to the room entrance. On his white cheeks was a hectic flush of excitement; his nostrils quivered like those of a hound on the scent.

"You were watching the door every minute?" His voice was unconsciously sharp.

"Yes."

The blind man turned to the chief, a curious smile on his face. "This is an instance of the blind's superiority. You and your man know that there is but one possible way for a man to get out of this room. You're as sure of that as you are of death. Yet you can't realise that that is the way Nelson got out because your eyes deceive your brain into thinking it impossible. Sight is the greatest handicap pure reasoning has. Even a man with eyes instinctively closes them when he is trying to figure out some particularly intricate problem. The trouble is that you haven't closed your eyes. Nelson went out through that door!"

"What?" The chief and his man chorused it blankly.

The blind problemist did not answer at once. He darted across the room. His stick found the chair at the fireplace.

"Nelson wanted you to turn this chair away from the fire?" he said suddenly.

"How did you know that?" asked the chief, and in his tone was wonder.

"Because it was necessary for his escape." The words came like staccato notes on a taut wire. "He knew that a man was watching that door. He didn't know what instant it might open an inch. But he knew that with the high sides of the chair toward the fire he would be invisible in the depths. He pulled his slippers off, and left one so that it could be seen—young

Nelson, who came to see his cousin last night, gave me most of the facts. Then he slid from the chair, and crawled across the floor to crouch down behind that other big chair near the door. From past tests he knew just how the servant would enter the room and just what he would do. It was the work of an instant to slip through the open door as the servant was crossing the room toward the fire-place. His stockinged feet made his exit absolutely noiseless. The very simplicity of the thing would deceive any man in the world who could see. Yet you knew it was the only way he *could* have gone!"

"I saw the door open!" gasped the secret-service man. "I thought it was a draught."

"Yes," nodded the blind man, "because your eyes saw the cigar-smoke and the slipper. They wouldn't let your brain get any idea but that he was in the chair."

"But the very simplicity of that would make elaborate preparations necessary," objected the chief. "The thing would have to be timed to the instant. Nelson hadn't a chance to communicate with any one without our knowledge. Jim, here, and the dictograph took care of that."

Colton's lips curved in a mirthless smile. "They made it possible! Their very actions prove that both Nelson and his daughter knew of the dictograph. They understood that, so long as you didn't suspect they knew, you would take no other precautions. They knew that you would depend on the instrument to hear every word, and on this man to see that there wasn't a written word of instruction put into their hands. And they fooled you! Tricked you every day!"

At the last word he dropped to his knees beside the big chair by the fireplace. His supersensitive fingertips brushed the carpet. Back and forth they went a dozen times, then stopped. "See that!" he cried. "See that!"

The two men leaned forward. For a minute they stared.

"Only a nail-hole through the rug," declared the chief.

"Yes, only a nail-hole," Colton repeated quietly. "That's the only thing your eyes can see. But my fingertip felt the point of a nail under the carpet and on a level with the floor."

"Nail?" repeated the chief dumbly. He had forgotten his superior attitude of a short time before. The dominant personality of the blind man; his absolute sureness of himself compelled respect, and brought a realisation that Thornley Colton was the master, he the pupil.

The blind man walked from the chair. His stick, poking in the corner beside the fire-place, found the tabouret. With an exclamation of satisfaction he pulled it out and touched its edge with his fingertips.

"You spoke of it as being 'teetery.' See how finely it is balanced on the two legs that are a fraction of an inch longer than the others. And see here!" His stick fell to the floor as he used both hands to turn it upside-down. The two secret-service men saw that all four legs were tipped with metal balls. "See the scars of the nail-point on the balls of the short legs?" cried Colton. He took his knife from his pocket, and tapped with the blade. A low, musical click-click-click that could be heard distinctly by the men resulted. "Hear that?" he demanded.

"What does it mean?" The chief made no effort to keep the bewilderment from his voice.

"It means that under the floor, and under that nail-hole in the rug, is a finely-adjusted magnet with a nail-pointed plunger in the centre of the coil. That's how Nelson beat your dictograph! That's how he beat your spy. Just as the girl inside understood the Morse messages I tapped with my cane."

"Telegraphy!" gasped the chief. "Nelson was chief staff-telegrapher in the army for years."

The blind man nodded. "The table was set here at eight because that is the time the person at the other end would be ready to send the messages. Nelson adjusted the tabouret so that one of the short legs would be directly above the magnet-plunger, which was as sensitive to the touch of the telegraph-key sending the current through the magnet-coils as the most delicate instrument in the world. To the trained operator who has learned to take a message from any single instrument in a room where a thousand others are clattering away, the click of the plunger against that hollow metal ball would be as easy to read as print to the average man. But ordinarily the dictograph would also hear. That's why the goblets were placed rim to rim—so that the ringing would drown the other sound over the wires of the dictograph, or to a man listening at the door. Acoustics would take care of that. The dot-dash of the magnet-plunger could not be heard five feet away, though the man in the chair could get every word."

"By God, that's clever!" There was admiration in Chief Whittson's tone. "Pull back that chair, Jim! We'll get the rug up and see the thing! We'll follow those wires and land the whole gang."

He stopped as Nadine Nelson entered the room. She wasn't the sobbing girl they had left who now entered; but a white-cheeked, white-lipped woman who did not speak until she had crossed the room and stood before the chief.

"I am the 'gang' you speak of," she said quietly. "The wires go to my room!"

III.

Calmly, disdainfully, the girl stood at the door of her room, and watched the secret-service men search it with no regard for care. At her side stood her cousin, looking on helplessly. His boyish protests had been stilled by a terse "Shut up!" from the chief. At the other side of the girl, his face black with a scowl, and his hands clenched at his sides, stood Sydney Thames. To the soft-hearted Sydney no crime was so great as that of causing a woman pain. So he gritted his teeth, and darted murderous glances at the secret-service men, and looks of pleading at the blind man who leaned against the wall, apparently watching the searchers.

The girl had shown them the room. She had flung open the door of the closet, and cleverly concealed behind hanging clothes they had found a telegraph-key on a small shelf. They had pulled out the wires, and found they led to the magnets in the library. Now they were beginning a systematic search of the room—and finding nothing. The girl had evidently told the truth. She, and only she, could have sent the messages.

"Where did you learn telegraphy?" demanded the chief suddenly.

"I can't remember when I didn't have a key to play with," she answered coolly. "Father was an expert telegrapher for years, and he taught us almost before we could read and write."

"'Us?'" snapped out the chief.

"My brother and me," she answered, and the ears of the blind man, trained to interpret every inflection of tone, caught the sudden forced note.

"Where is your brother, Miss Nelson?" he asked.

"He died ten years ago, in the tropics," she answered, and there was a curious break in her voice.

"And you left the library every night at eight so you could send your father messages?" asked the chief sarcastically.

"Yes. We did not dare talk because of your spy. And his eyes were never off my father."

"Well," the chief's tone was even more sarcastic than before, "*you* might have found an easier way."

She did not answer, but watched Thornley Colton as he stepped across the room to the closet. For a minute he poked inside with his cane, moving the hanging clothes away from the telegraph-instrument. He leaned over it, and seemed to be examining it intently. There was a frown of puzzlement on his forehead as he straightened up. It disappeared almost instantly, and in its place came a look of sudden enlightenment.

"Did you ever smoke South American cigarettes with licorice pectoral papers, Miss Nelson?" he asked.

"No, never!" She tried to make the denial indignant, but Colton's super keen ears caught the false note instantly, as did the keen-eyed chief of the secret-service. He opened his mouth to ask a question, but the blind man forestalled him.

"The next house is built right against this one, isn't it, chief?"

"Yes, but the crazy Frenchman next door is absolutely above suspicion. We looked up his whole life's history. He's a semi-invalid and nutty. He has a pet bear; also two servants to take care of the animal."

"Crazy, eh?" muttered Colton. He hurried across the room, his cane locating every piece of furniture. He stopped before the bureau, and leaned forward toward a drawer-pull. An instant he paused, and in that instant came the betrayal he had hoped to bring from the girl.

"Don't, please!" She stopped suddenly, biting her lips until the blood came.

Colton straightened up; his lips set grimly. "Pull out the bureau, and you'll find an opening into the house of the crazy Frenchman," he said.

"What!" The chief jumped across the room, and pulled out the heavy piece of furniture. Behind it was a jagged hole that a crouching man could go through with ease.

The two secret-service men jumped through the opening, but the chief paused. "How did you know that?" he asked wonderingly.

"Because the clothes in the closet held the faint licorice odour of the pectoral cigarette papers that South Americans affect. Therefore some man must have been sending those messages. It wasn't a man in this house. There had to be an entrance—and I tricked the girl into telling me that it was concealed behind the bureau. It had to be in this room because the message-sender wouldn't risk entering another to get where the telegraph-key was!"

The girl leaned back against the wall, and a sob came from her lips. "Oh, why did I ask Ned to find you!" she cried. "Their eyes could have seen nothing, and you—"

"It was necessary, Miss Nelson!" The gentleness that had been in the blind man's voice downstairs was missing now; it was brusque, sharp. "Better have one of your men remain here, chief," he said, and there was no mistaking his meaning. "I'd like to go through that house."

The chief looked at him curiously; then, with the docility that came to most men when the blind man advised or ordered, he whistled sharply. One of the men returned.

"Stay here!" commanded the chief, and he stepped aside as the blind man bent low and entered the next house. The chief followed.

"What do you know about the occupant here?" Colton asked the chief as he walked around the room, his thin cane locating furniture again, and giving his brain a mental picture of the whole chamber.

"He's lived here for some time. We looked him up from A to Izzard, also his three servants. About six months ago, it appears, he bought a pet bear, a nasty beast, and sometimes takes him out. Attracts quite a lot of attention because the old man wears a huge fur coat that makes him look like the animal's big brother."

"And because every man in your business thinks the crook is always seeking cover there would be no suspicion of a man who courts attention by means of keeping a pet bear. Clever game enough to throw any man that had eyes off the track!"

"Oh, the Frenchman's on the level," resented the chief. "He's getting worse, failing fast. Anybody can see that. Doctor comes twice a day to see him."

"And he comes every night about eight o'clock!" declared Colton suddenly. "He's the man that's been sending those messages. He's the chief of the gang you've been trying to locate so long. He must be, or he'd stay here all the time. He has to attend to the outside work while the men here do the actual counterfeiting. And it was never suspected because all you could see was a *pet bear!* Look!" He pulled open the drawer of a dresser. "Here's a dozen cigarette ends, all of pectoral paper and Brazilian paper. The doctor smoked them here the times he had to wait for eight o'clock and the time to talk to Nelson."

"By Jove! You're—"

"Hey, chief!" The cry came from downstairs.

"It's Jim. He's found something!" The chief started toward the door and stopped. "Do you want me to guide you?" he asked.

"Go ahead!" Colton said dryly. "My ears will follow your footfalls."

"This way, chief! Quick!" The voice directed them to the kitchen. The chief stopped with an ejaculation of amazement at the door.

The secret-service operative who had entered the house first was lifting an unconscious man from a heavy wooden chair. On the floor were the cut ropes that had bound him, and the wadded handkerchiefs that had prevented outcries.

"The Frenchman!" gasped the chief. "He's got to talk! Lay him down, Jim!"

The Frenchman groaned feebly as they put him on the floor, and choked when a pocket flask was held to his lips.

"*Mon Dieu!*" he moaned weakly. Then his dazed brain realised that men were standing over him. "Pleeze stop! I do nozzing!" he cried supplicatingly.

"We are friends—gendarmes." Chief Whittson said the words slowly and distinctly, so that the man could understand. "Who did this?"

The fear went from the Frenchman's eyes. "My servants," he whispered hoarsely. "Zay have kep' me prisoner for mont's; ever since my old servants go an' zay come."

"Damn!" jerked out the chief. "They've tricked us right along. We looked up the old servants' records, and didn't suspect for an instant the impersonation. Where did they go? When?"

The Frenchman fell back, his eyes closed.

"I think I can answer the 'when' part of that question," put in Thornley Colton, as he appeared at the doorway. "I apologise to the man here for the things I said upstairs. But even I didn't give the master counterfeiter credit for such diabolical ingenuity as this. The fake servants left the minute you entered Nelson's house to question the girl. And the man that went with them as the Frenchman was Dryden F. Nelson. That's the only way he could go!"

The Frenchman stirred, and tried to lift his head. "Zat is right," he gasped chokingly. "He—" His eyes closed.

"Get an ambulance, Jim!" ordered the chief. "This man's in bad shape. Get the boys from outside! Put two on the trail of the carriage. Nelson and his gang won't get far. Bring the others in to search the house!" The man darted out, and the chief picked the invalid up in his strong arms and carried him gently to a couch in the dining-room.

The Frenchman moaned, and a shudder shook his body. "Don't make ze bear hurt me!" he cried weakly. "Don't knock ze glasses togezzer and make him mad-crazee." He lapsed back into unconsciousness.

The chief looked at Colton significantly, but the blind man only nodded.

"But how did old man Nelson ever get a chance to get in here?" puzzled the chief.

"He didn't!" Colton's voice was sharp. "The man who posed as the doctor is the ringleader." There came a ring of menace in his tone. "I'll find him! I know him!"

"You know him?" The chief did not even nod to the three men who entered the room and stood respectfully by for orders.

"Yes! He's tanned a dark brown, an expert telegrapher, thirty-five years old, a man who likes to pet and fondle a bear, and his first name is Joe. There are a few other details I'll give you when the proper time comes."

"Great Scott!" Amazement, incredulity were in the chief's voice. He turned to one of his men.

"Was the doctor here last night, Tom?" he asked.

"We saw him coming out a minute before we got the alarm from you, chief. Said good evening, and told us it was only a matter of days for the old guy here."

"Eyes attach no significance to things they have seen a dozen times before," Colton observed.

The chief turned to him again. "Where did you get those facts?" he demanded, with the brusqueness of chagrin in his voice.

"The Brazilian tobacco and pectoral papers told me he had spent years in South America. Naturally he'd be tanned a dark brown. The fact that he must be an expert telegrapher is obvious. I know that he is thirty-five years old because I know that he is fifteen years older than Nadine Nelson. How I knew that you'll know later. This told me his name—and another fact." The blind man held out a charred fragment of paper scarcely two inches square, a deep brown in colour from heat and smoke. "The fact that the man you want takes pleasure in fondling and handling a bear my keen sense of smell told me. The bear-fur odour is unmistakable and clings to a thing for hours. It was on the handkerchief in the kitchen, and in the corner of the linen was the initial J!"

"It's impossible to decipher a word of this!" protested the chief, looking up from the charred fragment of paper.

"With eyes—yes. But my fingertips found the tracery of that name, even though the ink had entirely disappeared! The penridges remain, and would remain until the paper was consumed." He changed the subject suddenly. "There comes the ambulance. I want to go up and see the girl again."

"I'll go with you." Chief Whittson's tone was curiously humble. He turned to give curt orders to the men, and followed the blind man out of the room.

Despite the minutes that had passed, Nadine Nelson was just where they had left her. The secret-service guard sat easily on a gilt chair. Sydney Thames and the girl's cousin were alternately pleading with her to sit down. As the chief and Thornley Colton stepped into the room her teeth gripped her lower lip, and her hands clenched tighter at her sides.

"Who is the man who has been coming into this room every night to send those messages?" Thornley Colton's voice was hard, stern.

The face of the girl went white at the cruelty of it. Sydney Thames took a half step forward, and a gesture of the blind man stopped him.

"Who is he?" snapped the blind man again. She raised her head to look straight into his sightless eyes.

"My husband!" she answered defiantly.

"That isn't true!" The words came like the lash of a whip.

"Thorn!" In Sydney Thames's voice was agony that the man he loved could say such a thing to a woman.

"And you were the man I thought could help me!" Scorn, bitterness, self-accusation were in the vibrant voice of the girl. "You're worse than those curs who listened to every word! You've *killed* my father! If I were a man I'd kill *you*—even though you are blind!"

The last words came through her clenched, white teeth, and she advanced half a step, so that her hot breath reached the face of the blind man. But he only idly twirled his slim cane and looked down at her with a tolerant, amused grin that was maddening.

"You'll talk!" he promised curtly. "She'll talk in jail, chief!"

"I wouldn't talk if you tore me to little pieces!" she cried vehemently.

Colton did not answer; he nodded curtly to the chief, and with a "Come, Sydney!" he hurried from the room, and from the girl who stared straight ahead of her with dull, fixed eyes.

Sydney Thames followed him down the stairs silently. In the lower hall he spoke. "God, Thorn, that was barbarous! It almost made me forget—"

"Find the telephone and get me the number of the United Fruit Company," ordered the blind man sharply.

Without a word Thames found the 'phone in an alcove of the hall, and gave the number to Colton.

"What boat sails for South America today?" asked the problemist when the connection had been established. "The *Carracas*? Is there a bear consigned on that boat? Hasn't arrived yet? The sailing's at five? Thank you!"

As he hung up the receiver the angry boy's tone of Nadine Nelson's cousin came to them indistinctly. Sydney Thames jumped as though a pin had jabbed him. When he spoke to the blind man there was a look on his face that had never been on it before.

"Thorn," he said, and there was a break in his voice, "you've been the only father I ever knew, but I *won't* leave that girl to the mercy of those police brutes!"

"This is no time for sentiment!" snapped Colton.

"It is time for goodbye, then!" Sydney Thames, the colourless, the characterless, the counter of steps for the man who had picked him up, a bundle of baby-clothes on the banks of the English river that had given him the only name he ever knew, held out his hand.

The blind man's lips tightened; he ignored the outstretched hand as he pulled on a glove. "Make it *auf wiedersehen*," he said wearily. "Shrimp and I are going to catch the boat for Brazil at five o'clock!"

IV.

The Fee, red-haired, freckle-faced boy, who had become a member of the Colton household as the blind man's only pay for solving a particularly baffling murder case, eased his plaster-encircled arm on the rail of the *Carracas*, and watched with all the power of his round blue eyes the lowering of the big cage on the forward deck. As it swung for an instant on a level with the promenade deck on which they stood, the boy caught a glimpse of the shaggy animal under the canvas protecting-hood that covered the top and fitted tightly halfway down the sides.

"Gee, Mister Colton, it's certain'y got some claws on its feet!" observed the boy admiringly. A hitch of the rope jarred the cage, and brought forth a deep growl that could be heard above the creaking of ropes and the squeaky wheels of the stevedores' trucks as they rushed the last few cases of freight on deck. "There she bumps!" cried the boy as the cable touched the deck.

Then came a shriek of pain. "Gee whiz!" gasped the boy, and the blind man's cane felt him jump a foot. "One of the workin' men bent down to get the rope off the bottom of the cage, and the bear reached under the canvas, tore his arm with its claws. Darn it, but he's wicious!"

The bawling voice of an officer broke in: "Here, you men that own that bear! Unsling the cage!"

Three ragged, dark-skinned men jumped to the cage, and unslung the tackle ropes without arousing even a deep-throated growl from the animal.

The tense look left Thornley Colton's face as he heard the block slip to the deck, and for the first time in hours there came the slightest trace of satisfaction in the curve of the thin lips. He was right! Once more he had risked everything on his judgment and his wonderful mental ability to find logic in seeming chaos by following to their end the mind processes of men against whom he was pitted.

The proof had come with the shriek of the clawed stevedore. Thornley Colton's whole mind had been concentrated to catch one other sound among the multitude of noises. He had heard it and recognised it—the musical clink of glass on glass—the ring of a goblet! That had been the thing that had aroused the fury of the bear at exactly the instant that the workman was within reach of the tearing claws. That was the thing that had sent Dryden F. Nelson's daughter to jail, and had caused Sydney Thames to renounce the man who loved him.

"I'll bet nobody but them guys that own the bear'll go near him after this," observed the boy sagely.

"I don't think they will," the blind man said grimly. "Let's take a walk around."

The boy's eyes squinted along the deck from his feet to the rail at the other side. "It's ten steps," he calculated. "They's a man an' a fat woman five ahead lookin' down at the front deck, an' at the other rail there's a guy in a chair readin' a paper. Yuh gotta step out a bit for him."

"All right," nodded the blind man, as he started.

The boy walked at his side, and he avoided the man and the woman, but his foot seemed to slip at the steamer chair, and he fell sprawling into the lap of the seated man, sending the thin glass he had held in his hands behind the paper in a hundred pieces to the deck.

"What the devil!" snapped the hoarse voice of the man, as he angrily brushed away the sparks of fire that had fallen on his coat when the black-brown cigarette had fallen from his lips.

Instantly Colton was on his feet, apologising. "I am blind; I made a false step," he said contritely.

"Oh, all right," growled the man ungraciously.

The problemist started again on his walk. The grim lines had returned around his thin-lipped mouth, but there was no other change in the blind man's expression, not even triumph. Yet he had located the man he wanted; the man who had fooled the entire secret-service of the country for months! Reasoning had done it; the pure eliminative reasoning that was made possible by his lack of sight. The man into whose lap he had just fallen was the one who had aroused the bear's anger with the tap of his glass. He was the man whose pectoral cigarette papers and tobacco had scented the closet at the Nelson home. And he had recently handled a bear!

As his brain worked at lightning speed behind his high, white forehead, the blind man walked with the boy aimlessly around the decks, hardly hearing Shrimp's delighted chatter. The *Carracas* was in mid-stream now, her nose pointed toward the Narrows. Most of the passengers had gone to their staterooms, and the steam hissed from the winch cylinders forward as the last pieces of cargo were lowered into the hold. The blind man's ears were strained to catch each sound, or suspicion of sound that would tell him the things he could not see, and his brain counted the steps, measuring distance, memorising directions as years of training had taught it to do. Suddenly Colton realised that someone was following them, watching every move. A growingly familiar furtive footstep every little while as the shadow quickly dodged, whiffs of the Brazilian tobacco smoke wafted to his nostrils on sudden gusts of wind, told him more than eyes could have told. His fall, crude because of its necessity, had aroused the other man's suspicion.

"Show me our stateroom, Shrimp," he said finally. "Then you can come up on deck again. I'll remember all the steps."

"Gee!" grinned the boy, in huge relief. "I'm glad I don't have to stay down there. I wanta watch that little yacht that's comin' out."

Colton nodded. He knew why the "little yacht" was coming out. He knew she should be flying a flag with perpendicular red stripes—the flag of the revenue service. And he knew that on board her was Chief Whittson and his men, who awaited his signal.

The boy proudly opened the door of the little white room, and Colton closed it behind him. "Wait a minute, Shrimp," he said quietly. From his pocket he took a memorandum book and pencil. For a minute he wrote, then he handed the torn-out leaf to the boy, who read, with widening eyes:

> If you miss me for fifteen minutes, or see me on deck with the man I fell over, run to the wireless house and give the operator this message:
> John Jones, 56 Cedar Street, New York. Close.
>   Payton.

"Gee!" whispered the boy joyfully. "I *knowed* it was a case! I knowed you didn't mean what you said about not lettin' me in on anymore when I broke this arm. Gee!"

"Go up on the deck and see all the sights you can, Shrimp," smiled the blind man. "See you later."

The problemist sat down on the edge of the brass bed to go over the situation again and make sure that there was not a loose end. He had figured out on deck the only way, but he wanted to prove his reasoning by mental tests. The master counterfeiter, cunning, desperate, could do only one thing—eliminate the man he knew suspected him. And Thornley Colton could do but one thing—"watch" every minute the head of the gang. The success of the whole case depended on Colton's alertness in preventing the criminal from making one move that the problemist knew he would make the instant the master rogue discovered all was lost. Yet the presence of the man at the dénouement was *necessary!* Colton rose. He must take a desperate chance, just as he had taken them many times before.

He opened the door, and went down the narrow corridor, his brain automatically counting the steps it had registered when he entered. He stopped. He smelled the heavy licorice odour of the pectoral papers again. For an instant a grim smile flashed to his lips. He had followed the mind-processes of the man correctly once more. The smell of the smoke was too obvious; it had been overdone.

A stateroom door opened before him.

"Got a match?" asked a voice, and Colton understood the disguising of tone instantly.

The blind man held out his match safe; then the snarling whisper of the man cut the stillness, and he felt a gun-muzzle jab viciously into his ribs. "Get in here!" Colton quietly obeyed the order, and stepped over the threshold into the stateroom that was filled almost to suffocation with cigarette smoke.

"Put 'em over your head! Up!" The snarl changed to a sneer. "So you're the slick blind man that sister of mine talked about, eh? The lonehander that makes boobs of the police and secret service? Well, little bat-eye, I've been laying for you ever since I got wise to that slick fall trick. Got a damn' fine nose, eh, smelling that pec smoke I've been filling the lower deck with ever since you and the kid came down."

"Humour palls when the audience is forced to stand in so uncomfortable a position," said the blind man evenly.

He felt his own pistol snatched away.

"Back up a step, and you'll find the bed!" ordered the voice.

The blind man sat down and waited patiently. When the other man spoke again there was grudging admiration in his voice. "I've got to hand it to you," he admitted. "I didn't think there was one man on earth that'd get wise. Now I suppose you want the old man?"

"I want you first," Colton told him.

"You got me!" laughed the man with the gun. "But you haven't got me like you got that sister of mine, have you? She wouldn't say a word, would she? Well, it's a damn' good thing she didn't!"

"I knew that," said Colton quietly.

"You didn't think the wayward son could come back after ten years, with a counterfeiting process that couldn't be beat, and then get his father in on the scheme to pass the phony money through his bank, did you? And you didn't know that staid old Dryden Nelson would ever become head of the gang, and then slide out under the noses of the secret-service men. I guess he's the man you want to get, eh? Well, I'm the little man that's going to see that you don't!"

"I will find him when the time comes."

"You will, eh—you will!" Snarling viciousness dominated the voice. "Well, you won't! You, with your lone hand! Why, you poor boob, it'd take a gang to get me!"

"I had about concluded you were just taking a chance on a word dropped by Miss Nelson and a thing or two you might have heard of me," Colton said quietly. "I didn't think you'd dare have anyone near enough to get real information. This is one of the games where I don't play a lone hand. The boat that's been following us ever since we left the dock is the revenue cutter *Proctor*, with Chief Whittson and his men aboard."

The man ripped out an oath. "So that's it!" he snarled. "Fooled me, eh? Stand up! Put your hands behind your back! No funny work! I've tied men before with one hand."

Colton smiled at him sardonically. "If I am off the deck fifteen minutes Chief Whittson and his men will board the *Carracas*, and nab the fake owners of the bear. Quite a scheme, that. No one would ever suspect ignorant, ragged-looking, brown men with a dancing bear as counterfeiters, would they?" His tone was a burlesque of the man's own. "And what do you suppose the chief'll do when he finds me here? Tied up or dead makes no difference. I promised myself to get you, and get you alone.

But it'll be just as good that way." The mockery had died out of his voice at that last sentence; there was a tinge of bitterness that the man instantly recognised.

"Well, you couldn't put him wise to *me!*" gritted the man. "So you *are* a lone-handed worker, after all. Get up!" he commanded. Colton obeyed the jabbing gun-barrel. "I'm a single-hander, too!" went on the counterfeiter, "We're going up on the deck, and if there's a move to get me, out you go! This gun'll be in my pocket, jamming your kidneys every minute. Let 'em get the gang! I'm through with 'em! Let 'em have the bear, too! It'll be no good to anybody! I'll see to that. But if you even lift a finger to point me out—" He made a horrible gurgling sound in his throat that was more than significant. "Come on!" he ordered sharply.

They left the stateroom, Colton idly twirling his slim stick, the man at his side talking commonplaces in a grim tone that made them anything but commonplaces. To the passengers who saw them on the deck they were only ship acquaintances, but the blind man felt the gun-muzzle now and then in his side.

"We'll stop here," growled the man at the forward rail, overlooking the open deck below. "I want to be where I can watch those men of mine. Put your hands on the rail where I can see 'em!

Colton quietly obeyed, resting his elbows on the wood and dangling his cane over the edge. The crash of the wireless sender broke out; the blind man felt his companion grow tense as his trained ears read the dots and dashes. Then he knew that the message he had written so that the man who was an expert telegrapher could not suspect had flashed to the revenue cutter, "John Jones, 56 Cedar Street," meant nothing but a business deal.

Minutes passed. Below them the three ragged men lounged around the cage. Four or five other men, of the crew oft watch, stood around, scowling vindictively at the bear cage and its sleeping animal. Then came the thing that the blind man had been waiting for. He felt the big engines slow down. Not a muscle of his body seemed to move, but the knuckles of his right hand whitened as he gripped the end of his cane.

An oath came from the man at his side. "So you tricked—"

So sudden that it seemed but a whir in the light, the slim cane in the hand of the blind man swished around, straight for the other man's eyes. There had been not a warning move but a lightning turn of the wrist. The first instinct man has is to protect his eyes. The criminal obeyed it, forgetting all else. He dodged with a gasp. Colton's knees seemed to give way under him, he spun around on the balls of his feet like a cat; then his whole body straightened like a suddenly released whalebone, his right fist found the jaw of the other, and the master counterfeiter fell without a groan and lay still.

Colton's whistle rang out shrilly. A screamed oath came from the deck below. The sound of a struggle.

"Get the bear!" shouted Colton.

A shot rang out. Another. He could hear the big cage rattle and groan as the dying animal thrashed out its life. Around the cage seven men were struggling, the three ragged, dark-skinned men who had guarded the cage and the four men who had been apparently lounging sailors.

The blind man listened for a moment, then he smiled a grim smile. "A lone hand!" he murmured. "I hate assistants—but I'm not such an egotistical fool as all that!"

On the port side of the boat he heard the scrambling of men to the high, white deck. Then Chief Whittson's voice came:

"Did you get him?"

Colton touched the unconscious body of the man near the rail just as he would have touched the body of a snake with his foot.

"Where's Nelson?" asked the chief eagerly. "Down there in the false, canvas-covered top of that bear cage!"

"What!"

"Yes. Drugged! For God's sake get that suffocating cover off, and send for the ship's doctor."

The order was bawled to the men below. Willing hands ripped the cover to pieces, and on a thin mattress, in a steel-floored, steel-meshed upper compartment of the cage, was Dryden F. Nelson, white-faced, unconscious!

"By Heaven, he had his nerve with him to take that chance to get away!" gasped the chief, in admiration. "It's a new one! We'd never have suspected a bear cage in a thousand years. And we had every way out of the city guarded."

"Yes!" The word came as a half groan, half snarl, from the man on the deck, whom one of the secret-service operatives had just manacled. "He had his nerve! He's my father! And he's the greatest counterfeiter of them all!"

Thornley Colton leaned forward. He grasped a wrist of the man, and almost pulled the arm out of its socket.

"You dirty, lying cur!" he said, and his tone was one that he had never used before. "You forced that old man to serve you after he had discovered what you were doing! You forced the girl who thought you were her brother to protect you! By God, if ever a man deserved hanging you're the one!"

"He's my father!" grated the handcuffed man. "If I go to jail he'll go, too! He knows I'm his son!"

"You dog!" Colton's voice fairly shook with passion. "You fooled him into believing that you were his rotten-hearted son that died ten years ago. But you can't fool me! You may look like Joe Nelson! You may deceive even the eyes of a father! But I'm blind! Blind! I talked for an hour with a school chum who played in the football game in which Joe Nelson broke his wrist. You never had a broken wrist in your life! The bones are perfect!"

He turned to the chief. "Keep a careful guard on that cage, chief, until we get to the cutter. I think there's a million or so dollars that this dog got from Nelson's bank stuffed into that mattress!"

"Damn you!" The man half rose to his knees as he shrieked it. "I tricked them all! And you—"

"That's the confession I wanted to vindicate Nelson," said the blind man contentedly.

V.

Nadine Nelson rose as the blind man entered the room, her lips curved in a wonderful smile of joyous greeting, and she hurried across the floor to meet him.

"Can you ever forgive me?" he asked, in his rich, musical voice.

"Forgive you?" she cried happily. "Why, I could—kiss you!" She stopped, crimson-cheeked.

He smiled seriously down at her. "It was necessary, the way I spoke to you," he said gently. "Before, I did not realise how desperate the game was. I knew that your father's life hung on the thread of your silence. And I knew that the only way I could assure myself that you wouldn't break down and talk was to arouse every bit of that wonderful fighting gameness you have. The men who had your father would have killed him rather than risk getting him away if they thought there was a breath of suspicion."

"I know," she said; "I know—and understand."

"The ringleader talked a little to the chief on the way back in the revenue cutter," went on Colton. "He had been a pal of your brother's for years in South America. They worked together in a telegraph office in Rio."

"He was a wonderful operator," murmured the girl. "He is the only man I ever knew of who could imitate another man's touch on the key. That was the proof that convinced father that he was Joe. You know the touch of an operator on a sender is as individual as handwriting."

Colton nodded. "My knowledge of that fact is what threw me off the track at first. You knew your brother was implicated the minute you spoke of him in your room. I remembered then the stories I had heard of him. I remembered that he was fifteen years older than you, and was supposed to have been shot in South America ten years ago, where he went following some trouble here."

"Joe always was wild," the girl confessed softly, "though I only remember him as a big, strong brother who used to hold me on his knee while he told me wonderful stories. I couldn't believe sometimes that the man who was making daddy do such horrible things could be the brother I knew. But I couldn't convince father. The counterfeiter knew every incident of Joe's life, and there was the touch of the operator that father thought was so indisputable. I tried to get father to confess it all. I refused to carry him the messages that were left in my room after we knew the secret-service men were watching us, and that Joe and his men were next door. Then Joe—I can't call him anything else—"

"That is the name he has gone under for years," put in Colton.

"Then Joe rigged up the magnets and key," went on the girl. "He had to give father instructions every night where to distribute the counterfeit money that was packed in the vaults of the bank in place of the reserve. And he made father sell all his bonds to cover the shortage. Then, with the help of a watchman, who was another of the gang, they got the counterfeit money in to take the place of that father had gotten to make good. Every day Joe promised that he would make restitution, for he had made father believe that he had sent the money to Brazil for investment, and it would double in a month. So father hoped and prayed, and got years older every hour. The secret-service men were dogging every step, watching every move. Jail stared him in the face — and he believed the man he thought his son, believed that he would have the money to look the world squarely in the face once more.

"Then Joe told him one night, over the wire, that he had lost all. Father must go. I watched outside my door every night to see that Paul did not come near. I caught a word. I pleaded with father. For four days I fought against them. Then they won. I was at the door last night when father came running up the stairs, panting, half dead with the excitement of having slipped past the secret-service man. He darted past me. I followed. Joe grabbed me by the arm when I started to protest. 'Get downstairs and throw a fit because your father has gone!' he hissed. 'You'll be along in a little while, and be with him!' he finished, and there was a look in his eyes that frightened me. So you see it wasn't only acting in the library." She shuddered.

Colton understood, even more than she, for he had heard the confession of the master counterfeiter on the revenue cutter that had brought them all back to the city. He had learned then why he had taken such pains to get the old man away. The crook had not been satisfied to take every dollar of the old man's fortune. He had seen the girl; he had wanted her, and she was to have been the price of her father's life!

"The chief's men got the whole plant next door," he put in hastily. "It's a new process of bleaching one-dollar bills, and making hundreds from them with a new photographic process. The master crook had been perfecting it for years in Brazil, waiting for a big stake in New York. He put one of his assistants as correspondent of your father's bank down there. A year ago he had him write a humble letter asking for a position in New York. Your father gave it to him."

"Yes," admitted the girl. "And the man who took the position was the one who posed as my brother. He pretended to be very dull. That's why the secret-service men never suspected him.

When he had been in the bank three months, father discovered a shortage of sixty thousand dollars. He accused the man who came from Brazil. Father's bank, you know, is a private institution, and only has seven employees. The man confessed, and convinced father that he was Joe. He said he would make good the loss. And he did, with the clever counterfeits. That was the entering wedge. After that father was only putty in his hands. Six months ago he resigned, after seeing to it that one of his gang was put in as watchman and another took his place."

"That is when he took up his role as doctor," put in Colton, "and got his scheme of taking the poor Frenchman's house. And at the hospital they say the Frenchman will recover fully."

"And father is upstairs sleeping," she said softly. "You brought him back to me—and he knows that the man who tried to ruin him, the man who would have killed him if you had not been there to prevent him when the revenue men came, was not his son! That is the greatest of all! We owe you a debt that we can never repay; you and Sydney, here, who stood so bravely by when I thought all the world had turned against me."

She touched the arm of the black-haired man who had sat silent beside her, and he looked at her with a wonderful new light in his eyes. Gone, now, was Sydney Thames's great fear of women that had been his obsession all his life. He had met *the* woman.

"Can you ever forgive me, Thorn?" he asked, speaking for the first time. He had not even raised his eyes to the face of the man he had renounced that morning. Ever since Dryden Nelson had been brought back to his home, and the wireless message from the revenue cutter had opened the jail-door for the girl, his thoughts had been torturing him.

"I must forgive myself first," the blind man said quietly. "It hurt me more than anything else to talk to you like that. But a man's life hung in the balance. I could not tell you, for I knew you would tell the girl rather than see her suffer a minute." One of his rare smiles lighted up his face. "Let's make it a burned paper, more completely burned than the charred fragment I found in the Frenchman's house; the part of a note one of the outside men sent to the master counterfeiter. For on that my fingers read three words Joe, cage, *Carracas*. That finished the case—my case." And his sightless eyes seemed to look at them with understanding and joy.

8

The Eighth Problem:
THE EYE OF THE SEVEN DEVILS

I.

A jarring incongruity in the room of tapestries, silken-shaded lights, and furnishings of mahogany, the rough wooden box, with its dirty, scarred sides, scratched the top of the polished table in a hundred places without arousing even a murmur of protest from the four men who watched every movement of the little Japanese servant as he carefully pried the holding nails from the cover boards. A chorused "Ah!" came from four pairs of lips as the servant laid the chisel down and lifted the last board.

"Careful, Nesu," warned the frock-coated man with the white moustache and sun-tanned cheeks.

The dissipated-looking youth, with the Egyptian cigarette dangling loosely from his lower lip, rose to get a better view of the interior. "'Nough cotton stuffing there to fill a barrel, captain," he grinned, vacuously.

"Yes," nodded the white-moustached captain. "Nearly ten pounds, and the Devils are bound into place with nearly twenty yards of silk strips. A man takes a little care with a thing that's cost him forty thousand, Meynerd."

The Japanese servant pulled out a huge handful of cotton, and placed it on a spread newspaper as another of the group spoke. "Is it really worth that, captain?" he asked.

"Three times that, Joslyn. Forty thousand is only what I paid the hunchback outcast priest in the Yunling mountain monastery in Sze Chuen. He had had it hidden for nearly fifty years. The eye alone is worth sixty-five thousand, if it's worth a cent. The forty thousand I paid will buy the priest all the prayers he needs for the next hundred years; and they'll be the best prayers money can buy, at that." He smiled, grimly. "I needed a few of those same prayers on several occasions myself," he went on. "Especially on that three-hundred-mile journey through the Yunlings to Chingtu. I have an idea the priest wanted to steal a march on the prayers, and threw out a hint that the 'white dogs' had found the pearl-eyed Seven Devils of Sin. During the half century that had passed since he stole it, of course, it has been 'lost.'"

"Why didn't he return it instead of getting forty thousand dollars to buy prayer papers to burn for his soul?" asked Wilson, the fourth member of the group, taking his eyes from the busy-fingered Jap.

"Because he was a Chinese," explained Captain Richards. "He stole the thing when he had just entered the monastery, for a white man who bribed him—that's a long story in itself. The briber was killed the day of the theft. The young priest was suspected, and tortured until he became a hunchback and outcast, but no confession could be gotten. In the years the blame has been laid on the white man's devil, who stole the Chinese devils and took them to his home, when the white master was killed. The peculiar kink of the Chinese mind would not let the thief confess or return the devils. He couldn't see where the mere restitution would expiate his sin. The only way he could figure was to wait until someone came with enough money to pray him into heaven for a hundred years after he had gone. Peculiar cusses, the Chinese."

He rose at the last word, and the others rose with him. The Japanese was unwinding yard after yard of two-inch silken strips.

"Ah!" It was more than an exclamation: it was a three-manpower cry of amazement, wonder, and surprise as the captain lifted the thing from the box and set it gently on the table.

"Great guns!" gasped the dissipated-looking youth, backing away a step and stopping with a sheepish grin.

"The Seven Golden Devils of Sin with the single eye!" announced the captain, with a flourish.

The men stared at the most curious-looking object they had ever seen. At first glance it seemed merely a spidery collection of arms and legs; then seven figures stood out, separately and distinctly, grouped closely together. In the centre stood the shortest; around him, in every conceivable position, were six others. Their bodies were grotesquely deformed, their backs misshapen, their limbs twisted; and the genius who had fashioned the thing of his dull, hand-hammered gold in the centuries gone, had given to the bodies and limbs the distortion of horrible agony.

But it was the head; the single head that surmounted the seven bodies, which held their attention. The face was hideous; but in the very hideousness the gold worker had put cunning, power, strength. The thick lips leered a smile of satanic triumph; the cheek bones were high, oblique. And above the squat, wide-nostriled nose was a single eye! It was a pearl, perfect, flawless: milk-white against the red-yellow gold.

As they stared there seemed to come into the single eye of pearl a glow of red, as though the heart of the great jewel were a spark of fire that shone through the lustred surface. It was a trick of the lights, perhaps, or the reflected colour of the overhanging brow, but to the men who watched, it seemed that the eye held all the malevolence and cruelty of the Pit itself.

"The devilish thing gives a man the creeps!" growled Meynerd; and his hand shook a bit as he took the cigarette from his lips.

Joslyn laughed jerkily, for the spell of the thing was on him, too.

"Better cut out a few of those high balls, Mey," he taunted.

A flush of resentment mounted the youth's cheeks; but the captain forestalled his angry reply.

"Those figures represent the seven sins, each one enough to keep a Chinese from his heaven. The one in the centre, though the shortest and most horribly deformed of all, has the biggest and strongest body. That is Deceit, the most powerful of devils. The Mongolian reasons that none of the other devils can enter the heart of man unless deceit has entered first."

"Excellent philosophy, that," commented Wilson.

"That is why the head rests on the centre figure and the bodies of the others are bent forward to meet it," continued the captain. "Notice, too, that though the limbs are terribly twisted, and the bodies scarred to symbolize the awful punishment the gods have inflicted on the wicked seducers of men's hearts, the head is perfect, showing that the devils can still think with their one head, and plan traps for the unwary. And the eye"—his face lighted with the enthusiasm of the collector—"the wonderful eye that is all-seeing, alert to catch the first sign of weakening in the lowest coolie in the kingdom. That, gentlemen, is the thing I worked years to get; the thing that nearly cost me my life a dozen times—the Eye of the Seven Devils! The most wonderful pearl in the world; the pearl with a heart of fire!"

"Funny the thief priest didn't pry out the eye and sell it to buy his prayers, without risking getting rid of the whole thing," put in Joslyn.

"That's the wonder of the thing!" exclaimed the captain. "By some method that no one has ever been able to fathom, the maker of the thing set the stone in such a way that it can't be taken out without cutting the whole thing to pieces. The pearl appears merely pasted in its socket, but the microscope can see, in the space around it, that the jewel is gripped in four prongs that fit into tiny holes bored in the back of the pearl. The space around it is so narrow that no instrument of strength, sufficient to cut or break the prongs, can be inserted. And if it could, the very act would cause the gem to chip, and, perhaps, split. That is the way the maker made theft impossible!"

"Wouldn't mind having the pearl," growled Meynerd, "but I'd throw the rest of it in a sewer."

The tanned cheeks of Captain Richards went a dull red with anger, and his moustache bristled; but Wilson cut in to prevent an open break.

"Let's have a little drink."

The servant, who had stuffed the last silk strip into the empty case, straightened up.

"High ball," grunted Meynerd.

"Another absinthe drip," added Joslyn. "Bourbon," ordered Wilson, and the captain nodded.

Silence followed the going of the servant. The captain took out his watch, glanced at it, chewed his cigar almost nervously, and lounged back in the chair he had taken beside Joslyn. The eyes of the others wandered around the room, but always returned to the twisted bodies of the seven devils of the single eye. The thing of hand-wrought metal on the table seemed to exert an uncanny influence over men who had never known superstition. As the silent seconds passed there came a tension in the mood of all. Each found himself continually catching the other's eye, only to glance hastily and sheepishly away. And the twisted devil mouth leered at them; in the smouldering fire of the devil eye seemed infinite scorn.

The return of the servant with the tray of drinks made each one sit up eagerly. The Japanese went to the captain first and held out a card.

"Hustle the high ball," growled Meynerd. The Jap hurried over. Meynerd's unsteady hands had spilled a third of the liquor before Wilson took the small carafe from his shaking hands and poured the remainder over the ice. The youth growled monosyllabic thanks. Captain Richards whistled as Meynerd tossed his drink off at a gulp.

"Going to leave us, captain?" asked Joslyn, poking his straws farther down in the cracked ice of the absinthe.

Captain Richards looked up from the card he held between his thumb and forefinger. "Puzzling thing," he prefaced. "Here's the card of Ching Li Chu." His eyes went again to the pasteboard as he read: "Secretary to the ambassador at Washington of the Imperial Chinese Republic."

"What does he want?" asked Wilson. "That?" He jerked his head toward the table.

"How on earth—" Sudden decision cleared the look of puzzlement from the captain's brow. "Send him in, Nesu," he ordered,

"Chink devils, chink secretaries," grinned Meynerd. The liquor had pulled his nerves together again, and his lips curved in contempt when he caught Joslyn stealing a covert glance toward the table, as the door opened.

The man who entered, unquestionably a Mongolian, had a lean, intelligent face. The eyes, but slightly aslant, looked straight before him, giving no sign that they even saw the seated men, but stared fixedly at the table and its thing of gold. In the centre of the room the Chinese stopped and made a deep obeisance, once, twice, thrice. A low laugh of contempt came from Meynerd's lips, but the Chinese paid no heed. He walked to the table, and for several silent seconds gazed steadily into the eye of the pearl. With another deep bow he turned, his eyes searching each face.

"Captain Richards?" His voice was low, mellow, with no trace of accent.

"I am he!" The captain rose from his seat and bowed.

"So my information was correct; it is the Seven Devils with the True Eye." Again the Chinese bowed toward the figures. Once more Meynerd laughed sneeringly. This time the Mongolian turned toward him inquiringly.

"You do not mock me," he rebuked, mildly. "Your mockery is of the Seven Devils. I would be careful, were I you."

"Bah!" Meynerd set down his empty glass. "I didn't know you fellows worshipped devils, and little gold devils on a table, at that."

"Nor do we." Still that mild, even voice. "We worship our gods; but we are careful not to incur the wrath of our devils. The gods may forgive the ignorant mocker; the devils slay. That I believe, and I am no coolie, but a man educated in your own universities."

"Drunken kid!" muttered the captain, his fingers moving along the table-edge as he leaned against it. "You wanted to see me on business?" he asked the Chinese.

"Yes. I wish to pay you one hundred thousand dollars for the golden Seven Devils of Sin!" The amazement this announcement caused showed plainly on each man's face. The Chinese went on: "The new republic seeks to unite its people, but throughout the province of Chingtu it is known that the lost Seven Devils has been taken from the country. They demand that the new government see that it is returned if they are to believe that government's power. Our failure will mean a costly and bloody war, for the Yunling mountain men are fighters who know every inch of its vast slopes."

"So my six months of devious routes and constant guarding amounted to nothing." The captain's lips smiled grimly, but there was a light in his eyes that had not been there before.

"I suppose the priest is being honoured for having been told by the gods that the white dog had stolen the thing."

"Prayer papers have been burning this last five months for the hunchback," said the Chinese, quietly.

"Um." The smile left the captain's lips. He shook his head. "I will not sell," he declared, and there was finality in his voice.

It seemed a full minute before anyone spoke. The noiseless Jap servant industriously picked up small tufts of cotton that had fallen to the rug back of the table. Joslyn set his glass, with its green-tinged cracked ice on the table, clinkingly, and the captain's eyes left the Mongolian's face as the noise attracted them. Meynerd's lips still grinned contemptuously as he spun the piece of ice around in his empty high-ball glass.

"The devils can only bring sorrow to you." The voice of the Chinese was deep, full of sincerity. "Perhaps death, for in your country there will be mockers, and, as I told your friend, the devils slay those who mock them." His deep eyes rested on Meynerd. The face of the youth went red for an instant; then the sneer came back.

"Like to see 'em kill me!" he said, boastfully. "A chink knife in back might, but no pigeon-toed gang of devils with one eye could!"

"Do not speak that way!" There was stern reproof in the tone of the Chinese. "You may know the things of the West, but there are things of the East that you do not know!"

"Is that so!" Meynerd shook off the restraining hand of Wilson and stood up. The face of the captain went white with rage, and his hands fumbled with the handkerchief he had been in the act of lifting to his brow.

"Be a gentleman!" he snapped.

Meynerd paid no heed. "Here's to you devils!" he laughed, sneeringly. "Long may you wave—in a glass case!"

"The mockers kotow before they die!" The words came rapidly, almost hissingly, from the lips of the Chinese.

"Here's to crime!" Meynerd stood in front of the golden devils and drained the last drops of his drink. A gasp came from the Japanese as he backed away a step, his hand full of cotton tufts he had picked up from the floor. Captain Richards crushed the handkerchief in his hand as he brushed his lips. Every eye in the room was on the gently swaying man with the glass to his lips.

Suddenly Meynerd's face went livid; the glass fell to the floor. Slowly his knees bent. For a second he seemed to kneel before the leering face of gold. His body fell forward. His forehead touched the ground. Then the limbs straightened convulsively, and he lay still.

The seated men jumped to their feet, with exclamations of horror. The Chinese, face impassive, leaned over and touched the pulse of the man on the floor. Then he looked up into the faces of the three white-faced men who bent over him.

"He is dead," said the Mongolian, quietly. "The devils have slain."

Mechanically, involuntarily, they turned toward the hideous thing on the table. As one the startled cry came from three pairs of lips

"The Eye! The Eye!"

The twisted, thick lips of gold still leered at them, but where the eye of pearl had been, only an empty socket seemed to stare down at the dead man on the floor.

II.

"Pawn to king five and checkmate." Thornley Colton took a final puff of his cigarette, and dropped it in the ash tray beside the chessboard.

Sydney Thames, the apple-cheeked, black-haired secretary to the blind problemist, laughed ruefully. "I almost believe that you could beat me with pawns alone, Thorn," he declared, looking over the pieces on the board.

"Your whole game is attack," Colton observed. "You forget all about defence. Another?"

Thames merely nodded, and silently rearranged the pieces on the board. "Three and pawn again?" he asked.

"Yes, if you—" The ringing telephone-bell on the desk broke in, and Sydney rose to answer it. He returned almost on the run.

"It's Captain Richards, at the Wanderers' Club," he began, breathlessly. "He wants you at once. He said something about a murder, and the eye of some seven devils of sin, as near as I could understand."

Thornley Colton's mobile face, whose paleness was strikingly accentuated by the great blue circles of the tortoise-rimmed library glasses that shielded his sightless eyes from all glares, lighted up with interest. "Is he still on the wire?" He rose as he asked the question.

Thames shook his head. "He blurted out the message and rang right off. He seemed positive you'd come."

A faint smile came to Thornley Colton's lips. "I guess he knew that a single breath from the Orient would interest me." He touched the call-button on the desk that would summon the big black automobile instantly, at any hour of the day or night. "I hadn't any idea Captain Richards had returned. I haven't seen him for years." The smile left his face. "My fingers have been itching to see those wonderful Seven Devils I've heard so much about."

"Your interest in things Chinese is beyond me," confessed Sydney, as he followed the blind man out of the room and down the stairs.

"You were in college the last four years I spent in China, Sydney." Colton spoke as the chauffeur closed the tonneau-door of the touring car, and threw in the gears. "The lure of the East has never gotten out of my veins. To a man who can see, China must be wonderful. To me it is marvellous. Old, satiated of every human emotion before we discovered emotion; a viewpoint as incomprehensible as the hereafter itself; a character that cannot be visualized—why, Sydney, to men of eyes, the lure of China is the lure of a beautiful picture. To me it is the lure of the unattainable."

"Something like the mystery of woman?" asked Sydney Thames, seriously.

"Not at all." The slim cane waved an impatient gesture over the side of the car. "The so-called mystery of woman is her constantly shifting viewpoint dependent on outside influences; the mystery of the Chinese is his undeviating viewpoint."

"Too deep for me," laughed Thames; then he swung open the door as the car stopped before the great Gothic doorway of the Wanderers' Club.

The mantle of tragedy hung heavily over the luxurious, exclusive interior of the famous club as they entered. In the main lounging-room a small group of members talked in hushed whispers, and their nervous starts at each sound belied the reputations most of them had gained as travellers in countries where danger lurked constantly. The servitors, usually alert, swift to receive and execute an order, moved with lagging footsteps. Thornley Colton recognised the atmosphere of uneasiness immediately, and a cynical smile flashed across his thin lips as he understood the cause. The Wanderers, rich seekers of excitement and danger in foreign countries, hard-headed, with nerves of steel when face to face with violent death, had fallen under the spell of the uncanny, the supernatural.

The chief steward, from his vantage-point at the head of the stairs, spied them and hurried down.

"It's—they're upstairs, sir." A scared note was in his voice. "The physician has just this minute arrived. The police haven't been told. Captain Richards thought maybe—It's terrible, sir."

"Very, Peters," nodded Colton, absently, as he followed the man up the broad staircase, and to himself he muttered, "Lucky the police haven't had a chance to bungle it. Very, very lucky."

The instant they opened the door Captain Richards bounded across the floor to meet them. "Thank God you came, Mr Colton!" he cried, shaking the hand of the blind man with more than heartiness.

"Who was it?" asked Colton.

"Meynerd. The doctor's trying to find the cause of death now." He nodded his head toward the broad leather couch against the wall, with its grim occupant, and the physician bending over it.

Colton asked a dozen crisp, terse questions. The answers he got told him the whole story. The captain introduced him to everyone in the room, and Colton shook their hands, even to the obsequious Japanese servant, who stood patiently awaiting orders, near the wall.

The doctor finished his examination and straightened up. "Heart failure," he announced. "Brought on by alcoholic excesses, I should judge, and probably superinduced by excitement."

"Strange that the hand of God should have descended at the exact moment chosen by a thief to steal the pearl," remarked Colton quietly.

"You don't think it's murder?" There was a queer chokiness in Captain Richards's voice.

"*Yes!*" Colton shot out the word as he stood in the centre of the room, turning his head slowly, as though his sightless eyes were trying to surprise some expression of guilt on the white faces of the men. Wilson's hands gripped his chair-arms so tightly that the knuckles cracked. Joslyn stretched an arm toward the glass, with its green-tinged ice on the table, but withdrew it quickly, to let his hands fall on his knees. The Japanese servant's foot shifted nervously over a small wad of cotton that had fallen from his hands, minutes before. Only the Chinese was unmoved.

"Neither the gods nor the devils murder," he said. "They kill."

The blind man nodded toward him, slowly. "True," he answered, and his voice was serious. "But when the killing is done by human instruments, the law calls it murder."

"You are of the West," shrugged the Mongolian.

"But the whole thing is impossible!" There seemed almost a whine of incredulous protest in Captain Richards's voice.

"Does the impossible happen?" Colton's voice was sharp, curt. "No! But the improbable does! A hundred times a day! Every time a perfect match fails to strike an improbable thing has happened. Because that thing on the table hypnotized your eyes into waking the superstition that is the mental appendix handed down through the thousand centuries, you say that *it* is impossible. What is impossible? Meynerd's death? The fact that he was killed? My statement that he was murdered? Or do you mean that each one of you is so wise that no one could have deceived you? Yet the eye is gone! And even if the devils had killed Meynerd, would they have stolen their own eye?"

Each crisp sentence fairly sizzled as he shot it out. The hand that held his slim, hollow cane, that gave its messages to his supersensitive fingertips, waved up and down for emphasis, touching blindly the table, the golden devils, and some part of each man's body as he paced back and forth across the floor.

"A man can't give another man heart failure to kill him," declared the physician, pompously.

"Can't!" The smile on the problemist's face was sardonic as he faced the doctor. "Then no murder was ever committed. If a man's heart didn't fail he'd keep right on living. What caused Meynerd's heart to fail is the thing we've got to find out. Do you know how Meynerd fell?"

"No, immaterial details—"

"Very material!" The blind man interrupted brusquely. "Every diagnostician should be a detective, and I might mention right here that one of the greatest surgeons and diagnosticians in America is a blind man. You should know that a man standing as Meynerd stood, suddenly stricken with heart disease, would fall flat on his back. Yet he fell on his knees, his body bent forward so that his forehead touched the ground for an instant before it relaxed."

"By Jove—I supposed—" the physician sputtered his chagrin. Then his face brightened. "Some caustic, causing a griping in the intestines."

"Exactly." The sharpness had gone from the detective's voice now, and he spoke in his old calm, even tone.

"He drank a toast!" Even as he spoke, the doctor's foot crunched a bit of the broken glass on the floor.

"You'd have to analyze the rug," reminded Colton. "And who had the chance?" He looked around inquiringly.

"Wilson poured his drink!" The words came in a gasp from Joslyn.

Wilson sprang to his feet with an oath. "Are you accusing me of killing him?" He snarled the question, but his face was white.

"Meynerd had gulped his drink even before Ching Li Chu entered," suddenly remembered Captain Richards. "There was only a few drops of the melted ice-water in his glass when he stood before the Seven Devils."

"There are poisons that act after minutes have passed." The even, monotonous voice of the Chinese broke in.

"Do you think the poisoner knew to the second when Meynerd's drunken folly would take the turn it did?" demanded Colton; and each man in the room recognised the menace in his tone.

A gleam flashed to the eyes of the Mongolian for an instant, then vanished. "The instruments of the gods and the devils cannot fail," he answered, quietly.

"No poison known could be timed like that," declared Colton, positively.

"Right!" growled Wilson, as he resumed his seat and darted a glance of new-born hatred across the room toward the man who had virtually accused him of the murder.

Again came silence as the blind man stood in the centre of the room, alternately brushing the rug where lay the untouched pieces of the broken highball glass, and swishing at his trouser-leg. Across his high, white forehead, and at his eye-corners behind the round, blue glasses, innumerable fine lines deepened as his wonderful brain worked: visualizing each object in the room, every detail in the picture, every action that must have taken place at the instant of hopeless confusion when Meynerd had pitched forward on the floor.

Immovable, the men watched, each tense for the first word or movement to break the suspense. Sydney Thames sat in his chair, with his eyes fixed on the devils of gold. Ever since he had entered the room the thing on the table had held him fascinated. More sinister, more fiendish than ever, without its single eye of pearl, the empty eye socket seemed to glare at him as though it gloated over the repugnant fascination it exerted. Sydney had heard the captain's story; in his mind's eye he could picture the toast, the sneers, the fall. *Had* the devils killed Meynerd?—as the Chinese had said they would. Then his eyes narrowed slightly as they went to the Mongolian, whose impassive face showed nothing of the thoughts behind the bright, slit eyes. He had said that death would follow. He was a Chinese—of a race to whom a life means nothing; a race of mystery. Then his eyes went to the Jap servant who stood against the wall, patiently waiting permission to leave the room; then, at the two scowling men, who carefully avoided each other's glances as they stared straight ahead of them—at nothing. Wilson had poured the drink. Why had Joslyn been so quick to tell the fact?

Suddenly the swishing taps of the blind man's cane ceased; the lines across his forehead and at his eye-corners vanished. "There is one way." He spoke apparently to himself. "Only one way."

He crossed the room to the couch where the dead man lay, his face covered with a handkerchief. He pulled aside the coat, and unloosed a button of the thin silk shirt. From his vest-pocket he took a small rubber band, and the watching men saw him put it around the middle finger of his right hand, until the black rubber strands were deep sunken in the flesh. Then, gingerly, as though he were testing the heat of a red-hot stove, he opened the shirt, and with the tourniqueted finger gently touched the skin of Meynerd. Slowly, very slowly, the finger moved over the cold flesh of the dead man, then stopped.

"See, doctor!" He held the banded finger aloft. The physician's ejaculation of amazement was echoed by every other man in the room, but the unemotional Chinese and the well-trained servant. On the tip of the blind man's finger was a drop of blood!

"And see here!" His fingers, holding the shirt back, exposed an inch or so of the dead man's skin. Four men bent their heads to see the small smear of red Colton's finger had left when it had brushed away the single blood-drop.

"I don't understand." There was no doubt of the physician's bewilderment.

Colton pulled the coat back and stood erect. "The most diabolically primitive of all murderous weapons," he said. "A poisoned dart."

"But who? How?" gasped the captain.

"That's what we've got to find out," the blind man said, curtly. With his pocket-knife he carefully cut the strands of the rubber and gently massaged the swollen, blood-congested finger. "A nasty thing to try to locate with delicate fingertips," he remarked, casually. "A big chance that the thing hadn't penetrated its full length, as this one had, and a scratch would have meant another dead man."

Sydney Thames's face lost its last vestige of colour as he realized that once again the blind man had toyed with death. A hundred times had Thames seen the problemist—the benefactor who had picked him up on the bank of the English river from which came his only name—take his life in his hands for the sake of solving one of the crime-puzzles he loved; but always before there had been a chance for a fight against men with lesser brains. This time a single scratch of his feeling finger would have killed him instantly, horribly; just as the mocker of the Seven Devils had been killed by the man among them who had coveted the wonderful pearl that had been the eye. And that man—

Joslyn laughed a jerky laugh of nervousness as he turned away and reached out his hand for the glass that had held his absinthe. The ice had melted partially, and there was a half-inch or so of the pale-green liquid showing through the cracked-ice crystals.

"Don't touch that glass!" The command came, shot-like, from the lips of Colton. He lowered the slim cane that had touched Joslyn's leg and warned him of the movement.

Joslyn withdrew his hand as if it had suddenly touched fire.

"Why? Wh-y?" he gasped, and his face was pasty white.

"Because I don't want you to kill yourself!" The blind man's hand moved to pick up the glass. He held it up and gingerly poked into the ice with his fingers. A grim smile came to his lips, and he dumped the whole thing on the polished top of the mahogany table. Colton's eight fingers seemed to touch every piece of ice in a single instant, so quickly did they move. Then his forefinger separated a small pile of curiously-shaped crystals.

"Broken glass!" The exclamation came from the physician.

Colton corroborated him with a nod, and spoke to the still pasty-faced Joslyn. "Some of the smaller particles would surely have gone down your throat."

Joslyn's Adam's apple moved convulsively for a moment. "What is it?" he gulped, finally.

"The broken glass-tube that was used to shoot the poisoned dart; probably not more than two inches long, because of the short distance, and of the thinnest glass, with just this object in view."

"But how on earth did it get there?" puzzled Captain Richards.

"I'll bet it wasn't there five minutes ago Wilson cried; and every man in the room remembered Joslyn's movement toward the glass a few minutes before.

The suave voice of the Chinese cut in. "Might I be informed how one who is blind could know of the glass?" he asked.

"Because the cracked ice made an absolutely perfect hiding-place for fine pieces of broken glass. If dropped on the floor with the bigger, thicker pieces of high-ball glass, the difference would have been immediately noted. I discovered that it had been a frappéd drink when I walked up and down before the table and talked."

Ching Li Chu rose and bowed gravely toward the golden thing on the table. "Truly, the wisdom of the gods and of the devils is infinite," he said, in his even voice. "But one man has such a drink. The devils chose him to protect their emissary!"

"Pretty philosophy," admitted Colton, "made grim by the fact that someone must suffer for being the devils' tool." He turned to face the silent Japanese servant, who stood still by the wall. "Tell the steward he can notify the police now, Nesu."

The sunny Japanese smile that had been missing so long came to the little servitor's face, and he took a step forward to obey the order.

"What about the pearl?" asked Captain Richards, suddenly. "This man shouldn't get out until he has been searched. A sixty-five-thousand-dollar gem would tempt 'most anyone."

Colton broke in, amazedly: "Hasn't the search been made yet?"

"No." The captain stammered over the monosyllable. "I called you as quickly as I could get to a telephone, after warning everyone to stay in the room. I knew you were a member here, and clever at this sort of thing. The police are such assess, you know, and the scandal—"

Again the blind man cut him short. "Because there seemed no possible way by which the jewel could have been stolen—if the stories I heard of the famous Seven Devils, when I was first in China twenty years ago, are true—logically the jewel could be nowhere. Is that it?" he asked.

"Something like that." The tan on the captain's cheeks was a deeper tinge than usual.

"The jewel is nowhere." The Chinese spoke solemnly, earnestly, almost reverently. "The devils have merely hidden it from the sight of mockers. My government will give you one hundred and fifty thousand dollars for the Seven Devils without the True Eye."

"So that's it!" The captain's voice was almost a shout; the tone one of a man who has made a great discovery. "*You* have it! You killed Meynerd to make me sell, eh?" He advanced a step, threateningly.

"The police will attend to that part!" warned the blind man, curtly. "Search Nesu—or go yourself."

He turned to the table, and his wonderful fingers, each one an eye that could see things the eye of a normal man could not discern, touched the twisted limbs of one of the Seven Devils.

"Come over nearer the light, Nesu," ordered Captain Richards, and the serious-faced Japanese followed him around the table.

The attention of the silent men in the room was divided between the search of the Jap and Colton's examination of the thing on the table. At times the blind man's fingers moved swiftly over the dull-gold surface; at others they seemed to rest for seconds, unmoving, only to resume their journey, slowly. Each man in the room understood, subconsciously, that those marvellous fingertips would give to the sightless man a mind-picture as perfect as that their eyes had given them—more perfect, perhaps.

"All right!" There was a growl of chagrin in the captain's voice, as he finished the search. The little Jap pattered out.

"Didn't find it, eh?" Colton spoke idly, without raising his head. His right forefinger was gently probing into the empty eye-socket. He put his hand in his vest-pocket for an instant, then felt again where the pearl had been, first with one finger, then another.

"Strange," they heard him murmur. "Strange." Then he whirled to face them. "The prongs that held the pearl are unbent and unbroken! They are exactly as they were when they gripped the jewel! Yet it is gone!"

"I want to search you, Ching!" There was no mistaking the threat in Captain Richards's tone this time.

Calmly, disdainfully, the Mongolian raised his arms and stood ready. Richards explored every thread of his clothing. There was no doubt he had done similar things before; not a pin could have escaped him. He stepped back with a muttered curse of bafflement.

"Go through me, too." It was a snarl from Joslyn; the snarl of a man whose nerves are raw.

No second invitation was needed. Thornley Colton stood leaning against the table, his back toward the golden devils. He idly swished his cane and apparently watched every move. Wilson was searched—and there was nothing.

"The thief who had brains and nerve enough to commit that theft would certainly know enough not to have the pearl in his clothing," observed Colton, quietly.

"It's in the room here, then," growled the loser of the pearl, pacing the floor. "I'll tear it apart! That jewel was worth sixty-five thousand!"

"You haven't searched Meynerd's clothes yet. Everyone in the room had a chance to secrete it there—temporarily," suggested Colton.

The captain's face went white, and he shuddered as his eyes went to the body of the man whose death had been caused by the thing of gold he had brought into the room. "I'm not a ghoul," he choked. "The police can attend to that part of it."

"I think I hear them coming now; the tread is unmistakable." The problemist took a firmer grip on his cane with the hand that was not in his pocket. "They can mess things as badly as they want to now; I've finished." He took a step toward the door, then turned to face them—the captain, the physician, who had not spoken for minutes, Joslyn, Wilson, and the silent Chinese. "If you'll bring the Seven Devils to my house at six-thirty this evening, captain, I will show you the pearl, and handcuff the man who killed Meynerd!" Another step, and he halted again. "All of you must come, for only the guilty one will want to stay away. *All*, especially Ching Li Chu!"

III.

Guided by the touch of Sydney Thames's sleeve against his, the blind man made his way through the crowd of curious, idle persons, whom the sight of a policeman entering a building always attracts in New York. From the precinct station around the corner had come two uniformed men, and two detectives on the run, to answer the murder-call that had gone out. Colton and his secretary had met them coming up the stairs, and the problemist had given curt nods to their gruff greetings. Nearly every detective in the city knew the blind man and he knew all of them by the sound of their voices, just as he knew the voices of a thousand other men. A hundred times his abilities had made their efforts look ridiculous, and scores of the city-paid sleuths refused to believe that he was blind. Nor did anyone in the morbid crowd that opened before him suspect that the slight touch of cloth against cloth was guiding him in the darkness that had been his since birth.

Leaning back in the soft cushions of the tonneau, Thornley Colton lighted a cigarette and took several deep puffs. The machine had started without orders, as it always did when there was anyone around who might hear. For several blocks they went in silence; then Colton leaned forward.

"Osmuhn's, Fifth Avenue, Michael," he directed.

"A jewellery shop?" asked Sydney Thames, in surprise.

"Yes. I am going to make sure of every property for the last scene. There can't be a chance of failure!" There was an ominous ring in his voice.

"You speak as though you knew the murderer and the thief!" cried Thames, in amazement. "I don't see—"

"You *do* see!" interrupted the blind man, with unconscious sharpness. "Like the average person, you see too much. To any one with perfect eyes the whole thing is a jumble, for the murder of Meynerd was planned—devilishly planned—to make possible the one minute of hopeless confusion necessary to steal the jewel. The eyes of the men in that room could see but one thing, then—the mocker of the devils. Nothing could have drawn their gaze from Meynerd! That is the one fault of eyes. In great crises they numb every other sense!"

"But if you know the murderer, why not arrest him at once?" asked Sydney, his brain trying to fix upon the one man who could be guilty.

"Because I'm not a policeman. The arrest of the guilty person is always secondary, with me, to the complete solving of a problem. A crime-puzzle is never solved until the guilt of the prisoner is established beyond *all* question. No, Sydney, I'm not a detective, for a detective arrests, and then tries to fix the guilt. I fix the guilt first. That is the problem in this case!"

"Joslyn and Wilson certainly acted queer," mused Sydney. "The Chinese, too, seemed strange." A new thought flashed to his mind. "There is something Oriental about that murder!" he exclaimed, suddenly. "A dart, and a poison which could act like that!"

Colton nodded as he flicked his cigarette into the street. "Devilishly Oriental, Sydney," he said, quietly.

"Ching Li Chu!" gasped Sydney. "He—"

"Is secretary of a foreign legation, and therefore immune from arrest. Also, I think he could prove absolutely that he was standing in such a position that he could not have shot the poisoned dart at Meynerd!"

The machine swung into the curb before the shop of Osmuhn & Son. Colton alighted and hurried into the shop, followed by Sydney. He knew every step here, for he had learned them in the days when the problem of the Thousand Facets of Fire had interested him.

The elder Osmuhn came forward with a smile of welcome and extended hand. Colton swung his slim stick under his left arm and extended his left hand; the other had been in his pocket since they had left the room in the Wanderers' Club.

"I want to get an imitation pearl the size of this fingertip, with small holes drilled in the back at exactly these distances apart." He drew his right hand from his pocket, and Thames saw that his right index-finger was smudged with ink, and on the middle finger were four dots of black, at equal distances around the fingertip. "A bit of ink from my fountain pen on the four prongs, then I got the marks, to tell me where the holes had been, when I poked my middle finger into the eye-socket," he explained to his secretary.

"Come into my office," requested Osmuhn.

"We have some imitation gems that we use merely to show sizes. They wouldn't fool an expert for a minute."

"I don't want them to," Thornley Colton smiled, faintly. "I only want him to feel the gem."

"Ah, another of your problems." Osmuhn pulled open a velvet-lined drawer. "Hold out your finger, please." He adjusted a small caliper over the tip, and with a smaller one measured the distances between the dots. "How soon do you want it?" he asked, when he had made several cabalistic notes on his small desk pad.

"As soon as possible."

"In two hours, then."

Colton nodded and hurried out.

"Police headquarters," he ordered, when the tonneau-door had clicked shut behind Sydney.

"So soon?" asked the secretary, in wonderment.

"Griffith and Jensen, the two detectives we passed on the stairs, are, perhaps, the most dull-witted in New York. Naturally they'd be on hand in a case like this. The thing will be bungled hopelessly if I let them have their way. After they have been shown the facts I gathered"—a grim smile hovered on his lips for a second—"they'll have everyone in the room under arrest, even Captain Richards. I want them all—all—at my house tonight."

Thames knew the futility of further questions. Colton would do the thing in his own way, and explain when the time came. So they rode in silence to the big building that housed the central departments of the big force.

"While I'm inside, Sydney, call up Shrimp and tell him to get an inch auger and the most powerful pocket tubular flashlight he can buy."

"An auger and a flashlight?" repeated the secretary.

"More scenery," explained the blind man, laconically. "If I had been in the room when the murder was committed, my lack of eyes would have enabled me to detect the murderer-thief in the very act. Now I must carefully work on his nerves until I have the confession. And I'll do it!"

Again there was the ominous ring in his voice that Sydney had noticed every time the blind man spoke of the murderer.

With a curt nod of emphasis, Colton turned on his heel and walked briskly into headquarters, unerringly finding his way through the corridors he had travelled many times before.

There was no doubt of The Fee's delight when Sydney Thames gave him the strange order. "Gee! Anoder case!" came his squeal of joy over the wire. "An' the arm I got broke in the gilded-glove thing is all right. You bet I'll get 'em!"

Sydney smiled as he rang off. Nothing pleased the freckle-faced, blue-eyed boy, with the slightly-twisted nose, who had become a member of the Colton household at the conclusion of a particularly baffling murder case, like participation in one of the blind man's problems. But since the affair of the gilded glove, Colton had been careful to keep the irrepressible youngster out of all harm's way.

For half-an-hour Sydney sat in the automobile and puzzled over the theft and the murder, the use of the imitation eye, the request for an auger and a flashlight. Then Colton came out of headquarters.

"One more stop," he said, as the car glided away from the curb. "Five o'clock," he announced, as his fingers touched the face of the crystalless watch in his pocket. "Just time for the call, a hurried bite, and then the dénouement." He leaned forward to speak to the driver. "The Waldorf," was the order he gave.

At the big desk of the famous hotel, Colton's low-voiced inquiry brought an involuntary ejaculation of amazement from Sydney Thames. The blind man had asked for the Chinese ambassador.

"Not here!" declared the man at the desk with a positiveness that only hotel-clerks can assume when they are lying.

"Tell him I'd like to see him in regard to the Seven Devils of Sin." Colton's voice was quiet and even, but there was something in it that commanded respect—and got it.

"I'll see!" The clerk turned to the house switchboard, and a few minutes later Thames and the blind man were being ushered to the suite of the diplomat. The ambassador, unlike his secretary, who had worn clothes of the latest cut, was dressed in robes rich with embroidery. He looked at them inquiringly as they entered, and the man at his side bowed deeply.

"His excellency bids you welcome," the interpreter said, in precise English.

"I came to tell you that the eye of the Seven Devils has been stolen, and one of my countrymen murdered to make the theft possible," Colton said, without preamble or preface.

The interpreter might have been a graven image for all the expression that came to his face. He bowed again, and spoke in Chinese to the ambassador. When the diplomat had answered him, he spoke again to Colton.

"His excellency says that the thing of which you speak is impossible. The devils would not allow it. The eye of the Seven Devils of Sin disappears for a week every hundred years, and has done so for centuries at the Yunling temple."

"Ah!" There was a note of quiet satisfaction in the problemist's voice as though sudden light had been thrown on an obscure point. "How did his excellency know where the devils were?" he asked, gravely.

For several minutes the two Chinese talked. Colton stood in the middle of the floor, idly switching his trouser-leg with his slim stick, apparently paying no attention to the two Chinese. But Sydney Thames knew that the keen ears of the blind man were taking in every word; for he knew that the problemist understood the language perfectly! What were the two Mongolians talking about? Why the discussion before such a simple question could be answered?

Then the interpreter spoke. "The gods decreed that his excellency should know the exact place and the hour at which it would be ready," he said, solemnly. "The devils stirred to anger the people of Chingtu against the white rogue who so cleverly outwitted the Yunling mountain men. But the gods found him, after months had passed, so the anger of the devils might be appeased and the people made content."

"Thank you."

Sydney Thames thought he detected a dryness in the words, but the look on the blind man's face as he left the room augured ill for someone.

"I can't see how apparently intelligent men can believe such rot!" declared Sydney, impatiently.

"The undeviating viewpoint, Sydney, the undeviating viewpoint. That religion has been ingrained for centuries and tens of centuries. No Western knowledge can ever change it." A peculiar smile came to his lips. "They never consider the incongruity of the gods helping them find devils—no more than they would consider a human life beside that thing of gold we left on the table at the club."

Thames tried to read the expression on the blind man's face; but there was no expression. Was the Chinese the murderer? Then what could the problemist do alone? What had been the object of those apparently irrelevant questions? And why had Colton pretended he knew no Chinese?

"One thing more, Sydney." The problemist stopped beside the operator's desk at the telephone-booths. "Call up the club and tell the president that I'll contribute enough to have that upper hall re-decorated. Tell him that the workmen will be there tonight. It's about time it was fixed."

Sydney asked no questions this time. He merely obeyed the order. During the hurried, silent meal that followed, he was all at sixes and sevens, and his brain fairly reeled as the questions raced, shuttlelike, through his mind. The Chinese had known the exact hour the thing would be unpacked at the Wanderers' Club. The secretary had virtually threatened Meynerd with death. Yet Colton had said Ching Li Chu had not been in a position to shoot the poisoned dart. Who had been in the right position, and how did the blind man know? He had not asked the positions of the men. There were Wilson and Joslyn. What of them? He remembered stories he had heard of the men. Joslyn was an absinthe-drinker, supposed to have an independent income. But what was the source of that income? Sydney had never heard. Wilson was noted for his temper—but the crime was not that of a man with temper. It was cold-blooded, devilish.

"Six o'clock." Colton paid his check and hurried down the winding aisle of tables, his brain unconsciously counting the steps it had registered when he entered. "Get me a paper, Sydney," he asked, when they were on the sidewalk once more.

Sydney hailed a boy and bought one. At the first sight of the black headlines he gasped aloud.

"They've arrested Nesu!" he cried. "The two detectives took him to headquarters!"

He saw again the quiet little Jap; the one man he had never suspected! Colton had said that the murder was devilishly Oriental; he had said that the Chinese had not committed it. The Japanese was the guilty one! He must have been standing at the side of the table opposite Meynerd, for Sydney had seen the cotton tufts he had dropped. And the police had beaten the blind man; they had gotten ahead of the problemist who had scorned them so often. Sydney could see them laughing up their sleeves at the man he loved.

"It's a shame, Thorn!" he choked.

"It is," admitted Colton, quietly. "But better a live prisoner than a dead freeman. I asked the chief to arrest Nesu, for he would have been the next victim of the poisoned dart!"

"The next—" began Sydney, dully; but Colton did not let him finish.

"Yes, but we haven't time to discuss it now. Run up to Osmuhn's, and get the fake pearl. I'll take the car, and you can come home in the subway. There's a little job Shrimp and I have to do."

Once more Thames silently did as he was told, and when he got back to the old-fashioned, brownstone house in the upper eighties, he found the blind man carefully studying two deep scratches in the polished top of the library table.

"All right, Shrimp," called Colton, without raising his head.

Thames looked around, but could see no sign of the boy; he was not in the hall, nor in the music-room. He opened his lips for the question, then the electric front-door bell tinkled its announcement.

"The jewel! Quick!" Sydney Thames thrust the imitation pearl into Colton's hand. For a second the blind man rubbed it between his flexible fingers. With a nod of satisfaction he dropped it carelessly into his lower vest-pocket, and was sitting on the table, feet dangling, smoking a cigarette, when the servant entered to announce the four men.

Captain Richards came first, and in his arms, held as carefully as though it were fragile glass, was the Seven Devils. He grunted in relief as he set it down on the table and mopped his sweat-beaded forehead. Ching Li Chu, who had been at his heels, remained standing, straight and rigid, beside the thing of gold on the table. Joslyn, who could not seem to keep his twitching fingers still, flopped into a chair without even a grunt of greeting. Wilson seemed strangely cool, and calmly chewed an unlighted cigar as he shook hands with the blind man and his secretary.

"No trouble getting us all here together," he grinned. "Not one of us has dared leave the other's sight all afternoon. Sat like bumps on a log glaring at each other, and trying to figure which of us was a murderer."

"For God's sake, get it over with!" Joslyn licked his dry lips with his tongue, and his voice was shaky. "The police were going to arrest all of us until their brains got untangled, and they took the right one. What d'ye want us here for, anyway?" he demanded.

"To show you the eye of the Seven Devils," Colton said, quietly. He moved the golden image along the table, and carefully placed it in the centre, facing the five chits that were drawn up against the wall. The blind man was very careful of the placing, and his secretary knew that he was putting it exactly over the scratches. Why?

"I told you not to drink so much absinthe this afternoon, Joslyn," put in the captain, impatiently. "Your nerves are all gone." He spoke to the problemist. "Are you really going to find the eye?" he asked, and there was a note of disbelief in his voice that Sydney Thames instantly resented.

A nod was Colton's only answer.

Richards shook his head doubtfully. "Where that infernal Jap could have hidden the thing is beyond me. We literally tore the room to pieces, and picked the cotton apart, tuft by tuft." His voice changed suddenly. "Did you find it?" he demanded.

The blind man straightened up. "Take seats," he invited, for he had apparently not even heard the question. "You, too, Ching; the devils won't get away."

"The ambassador said that I must guard them," replied the Chinese, simply.

"I expected he would," declared Colton. "I saw him for a few minutes this afternoon."

"You did!" The exclamation came from Captain Richards.

"Yes. I'd like to speak to you a few minutes in private, if the others will excuse us?" he turned to them, apologetically.

"Long as you like," granted Wilson, lightly.

"Have it over with!" snarled Joslyn.

Colton put his hand on the captain's shoulder and drew him to a far corner of the room. For several minutes they conversed in earnest whispers. The blind man's back was toward the seated men, but they could see him making gestures of emphasis with the hand that was not resting on the captain's arm.

The captain nodded emphatically, and they returned to the others. His face was grave, unreadable, but Sydney Thames saw a look of satisfaction gleaming in his eyes. So the blind man had convinced him that the pearl would be recovered!

They were all seated now, even the Chinese. Colton leaned against the table beside the seven golden devils, and faced them. His fingertips felt of his crystalless watch.

"Ten minutes of seven," he said. "At seven o'clock the jewel will be returned. Seven has been a mystic number for centuries."

Wilson laughed shortly. "You're worse than the Chinese, Colton," he accused.

"Rot!" growled Joslyn.

"You know that seven is the number sacred to our devils?" asked the Chinese, gravely.

An inclination of the blind man's head was his only answer. Silence came. The minutes slowly ticked past. As time went the men again felt the sinister influence of the thing of gold before them; just as the blind man had intended they should. Joslyn could not keep his twitching hands still. Wilson bit through his cigar and muttered a curse as it fell to the floor. Even Captain Richards nervously tapped his vest-front with his fingers. Sydney Thames shifted uncomfortably. What was going to happen? Was this merely another of the irrelevant, apparently senseless things?—like the others of the afternoon.

Colton's voice, low, solemn, broke the stillness.

"The murderer of Meynerd can never receive his full punishment on this earth. He has murdered thousands!" Every man straightened in his chair. "For years he has lived on the blood of innocent women and children, and for years I have waited this opportunity. Thank God it has come!"

From the lower hall came the first stroke of seven. The blind man stood facing them, hands resting lightly on the table at his sides. The mellow note of the second stroke came. Unconsciously each man's muscles tightened for something—they knew not what. Week-long seconds passed before the gong sounded the third time. Still the blind man did not move. He stood there as rigid as the hideous, eyeless thing of gold beside him.

"Do not move!

With the snapped-out order came darkness, black, impenetrable. An indrawn breath sounded hissingly, sucked in through tight, clenched teeth.

Again the clock sounded. From over their head, behind them, came a single shaft of soft, white light. In the small circle of brightness the face of the Seven Devils leered at them. And over the squat, wide-nostriled nose the single eye of pearl, perfect, flawless, gleamed with its spark-red heart!

An animal-like snarl broke the silence. Sydney Thames felt the sweeping rush of a body past his chair; heard body meet body in struggle. He knew one was the blind man. The other—

He made a move to rise and snap on the lights. Some subtle fifth sense of the blind man seemed to tell him the very thought in his secretary's mind. "Stay where you are!" came his command. "Don't touch the lights!"

Came a crash of a falling body.

The blind man's voice cut the blackness. "You would, eh!" He followed in with a half-dozen words in Chinese. In the tone was some terrible accusation, and they seemed to goad the other to madness.

"Your devilish Oriental poisons will never kill another!" There was not even a catch in the blind man's breath; but the men who could not move a muscle heard the sobbing gasps of the other. Suddenly came silence. Then two sharp clicks of snapped handcuffs.

And as though the clicks had been a signal, the lights came, and with them the voice of Thornley Colton, quietly triumphant:

"The murder of Ralph Meynerd will at last bring you the death you have deserved so long, *Captain Richards!* Yes, the pearl you have been assuring yourself you still had in your pocket is an imitation. I took the real eye from you while we were talking in the corner. My fingers might make me a successful pickpocket."

He turned to face the doorway, and there the dazed Sydney Thames saw the wide-eyed Fee. Behind him were two stalwart detectives.

"The prisoner I promised your chief," Colton said, shortly.

They came forward and jerked the cursing man to his feet. "One minute!" commanded Colton. He faced the Chinese. "The Seven Devils was stolen from your temple. It is yours. Take it."

"Damn you!" shrieked Richards. "You—"

For a silent second Colton's eyes seemed to stare at him, then his eyes dropped.

"Take it to its true owners," repeated Colton.

"But first, see!" He went to the golden thing on the table. One hand, held cuplike, under the eye. A finger touched the toe of one of the figures. The eye dropped to his hand! "The true secret of the image," he said, quietly. "The prongs, by some method of a forgotten genius, open by the pressure of one of the toes. That is how it was stolen in the instant you could see nothing but the dead man before you!"

IV.

An alcohol-soaked bandage around his eyes to ease the splitting headache the loss of four hours of sleep in the afternoon had caused, Thornley Colton sat in the darkened music-room. Hours before, the hand-cuffed Captain Richards had been led away, cursing, raving, blaspheming. The table in the library where had been the wonderful Seven Devils of Sin, was empty now, but in a room at the Waldorf four sleepless Chinese guarded the sacred thing with their lives; praying alternately to it and to their gods in thanks. Under the waters of the Pacific had already sped the news that the True Eye would again look from the altar of the Yunling monastery. The Chinese ambassador had come personally to thank Colton. He had promised the blind man honours, decorations, and Thornley Colton had smiled them aside.

"A curious crime; that of committing a murder to steal the thing he already owned?" The blind man repeated the question Sydney Thames had asked minutes before. "Yes, it was a curious crime, Sydney. But Richards knew that he was dealing with a curious people; he had dealt with them for thirty years. He understood perfectly that a Chinese who knew the legend regarding the impossibility of theft would not deviate a hair's breadth from his century-old ideas. The devils would not let it be done; therefore it could not be done. The disappearance of the eye—coupled with the century vanishings which, of course, the captain knew all about—would only make the Chinese more anxious to get the image. It would prove to his peculiar mind that the devils had not lost their powers in the years they had been gone. You heard him raise the price. You saw Richards's clever acting then; though he must have known that Ching couldn't be found guilty of the murder. He would have seen to it that at the time of the killing the Chinese was in the wrong position to shoot the dart. He was wise enough to know that police suspicion would be immediately directed toward the Mongolian, but it was no part of his game to have him arrested. The others could have sworn Ching could not have committed the crime.

"The reason for it all is very simple—money. Richards, temple-looter for years, knew that this was his last game. No collector would have given him more than a hundred thousand, and that would have included the eye. He could not have substituted a gem that would deceive an expert. And by murdering in such a way as to make the Chinese think it was the work of the devils, he could have sold the image to the Chinese government for two hundred thousand *without the eye!* They would have staked their lives on the pearl re-appearing in some supernatural manner the minute the thing was restored to the monastery. And by killing Meynerd, Richards would gain the eye; an extra sixty-five thousand dollars. That was the price of the boy's life. It was Richards, too, who sold the jade god that caused the Boxer trouble that cost the lives of a thousand innocent women and children, and lives of ten thousand men to net him twenty-five thousand dollars!"

"He did that?" gasped Sydney, horror in his tone.

"Yes. He stole it and laid the blame on a white missionary to save his own worthless hide. That caused the first massacre. How he aroused the people of Chingtu over the Seven Devils I don't know, but he had been in China long enough to learn all of the underground methods. He must have stayed there months to get the people in a proper spirit to make the government willing to go to any lengths to prevent an insurrection. Then he picked New York for the final scene. He joined the Wanderers' years ago, and no one knew that his money came from the loot of temples and the blood of massacred women and children. I did, but I could do nothing but wait.

"See how carefully he picked his audience. Meynerd, drunken kid, could be depended upon to mock the serious

Chinese. Joslyn, whose nerves were shattered by absinthe, would surely act suspiciously because of his very nervousness. Then Wilson to add fuel. And the Chinese! The scene was laid just as he has probably laid dozens of others.

"How he learned the secret of the devils' eye I don't know, nor care. Perhaps he learned it accidentally. Perhaps he picked it up in some obscure corner of the kingdom during his years of wandering. But he never thought that my supersensitive fingertips would discover it, though his bringing of Nesu to the window was done so that he could get into a position where he could watch me. But I had found the thing in an instant, and while he watched I carefully kept away from it. The minute my finger felt the unbent prongs I knew they must have opened, and the toes would be the most ingenious place for the manipulator of them.

"It was he who notified the Chinese ambassador the exact hour he would unpack the image. I wanted to make sure of that, so I went to the Waldorf. I knew the thing was important enough to bring the diplomat all the way from Washington, though I knew, too, as Richards did, that a secretary would make the first visit."

"How do you know that Richards told them?" asked Sydney. "Was he the 'gods' they spoke of?"

"The discussion between the ambassador and the interpreter before they answered my question told me that. While they spoke of the gods they mentioned a note sent the night before from New York. Of course, I was careful to conceal the fact that I understood Chinese, because I knew they would never tell anyone of that. To them it was a decree of the gods; and a state secret."

"And Richards deliberately killed Meynerd to make the one necessary minute of confusion?" put in Sydney.

"It didn't matter whether it was Meynerd or not. But luck was with him; luck and the working out of the chance on which he had invited Meynerd as one of the party. The poisoned dart, in its short glass-tube, was in his handkerchief. I also took that from the pocket of his frock-coat when we talked in the library, and in it were fine glass particles. He hadn't even thought it necessary to get rid of the thing. A simple crushing of the tube in his handkerchief when a breath had sent the dart on its journey of death, the dropping of the pieces into Joslyn's drink, where eyes would never have seen them, was the work of an instant. Of course, if Joslyn hadn't had the frapped drink Richards needed as a hiding-place, the captain would have ordered one for himself. But there was one break in the programme. The Jap saw the theft of the jewel."

"How did you know that?"

Colton smiled grimly. "The keyboard of silence again. When I shook hands my index-finger on the Jap's wrist told me that his heart was pounding like a trip hammer. A mere death would never have excited an Oriental like that. For a time I suspected that he had shot the poisoned dart, and the captain had stolen the jewel. But the glass in the ice instead of the cotton, and the captain's gentle manner toward him, proved that they were not working together. If they had been accomplices Richards would have acted harshly to avert suspicion. He was trying to convince the Jap that silence would mean a share of the theft. But I knew Richards wasn't the kind to divide, or pay blackmail. The poisoned dart was too easy. There wasn't a chance to end the Jap's life in the room, for I knew the captain would have hardly dared bring two darts and tubes. There was always a possibility of his being searched by the police. At the first opportunity outside, though, puff! A dead Japanese who would tell no tales. Therefore I had the police arrest Nesu because Captain Richards probably had another one of his devilish darts somewhere around the club."

"But the pearl?" demanded Sydney. "Why didn't you search Richards before we left that room?"

"Do you think he would have taken such pains to hide the broken tube and then have kept the Pearl?" asked Colton, dryly. "He hid the gem in a previously picked-out place when he left the room to call me on the telephone. Suppose I had arrested him; suppose we had torn the club apart and found the jewel. Would Captain Richards have gone to the chair for murder? Not with an American jury, and the mass of other suspicious things that would make more than a 'reasonable doubt' of his guilt.

"So I arranged tonight's affair for a denouement. I knew his nerves weren't steel, for he had shown that when I told him to search the body of the man he had killed. That was a little too much even for him. Then I got the 'eye' while I pretended to tell him of a plan I had to make Joslyn confess. I substituted the fake pearl that would feel just the same in the darkness, because the whole thing depended on his having no premature suspicion. My announcement that workmen would be on hand to re-decorate the upper hall of the club, the place he must have chosen because of its nearness, forced him to take the pearl from its hiding-place tonight. He had to bring it here because I timed the thing so that he would have no chance to find another hiding-place. During the afternoon he probably saw to it that Joslyn kept on drinking absinthe, though Wilson's drinks only seemed to straighten out his nerves.

"It was simple, very simple, but I have waited years for the opportunity; ever since I heard the true story of the Boxer uprising from the lips of a dying coolie who had helped to steal the jade god. I knew my chance would come some day, and the cocksure attitude I always took when Captain Richards was around, I knew would make Captain Richards welcome the opportunity to amuse himself by watching me try to solve a puzzle. That Chinese sentence I used there in the darkness told him for the first time that I knew all about him, and he realized then that I had been waiting for the chance his egotism had brought me."

Sydney Thames's lips curved in a superior smile. "And the Chinese can only see it as the working-out of the gods' decree," he murmured.

The blind man leaned back in his chair and blew a thoughtful smoke ring toward the ceiling. When he spoke his voice was low, almost reverent. "A half-century ago the thing was stolen by a young priest who did not know the secret that had been carefully guarded by the highest priests for centuries. Fifty years later it passes into the hand of a white man, and is brought thousands of miles to New York. A man is killed, another is in a prison-cell, and the devils are returned by one who is blind. The working of the gods? I wonder, Sydney, I wonder."

Silver Sandals

PREFACE

As you read this story you may be inclined to remark: "His perceptions are too remarkable." "A sense of touch too delicate." Yet here is an article which appeared some time ago in *People's Magazine* preceding a short story which contained the same character that appears in "Silver Sandals," and which will probably make interesting reading to you. To the great majority of people blindness is a synonym for helplessness. This isn't at all remarkable. The mental conceptions of most humans are based on what their eyes have seen. The hobbling blind beggar, with his cane and dog, comes instantly to the mind when one's thoughts turn to those who are sightless. But have you ever realized that the straight-shouldered man with the confident stride and the snappy step of health, who makes his way through the Broadway crowd, may be as blind as the beggar who shuffles along the edge of the pavement? You wouldn't believe it, probably, if someone told you; simply because his actions are the actions of a man in possession of all his faculties. But there are men to whom, for all practical purposes, eyes would be almost as superfluous as the vermiform appendix. Does that sound ridiculous?

*****

Of course, you have heard, or read, or perhaps have seen, the wonderful Helen Keller. Helpless? A thousand times no! Helpful is the word. But did it ever occur to you that the very lack of sight might be itself a big factor in the development of her wonderful insight, her remarkable grasp of big subjects, the human appeal in her written words, her beautiful viewpoint, and the all-enduring optimism that has made her one of the best-loved women in the world?

It is Thornley Colton's astonishing physical abilities, however, in which you don't quite believe: the delicate touch, the step counting, the independence of action. Have you ever heard of America's wonderful blind surgeon and diagnostician, Doctor Jacob W. Bolotin, of Chicago? Born blind, he has a mentality and has acquired physical abilities that, to the average person, seem absolutely superhuman. Below, in tabular form are some of the things this sightless doctor does, and remember this is not fiction, but *fact*.

*****

Doctor Bolotin is twenty-five years old, and is a specialist in diseases of the heart and lungs. He has been appointed attending physician at the Illinois Tuberculosis Hospital at Dunning.

He takes the temperature of patients by a touch of his finger, and is usually nearly exact—never more than a fraction of a degree wrong.

He is such a keen judge of time intervals that he is able to get the number of pulse beats to the minute correctly without a watch.

By feeling the patient's chest he diagnoses tuberculosis and all heart troubles.

He lectures twice a week before two medical colleges, talking from two to three hours, and never uses a note.

Of the thirty-five hundred patients he has examined, not more than fifty ever guessed that he was blind.

He knows two thousand persons by their voices. He knows several hundred by their hands alone.

He goes all over Chicago without a guide, and makes all his calls unattended.

To earn money enough to pay his college expenses he traveled alone all over the United States as a typewriter salesman for four years. He made such a success of the work that, when he resigned to enter medical school, he was one of the highest-paid sellers of writing machines in the West.

He is an expert typewriter.

His sense of touch is so delicate that he can read the raised Braille letters for the blind through the thickness of *sixteen* handkerchiefs.

*****

Would you believe some of those things if you read them in a fiction story? Yet every fact can be verified by the physician himself, or any of his hundreds of friends. And Doctor Bolotin says there is no reason why a blind person should not be as successful as one who can see.

You may have heard of the "Lighthouse," New York's club for the blind. Here a magazine for the blind is issued; also one for persons who can see, and who are interested in those who walk in the darkness. Both are written, edited, and printed by blind men. In the clubrooms there is always a game of chess, checkers, or dominoes going on. And card games are favorite amusements. The blind people use the cheap card decks on which the corner marks can be easily read by their delicate fingers. But an outsider must always deal. Otherwise the dealer would know every card going to his opponents, as they slide through his fingers.

A blind man, secretary to a New York millionaire, read this story from proof. Proof sheets are only printed on one side, and his fingers, brushing the back, gave him the words. When he had finished it he smiled quizzically.

"Colton is quite clever—mentally and analytically," he commented. "But not remarkable for his physical abilities, for he is usually accompanied by a man to guide him, his secretary. There are a hundred blind men in New York who do not need the touch of a sleeve to guide their steps. I go all over the city alone. I used to give the big traffic policeman at Forty-second and Broadway heart failure by the way I crossed the street. But after a while he got used to me, though he doesn't know today that I'm blind. I've spoken to him every morning for three years, too. It's a lot safer for me to cross the crowded streets than it is for a person who can see. Every accident you ever heard of is caused by a pedestrian failing to see an automobile or car behind him, or approaching from the side where he doesn't happen to be looking at that particular instant. That couldn't happen to me. My ears, twice as keen as the average, and trained to locate sounds, tell me instantly everything that is happening on *all* sides of me, back or front, left or right. The man who can see, sees only in one direction; I have 'eyes' in every part of my head."

*****

"Colton's sense of touch too fine?" Seriousness took the place of the quizzical smile. "Not at all. Some of the things the blind can do with their fingers seem positively uncanny to the average person. I, myself, can locate exactly a human hair under eight sheets of note paper.

"Step counting? If you've been much in downtown New York you've seen 'Paddy the Beggar.' Paddy always has a boy and a cane, because they are a necessary part of his business. But when the day's 'work' is over he dismisses the boy, and has a good time in Greenwich Village, where he has lived for fifty years. Paddy can tell the distance, *to half a step*, from any given point in the Village to any other, and he could find his way unerringly—if he wasn't a beggar who needed his 'props' to any cafe in the downtown section."

1

THE AMAZING ENTRANCE

The wine-born laughter softened, ceased; blatancy became solemn hush. The life and color of the big restaurant seemed chilled, as though some icy wind had come, unheralded, to destroy. Jewel-panoplied women lowered their eyes, only to raise them again and stare. The movements of the waiters, silent always, seemed more ghost-like than ever. The ringing click of silver on china was stilled as diners forgot food, to watch the three persons who were entering the big dining-room of the Beaumonde.

It was the man who attracted the eye first; it was the woman who held it. The third of the trio was merely a waiter, whose arm through the man's arm helped support him as he walked through the aisle of tables with a peculiar, stumbling, stiff-legged gait, that reminded one instantly of the mechanical walk of an automaton or a paralytic. At first glance, the man appeared intoxicated, until one saw that his chin was held high, and that his eyes, almost met by the gray-streaked brown whiskers that came halfway down his vest, stared straight ahead of him unblinkingly. But his whole weight seemed supported by the locked arms of the waiter and the woman.

It was the woman who brought the hush; the chill. Tall she was, regally erect, gowned in black satin, with a wide, silver girdle that accentuated the sheen of the silk strikingly. But the face under the snow-white hair exerted an instant spell of repellent fascination. Age, terrible age; a hundred years, or just as well two hundred, was depicted in the network of deep-graven lines, woven, interwoven, crisscrossed with their thousand intricacies in the chin, the forehead, the hollowed cheeks. None of the softness of age was there; only the coldness, the bleakness of life's winter. Even the eyes, coal-black under the white brows, seemed to glitter with the coldness of black polar ice. The specter of age had stalked into the realms of youth, frivolity, devil-may-care.

The moment of hush became a low-voiced murmur as she helped guide the man, with her arm through his arm, down the aisle of tables.

"Silver sandals! See the silver sandals!" were the words that made the murmur as the diners caught flashes of them when her feet moved under the satin dress hem. They weren't of silvered leather; that was seen immediately. They were of the metal, burnished, with straps of finely meshed links.

The woman paid absolutely no attention to the overt watching; she seemed unaware that anyone else was near. She walked as a queen would have walked between rows of curtsying women and bowing courtiers, accepting the attention she attracted as a queen would have accepted her homage; unheeding, uncaring. After the first instant, the diners did not even see the man whose automaton like walk seemed only possible with the aid of the holding arms. The woman held all eyes; she was the whole picture.

A waiting captain, with the acumen of his kind, felt the chilling influence of the newcomers, and resented it; just as he resented anything that would detract from the life and gayety of the aftertheater crowd in the restaurant. He knew, too, that the man and woman were not of the type his men were in the habit of serving. And the waiter who helped the man was doing an unheard-of thing! His business was to serve food and wine. How he had happened to be at the entrance of the dining-room to offer his help was something the waiting captain was going to find out. There was a scowl, just a slight, apologetic scowl, on his face as he approached. He opened his lips to speak. The woman's eyes met his, and the apologetic smile went instantly. Servility, humbleness covered the waiting captain like a cloak. There had been no words because there had been no need of them. The cold eyes had commanded.

"Madame wishes a table?" He backed before her.

"It has been reserved." The heavy, gutturaled words came from the man with almost uncanny effect, for there was no motion of the head, and the thick beard hid from sight any movement there might be of lips.

"Ah, your pardon!" The head waiter apologized humbly with his lips and back; but there was a strange expression in his eyes as they darted toward the waiter, whose arm supported the bearded man.

"Mr Carl took care of the reservation," explained the waiter simply.

The waiting captain's eyes cleared. The manager had attended to it personally. The woman of the queer costume and the man in whose limbs was paralysis were evidently persons of importance. Their table must be one of those attended to by the waiter who had been ordered to assist the invalid. The captain backed rapidly, still bowing, still under the spell of those cold eyes that had never glanced in his direction but for that single instant. Though the man had spoken, the waiting captain realized, as did everyone else who saw, that it was the woman who was to be obeyed—to be honored with attention.

He pulled back a chair at the one empty table of the two the waiter served. Carefully, gently, the servant and the woman helped the man seat himself. The woman's hand on her escort's elbow rested his arm on the napery with a gentle, caressing motion. There was affection in that simple thing, and for an instant the wrinkled face seemed to contort with some inner emotion; but so quick was the transition that not even the waiter who held the other arm as the man's hand touched an empty wineglass appeared to notice it. Then the woman took the chair at the other side of the table.

Again the man spoke, with that curious lack of movement: "You have our order. Attend to it. We are on this earth but a little while. We come. We go. Wraiths in a dream we live. The end of one dream is but the beginning of another."

The heavy voice that came from the thick beard was pitched so low that it was but a wordless rumble a few feet away, yet the girl who sat at the next table, alone, seemed to hear. A shudder shook her slim body. The hand that held her wineglass trembled so that a few drops of the straw-colored liquid spilled on the cloth. The eyes of the silver-sandaled woman turned to meet those of the girl. The coal-black eyes seemed to soften as they rested on the beautiful face, with its full, red-curved lips and pink, health-tinted cheeks that were framed in great waves of burnished gold hair, dressed low over her ears. Then the coal-black eyes went hard again; the lines around the withered lips tightened as the teeth clamped together behind them.

The captain hovered over the table, fearful lest these favored guests should find something wrong. The woman glanced at him once more; he bowed, and hurried away, obeying the unvoiced command as though it had been spoken. Something in that look had told him that he was not wanted; he understood without knowing why he understood.

The girl's hand shook as she lifted her glass to take a sip of wine. But she did not look toward the other table. She, too, had obeyed the unspoken command.

The other diners, more blase, probably, or more typically New Yorkers, stared frankly at the strange couple. The woman sat straight in her chair, unmoving, fingertips touching the table edge. The man's left hand still rested, palm down, on the cloth, where the woman's hand had left it. The fingers of his other hand, relaxed, were around the stem of his wineglass. His gaze never left the woman's face; his stare was unblinking, uncanny; his eyes were bright.

The murmur of comment still went the rounds of the tables. The silver sandals, the silver girdle, the gown of black satin, that was cut according to no prevailing mode, but seemed, somehow, to be eminently in keeping with the age-lined face, were discussed, speculated upon, wondered at.

The waiter approached the couple's table with a silver wine-cooler. The dining-room captain hurried over, napkin on arm, to assist. The waiter was a new man, and nothing must go wrong. The waiter held the bottle so that the man could see the label.

"That is right." Once more the words came from the beard with no movement of head or body.

The dining-room captain saw the label, and a look of wonder crossed his face. The wine was Pol Roger '56. In all his years of serving he had never known of a bottle of the famous wine being in the place. He watched every movement of the man as he poured the wine into the woman's glass; a look cautioned care as the serving man turned to pour the wine into the glass loosely held by the man's relaxed fingers.

The man spoke again slowly, solemnly: "Life is wine. Wine is life. Its bubbles come from the depths, to break into the free air of the higher above. But half a glass, man. I do not wish to drink."

The waiting captain turned away. A strange man, surely! He glanced at the lone girl, and surprised a startled look of fear on her face before she lifted her wine again to her lips and lowered her head. A girl without an escort in this Broadway dining-room! How had she entered? How had she passed the men at the door? He must tell her of the Broadway rule regarding unescorted women.

As he took a step toward the table, the waiter unceremoniously brushed past him and spoke to the girl.

"Mr Smith is at the telephone, miss. He will return in a minute."

He took the bottle of wine from the cooler on the stand at her side and filled her half-emptied wineglass. There was no doubt of the captain's scowl this time. He knew that the waiter had deliberately pushed past him to forestall his request that the girl leave the restaurant. And the lie had been so obvious! What interest had the new waiter in the girl with the hair of burnished gold? Why was she waiting, alone? His raised finger beckoned the waiter. The thing must be settled. The man must know his place.

"Man!" The command came sharply from the bearded man at the table with the strange, silent woman.

The waiter, who had started to obey the raised finger, hurried back to the table.

"Fill my glass. The bubbles of life have ceased to rise."

Silently the serving man obeyed, pouring the wine slowly. When he straightened up to replace the bottle, the captain had gone to attend another table. His eyes met the eyes of the woman. His head lowered slowly in a nod of thanks!

The silent woman of the silver sandals lifted her untouched glass. For a moment she held it toward the man at the other side of the table. Then, with a motion as graceful as that of a queen drinking the health of her liege lord, she slowly drained the bubbling wine. Almost reverently she set down the empty glass and brushed her withered lips with a napkin. Rising slowly, as unconscious as ever of the watching eyes, she walked around the table, her silver sandals flashing under the satin dress. Diners held their breaths as she laid one hand gently on the bearded man's shoulder. She leaned forward, and a hundred half-suppressed gasps went up as her lips lightly touched the forehead of her escort. The man did not move under the caress. Only a heavy-voiced, simple "Thank you" came from the beard-shielded lips. The silent woman turned, bowed her head for an instant, and left the dining-room as she had entered it, cold eyes apparently seeing nothing, body erect, regal.

The waiter filled her empty glass again. The girl at the next table called him, spoke to him in a tremulous undertone. He nodded, and, in picking up her fallen napkin, touched her arm. He left her, apparently to execute some order she had given.

The bearded man never moved in his chair at the table in the center of the big dining-room, with its wine-livened men and women, who still watched covertly. The waiting captain came over and touched the bottle in the cooler to see that the temperature was keeping right. He glanced up inquiringly, but the man paid no attention.

The fingers of the girl at the next table toyed nervously with the stem of her wineglass. That reminded the captain of the waiter from whom an explanation was due. The serving man was not in the dining-room. He hurried over to the door through which his men entered the dining-room. Where there would be no possibility of the diners hearing would be the proper place to speak to the waiter. The man was not in the kitchen, nor in the private bar, where the 'bus boys got the ordered drinks. For ten minutes he searched, neglecting his men and tables in the big restaurant. Then a word to a page summoned the manager. Mr Carl should know the incompetency of this new serving man.

The manager came, low-voiced, suave. He listened, nodded, and walked over to the table. He addressed a polite query to the bearded man. He received no more attention than the Sphinx would have given. A startled look came to the manager's face; then he seemed to remember the hundred other diners who must not suspect that he thought anything was wrong. His eyes swept the big room, and his face lighted as he saw a white-haired man with a pale, intellectual face, lean, cleft chin, delicately nostriled nose, whose eyes were concealed by the great, blue circles of the smoked, tortoise-rimmed library glasses he wore.

"Attend to your duties," he ordered the captain, as he started through the aisle of tables to the other side of the restaurant, bowing and smiling to the diners whom he knew, as though not a trouble was on his mind.

"Good evening, Mr Carl," greeted the man with the smoked glasses, as the manager neared the table.

"How d' do, Mr Colton?" There was a nervous tremor in the manager's voice that the seated man detected instantly, for a look of interest came to his face as he asked: "That strange couple Sydney has been telling me about? The man who is sitting there alone?"

"Yes. I think there is something wrong. Would you mind going over there with me, as though you wished an introduction? If there is nothing wrong, I can apologize. If there is, you can tell me without alarming the guests. The man did not move nor answer when I spoke to him."

Thornley Colton, blind problemist, to whom crime puzzles were the one great recreation of life, rose. "I will return in a few minutes, Sydney," he said to the apple-cheeked, black-haired young man who sat at the table. Then he spoke once more to the manager. "The two interested me from the moment they entered; especially the voice of the man. Is he still sitting with one arm resting on the cloth and the other hand at the stem of his wineglass?"

"Yes. The captain says that he has not moved since he sat down, and he hasn't said a word since the woman left."

Back between the tables they went. On all sides of them were laughter and gayety, richly dressed women, and wine-flushed men, who had already ceased paying attention to the lone man at the table, and were once more thinking only of their own good time. The manager stopped at the table as though to speak. Colton stepped around him and touched the wrist of the arm that lay palm down on the table. His long, slim fingers encircled the wrist. He raised his head. His nostrils quivered as though some strange odor had come to them.

"The wrist artery has been slashed in three places," the blind man said quietly. "He has been dead for hours!"

A tingling sound came from the next table as a convulsive movement of the girl's fingers shivered the straw stem of her wineglass.

2

THE PROBLEMIST

"Dead!" The horrified whisper came from the lips of the manager before he could choke it back. Then he remembered the crowded dining-room. The axiom of his business, made a very part of him by the years, governed his next speech. Experience had taught him that paying guests should never be disturbed or annoyed.

"Come outside to my office," he pleaded huskily.

Colton nodded. "A moment, please; I want to speak to my secretary." He turned and retraced his steps through the winding aisle of tables swiftly, unerringly, his trained brain counting the paces automatically and with no conscious effort. He spoke a few low-toned words to the apple-cheeked young man who had patiently waited. Sydney Thames' face, which could never mask emotion, lost its color as he glanced at the table with the silent dead man. Then he inclined his head in acquiescence to the evident order.

The manager waited at the door, his eyes troubled as they looked over the big room. He saw that the diners were beginning to whisper among themselves as they watched the bearded man at the table and the blind man who had touched his shoulder and felt of his wrist. Quick to catch the influence of the unusual, the tragic, as are all highly keyed New York habitues of restaurants, the suspicions of the diners had already been aroused; the gayety and laughter were becoming strained. The manager glanced in the direction of the orchestra leader, and a jingling cabaret air filled the big dining-room as he led the way to his private office.

Behind the closed door Manager Carl mopped his sweating brow with a handkerchief held in a trembling hand. His face was colorless, and the strain of having concealed his feelings outside showed in the haggardness of reaction.

"My God, Mr Colton!" he choked, flopping into a chair with the inertness of a jellyfish. "This is terrible! Terrible!" His tone suddenly became vehement. "It couldn't be! It isn't possible! His wrists couldn't be cut without attracting attention, and"—his voice was almost childishly triumphant as he jumped to his feet—"there would be blood!"

"You forget that dead persons don't bleed," Thornley Colton reminded him seriously. "The death of that man occurred at least five hours ago."

"Why, that's ridiculous! Ridiculous!" Manager Carl was pacing the floor like a caged tiger. "He has not been at the table more than half an hour."

"Thirty-three minutes, to be exact," Colton said, his sightless eyes apparently fixed on the ceiling, his slim fingers in his vest pocket touching the face of his crystalless watch. "The strangeness of the couple, described by my secretary, immediately attracted my attention. Time usually has a peculiar significance in cases like this, and I try never to overlook the significant!"

"You—you mean he was dead when he came into the dining room!" gasped Carl.

"Naturally." Colton's voice was dry.

"But he walked into the dining-room, man! He walked!"

"With the assistance of the woman and the waiter, yes." Colton's sightless eyes were still fixed on the ceiling; across his forehead and at the corners of his eyes was the fine tracery of lines that always came when his wonderful mind was working to visualize each detail of the picture other eyes could see but could not understand.

"Do you mean to say that a dead man could walk, even with the assistance of two persons, and not show immediately that he was dead? "

"With proper preparation, yes. The touch of my hand on his shoulder told me that under the clothes was an ingenious steel framework to support it naturally, and give to the limbs the peculiar automatonlike movements that were so noticeable before the woman attracted all the attention and made the watchers forget even the existence of the man. Her dress, her looks, everything about her, were intended to distract attention from the man."

"Far fetched!" snorted the manager, petulance coming to cloak his nervousness. "The waiter could not be deceived like that! Why, his hands would have felt the steel framework and the dead weight of the body at once!"

"Certainly!" assented Colton readily. "Where is the waiter?"

Halfway across the floor, the manager stopped his pacing to whirl. "What do you mean?" he demanded, and there was a tremor in his voice.

"Merely that the waiter was there to help the woman get the man to the table. When his work was finished, he vanished. I had my secretary watching him."

"You think he secured the position for just that purpose!" The manager slammed the top cover of his rolling desk, and his trembling fingers pulled out a card index from the drawer. He found the card he wanted, read it, and a groaning curse came from between his set teeth. "You're probably right! He's been here only two days."

"Tell me his name, and the facts you have," suggested the blind man, his tone merely interested.

"George Nelson."

"Fictitious, of course," put in Colton.

"Age twenty-seven. Four years' experience in London and Continental restaurants. That's a lie, too, I suppose." His eyes lifted from the card, as though he had forgotten he was speaking to a blind man.

Colton nodded. "He wasn't a waiter, that's sure. He was too clever and nervy. It takes some nerve to do the thing he did, even with that remarkable woman at his side. How about references?"

Carl shoved the card back in the box and went to the small steel safe. He took an envelope, ripped open the flap, and almost dropped the inclosure when his eyes saw the signature.

"He was personally recommended by Mr Bracken!" he exclaimed.

"The owner of the hotel?"

"Yes. The man had served on his private yacht coming over, and wanted to stay in America a while. Of course, being recommended by Mr Bracken, we never bothered to look into the authenticity of the references."

"Um!" murmured the blind man. "No chance of forgery?"

The shake of the manager's head was positive. "I'd stake my life on that signature!" he firmly declared. "I'd forgotten the thing because I put it into the hands of my assistant."

"Where is Mr Bracken?"

"He put to sea again this morning. You know he never spends a minute more than he has to on dry land." Then came the inevitable question: "But what could he have to do with the man inside; the dead man sitting there with all my guests?"

"That's the thing we'll have to find out," answered the blind man grimly.

Carl again took to pacing the floor, his lower teeth gnawing at the stubby mustache on his upper lip. "It's devilish!" he groaned. "Positively devilish! How am I to get the body out of the dining room without disturbing my guests?" The rules of his business seemed to overshadow every other consideration in the manager's mind.

"The police will probably have a whole lot to say if you move it before they arrive," reminded Colton.

"Do you mean that they'll have to troop into my dining-room, a bunch of big-footed, fat-brained louts?" moaned Carl, with visions of his paying guests in a panic of fear, and rough-voiced men swarming into his dining-room.

"Yes," nodded Colton. "And they'll demand an explanation as to how a dead man could be brought from an automobile or carriage into the dining-room, to be met by the waiter, too. That is what will require considerable explaining. The whole thing is too extravagant, too bizarre to be ordinary. The strangest case I have ever been connected with, yet with a solution that must be simple."

"Simple!" The words came as a choking gasp from Carl. "Why do you say that?" His voice trembled with fierce impatience.

"Because of its very extravagance; its obvious preparation. I have found that the cases with the apparently simple climaxes, or beginnings, from the detective standpoint, are the ones with involved explanations. There must be some simple explanation of how and why the dead man was brought into your dining-room."

"He couldn't have been dead! He spoke! He must have been alive!" Again there was vehemence in the manager's tone as the blind man's words brought his thoughts back to the thing he refused to credit.

"Your opinions die hard, don't they, Mr Carl?" A slight smile curved the blind man's thin lips for an instant. "It has always seemed strange to me how people refuse to be convinced of the falsity of a thing they think their eyes have seen. I have told you that the man was dead. Any physician in the world would place the time of death within an hour of the time limit I put, yet you won't believe because someone else's eyes deceived you into believing the man talked."

"But the waiter heard him! It was the woman who did not speak a word!"

"It was the woman who said everything. A strange woman; a wonderful woman whom I shall know!" The blind man's lean, cleft chin was set at an ominous angle, but on the intellectual, patrician face was a look of intense interest. The problemist had a problem that he knew would take every ounce of power in the wonderful brain behind the high, white forehead.

"You mean ventriloquism?" Carl sat inertly in the chair once more. He had apparently given up rebellion against the crisp, terse statements that came from the lips of the blind man.

"Yes. The false huskiness of the man's voice aroused my suspicions immediately."

"You were across the dining-room!" interrupted the manager.

"My ears are supernormal to recompense my lack of sight," put in the blind man seriously. "But ventriloquism can never deceive them, *because* I am blind. The ventriloquist does not throw his voice, despite the popular fallacy. It is merely pitched so that the ear can't locate it. A look, a motion of the hand tells the listeners' eyes where the ventriloquist wants them to imagine the voice comes from. Though the scores of the eyes saw no movement of the man's head, or of the beard over the lips, there was never a suspicion of trickery. My ears have been trained for years to locate sounds unerringly. They never fail!"

"Then the whole crime was devilishly planned for my restaurant! I should have known it!" Manager Carl's voice was almost a wail. "The way the reservation was made should have told me not to touch it."

"How was the reservation made?" asked Colton quietly. A problemist before all else, he would get each vital fact in the case while he had the opportunity. In a short time the police would be on hand with their badgering questions and confusion. Carl was now in the mood, seemingly, to give information. Later, he would close up like a clam. When the shock of the thing had passed, he would remember that he was a hotel manager, and would try every means in his power to cover all facts. But now he was ready to fall in with every suggestive question the problemist put.

"That was as strange as the rest of it was awful." The manager rose, with a huge sigh, and took a note from his desk. He held it with outstretched hand toward Colton, then suddenly remembered that the man to whom he was talking was blind. "Shall I read it to you?" he asked.

"Let my fingers look it over first." The problemist took it in his hand, and his supersensitive finger tips felt every fractional inch of both sides. A low-toned whistle came from his lips, and his face lighted with a new look.

"Papyrus!" he exclaimed. "Papyrus!"

"The stuff the old Egyptians used?" queried the manager, wonder in his tone. "I thought that was darn' funny paper."

Thornley Colton's voice was a murmur as he spoke, apparently to himself: "Silver sandals. Silver girdle. Age! Can it be! Reincarnation? Is it possible?"

"You don't believe that?" The question came breathlessly from the manager.

"No." A cynical smile crossed the blind man's thin lips. He shook his head, as though the thought was not worthy of serious consideration.

His fingertips slowly brushed the writing.

"Can you read it?" asked the manager.

"Yes. The words have been written with an ink-dipped stylus instead of a pen." He raised his head, with an ejaculation of wonderment. "Fifty dollars for reserving a table and serving a bottle of Pol Roger wine that was sent with the note! No wonder you granted the request for the particular table this mentions, undoubtedly one at which the pseudo waiter served."

"And it was all a game to have my place overrun with police!" groaned the manager. "A game to ruin me! I won't *let* the police into that dining-room tonight, with my people there. I'll get the body out the way it came in, and hush the whole thing up. I've got pull enough to do that! I've—"

He stopped suddenly as the door of the small office was unceremoniously pushed open and a red-faced man in a brass-buttoned blue uniform strode in. The newcomer's heavy jaw was thrust out belligerently as he saw the seated blind man, and a black scowl came to his face.

"Trying to steal a march on me, eh?" he snapped.

"Good evening, Captain McMann," greeted Colton suavely, removing his hand from the inside pocket where he had thrust the note when the door opened.

"Huh!" growled the police captain; then he stepped forward, to face Manager Carl. "Trying to put one over on us, eh? Where's the murder that was pulled off here tonight?"

3

EVIDENCE

Having thrown his bomb at the startled manager's feet, Captain McMann, whose sense of the dramatic had not been dulled in the least by his twenty-two years on the force, watched the effects of the explosion with narrowed eyes. They were immediate and instantaneous. Manager Carl drew back with a squeal that was half fright, half incoherent protest.

"Why—why, that's ridiculous!" he gasped.

"I know! Oh, I know!" Captain McMann's voice was sarcastically soothing. "A thing like that couldn't happen because it would get on the nerves of the people that's spendin' their good money. I know!"

"Oh, Lord!" groaned Manager Carl prayerfully. "My dining room! Ruin!"

The police captain's lips pursed in a whistle. "The dining room, eh?" There was amazed surprise in his voice. "A murder pulled in a crowded restaurant!" His tone on the last exclamation was one of snappish incredulity.

"That is where you will find the body." The blind man spoke very casually; his whole attention on the match he was holding at his cigarette end.

"What d'ye mean by that?" The police official turned upon the agitated manager to growl the question.

"There is nothing subtle about a plain declarative sentence. The body is in the dining-room, seated at a table, with one hand loosely around the stem of a wineglass."

"Poison, eh?"

"If you know of a poison that causes slashes of the wrist arteries, yes."

"Slashed wrists!" Captain McMann's eyes narrowed once more to pin points as he stared at the blind man to see whether or not he was in earnest. Then he remembered the futility of trying to read the problemist's expression. He whirled on Carl. "Is that true?" he demanded. The manager's expression was answer enough. "Show me where it is!" he ordered.

"My God, man!" pleaded Carl. "Can't you wait for an hour or so, till the dining-room is closed? Why, if the guests supposed that the man out there had been murdered, and that they had been sitting in the same room with a dead man, I would be ruined!"

"That cuts a whole lot of ice alongside a murder!" snapped the captain. "Putting a few sordid dollars above a human life!"

A black scowl came to his face as he saw the blind man smile at the obvious quotation. "Oh, I suppose you're so devilish smart you've got the whole thing solved?" he sneered.

"We start pretty even on this case, captain." There was no trace of rancor in the problemist's tone; but the tolerance there was maddening. For years Colton and the police had been sworn enemies. The paid investigators of the city always resented the blind man's presence at the scene of a crime. Time after time he had shown them the falsity of their premises, and his reasoning had led him unerringly to the solution of the mystery when the police detectives had been circling wildly. Of all the hundreds of detectives and policemen whom Colton knew, but a scant half dozen or so ever appreciated his ability or help. The others, with the superiority of professionals in all lines, went out of their way to confuse the blind man whenever possible. So Captain McMann curved his lips in a wider sneer as he said:

"We won't be that way long. That luck of yours can't last forever."

"A race for the solution?" It was but a quiet question, but there was a challenge in it that the captain took up instantly. He nodded.

"Try out your fool theories." It was his turn to adopt the tolerant tone, and he took full advantage of it. "This looks as though it might be a real case, and a thing for practical men, not amateurs."

"Very well." Colton rose, with an assumed languidness that concealed the physical and mental tenseness of a hound held in leash the instant before release. "You haven't any objections, I hope, to my waiting till the coroner arrives?"

"Go as far as you like — *as* far as you like!" granted Captain McMann, with magnanimity.

"You aren't really going into my dining-room while all the people are there?" Manager Carl had come to life again.

"Come on!" Captain McMann said brusquely, as he started for the door. "I'll get a line on this thing before the cor' gets here." With his hand on the knob, he turned, as he remembered something. "Like to know how I got wise so quick, wouldn't you, Colton?" he asked, with a grin of knowledge withheld.

A slight motion of the problemist's hand dismissed the possibility.

"Immaterial," he declared. "Salient facts are all I ever worry about. I haven't the police practicability, you see."

"Oh! O-oh!" The two exclamations were almost a chuckle. "Wise to the fact that I wasn't going to hand up, eh?"

"Something like that." Colton rose and took from his pocket the strange note reserving the table, "Here's that papyrus table reservation, Mr Carl. I'm through with it."

The superior grin faded from the captain's face with a suddenness that opened his mouth and caused a gasping sound to come from his lips before he jumped forward with outstretched hand.

"Let's see that! Give it here!"

The blind man extended it politely. "Looks exactly like the one you got, doesn't it, captain?" he queried.

The captain's eyes seemed fairly to jump from the note to search the expressionless face of the blind man. "How did you know that?" he demanded, anger in his voice.

"You have just told me. Merely the proof of one of the theories you consider so uselessly foolish."

"Clever!" Carl put in the compliment excitedly, evidently not ill-pleased at anything that reflected on the police captain.

Colton paid no attention, but went on: "To save your practical men the trouble of tracing that curious paper through a hundred mills, I'll tell you that it is papyrus, made of crushed reeds that grow only in Egypt. Material like it for conveying the written word hasn't been manufactured for two thousand years."

"Huh!" The captain's grunt was suspicious, his face still showed the flush of anger the manager's exclamation had brought. "Why are you so anxious to give this information?"

"Merely so that we can start out even, that's all." Thornley Colton's tone was impatient. "I've tried to help you and your men out several times, and you've always taken this supercilious attitude. I welcome this opportunity to match my wits with your"—the pause before the next word was pregnant with meaning—"practicability." He dropped his cigarette in an ashtray on the desk, locating it with his fingers without turning his head. "If you want to get ahead of the coroner you'd best hustle," he observed quietly. "This is Bierbauer's district, and his car with the loose-chain drive he never seems to have time to fix has just drawn up to the curb outside."

Again Captain McMann shot him a suspicious look, and some subtle sixth sense of the blind man seemed to instantly detect it.

"Another of the papyrus notes," he made answer simply.

"When I get time, I'm goin' to find out how much you know," promised Captain McMann grimly, as he opened the door, silencing Manager Carl's unvoiced protest with a single look.

"That makes it even again." The blind man smiled slightly as he followed into the main body of the hotel.

"'Lo, cap!" greeted the thick voice of the loose-jowled, purplecheeked man who puffed as he wiggled out of his heavy coat. "Devil of a time to break up a man's party. Where's the body?" The cordiality went from the voice as he apparently saw the blind man for the first time. "'Lo, Colton! In on this, too? Goin' to make another flying-death mystery, and go over our heads?"

Coroner Bierbauer, like Captain McMann, had never forgotten the blind man's solving of the girl violinist's death at the theater, and the sequel murder of the theater manager, Crawford, in the rathskeller, by the insane knife thrower. Both had occurred in their precinct; and, while they had bent every effort to fasten the guilt on two wholly innocent persons, the blind man had gone over their heads to the chief of the detective bureau, and had forced a confession from the real murderer.

Thornley Colton merely contented himself with a nod of recognition as Captain McMann took the coroner aside. For several minutes the two held a whispered conversation. The talk was official, uninteresting, and Colton did not even attempt to hear, but his super keen ears, trained to locate sounds unerringly, and to tell his brain their meaning, were strained to catch each significant sound in the lobby. He knew that there were groups of men on the seats' and divans conversing in tremulous whispers. Manager Carl had left them the minute they came out of the office, and Colton knew that he had gone to the door of the dining-room.

The blind man did not need eyes to tell him that the suspicions of the diners in the restaurant, aroused by his action of feeling the wrist of the dead man, had become tangible certainty. With the typical New Yorker's fear of the witness stand and the House of Detention, the diners had gone scurrying away, with nervous glances at the unmoving man. The brusque entrance of the uniformed captain, known immediately through the whole floor, proved these suspicions. Those remaining in the lobby and dining room were only the morbidly curious waiting for something to develop.

Captain McMann turned from Bierbauer and nodded to a square-chinned, square-toed man, who puffed a black cigar in a leather wall chair. The man rose and walked over leisurely.

"Cover the doors, Tom," Captain McMann ordered.

"Done, cap."

"Anything?"

"Nope."

"See the book?"

"Every name. Reg'lar hotel bunch."

"New men?"

"Waiter. Been here two days."

"Details?"

"Nope. Not yet."

"Get 'em. Have a couple of uniformed men cover the dining room doors."

"Yep. Heard talk of the thing. Took a peek. Queer case, cap."

"Uh-huh!" The captain nodded toward the waiting coroner, and started toward the restaurant.

"You didn't lose any time, captain," Colton said, and there was sincere compliment in his tone. The police official had had his men take care of every possible end, from a police viewpoint, except examining the body and scene of the crime. That was the work of the superior.

If the captain understood the compliment, he refused to recognize it.

"No grass'll grow under my feet in *this* case, believe me!" There was a grim emphasis in the remark that did not escape the problemist. McMann had confidence, and more than the usual allotment of police-detective ability.

At the door of the restaurant the captain waited for the two uniformed men the plain-clothes man had summoned, and he placed them at the kitchen and main doors of the room. Then an unnecessary snap of his fingers attracted the attention of the handful of diners who were still sitting at the tables waiting for the denouement they were sure would come.

"Clear out!" he ordered. "Get! You'll find out all about it in the morning papers, I suppose."

Meekly, disappointedly, they obeyed the blue uniform, and a glance told the waiting detective to find out whether or not they knew enough to make them valuable as witnesses. Then the three men, with Manager Carl almost on the verge of nervous collapse bringing up the rear, started toward the table of death.

The bearded man still sat in his chair; his relaxed hand was still around the stem of the wineglass, in which the bubbles had ceased to rise. His eyes, bright, with none of the fishy dullness that comes to dead eyes usually, stared straight ahead. The bearded chin was still held high. The arm with the slashed wrist was unmoved. Nothing was changed; yet everything was different. An hour before, there had been laughter and gayety on every side. Now death reigned supreme in the big dining-room. The waiters, the captains, leaden-footed and torpid-brained with the demoralization that had sent the diners bustling away, were gathered in small groups, whispering, glancing apprehensively at the single occupant of the big room. Empty dishes, empty glasses were still on the tables, because discipline had gone.

Captain McMann's eyes took in every detail of the picture as he walked to the table. Then he turned over the hand that was palm down and whistled a combination of surprise and professional satisfaction as he saw the three gaping slashes across the wrist artery. Then lines of puzzlement came to his florid brow.

"How long ago did this happen?" he demanded of the nervous manager, who stood back, wringing his hands.

"I—don't know," stammered Carl. "Mr Colton says that he has been dead for hours."

"Right, at that!" The admission came scowlingly from the coroner, who had lifted the glass of dead wine from the relaxed fingers, and was feeling the wrist that was uncut.

"Why didn't you notify us before, then?" asked the policeman sharply. "Don't you know that there's a jail penalty for concealing crime?"

"You came within three-quarters of an hour after the discovery," put in the blind man quietly.

"How's that? The man's been dead hours! How'd he get here?"

"Walked," answered Colton shortly.

An exclamation came from the coroner, as he rolled up a sleeve to the elbow and ran his hands up the arm to the shoulder and then down the back. "The body is in a metal brace!" he ejaculated. "Silver, by the Lord Harry!" He exposed the silver, cleverly hinged double circlets around the arm above and below the elbow.

"Mr Colton said it was steel," declared the manager nervously.

"Mistake number one," admitted the problemist candidly; then he spoke to Bierbauer: "Those gaping slashes weren't made after death, were they, coroner?"

Bierbauer darted him a sharp glance before he took the wrist in hand to examine it.

"No!" The negative came with an air of finality, and the explanation that followed showed that he respected the ability of the blind man. "The 'lay' of the slashes was made by the flow of blood from the artery. If the cuts had been made after death, they would be straight, and cleanly open. These 'lip' a trifle where the blood has forced them up over the arterial passage."

"Then death was caused by arteriotomy?"

"Yes," nodded Bierbauer. "No doubt of it."

"What's that arter'omy thing?" growled Captain McMann.

"Bleeding to death." Colton put it into simple words. Then he spoke again to the coroner: "Aren't his eyes unusually bright?"

"How'd you know that, if your blindness isn't bunk?" snapped the short-tempered police captain. Thornley Colton had taken the principal part away from him, and he resented it.

"The dullness of dead eyes would have attracted immediate attention," Colton explained frankly.

"Chemical," declared the coroner, a trifle ungraciously. The captain and he were old friends. But he was going to show the interloper that he knew his business, and knew it well. "Atropine," he added.

"Uh!" Colton turned away and spoke over his shoulder as he went to the next table. "I thought belladonna merely dilated the eye pupils, to make them lustrous. I had no idea it would act on dead eyes!"

The coroner's face flushed as he realized his mistake, and he muttered something under his breath. But the blind man had apparently forgotten the two men. His back was toward them, and his sensitive finger tips were gingerly brushing a damp spot on the cloth of the next table, moving gently the sharp fragments of a broken wineglass. With a quick motion, he thrust his fingers into his vest pocket; not quickly enough, however, to escape the sharp eyes of McMann.

"What was that?" he demanded, as he strode over. "What was it?"

Thornley Colton reached into his pocket again and held out the thing he had picked up. "Merely a fragment of broken wineglass, captain. There are others there; take all you want."

McMann took the small piece of glass from the outstretched palm with no word of apology. His brows beaded as he looked at it, trying to puzzle out the blind man's object in attempting to conceal it. It was nothing but a broken piece of thin wineglass stem, like half a dozen others on the table next to the one where sat the dead man. But McMann was nothing if not cautious.

"The police are in charge of this case. I'll take care of this."

"Very well," assented Colton. "Goodnight, captain!"

Colton's ready acquiescence struck the captain as suspicious.

"What is it?" he asked again, his tone this time one of assumed amusement.

"The race has ceased to be even, that is all."

The problemist nodded a goodnight to the coroner, and walked leisurely away, a peculiar smile curving his thin lips. His lightning-moving fingers had picked up two of the glass fragments. The one that the captain had not seen was still safe in his vest pocket.

4

THE TRAIL

Sydney Thames had drained his drink gulpingly to hide the nervousness the blind man's words caused as Thornley Colton had followed Manager Carl from the restaurant. There had been but three terse sentences in the minute the problemist had leaned across the table to whisper while the nervous manager waited at the door; yet they put a responsibility on the shoulders of the applecheeked secretary that had never been there before.

"That bearded man you noticed is dead," Thornley Colton had said. "It looks like murder. Watch the girl at the next table whose fingers snapped the stem of her wineglass, and see where she goes."

That was all. There had been no time for question nor explanation. The blind man had requested, and there had been no thought in his mind that the secretary would do anything but obey. Nor was there any other idea in the mind of Sydney Thames, whom Colton had picked up twenty-five years before as a bundle of baby clothes on the banks of the English river that had given him the only name he had ever known.

Sydney's nervousness was tinged with a bit of pride. This was the first case in which he had ever been intrusted a responsible part. Always before he had acted merely as a guide, the eyes of the man who had walked in the darkness always. He realized that the problemist had recognized in the presence of the dead man at the table evidence of a crime more complex, more sinister, perhaps, than any he had ever come in contact with before.

Had it been like any of the other cases he had watched the blind man solve while others stood helplessly by, Thames knew that Colton would have traced the girl himself, trusting to his extraordinary powers of mental visualization and elimination to find unaided the end of the tangled thread that led to the center of the maze. Interesting crime puzzles were the blind man's one great pleasure in life, and a peculiar vanity of his nature made him handle every possible end of a case alone.

Sydney Thames, after that first nervous glance toward the bearded man, kept his eyes on the girl and her every movement. Her back was toward him, so that he could watch unobserved. Under the broad velvet rim of her Gainsborough hat, more striking because it was the only one in the restaurant, and plainly worn because the girl cared more for becomingness than ephemeral style, Sydney Thames saw the white curve of neck and the shell-pink ear lobes that peeped from beneath the great coils of burnished gold hair. Her evening wrap had fallen from one white shoulder, showing her left arm. The right arm and hand were hidden under the folds of her wrap.

She had pushed back her chair a trifle when the glass had broken and the wine spilled on the cloth. Her waiter had disappeared, and the captain was busy at another table. The girl turned her head impatiently, and Sydney Thames saw her profile; Grecian, the face of a young goddess, as clear cut as a cameo. The blind man's secretary, who deified all women, drew in his breath sharply. She was beautiful, wonderfully beautiful!

What could a girl like that have to do with a murder? Why had Colton watched her? What significant message had the stem of the wineglass given the wonderful brain of the blind man? Sydney Thames did not know. He had no means of knowing. The same question flashed to his mind that had occurred to the waiting captain minutes before. What was she doing in a Broadway restaurant unescorted? Where was her escort? Was he the one Thornley Colton hoped to find by watching the girl? No. The problemist's instructions had been specific. He was interested only in the girl.

The waiting captain finally turned. He saw the broken glass, the stained cloth, and hurried to the table. Sydney saw him begin to remove the pieces of glass. He saw her imperious gesture demanding her check. The captain asked a question, plainly to ascertain the amount of her check, because the waiter who served her had gone. She told him, and paid with a bill from a silver-mesh purse. Without waiting for change or assistance with her wrap, she rose. A shrug of her shoulder and a sweep of a left arm put the wrap into place with no sign of the hidden right arm or hand.

Sydney Thames hurriedly pulled out a bill as he watched the girl start toward the door. Even across the room he could see that her wrap brushed the cloth of her table to keep as far away from the bearded man as the narrow table aisle permitted. He could see, because he was looking for it, a shudder shake her body as she passed. So she knew that the man was dead! How did she know that? Thames understood that Colton, if he had spoken at all, had pitched his voice so low that there was no possibility of anyone hearing his words but the manager, who had summoned him to investigate. He could see that the other diners were casting uneasy, apprehensive glances toward the table, and he realized that they knew something was wrong. But there was none of the fear, the evident repulsion that the girl had shown in the brief instant she had passed the table. She knew that the man was dead, and that he had been murdered!

Sydney Thames got his hat and coat and left the main entrance of the hotel a few feet behind the girl. On the sidewalk she stopped and glanced swiftly from right to left. One of the uniformed men Captain McMann had stationed at all entrances of the hotel moved near her as he shooed away a small group of loungers the sight of his blue uniform had attracted. The girl shrank back into a knot of men standing beside the main entrance. A low-toned, leering salutation drove away the momentary panic, and she started for the curb. The cab starter held open the door of a taxi, and she entered. It was her left hand she put out to touch the door.

Sydney Thames' eyes swept the line of waiting taxi's and automobiles, and located Colton's long, black car, with the alert Michael at the wheel. He hurried down along the curb line. The stolid chauffeur looked surprised when he saw Sydney alone; but understanding quickly replaced the surprise when Sydney gave his order:

"Follow that first taxi that is just pulling out."

Expertly Michael swung his car away from the curb. Sydney Thames lay back in the cushions. Michael could be trusted to carry out instructions. He had trailed cars many times for the blind man in every section of the city.

Straight down Broadway to Thirty-third the taxi, went, then it turned toward Fifth Avenue. Evidently there was no thought or fear of pursuit in the girl's mind, for her car came to a stop before the Thirty-third Street entrance of the Waldorf. A plain trail, thought Sydney, and he was disappointed. Michael made no attempt to stop his machine until he had rounded the corner into the avenue, then he turned in his seat to speak.

"'Tis more than likely she came here to get away from any one follerin' her," observed the wise chauffeur.

"'Tis the best place in the city fer that. Like as not she will go through the lobby an' get another car that'll be waiting in the court at the other side. They have done that before on Mr Colton and meself."

"All right, Michael." Sydney Thames was perfectly willing to take tips from the more experienced chauffeur.

The car turned the corner, went around Fifth Avenue, and stopped a short distance from Astor Court. Michael swung round in his seat, as though Sydney had given an order, but it was he who spoke: "Sit back in the cushions as though you cared fer nothin'. I will watch fer her in the mirror-scope, which I can do easylike, and widout turnin' me head." He swung the arm of his mirror at the proper angle, and Sydney Thames, appreciating the suggestion, obeyed literally.

It was fully fifteen minutes before the low hum of the gears sounded as the black car moved silently from the curb. Sydney saw that they were following a low-hung, single-seated car of the racing type. The big hat of the girl was unmistakable. The man beside her, driving, was hunched low over his wheel.

Down the avenue to Madison Square, with wise Michael keeping well in the rear, the two cars sped. Then the low-hung machine turned east, turned again, down Third Avenue, under the clank and clatter of the L trains; down past Chatham Square and Chinatown. Then the car they were trailing swung sharply into a diagonal street. Sydney caught a glimpse of a street sign as they passed, and read the name of Roosevelt. The big machine crawled along the narrow, dirty street, more than a block behind the smaller car. Another corner was turned. Another. The streets, narrow, dark, seemed to twist like snakes. It was an absolutely new district to Thames. Warehouses, tenements that defied every article in every building code that ever passed a board of aldermen or legislature, cluttered sidewalks, dirty gutters, lights few and far between, and in the distance the rattle and clang of the L trains and below the gongs of the bridge cars. At a street corner, narrower than any of the others, Michael stopped the big car.

"'Tis in the Peck Slip district we are. You had better walk, now. There is nothin' but Roosians down here, and two cars in the street is like to bring them out. The other car will have to go slow, an' you will have no trouble follerin'."

"Thank you, Michael." Sydney stepped to the sidewalk. "Go back to the hotel and get Mr Colton. I can find my way to the bridge, all right, and I'll take an L train uptown."

"'Tis a bad place at this time of night," observed Michael dubiously.

"Everyone's in bed by this time," laughed Sydney; and, with a wave of his hand, he started down the dark street in the direction the other car had taken. At the corner, he drew back into the shadow of a ramshackle building with scrawly Russian characters on the window and dirty, fly-blown piles of canned goods behind the dusty panes. Michael had stopped just in time. The other machine had halted, and the girl was stepping down to the sidewalk. He saw the driver put his hand on her shoulder, as though he was encouraging her to do something she feared. Suddenly she lifted her head in a pretty, significant gesture, and her left arm went around the driver's neck. Always her left arm, thought Sydney. What was the trouble with the right one? The driver patted her on the shoulder once more, a low-voiced word or two, and the girl started down the street alone. Sydney drew farther back in the shadow as the car backed along the curb to the corner. It turned, and crawled slowly past his hiding place out of the street. He tried to see the driver's face, but it was covered with big, mask-like automobile goggles.

Keeping in the shadow of the buildings noiselessly, Sydney slid along in the wake of the girl. In the stillness of the deserted street every sound seemed magnified, intensified. He could hear the pounding of his own heart, and his footsteps sounded, to his highly strung nerves, like the clank of horses' hoofs on cobbles. He could imagine the feelings of the delicate girl as she made her way alone through the street, where every house was a hive of bewhiskered, ill-smelling foreigners, who would come swarming out at the least sign of anything unusual. But she went resolutely ahead, never once turning to look back.

Halfway down the block she walked nearer the houses, and Sydney saw that she was looking for some number or sign. She stopped before one with brownstone steps, a relic of the days when aristocracy had reigned, and powdered, bewigged women and men had walked the rutted dirt road of old New York. But now the building was wedged between a tottery wooden warehouse and a tumbledown structure, outside of which a great, rusty anchor and huge pile of chain proclaimed the owner's business. The girl hesitated a moment, squared her shoulders, and hurried up the steps as though she was afraid her courage would desert her before she reached the top. She put her hand on the door handle and turned it. The door opened creakingly, and she entered.

For several minutes Sydney Thames crouched in the shadows, staring at the house. The unexpectedness of the girl's action had stunned him. He had thought of every possibility but her ready entrance. He had seen fear in her manner as she paused at the bottom of the steps. Yet she had gone into the dark house as though she belonged there. Why should a girl like that be in such a section of the city at such an hour?

Taking advantage of the shadows, he crept nearer the grim-looking house sandwiched between its grimmer-looking mates. There was not a light. He could see the end windows, thick with years' accumulation of dust and dirt. One heavy green shutter hung by a single hinge. An empty house, certainly. Yet the front door had been open and the girl had entered. Fifteen minutes passed, a half hour, three-quarters. The noise of the bridge cars sounded in Sydney's ears. On a street far over, a milk wagon clattered over the uneven street pavings. But the girl did not reappear. Sydney Thames' brain conjured up all sorts of terrible possibilities as he crouched in the darkness of the shadows. Where was the driver of the car who had left her? Why had she shown such fear at the bottom of the steps, then entered the house so boldly and without knocking? What kind of a place was it?

Sydney Thames went forward carefully. Colton had told him to find out where the girl went. He would! The big pile of rusty chain threw a mantle of blackness over the stone steps. He ascended them carefully; but there was no sound, nor a chink of light. He saw a heavy brass knocker on the green-painted, unpaneled door. A battered brass sign, slightly askew, showed outlines dimly in the lesser shadows of the house front. He bent forward to make out the letters in the darkness, but could not. He put his fingers up to feel the first letter, deeply bitten into the metal. As the blind man would have read, so Sydney Thames spelled it out slowly, and when the last letter on the dull brass sign told him the words, his sharp indrawn breath sounded hissingly in the silence. His fingers had read:

SILVER SANDALS,
CLAIRVOYANT.

The shooting of a heavy bolt behind the wooden door grated on his ears. He heard the first creak of the hinges before he had a chance to move. The door swung open, and, standing before him, terrible, more sinister than ever against the heavy black of the wall hangings, was the woman of the restaurant; the woman whose face was seared with years uncountable. The lighted candle she held over her head accentuated her age with its garish, flickering light. She peered out into the darkness, and the lined face contorted with passion. A queer, parrot-like cry issued from the withered lips, repeated shrilly as he stared dully. She opened the door wider. He wanted to get away, to dash down the steps and run, run, but something seemed to hold him there before her. Again came that curious sound from her lips, eerie, unhuman; but in it was command.

Then Sydney Thames understood. The woman who stood before him with one silver sandal showing under the hem of her black satin dress was deaf and dumb—a mute!

5

THE HOUSE OF MYSTERY

Thornley Colton's slim fingers unwound the alcohol-soaked bandage that covered his sightless eyes and forehead, saturated it again from the bottle at his elbow, and carefully replaced it. For five hours the blind man had sat in his chair before the oak desk in the library of the old-fashioned uptown house, his mind visualizing each separate piece of the new crime puzzle; arranging, rearranging, spending an hour over a piece that seemed to fit, only to cast it aside finally because it was wrong. At times the skein seemed straightened, the end appeared plainly in sight. Then some new tangle came to snarl the whole thing once more.

The blind man touched the face of the crystalless watch in his pocket. It was seven-thirty. In the five hours after his return from the hotel, Colton's only movement had been to change the head bandage, which relieved the splitting headache too many hours of light always caused. There had been no sleep; nor would there be, until the building up and tearing down that was going on in his mind resulted in some definite point of starting. His fingers touched two of the buttons in a row on the flat-topped desk.

Light, running footsteps sounded in the hall as: the Fee—red-haired, freckle-faced boy, with the slightly twisted nose, who had become a member of the Colton household as the only fee in a particularly baffling murder case, hurried in answer to the summons.

The boy made his way into the darkened library without hesitation; for he knew every step of the house, and his hours were spent figuring steps for the blind man so that he could be as valuable an ally as Sydney Thames. In the center of the floor he waited patiently for Colton to speak.

"I've just called the car, Shrimp," Thornley said. "Tell Michael I want to see him when it arrives."

"Yes, sir." The boy hesitated a moment, then asked his question: "Yuh ain't heard nothin' of Sydney yet, Mister Colton?"

"No, Shrimp."

The boy's feet shifted on the rug, as he hesitated again before the next question: "Yuh don't suppose he got black-jacked, or nothin'?" he finally ventured, remembering his own experience with certain ruthless men.

"I think not, Shrimp. The principals in this case are a very different sort of people."

"Gee, I hope so!" The boy darted out, then, to obey the order.

Michael's brief story of the district in which he had left Sydney Thames had overthrown a complete theory; necessitated a whole new structure in place of the one that had toppled in the Peck Slip section of the city. Colton had come directly from the hotel to wait for the return of his secretary. As the hours went by, and Thames did not return, Colton realized that he had gone further than his instructions warranted. The blind man had expected the trail would be an easy one, ending at a hotel or private house in one of the better sections of the city. But the dark, dirty part of the old city near the river upset everything. Thornley Colton's intuitive reasoning, which the years of visualizing and projecting, made necessary by his lack of eyes, had made almost superhuman, seemed wholly at a loss to understand this new turn of events. There could be no police search started for the missing secretary. Captain McMann's attitude had put the blind man on his mettle. He would find Sydney alone. He must find him, for the secretary was the only eyes he had used in years. And this was apparently a case where eyes would be essential. So the blind man sat quietly in his chair, planning, figuring.

The sound of the chauffeur's approaching footsteps came to the problemist's super keen ears, and he snapped on a light so that Michael could find a chair.

"Ain't no word yet, sorr?" Michael spoke with the familiarity of long service and years of confidence as he seated himself.

"No." Colton snapped off the light again.

"I tol' him it were a bad distric', sorr."

Colton dismissed the apologetic words with a nod, and went right to the heart of things: "The girl left the public taxi at the Thirty-third Street entrance of the Waldorf, walked through, and took another car that was waiting?"

"Yes, sorr. A runabout wid a racer body. I didn't wait fer it to come out after leavin' the girl. 'Twould be suspiciouslike."

"Did you see the number?"

"Yes, sorr. I've been too long here to miss a thing like that." Michael gave it with a distinct air of triumph.

"Fine work!" declared Colton appreciatively, and he reached for the desk 'phone. "Bureau of automobile licenses," was what he asked for, and he got the State secretary finally. A question, a wait, then a thank you.

"Them numbers is great things," observed the chauffeur, as he heard the receiver click back into place. "They makes it easy."

"Not very, Michael, not very." Colton spoke quietly, but if it had not been for the darkness of the room the Irish chauffeur would have seen the grim tenseness of the blind man's lips. "The number on that machine is the one allotted to the personal car of the district attorney of New York!"

"The devil it is!" Michael's chair fell over as surprise jerked him to his feet. "What would he be doin' in the case—an' gettin' away a girl that did have a hand in killin' the old boy at the Hotel Beaumonde?"

"Where did you get that idea?" asked Colton sharply. "Have the papers got her connected with the dead man?"

"No, sorr." Michael hastily disabused the blind man's mind of any such impression. "The mornin' papers have but a bit, 'twas too late fer them. They know nothin' of who the man was nor the woman wid him. They couldn't even seem to find out how he got into the hotel. As fer the girl, she was not even writ about. But Sydney follerin' of her, an' you at the hotel—" Michael knew that his own astuteness was obvious.

"Um!" Colton's fingers played a devil's tattoo on the desk for several seconds. "So they don't know how he got from the sidewalk to the dining-room entrance?" The words seemed a low-toned, musing question. "I didn't think they would, Michael; I didn't think they would."

"What's that, sorr?" The chair Michael had righted as he talked, creaked as he leaned forward.

The drumming fingers stopped. "You can take me to where you left Sydney?" the problemist asked.

"Sure, sorr. 'Twas old Cath'rine Street, or thereabouts."

"All right." Colton snapped on the light so that Michael, unaccustomed to the darkened rooms of the blind man's house, could find his way out.

As soon as the chauffeur had gone, the light went out again, and Colton's fingers unwound the wet bandage from his sightless eyes and put in its place the tortoise-rimmed spectacles of smoked glass that protected the tender eyeballs from the glare of all light. A touch of a button brought the Fee with suspicious dispatch.

"Yes, sir, Mr Colton?" There was an eagerness in the boy's voice that told plainly Shrimp hadn't been out of earshot.

"Hat, coat, and stick, Shrimp!"

"Yes, sir, here they are, Mister Colton." The boy held them out. "We're goin' t' find Sydney, ain't we?"

"We're going to try, Shrimp." Colton took the things smilingly. He knew that the boy, whose one ambition in life was to help the blind man solve his crime puzzles, had been listening to every word. He knew, too, that every nerve in Shrimp's body tingled with the prospect of having an active part in one of the cases on which the blind man was working.

The car was at the door, and within two minutes Shrimp and the blind man were on their way to the starting place of the long trail. Michael went across the city to Third Avenue, and followed the same route he had taken the night before, when the low-hung car had taken the girl down into one of the darkest, most narrow-stretched, least-known parts of the big city. The boy's alert mind was teeming with a hundred unasked questions; a thousand possibilities; a million pictures of what the blind man would do and could do. To the boy there was nothing impossible, nothing too difficult, no case too complex, for the master mind of the man he worshiped. But he was silent, knowing that the blind man wanted silence.

Michael drove the big car slowly through the twisting streets, stopping at the narrow corner where Sydney Thames had alighted early the same morning. The chauffeur turned in his seat. "Down this street, to the first turn on the left," he said.

Colton nodded, and scowled as his ears told him of the small group of staring urchins who crowded around the car. Shrimp, visibly swelled with vested authority, curtly ordered them aside as he stepped out of the machine and held the door for the blind man to alight.

"Wait," said the problemist to the chauffeur, and, with the touch of the boy's sleeve against his arm, he walked through the crowd and started down the sidewalk, perfectly conscious of the staring eyes of bearded men and kerchief-hooded women from doorways and curb.

A blear-eyed man sidled from a dingy hallway.

"Guidechu t' Silver Sandals, sir?" he wheedled huskily. "Do it fer a quarter. Wonder, Silver Sandals is. Past, present, and fucher. Love, business, an' domestic troubles. Investments, lucky days, an' women. First name, hor'scope, picher of yer wife. Spir't control, hyp'tism, an' mind-readin'. Slate-writin', cab'net mystery, an' wishin' charms. One dollar, two dollars, an' five. Can't make a mistake, or your money back. Best fortune-teller in the world. On'y def-and-dumb cla'r'v'ynt in America. Guiddechu, sir, a quarter!"

The words came rapidly, in a husky singsong, as the blear-eyed man shuffled along beside them.

"All right," nodded Colton, but the words of the guide had put a dozen new kinks in the snarl the blind man was trying to straighten. There was no doubt of the fact that at least some of his bleariness of eyes had been caused by the quarters this professional had got for guiding well-dressed people to the house of the clairvoyant. His patter had been too glib, too well learned to be new, and his voice had the whisky huskiness, of the hard drinker.

A common fortune-teller in such a district! Colton's mind picture of the woman who had guided the bearded man to his table in the restaurant had been entirely different. But she was evidently well known. There was no question that the woman of the night before and the clairvoyant of the blear-eyed guide were the same. The girl of the burnished-gold hair would have had no other reason for visiting this part of New York. Sydney had disappeared here. And there wasn't one chance in ten thousand of two women who wore silver sandals being connected with the case.

"Silver Sandals is quite old, isn't she?" Colton asked the question in the tone of nervous anticipation that a seeker of a new experience in a strange section of the city would use, and his hands fumbled around the guide's arm and hand with the nervousness of a stranger in the section.

"She's a thousand if she's a day!" declared the guide positively, figuring that the tone of the blind man was worth at least an extra quarter, and determining to give full value. "I been in this section twenty years, an' she was here when I came. Folks said she'd always been here. She's got a crow what talks fer her that's older'n she is. Says it's a carnation of some 'Gyptian ram. I don't know how she figgers a crow bein' a flower an' a goat, but then I don't figger nothin' *she* does!"

Colton understood that the woman had impressed the guide, and probably others, with the fact that her crow was a reincarnation of a Rameses. A trick of the charlatan to impress the gullible! But why the pretended deafness and dumbness? Colton, who prided himself that his ears could not be tricked, had declared it was the woman who had spoken in the restaurant the night before. He could not be mistaken!

"It must be quite difficult for a deaf-and-dumb person to be a clairvoyant," remarked the blind man.

"Not fer her!" There was no doubt that the guide was profoundly impressed. Colton's super keen ears told him that there was no hypocrisy in the blear-eyed man's statement. He spoke as a man who would stake his life on his statements. "She kin tell what you say by lookin' at yer lips. You needn't make a bit of noise, if you don't want to, on'y move yer lips like you was talkin', and she gets everything. Some of the swells as comes to her does that so's there'll be no chance of anyone hearing what they has to say. An' she couldn't hear a house fall down. That's right! One fell down 'cross the street, an' she never knew it till I tol' her. She just makes a sorter squealin' noise in her throat. Nobody 'round here ever heard her say a word, an' I know people as knew her fifty years ago."

"Strange I never heard of her until a friend told me a few days ago," Colton said casually.

"Ye'r' lucky," confided the guide. "Ain't many people hear of her. She ain't the kind that reads yer hand fer a quarter. On'y swells is what she handles. Chee, some of the people that come! Women with diamonds enough to make the bridge cables stretch when they go over. An' men! Honest, mister, if I tol' you some of the guys come to find out things from Silver Sandals you'd call me a double-barreled liar, with a tied tail. I'm the on'y one ever dares guide new ones. These Roosians is scared t' death to go near her house. Not that I blame 'em, either."

"Perhaps you know my friend?" suggested Colton. "You couldn't mistake his heavy, brown beard streaked with gray."

"Him!" The blear-eyed man stopped dead in his tracks. "Him!" he repeated in a tone of dull wonder. Then suspicion came to his voice. "He ain't yer friend. Yer kiddin' me!"

"Not at all!" protested Colton. "His name is Johnson; he's a lawyer."

"Oh!" The guide started again. "No, I don't know him."

"Someone who looks like him, eh?"

"Nope!" declared blear-eye positively. "I don't know *nobody* that looks like that. The feller you described *ain't* nobody. He's just one of her controls."

"Controls?"

"Yep. One of the spir'ts she brings outta a cabinet. She's got two. One's a girl with red hair. She's Golden Locks. The guy's name is The Prophet. Him an' the crow is the profsizers. They tell you what to do when the girl ye'r' strong fer ain't strong fer you. See!"

"Strange combination," mused the blind man. The feeler had brought more information than he had even hoped for. So the girl and the dead man who had been at the table in the restaurant and the woman with the face of terrible age had been together in the house toward which they were going. The blear-eyed guide had seen them. They must be well known in the district; but only as "controls" of the charlatan. Who were they? Who was the woman; the director, the controlling mind? Why should she have buried herself here in this part of the city? She was no common fortune-teller, dependent on the tricks of the trade to bring her dollars. Why the dead man in the restaurant? Why the girl whose hand had broken the stem of her wineglass?

"Here's the place!" The blear-eyed man stopped before the brownstone steps between the rusty iron rails. The windows, with their shutters hanging awry, still gaped emptily. "I'll ring the bell fer you."

He started up the steps; then the unaccustomed sound of an automobile horn in the street caused him to turn.

The silent Shrimp turned, too. He saw the car, and he spoke for the first time, in a tense whisper:

"It's a runabout, with a racer body, Mr Colton."

The guide almost stumbled as he jumped down the steps to the side of the blind man. "Gimme my quarter," he demanded. "Me wife's callin' me. Gimme it, quick. I gotta get!"

"Is this the place?" There was suspicion in the blind man's tone; though he knew the guide had led him right. He knew, too, that the sudden fear had been inspired by the coming automobile, a car like the one Michael had followed the night before.

"You damn' piker!" snarled the blear-eyed man. "I hope you get pinched!" He turned on his heel and darted away, a string of oaths trailing behind him as he disappeared into a dark alley.

The low, black car drew up to the curb.

"Good morning, Mr Colton!" greeted a hearty voice from the car. "What are you doing in this section of the city?"

"Just exploring," answered the blind man quietly, but there was a big question in his mind that demanded answer.

The voice of the man in the runabout car was the voice of the district attorney of New York City!

6

ANOTHER VICTIM

It seemed minutes that Sydney Thames' eyes were held by the strange eyes of the woman who stood in the doorway of the house with the dark, cobwebby windows and hanging shutters. It was only seconds, probably; minute-long seconds of silence. There was no repetition of the strange, eerie throat sound of command; nothing but the coal-black eyes that never wavered. Sydney took a step forward. He did not know why. There was no reason why he should have taken that step; no reason why he should have taken the next. No reason on earth but the woman, who was slowly backing before him; the woman with the coal-black eyes.

He heard the door close behind him creakingly as one sandaled foot of the woman pushed it shut. There was no movement of the eyes that held his; no movement of the flickering candle she held over her head. Behind the woman, on both sides of her, were hangings of dusty black velvet over which weird, cabalistic figures ran riot; signs of the zodiac, freakish figures of animals out of all anatomical proportion, suns, moons, stars. All were of silver, the burnished metal that showed in the stiffness of the thick velvet.

The woman's back bent in a curtsy, both arms swept wide, and the candle in its silver holder flickered above her head, where her hand had left it! Sydney Thames knew it was a trick of a hanging wire. He knew it was all trick; the velvet hangings with the silver designs to impress the impressionable; the silver sandals; the tomb-like silence; the garish light of the single candle that accentuated the weirdness of it all. All a trick! Yes! All but the unwavering, unyielding eyes in the unfathomable depths of which seemed to lurk the wisdom of centuries dead and gone.

The arms swept together, the palms met in a sharp, pistollike slap in the silence of the hall. A swift, darting shadow enshrouded the flickering light for an instant, and a crow, black, monstrous, thing of evil, perched on the outstretched right arm.

"What is it, sir? Your business at this hour?"

The rasping questions came from the bird on the woman's arm! This last, uncanny detail in the whole uncanny picture stirred the latent superstition in Sydney Thames despite himself. He shot a glance over his shoulder toward the door through which he had entered. But behind him, as in the front, the heavy velvet hangings covered everything. The door was hidden.

"Your wishes, sir? Your wishes?"

In the scratchy, grating voice of the bird there was impatience.

What did he want? What could he say? That he had followed the girl? That he wanted to find out about the murdered man at the restaurant? That he wanted to know why the woman of the silver sandals had drunk her toast to the man with whom she had sat at the table? Why the man was killed? Who was he? Who was she? Who was the girl he had seen enter the house a few minutes before?

These were the questions that flashed through the mind of Thornley Colton's secretary as he stood there. They were the questions he wanted answered. Those were the things he wanted explained. But he could not ask them. The woman before him must not suspect any connection with the murder at the hotel. But even as that thought came, Sydney Thames knew—*knew*—that the coal-black eyes of the woman that seemed to read his very soul must understand his visit and its reason. He could not lie!

"The murder at the hotel!" He blurted the words, and cursed inwardly because there was a tremor in his voice that all mental striving had not been able to keep out. "The murder at the hotel," he repeated inanely. He knew it was inane, foolish, but the words seemed to come before he could hold them back. He realized that he had probably spoiled everything; that he had failed at the first responsible part Thornley Colton had ever given him. But the blind man was far away; the coal-black eyes were very near.

"There was no murder." Again the metallic voice of the crow answered, as a parrot would have answered; repeating a thing it had learned by rote. The woman did not move a muscle, her arms remained outstretched at her sides, there was no expression on the wrinkled face. She stood like a statue against her background of black, her arm a perch for the crow who spoke because she was deaf and dumb.

"The bearded man at the restaurant—the dead man there!" Sydney's words were puerile, and he knew it, but some separate consciousness seemed speaking while another part of him stood aloof, unable to combat the thing that was leading him to say words he did not want to say.

"The Prophet?" rasped the crow. "The Prophet? You want to speak with the Prophet? He knows all things, sees all things, tells all things that you wish to know. Come!"

Again came the shadow across the suspended candle, as the crow left the woman's arm. Its wings flapped softly against the black velvet. Its bill pecked at the hangings a moment, and they swung back, revealing a door. The woman's arm moved upward, she seemed to pluck the candlestick from the air, and with a movement of her eyes she commanded Sydney Thames to follow her.

The moment the eyes of the woman turned from his, Sydney Thames shook off the spell of them. He was himself again. But there was no turning back now. He would see all there was to be seen, hear all there was to hear. There was no thought in his mind of danger. The hanging candle, the crow, the cord he saw that had released the swinging velvet curtain over the door, were all parts of the charlatan's stage setting. A fortune-teller, a clairvoyant. He could take care of himself, and he would have even more information than Thornley Colton expected. He had failed in the first part. He would more than make up for it now. So he followed her.

The room they entered was but a counterpart of the hall on a larger scale. The same velvet wall covering with the strange silver figures was there. A stuffed owl perched on a big cabinet in a corner. A skull gaped grinningly from a black wooden table in the center of the floor. Silver scarabs spread their wings over the black wooden chairs. A typical clairvoyant's room, thought Sydney, and a cynical smile came to his face for an instant. He had seen them before. Did the woman hope to impress him with such tawdry fake? Did she think to frighten him with her spirit manifestations? That was the old, old game. The Prophet! Bah!

He pretended semi-hypnosis as he seated himself in the chair which a motion of the woman's arm indicated. She sat facing him in another chair, beside the black table. He met her eyes fairly, but every part of him was fighting against them now. The surprise at seeing the woman in the doorway when he stood on the brownstone steps had taken him off his guard, and he had obeyed the commands of her eyes before he had had a chance to recover himself. Now he and she were starting equal. But the coal-black eyes seemed to make no fight for the mastery of Sydney's mind. They flashed their glances on all sides of the room, following the flight of the black crow as it slowly circled the walls; following the bird till it alighted on the skull on the table beside her. She was neglecting no detail of the stage setting, Sydney told himself.

But a shiver went down his spine as he watched the crow. It flapped its wings; it cawed raucously, once, twice. Then it slowly turned to face the woman.

"Sleep, Silver Sandals!" came its sharp voice. "Sleep, Silver Sandals. Command the Prophet to appear. The young man before you wishes speech with him. It is I who command you; I, the vested spirit of the great Rameses. You, who can hear no human voice or earthly sound know what I say, because I speak from another world. Obey! Obey!"

The remarkable eyes of the woman closed, the head with its white hair and wrinkled face nodded back and forth slowly in time with the solemn, metallic voice of the bird. Sydney Thames knew it was the old trance-medium trick. There would probably be mysterious rappings produced by mechanical means; perhaps the slatewriting hoax. But the single candle, the old, old woman with her silver sandals and black satin dress, and the crow were uncannily impressive. With the closed eyes, the age-lined face of the woman seemed softer, the repellent expression melted into peace, repose. The regular breathing was that of a little child. It was impressive, but Sydney refused to be impressed. Colton had explained to him all the tricks of the spiritualist charlatan: the magnetic rappers, the thin wires that tilted tables, the false black cardboard on which the slate writing was written, the tricks of lights that produced diaphanous spirits with Indian names. This would be the same, despite the elaborate stage settings.

Around the cabinet in the corner came a ghostly glow, whitely phosphorescent. Slowly the black velvet curtains parted. Sydney Thames' chair pushed back as his whole body jumped; his breath choked in his throat. Standing before him in the light, head held high, bright eyes staring straight ahead, was the bearded man of the restaurant; the dead man he had left sitting at the table!

There was no doubt of it—no doubt of the bushy brown bread streaked with gray that almost met the eyes and covered half the vest. There was no doubt of the clothes, cut according to the fashion of half a century past. The bearded man took a step. Another. There were no supporting arms now, but the leg lifting was that of an automaton, jerkily mechanical, as had been the gait of the man he had watched enter the dining-room an hour before. The man was coming toward him. Sydney Thames sat rigid in his chair. There was but one thought in the mind of Colton's secretary then: to get away. But his muscles refused to obey the dictates of his brain.

It wasn't a trick of the lights. It wasn't a trick of anything. The man was there. He was before him. He was flesh and blood; alive! Yet the blind man had told him the man he now saw was dead—murdered! The arms that were now bent at the elbows and held away from the body, as though invisible hands were aiding the paralytic steps, had rested on the restaurant table, one hand loosely around the stem of the filled wineglass, the other palm down on the cloth, when Thames had last seen them.

Each halting step of the man brought him nearer Sydney. Each inch Sydney Thames moved back his chair seemed to take all the strength from his body. An arm of the bearded man straightened out slowly, the hand rested on Sydney's black hair. A chill shook Thames' body, but he did not move; he did not even look up.

"You wish the aid of the Prophet?" The words, solemn, spoken slowly, came in the heavy voice of the man who stood over him.

"The Prophet wishes to aid you. Speak!" There was the same solemnity in the resonant words, but in the tone seemed kindliness; just a hint of gentle command. Sydney Thames felt the hand resting lightly on his head; about the man who stood over him seemed to hover the scent of some subtle Oriental perfume, as of incense burning. But there was no brazier, no smoke, and there had been no smell until the man's hand had touched his head. The woman in her black chair swayed back and forth, her eyes closed, her withered lips curved in a smile. From the skull top the crow blinked at him wisely.

Every bit of will Sydney Thames possessed fought back the fear, the superstitious awe, that was in him. His fist clenched at his sides; his jaw set—then relaxed as he asked his blunt question, the only question that would come to his atrophied brain:

"Why were you at the restaurant—dead?"

In type, the question sounds silly; but there was nothing silly in it to Sydney Thames as he felt the hand of the bearded man on his head, as he saw the woman before him who was apparently sleeping, as the black crow blinked at him from its perch.

"I was not dead—I slept." The kindly note was still in the heavy voice.

"But why did you choose such a place to—sleep?" Sydney Thames asked the question doggedly. The strangeness of the thing was making him forget the superstitious awe. Somehow he wanted to smile at the grimness of it—of asking a man he had last seen dead the whys and wherefores of it all. Surely no one had ever had such an opportunity before!

"Because there was feasting and merrymaking. Death should always come to the banquet board to remind the living that the body is but an ephemeral wraith inclosing the restless spirit."

"The old Egyptian idea of the mummy at the feasting board?" asked Sydney. His only feeling now was one of curiosity to see how far he could go. He forgot the sleeping woman, the crow, the single candle in the velvet-hung room. He thought only of the voice in which was a note of kindliness, and the gentle pressure of the hand on his head.

"I was in Egypt ten centuries agone. My beliefs are the beliefs of the wise men of the Nile." The solemn sincerity of the words was unmistakable. It drove all thoughts of amusement from Thames' mind. The man standing over him believed what he said! But Sydney Thames refused to be sidetracked. The man who spoke might believe such a thing, but Sydney Thames refused to credit such belief. The man was there, and Colton had said he was dead in the restaurant. The blind man did not make mistakes!

"You were murdered in the restaurant!" Sydney snapped out the words, and his muscles grew tense for the explosion he expected. The hand on his head did not move; there was no new note in the voice that answered:

"That is untrue. I went to sleep hours before you saw me. The two who guided me knew I was sleeping; but years have obscured the true belief, and preparation was necessary to carry out my wishes. When the day came for my sleep—forecasted by the oracles centuries back—everything was ready. Those who carried out my wishes will be rewarded."

The words carried conviction! Sydney Thames shivered under the touch of the hand as his mind went back to the picture at the restaurant: the mechanical walk, the waiter, and the woman who not only guided but supported. Dead when he entered the restaurant! The thing seemed absurd. A dead man could not walk even with supporting arms! And Colton had remarked the strangeness of the bearded man's voice!

"You do not believe!" The kindliness was gone now. Anger had taken its place. "See!"

The hand was lifted from his head. The man stepped back. Slowly he rolled the sleeve from his left arm, baring the thin, corded forearm. Around the flesh, above and below the elbow, Thames saw cleverly hinged, double circlets of silver!

"The preparation!" said the solemn voice. "Years of thought, and of toil wrought by mine own hands; of bands of silver, of coils, and springs and braces of your new metal called steel."

The mechanical walk! The automaton leg-lifting! The unmoving head, held high! All those things came back to Sydney then. There was no lie in the speaking voice. Sydney knew that. And his eyes had seen!

"So you died naturally?" the words came slowly from Sydney's lips. "The bringing you to the restaurant was but the carrying out of your desires?"

He remembered the toast the woman had drunk; the touch of the woman's lips to the man's forehead, the moment of bowing before she walked out of the restaurant. It must be true, all true. Thornley Colton had been wrong! There had been no murder; only the obeying of a curious wish of a strange man.

"Yes." The bearded man answered the question as he slowly backed toward the cabinet in the corner. "Yes. So you may tell your blind master."

His blind master! The words aroused Sydney Thames' numbed brain like a sudden plunge into cold water, and brought back to his mind all the suspicion the words of the man had allayed. He knew of Colton! He must know of the trailing. So it was all a trick. He realized then that he had left the bearded man at the restaurant. There was no way he could have gotten here. Who was this man? Who was the man with his fingers around the stem of the wineglass? Who was the woman? The woman! He'd forgotten her completely!

He moved his chair as the curtains of the cabinet closed before the backing man. Silver Sandals' eyes were still closed, her body moved back and forth in her chair. He started to rise. He'd find out what it all meant! The sharp voice of the crow cut the tomblike silence.

"Wake, Silver Sandals!" it commanded. "The young man has seen and heard. Wake, and touch him with your hand, that he may know it is not all a dream."

The body swaying ceased. The coal-black eyes opened slowly, stared straight into his. Again Sydney felt their uncanny power. His tense muscles relaxed as he sat back in the chair. The woman rose slowly from her seat. She came toward him, her silver sandals moving slowly under the black silk of her gown, her hands rigid at her sides. Once more Sydney felt the wild impulse to get away, and once more his limbs refused to obey the dictates of his mind. She stood before him, over him, as the bearded man had stood a few minutes before. She raised her hand. His eyes, moving to avoid her gaze, caught the bright, silver flash of something in her hand. The hand came nearer. He raised his arm instinctively to protect himself; his chair moved back as his heels dug into the velvet carpet. Then the woman's arm moved like a flash of light. He felt a stinging, burning sensation in his left side. The woman seemed to sway dizzily before him, then she went farther and farther away. For an instant he saw a new figure standing against the black velvet hangings of the corner cabinet. It was that of a girl, her eyes wide with fright and horror, the fingers of her left hand gripping tight at the velvet, the burnished gold of her hair glinting in the light of the candle.

The girl's lips moved. Faintly he heard the sobbing words:

"Another! My God, *another!*"

Darkness came to hide all things from the eyes of Thornley Colton's secretary.

7

THE PANHANDLER

To the blind man there were a thousand voice inflexions which told him a thousand little things that the eyes of the seeing missed. In his brain were catalogued hundreds of men by their voices alone. His memory, trained wonderfully by the constant use necessitated because of the lack of eyes, never forgot a voice nor the man who used it. So Thornley Colton's blindness was an asset rather than a handicap. Faces may be disguised so that the sharpest-eyed will not recognize them, but the vocal cords have been attuned by nature to a pitch that cannot usually be radically changed.

The problemist, with one hand on the rusty iron rail of the brownstone steps that led to the door of the old house, waited for the district attorney, who had greeted him from the underslung machine. Another new twist to the case that had already involved the coroner and a precinct captain.

The district attorney hurried across the sidewalk, nodded cheerily to the silent Shrimp, and took Colton's extended hand. "If you're exploring," he smiled, "we might just as well explore together. Our paths lie in the same direction, I think."

"Silver Sandals?" queried the problemist.

The district attorney nodded, losing sight of the fact, as most people did, that Colton was blind. "A queer character," he said. "For more than a quarter of a century she has escaped the periodical crusades against fortune-tellers and their ilk. Men have been sent to get 'false pretenses' evidence, and they've come back to report the wonderful things she did. I'm going to see for myself, this morning."

"I think you've waited about six hours too long," declared the blind man, with quiet certainty.

"What do you mean?" In the voice of the district attorney was the inflexion Colton had been awaiting. The previous statement regarding the "exploring" had been no more true than Colton's own.

The problemist answered the question simply: "I mean that Silver Sandals has gone, taking with her the explanation of the dead man in the restaurant of the Beaumonde."

"How did you connect the two?" The official was plainly chagrined.

"Silver Sandals are not common pedal coverings in New York; nor is it a common *nom de guerre*."

"That's equivocation!" The lawyer's training made the statement a trifle snappish. "*When* did you know that a clairvoyant in a section like this was connected with a murder in one of the biggest Broadway hotels?"

"My secretary visited this house a short time after the bearded man was discovered to be dead."

"Why, the police haven't connected the two yet!"

"I am not a policeman." Colton was gently ironic.

"No, you aren't!" stated the official positively. Then, frankly: "Look here, Colton, why can't we work together? I know the police have nettled you, and you're human enough to resent it. But this case has all the earmarks of the unusual. That's why I'm on the job myself. Things were dull yesterday, and I happened to come across some of the reports regarding Silver Sandals. When I heard of this case I immediately took a chance of connecting the two. I understand and appreciate your abilities, and I've got sense enough to know that my official position doesn't imply that I know it all. What say?"

The frankness of the appeal touched Colton as nothing else in the world would have done. Perhaps the district attorney had been clever enough to understand that; but there was sincerity in his tone and words. The official had been keen enough to know that the problemist was human; that he *did* resent the supercilious attitude of the professional investigators of crime whose record was based on the number of convictions and not the number of correct solutions they found. With the police, the arrest and conviction of the man they had picked up ended the case, and added to their prestige. With the blind man, the solution of the problem was the great thing in the crime puzzles he loved. He realized the fairness of the district attorney's proposition, and he met frankness with frankness.

"I'll give you all the help I can," he promised, and there on the brownstone steps their hands met in an oath of allegiance.

"Now we'll go inside. Frankly"—the district attorney smiled apologetically—"I can't quite credit the disappearance of Silver Sandals. For years she has been a sort of institution. No one seemed to know where she came from, nor what her real name was. The files at my office cover her for years back."

"Anything criminal?"

"Nothing. She is merely a high-class clairvoyant. Deaf and dumb, with a wonderful crow that does all the talking for her. That seemed to be merely a trick, but dozens of tests have been made to see if the woman really could hear or speak. A building was to be torn down across the street, and men were watching her to see if the noise would bother her. It collapsed one day, and she didn't even hear the crash. She is deaf and dumb, all right, and a list of the persons who visit her would surprise you: members of the four hundred, politicians, hardheaded bankers, Wall Street operators, gamblers, and men-about-town."

"The superstitious streak is in all of us," nodded Colton. "Even Napoleon had his dream-book."

The district attorney took a step toward the door. "Ready?" he asked.

"One minute." Colton turned to The Fee. "How clean is that suit of yours today, Shrimp?" he wanted to know.

The boy's face went as red as his hair. "Honest, it's clean, Mister Colton," he protested. "I only got a little dirt off the car when I helped Mike clean it yesterday." He turned to the district attorney pleadingly. "It is clean, ain't it?"

The puzzled official agreed that it was.

"If it's that clean," smiled Colton, "get around the corner and roll in the gutter. Then slide down the alley to our right. You'll find a small gang of Irish kids playing there." He added a word to clear the lines of bewilderment on the district attorney's face. "My ears are three times as sharp as yours. I can hear them plainly, though you can't hear a sound. This used to be a great Irish district, you know, and several of the old families refused to be chased away by the foreign invasion." He spoke again to Shrimp. "Get that?"

"Yuh bet I did!" The boy's eyes were aglow with joy. He knew that he was going to do some of the work he loved; real detective work, helping the blind man.

"Fall in with them, and find out the name of the man who guided us here. Don't do anything else. Don't attempt to locate him alone. If you do, I'll never let you work on another case!" There was no mistaking the severity of the tone, and the boy agreed soberly before he darted away gleefully to get himself as dirty as his boy's heart desired before doing his share of the work.

"Mind telling me what that means?" asked the district attorney when the boy had disappeared from his sight.

"Did you see the man who was with us as you came?"

"Merely as a type of panhandler, who had apparently been turned down when he asked you for the price of a drink."

"You only heard the end of it. He seemed to be an official guide to Silver Sandals' place. It was when he recognized you that he ran away without getting his quarter."

"Recognized me!" ejaculated the district attorney. "I never deal with his kind. There isn't one case in fifty on which I ever go out, and—Silver Sandals never sees anyone without an appointment."

"He was waiting for someone," declared Colton.

"I was the first to arrive, or—" The words trailed off thoughtfully.

"That's a queer one," mused the district attorney.

"There are several queer ones. Why should he fear you, if Silver Sandals has been wonderful enough to keep beyond the law for a quarter of a century? And, speaking of queer ones, here's another."

He stepped from the rail against which he had been leaning while the fingers of his right hand idly rubbed the rusty iron behind him. His fingers touched a spot on the metal that seemed darker than the brown rust.

The other bent down to examine it, then straightened, with a sudden whistle. "Blood, by Jove!"

"Yes. My fingertips felt the unmistakable silk hardness of it when there should have been nothing but the flaky corrosion of the iron."

"It's all up the rail," discovered the official, as he walked up the steps.

"Down the rail, you mean," Colton corrected. "It was made by a person coming down."

"Where do you get that?"

"Because it is on your left, and would be on the right of one descending the steps. The blood came from the right hand of the person who left it."

The district attorney shook his head helplessly. "That Sherlock Holmes stuff is too much for me," he admitted.

"Nothing of the Holmes type of deduction in that," Colton deprecated. "I merely happen to know that the person who made it had blood on her right hand!"

"Her?" broke out the official quickly. "You mean Silver Sandals?"

Colton shook his head. "No. Golden Locks!"

"Golden Locks?" The district attorney's tone was a combination of surprise and sudden recollection. "I saw that name in the reports on the clairvoyant. Golden Locks is supposed to be one of the spirits she controls."

"A spirit of very healthy flesh and blood," averred Colton. "She was sitting at the next table to the dead man at the Beaumonde."

"What?" There was distinct shock in the district attorney's tone.

"True," the blind man said quietly. "My secretary followed her to this place when she left the dining-room. She came here in a car like the one you own, and which bore the same license number."

"My car?" The exclamatory question fairly popped from the lips of the official.

"The same kind of a car, with the same license number," repeated the blind man.

"Certainly! Certainly! Of course!" There seemed almost suspicious hastiness in the staccato sentences. Apparently the district attorney realized it, for he veered quickly. "What did your secretary discover?"

"I don't know." Colton spoke soberly.

"Don't know?"

"He has never returned."

"Never returned?"

In the repetitions the blind man recognized sparring. But why should the district attorney of New York spar in a case like this? How could his automobile be connected with the murder?

"You mean he is there yet?" asked the attorney eagerly, with a flirt of his hand toward the green-painted door, with its heavy brass knocker.

"No. He has gone."

"You don't know! You haven't looked!"

"Diagrams aren't necessary in a case like this," the blind man said grimly. "A few blood spots on a rusty rail and a little knowledge of feminine human nature are sufficient."

"I don't quite follow." Real bewilderment was in the voice.

"You know that a woman is instinctively careful of beautiful clothes, when she wears them."

The official's nod told that he did, but it also told that he didn't see the connection.

"If she cuts her hand, she is mighty careful to hold it so that it won't touch any part of her wrap that can be seen. She wouldn't use it for fear of spotting the cloth. That's an inborn something in a woman that a man lacks. When a girl forgets that, as she did when she put her hand out to touch this rail, and leave the evidence of her forgetting, then something has happened to drive away the deepest ingrained instincts of her sex. No ordinary thing would do it."

"You mean that something happened to your secretary, and she knows of it?"

"She saw it!" Colton spoke positively. "She knew of the dead man at the next table, yet she did not forget to hide her hand when she had cut it on the broken wineglass. If she had, my ears would have caught the whispered comment of the other diners who had seen the blood. She saw what happened to Sydney, and she left this house before she recovered from the shock of it."

"You don't suppose he was murdered?"

The blind man shook his head slowly. "No. I am working on a strange theory here. What it is you'll know later—if it's the right one. But I am positive Sydney is not in that house."

The district attorney had no answer for this. He stood on the lower step without speaking, his head lowered in thought, his hands deep in his trousers pockets. Colton stood on the step above him, idly swishing his trousers leg with the thin, hollow stick he always carried, and which gave to his supersensitive finger tips its messages.

Suddenly the official looked up. "Do you know where my car was last night?"

"Naturally not," the blind man said, a trifle dryly.

"I loaned it to a friend of mine." The statement was lame, and the attorney knew it. "Bracken," he added.

"The owner of the Beaumonde?"

"No. His son." The district attorney walked from one end of the steps to the other. Down the street stolid-looking foreigners were going about their business, children were playing in the streets, but none came near. The fear the old woman and her house had inspired kept them at their distance. Even the presence of the automobile and the two well-dressed men would not lure the staring children from the places of safety a hundred yards or so away. The two men were as much alone as if they had been miles from the teeming city. "Bracken and I were college roommates," the district attorney went on. "I'd do anything in the world for him. His son has always been a little wild, and hasn't been around New York for nearly five years. Day before yesterday he came to see me. He'd been working upstate somewhere, and he'd fallen in love with a girl, he said. She was coming to town last night, and he wanted to take her to the theater. I offered to lend him money, but he said he had enough of what he had earned. Then, shamefacedly, he told me what he did want. He wanted to borrow my small car for the evening. He'd told her, lying, as he admitted, that he owned a machine. Colton, he was the son of the greatest friend I have on earth. He had apparently braced up. The thing he asked was a simple thing; perhaps it meant a whole lot. Women are funny, you know." He walked the length of the steps again; his face seemed to have aged years in the seconds. He spoke again. "But there was a bigger thing than friendship involved in the oath I took when I became district attorney."

Colton's cane still swished his trousers. His mind was back in the office of Manager Carl at the Beaumonde. He was listening again to the facts regarding the waiter who had helped the dead man to his seat. He had been personally recommended by Bracken. Here was the son! How easily the recommendation could have been secured! How logical the choosing of the Beaumonde! He remembered the pedigree of the serving man who had secured his position but two days before, and had disappeared when his work was done. *He* was the man that must be found!

"When was your car returned?" asked the blind man.

"My chauffeur says it came back about two o'clock."

"Bracken return it personally?"

"My man doesn't know him, but he says a blond chap brought it back."

"Blond? Um!" Colton stood in thoughtful silence, then: "It was he who met the girl at the Waldorf, where she tried to avoid pursuit. He didn't wait to take her and Silver Sandals, and perhaps my secretary, away. There wasn't time enough."

"He might have taken her to the station."

"No. They wouldn't risk trains. The old woman would be too unmistakable."

"We'll look over the house," suggested the district attorney. "We may find the clues we need there."

Colton followed him. As the other put his hand on the door handle Colton suddenly swung to face the street. Fine lines came to his eye corners and across his forehead as his ears strained to catch some far-off sound.

"Shrimp's footsteps in the alley," he said. "We'll wait for him."

They stood on the top step, the blind man getting everything with his ears, the district attorney with his eyes, when the boy came into sight. The red-haired kid, face dirty, clothes muddy, bobbed up the steps with a twisted grin of triumph on his freckled face.

"It was easy!" he exclaimed joyously. "The kids knew him. His name is George Nelson, an' he's a waiter!"

8

QUESTION AND ANSWER

Unique in the annals of New York death mysteries, and with none of the sordid, revolting details that usually mark the daily murder of the metropolis, the strange dead man who had sat with his glass of wine at the table in the fashionable Beaumonde had aroused the interest of the whole city. Two million insatiable readers of the daily newspapers waited eagerly for the meager facts each edition brought them. The stories in the morning papers but whetted their appetites for more. In the early evening papers, on the streets before the average business man had even thought of leaving his bed, were stories that bristled with lurid speculation. But that was all. There was nothing beyond the actual finding of the dead man, the woman who had come with him, and the astonishing fact that he had been brought to the restaurant dead.

There all facts ended and reportorial imagination ran riot. Every paper had its own theory, weird, wonderful, ridiculous. Each proved its facts after its own style. But what everyone who had been in the dining-room had seen was all that any one seemed to know. There was not a thing that would tell who the man was nor whence he had come. The pockets had been absolutely empty. The woman was a mystery; not one of the hundred of keen-nosed newspaper sleuths who were scouring the city had had time to connect the clairvoyant of the Peck Slip district with the strange woman who had entered the restaurant. The waiter who had helped, and then disappeared, was being searched for in every nook of the city. But he had disappeared completely. The woman, too, had gone from the hotel to step into oblivion.

According to the taxi starter, she had refused a cab, and had walked around the corner. If there had been another machine waiting there no one had seen her enter it.

An interview with Manager Carl at the Beaumonde was very brief. It consisted of a newspaper man's questions and a slam of the office door in his face. Interviews with Captain McMann and Coroner Bierbauer were equally terse. "Come to the coroner's inquest at ten o'clock," was the gist of both.

So the coroner's suite was filled when Bierbauer, with the pompous authority that marks the official business of the city, started the proceedings. Newspaper writers jostled elbows with newspaper artists in their cramped space. Women sob writers, who sought eagerly the one touch of human nature in the case that yielded no straight facts, wrote notes about the crowd of morbidly curious that infest such places at such times. Bierbauer selected his jury with the dispatch of long practice, and necks were craned eagerly for the first witness.

"Doctor Brown!" called the coroner, and a well-known police surgeon took the stand, crossed his legs, uncrossed them, cleared his throat importantly, and leaned back comfortably, conscious that he had made a good impression on the newspaper men. He carefully kept his profile toward the lean-faced young man whose pencil was busily working over a "sketch from life."

"Going to take no chances of his own judgment being wrong," went the whisper among the reporters.

The surgeon's name, age, official capacity, and length of service were established and then came the first question.

"What, in your opinion, was the cause of the victim's death?" asked Bierbauer, "victim" evidently being the official designation of the bearded man.

"Arteriotomy. The wrist arteries were slashed, and the man bled to death."

"Isn't this supposed to be a painless method of suicide?"

"Yes. After the first sharp sting of the incisions the victim feels about the same sensation as that of morphia; the dreamy, floating-away feeling, lassitude, and then gentle sleep. It is, of course, much slower than an opiate, and never gained wide favor among the unfortunate victims of melancholia because of the innate horror most persons have of blood."

"Would you, as a practising physician and surgeon, on your oath, give it as your opinion that the victim in this case might have been a suicide?"

"No!" The negative reply came sharply.

"Why not?"

"There were unmistakable marks of violence on the body!"

Heads lifted in all parts of the room. The inquest was surely carrying out its promise of startling developments.

"Tell the jury the nature of the marks?"

The police surgeon uncrossed his legs and recrossed them again. He saw that the artist's pencil was idle, and fixed his body in a more comfortable position.

"The largest mark was on the left side, directly over the heart, starting almost at the breastbone and extending under the left arm at the armpit. It was a bruise, six inches long and nearly two inches wide."

"This could be made, how?" interjected the coroner.

"I should say"—the witness cleared his throat impressively—"that it had been made by a heavy club. The blow was struck over the heart while the victim had his arms raised, probably in an attitude of pleading for mercy."

"Were there other marks?"

"Two: A wide welt on the left forearm and a bruise on the shoulder that could only have been made by a terrible grip of fingers."

"Could you tell, by the marks, whether they had been made by the hand of a man or a particularly strong woman, such as the one who supported the dead man?"

"No. The hand that made the shoulder mark, and probably the welt on the wrist, was heavily gloved, to prevent Bertillon measurement and comparison. The arm bruise is a welt because the fingers entirely encircled the thin forearm. The man could not have weighed more than a hundred pounds. Age and a sedentary life had wasted the body. On the narrow shoulder, the finger ends sunk into the flesh."

"How would you place the time of death?"

"About seven hours before I examined the body, or about six hours before you first saw it."

"Then there is no doubt that the man who apparently walked to the table was dead?"

Again all heads lifted and all ears strained for the answer. Each person in the room knew what it would be; yet each wanted to hear confirmation of the thing that seemed so impossible, so absurd. Never before had such a question been asked by a coroner of a witness. Had the dead walked! Question of a hundred possibilities; of endless complications!

The surgeon nodded emphatically. "He had been dead for hours!" Unconsciously he repeated almost verbatim the words the blind man had used.

"You examined the framework that supported the body and gave the impression that the dead man was merely a victim of partial paralysis."

"I did. It is the most ingenious thing I have ever seen. It must have taken years of study and work. Its designing and building show a keen insight into the anatomical structure of the body."

"Would it be possible, in your opinion, for such a frame to be fitted to any body?"

"Most emphatically not!"

"You mean that the frame was made for the body it fitted?"

"It would work on no other, unless the one chance in a million of another body with exactly the same measurements and of exactly the same weight."

"Could the frame have been fitted quickly to a dead body?"

"It could not. The fine adjustments of the thirty-three places where the silver circlets and steel springs were placed would have taken hours."

"Five?"

For a full moment the police surgeon sat in deliberative silence. His eyes looked over the heads of the eager men and women who leaned forward so that they would not miss a word. Finally he answered the question.

"My own personal opinion is"—came another of his impressive pauses—"that *one* person could not have fitted the frame on the dead body. It was the work of two, or probably three, persons. One person could not have committed the murder and attended to its following details."

"Then it is your professional opinion that it was murder?" The tone of the coroner told that this was his last and clinching question.

"Unqualifiedly yes! Fiendishly planned and devilishly executed!" The surgeon's eyes searched the faces of the newspaper men to see that they had gotten that last well-turned sentence.

"Thank you, doctor; that is all."

Coroner Bierbauer waved a dismissal with one pudgy hand, and glanced at a sheet of notes at his elbow. As the physician stepped down, a buzz of excited comment went up. The newspaper men were writing. The morbid element whispered its satisfaction. A good murder! This was the unanimous verdict of all who had heard the doctor testify. A brutal killing, with a strange new twist of the restaurant and the silver-sandaled woman, and the framework that had been made for the body of the murdered man!

Feet scraped expectantly as the coroner looked up from his notes.

"Adolph Heindle!"

A well-fed, well-dressed German mounted the stand nervously.

"Business?"

"Captain of waiters at the Beaumonde." There was just a trace of accent, but it was in the harshness of consonants rather than the pronunciation of words.

"How long have you been at the Beaumonde?"

"Fifteen years."

"The dead man, and the woman who accompanied him, sat at one of your tables?"

"Yes."

"Tell us what you saw."

The captain described how he had seen them entering the restaurant with the waiter who should have been at his tables. He told of the effect of the woman's eyes on him, the bottle of rare wine, the curious words of the man, and the reservation of the table through the manager. This last with a trace of hurt pride, and a glance toward where Carl sat scowlingly awaiting his turn to testify.

"The waiter was a new man, wasn't he?"

"He had been at the hotel two nights."

"An experienced man?"

The waiting captain hesitated before he answered. "He seemed to know the dishes and silver," he said slowly, "but he was a poor carrier. Had he not been put on by Mr Carl, I would have spoken for his discharge."

"Was there anything suspicious in his actions?"

Again there was hesitation before the captain's answer. "A girl was sitting at the table next to the dead man," he said slowly. "The waiter seemed to know her. She was unaccompanied, and I was about to tell her of our rule regarding unescorted ladies, when the waiter prevented me."

"How?"

The captain told of the brushing past and the allusion to the mythical Mr Smith.

"Describe her!" There was real animation in the coroner's tone this time. The newspaper men, alert, to catch this new turn, stopped their writing to get every word. The group of detectives in the rear of the room, whose eyes had sized up and properly classified every person in the room, stretched their necks as an aid to ears. Bierbauer glanced over them, and a look of disappointment came to his face when he did not find the person he sought.

The waiter described the girl in a way that showed plainly his fifteen years of experience in a Broadway restaurant had not destroyed his eye for feminine beauty. The women sob writers' pencils were flying now; their part of the story had come.

"Did you see her enter?" quizzed the coroner.

The captain shook his head.

"Is that usual?"

The captain seemed to take this as an implication of personal neglect. "Not at all," he assured, darting another hurt look at his manager. "But two of the other captains had been allowed a night off, and I had three table groups to attend."

"Then you did not see the couple enter the restaurant?"

"No. When I first saw them they were at the fourth table from the lobby entrance. It was early, and the diners had all been shown to tables in the center of the room."

"That is all. Thank you."

Again the coroner referred to his notes. Heindle made his way nervously down the center aisle with an uneasy glance or two over his shoulder as a small group separated from the crowd of reporters and started after him. The uneasiness became real fright when a square-jawed detective took him by the shoulder and whisked him out of the room before the newspaper men had a chance to pump him further.

Two pages, whose duty it was to stand at the lobby entrance of the restaurant to take hats and coats that had passed others of their kind, added a new element of mystery. They had not seen the strange couple enter from the lobby. Both had been busy with hats and coats inside the room. The hotel clerk declared that the man had not been registered as a guest, and he had never seen him.

There was a stir when Manager Carl was called. The table had been reserved through him. He must know something of the strange couple. But Carl was sullenly antagonistic, and showed it in his manner, his words, and the very way he sat in the witness chair. The police had evidently badgered him to the point of distraction, and he apparently saw his dining-room business ruined.

"How long have you been manager of the Beaumonde?" Coroner Bierbauer asked the question brusquely, and his manner showed that he was not to be trifled with. He had evidently had enough experience with the irate manager the night before.

"Nine years," answered Carl curtly.

"Do you know anything of the man and woman who came into the restaurant last night?"

"No."

"The table was reserved through you, wasn't it?"

"Yes."

"How?"

"Note."

The red flush mounted the purple jowls of the coroner. "Show me the note, and answer the questions fully!" he snapped.

A sneering smile on the lips of the hotel manager was the only answer to this as he handed over the papyrus note. The coroner took it scowlingly, cleared his throat ponderously, and read to the jurymen:

> Manager Carl: With this note are fifty dollars. Is this sufficient to reserve the fifteenth table from the lobby entrance, which is the fourth table from the east wall, for an hour before your time of midnight? The service must be for two. I wish to be served this bottle of wine, which I send.

The coroner made no effort to still the loud whispers of surprised comment the reading of the note caused. In fact, there seemed a bit of pride in his manner as he glanced down at the long table with its rows of newspaper men; as though each new twist of the case was of his own devising. There came a glow of professional pride as he realized that this case would spread his name all over the country.

He handed the note to the jurymen, and they read it one by one, nodding wisely. Meanwhile the talk went on in the room. The curious phraseology of the table reservation was discussed fully.

"'Inclosed *are* fifty dollars,'" repeated a *Times* man to a *World* reporter, who sat beside him. "Not one person in a thousand would put that sentence in that way. It's too stiltedly correct."

"'After *your* time of midnight!'" exclaimed a *Sun* man. "There isn't a spot on earth, where time is kept, that midnight isn't universal. Why '*your* time'?"

Coroner Bierbauer interrupted the speculation to speak: "Those words are written on papyrus, a kind of paper made in ancient Egypt"—from the corner of his eye he saw the impression this new information made—"a writing expert declared that the words had been written by a man. There are two other notes, written by the same person within the last few days, according to the expert. One, addressed to myself, I will now read you:

> Coroner Bierbauer: At the Beaumonde Restaurant you will find a dead man. Kindly proceed at once to make your official investigation so that the body may be sent as quickly as possible to the Fresh Pond Crematory for incineration.

"As in the case of the other note, there is no signature," added the coroner. "This note was delivered about eleven-thirty last night by a messenger boy from an upper Broadway office. There is no record of who left it. Here is the other note, directed to Police Captain McMann:

> Captain McMann: At the Beaumonde Restaurant you will find a dead man. How his death was caused a superficial examination will probably reveal. Unwind police tape as quickly as possible so that the body may be sent to Fresh Pond, where arrangements have been made for incineration.

Coroner Bierbauer made several notes on the paper at his elbow, glancing toward the door from time to time. A frown came over his nose as the man for whom he was looking did not appear. Manager Carl fidgeted as the minutes went by and no attention was paid to him.

"I've got work to do!" he snapped finally.

Bierbauer's frown deepened. Another glance toward the door, then he put another question to the short-tempered manager, who was being kept away from his hotel.

"Did you see the couple enter the hotel?"

"No. I didn't see the couple at all. I only saw the man when the captain sent for me."

"Where were you?"

"In the café."

"Then you couldn't have seen them if they had entered the hotel through any of the entrances?"

"No."

"Why didn't you notify the waiting captain of the table reservation?"

"Forgot it. I received the note early yesterday morning. I had an important engagement in the afternoon, and turned it over to my assistant because the night-room men don't report until five o'clock. Why he didn't tell the captain I don't know."

"Where is your assistant?"

"He started yesterday on a month's vacation."

"Where?"

"He didn't tell me. It was none of my business. The vacation was coming to him, and when his time was up at six o'clock he went."

"Did you examine the waiter to see that he qualified for a position in your restaurant?"

"No. My assistant has charge of the dining-room force."

"What's his name?"

"John Norman."

The coroner made several notes before he asked the next question, and two of the square-jawed detectives hurried out to get the wheels of the police department started on this new lead.

"What did you do when you saw that the man was dead?"

"I didn't see that he was dead. I asked a friend of mine, Mr Colton, to find out what was the trouble with him."

"Why Mr Colton?" scowled the coroner.

"Because he's cleverer at finding out things than the whole darned police force put together! That's why!"

A bang of the coroner's gavel chased the smiles from the faces of the spectators.

"Didn't you think it strange," demanded Bierbauer angrily, "that such a note should be sent with a bottle of rare-vintage wine? Wasn't that worth looking into a bit instead of handing it casually to your assistant?"

"Nothing's strange in my business. I've had tables reserved for tame monkeys and pet lion clubs, and there have been banquets for South Sea Island chiefs with blue baboons tattooed on their cheeks. If anyone wants his own wine served, it's none of my business, if he pays for the service."

Bierbauer had an angry retort ready, but a quick separation of the crowd at the door drove it from his mind, and a pleased light came to his eyes as the burly form of Police Captain McMann pushed his way through the throng.

"Is there any way the man and woman could have entered the restaurant without someone seeing them?" Bierbauer put the question as though it were merely a matter of duty, and he wanted to get it over.

"No. Someone's lying!" growled the manager.

"What's that?" Bierbauer straightened in his seat.

"Do you suppose crooks and pickpockets could enter a hotel like the Beaumonde?" asked the manager sarcastically. "Someone sees everyone who comes in. I thought I was paying men to watch!"

"Do you own the Beaumonde?"

"Philip J. Bracken owns it."

"Has he been notified of last night's occurrence?"

"I've been trying to locate his yacht by wireless all night. When he comes you can question him. He knows as much about it as I do."

"That's all!"

Carl growled at the dismissal, and pushed his way from the room, turning a persistent reporter aside with a snarl.

"Captain McMann!" called Bierbauer, and the police captain, with a conscious air of his importance, mounted the stand and took the oath.

"You investigated the case at the Beaumonde last night?"

"I did. I was on the job fifteen minutes after I got the note. It might have been a fake, but I wasn't taking any chances in my precinct!" The captain's eyes were on the newspaper men, to see that they got it right. Then he glanced up as there came another movement of the crowd at the door. A look of triumph flashed across his face for a minute before the official mask fell again. The man who entered the room, his thin stick held loosely in his fingers, the blue lenses of his spectacles looking straight at the captain, was Thornley Colton.

The coroner saw, too, and his eyes met those of the captain before he put the question.

"From your experience, would you classify the death of the man at the restaurant table as murder?" he put bluntly.

"No doubt of it!" The emphatic statement came unhesitatingly.

"Will you tell the jury why you say that?" The coroner's voice indicated that he knew the reply, and his eyes swept the room, resting on the face of the white-haired man who leaned easily against the back row of seats.

"I will." The captain spoke the two words slowly and a dozen keen ears caught the note of gloating in his voice. "I know it was murder because the murderer is under arrest at police headquarters! His name is George Nelson, and he's the waiter who disappeared from the Beaumonde last night!"

The silence that followed this startling statement was broken as the slim cane fell from Thornley Colton's fingers to the hardwood floor at his feet.

9

A SMOKING TRAIL

A quick clean-up! This, in police and newspaper parlance, is the phrase which describes rapid action, quick solution of a case, and landing the prisoner in a cell. In the four-word terseness of the sentence is the highest praise, the greatest encomium that can be given a police officer. Captain McMann had made one of the quickest cleanups in the history of New York crime. Eight hours after one of the most mystifying murders that the city had known the murderer was in a cell.

The police captain was the last witness called. He told of the all-night search for the man on whom suspicion had instantly rested; the waiter who had assisted the man to the table. He told of finding him in the back room of a café on Park Row, above the bridge, babbling drunkenly of silver sandals, of a walking dead man, of his failure to receive the money he had been promised for "pulling off the greatest stunt New York ever saw, right under the noses of a hundred people."

The prisoner was well under the influence of liquor, and at police headquarters heroic methods were being adopted to straighten him out sufficiently to get a confession. Headquarters detectives were already on the trail of the silver-sandaled woman, and an arrest was expected there in a few hours. And on the testimony of Police Captain McMann, "George Nelson, waiter, age twenty-seven," was held as a "material witness."

Before the captain had left the stand, the reporters had disappeared in search of telephones, and members of the coroner's jury crowded forward to shake the hand of the police captain and congratulate him. Why a coroner's jury should do such a thing is one of the higher mysteries; but it is characteristic of all jurymen to congratulate someone. Prisoner or prosecutor makes no difference. The morbidly curious joined the jurymen, and Coroner Bierbauer, relieved of the tremendous weight of official dignity, smiled genially on one and all. His duty had been done, and done well.

At the rear of the room, Thornley Colton stood alone, carelessly tracing diagrams on the hardwood floor with the end of his recovered stick. The red-haired boy, whose clothes had apparently been rolled in the mud, had wriggled through the crowd to pick up the fallen stick, and had wriggled out again.

Captain McMann finally spied the blind man, and made his way toward him, nodding to the men on all sides his appreciation of the compliments he was getting. The hangers-on of the coroner's office kept a respectful distance from the greatness of the police, and talked it over among themselves with many a whispered "I told you he'd do it!"

"Congratulations in order?" asked the blind man smilingly, with hand extended.

McMann accepted the words and the hand as matter of fact. "You're a mighty good loser," he conceded generously. "But I said before it was a job for practical men. You're all right; you've done good work, but on a real case it's the police every time."

"No doubt of it being a real case." Seriousness took the place of Colton's smile. "Have you cleared up all the peculiar ends yet?"

"We will before night!" was the way the captain dodged that question. "We only landed the waiter an hour or so ago. I telephoned the coroner that I'd be right up, so I didn't have much of a chance to get anything on the detail part."

"Mind telling me how you located the waiter so quickly?" The problemist seemed really anxious to know.

"Little reasonin', little knowledge of human nature, and a practical way of going after what you want." McMann could afford to be magnanimous.

"If you know much about human nature, you know a man can't pull off a stunt like last night without needin' a couple of drinks or so to make him forget. But after that first couple he only remembers worse, and he needs some more, and when he gets more he talks. That hunch works eight times out of ten. Bein' practical, we watched the saloons. We knew he was a new hand, because the description didn't fit the old ones. We got him, and that shows you that while theories are all right in their places, there's a practical side to this game you ain't had a chance to learn with dark eyes—that's unusual enough. We sent out an alarm for a blond feller to narrow it down for easy spotting."

"Um!" Colton's cane resumed its tracing on the floor. "Looked as though he'd been drunk about five days, didn't he?"

The grin faded from the captain's face. "What d'ye mean by five days?" he wanted to know.

"That's the time Bracken's yacht landed. I looked that up. He sailed again yesterday. I had an idea someone might have gotten the waiter drunk and have stolen the recommendations to get the job."

The grin came back. "We had the same sort of a hunch," he declared warmly. "But this guy *talked!* He told us about doing the job and not getting his money. He knew the woman that wore the silver sandals!"

"I'd forgotten that." If the captain could have read the mind of the problemist he would have seen real puzzlement there. But there was no trace of it in his tone as he asked the next question: "Have you learned the name of the dead man yet?"

"Not yet, but we'll get it before night!" declared the captain positively.

"Perhaps I can help you." Thornley Colton took his wallet from his pocket and handed the police captain half a dozen clippings from newspapers. McMann read from one:

> In New York, suddenly, December 3, Sladnas Revlis, age 63. Incineration at Fresh Pond.

Rapidly the police captain glanced at every clipping. They had been in every New York paper, and the date they bore was that day!

"Where'd you get these?" demanded the policeman.

"At the home of the silver-sandaled woman who led the man into the restaurant."

"Have *you* found that place?" There was wondering respect in the captain's voice. The police had evidently kept the discovery of the clairvoyant a dark secret, and the blind man had been there before them! "Come outside." There was the habitual growl in the captain's words as he saw the loungers in the room staring at the two.

Colton nodded, and followed. In a corner of the corridor the captain stopped to glance again at the clippings, his heavy brow wrinkled and creased.

"Sladnas Revlis," he repeated. "A foreigner."

"Merely Silver Sandals spelled backward," Colton pointed out.

"D'ye mean to say this is the death notice of the man that was murdered?" the captain asked sarcastically.

"Yes."

"Bosh!" The expletive was fairly sneezed. "It's a fake! Whoever heard of publishing a death notice?" A new thought changed the trend of the sentence. "To get in this morning's papers, the copy for the ad would have to be sent before the man was murdered!"

"Before his death was discovered, you mean," corrected the blind man mildly.

"Who'd do it? Who'd do it?"

"The same person who wrote the three papyrus notes."

"May be you know who that was?" The captain put the question belligerently.

"I do." Colton was serious. "It was the man you found dead at the table; the man who was murdered!"

"*What!*" All the other verbal explosions had been mild beside this one.

"That is true." Colton's tone carried conviction. "Those notes and that notice were written by the man we found dead. Here's a picture of him writing them!"

From his outside coat pocket the blind man took a photograph. In the light from the big window, the police captain saw the picture of the bearded man. The captain had had twenty years' experience comparing photographs, and he could not be deceived.

It was the same man. He was dressed in a long robe, with huge Egyptian scarabs showing on the front and sleeves. He was writing at a small table on which a black crow perched with outstretched wings on a grinning skull! Another, and smaller, photograph pasted on the back showed the man's hand with a curiously shaped pen resting over the unfinished note that had been sent to the captain.

"Writing with a stylus," explained the blind man. "It makes a deeper line on the papyrus than would an ordinary pen. My fingers had no difficulty in reading the one at Carl's office."

"Where did you get this?" The captain's voice was growing humble.

"On the table you see in the picture, together with the clippings. They had been left to find. The rest of the house had been cleaned out before Silver Sandals left it. They were very careful; there wasn't much left for eyes to see."

"Can I have this for a while?"

Colton resisted the temptation to smile. He understood, now, the humility of the previous question. "Certainly," he agreed. "A photograph isn't of much use to me," he added dryly.

"Thanks. I'll do something for you some time." The captain actually sighed in relief as he shoved the picture into his pocket.

"You might allow me to interview your prisoner," was all the problemist asked.

"Sure! Sure! Any time!" The police officer gave the permission hurriedly. He backed away a step. "Goodby!" He was on his way even before he finished.

Colton heard him go, and a half smile curved his lips as he took out his cigarette case. He put his slim stick under his arm as he lighted the paper roll. For several minutes he smoked in silence; then his ears told him that the last of the hangers-on had left the coroner's suite. The cane clattered to the floor as it fell from under his arm.

Down the corridor came the pat-pat of light-running feet. A red-haired boy leaned over to pick up the stick.

"Did you get the district attorney, Shrimp?" queried the blind man.

"Yes, sir." The boy handed the cane to the problemist. "The cops didn't get the same one. The D. A. says his men ain't located the waiter that guided us to Silver Sandals' house. An' say!" The boy assured himself that there was no one within hearing distance. "When I got that cane signal inside an' called up what yuh whispered when I put it in yer hands, the D. A. was just gonna call up."

"Any news of Sydney?" The question came with a quick eagerness that seldom marked the blind man's tone.

"Nope, not yet," the boy answered solemnly. "They're lookin' fer him. But the D. A. says the two women left the house about three o'clock. A Hun s'loonkeeper that was just closin' up saw 'em. They went down toward the river."

"Three o'clock!" mused the blind man; and he went on, apparently to himself: "That waiter was the one who waited for the morning papers so that he could put the clippings where we could find them. I wonder—"

"They on'y had a satchel," put in the boy. "The D. A. remembered that yuh wanted to know what they carried."

"Sure?"

"Certain. The D. A. said he didn't know what you was so anxious about that fer, but he made certain. He says the police have just finished searching the house, and they didn't get a thing."

Colton nodded. "All right! We'll have to see for ourselves. Come on!" He started briskly toward the elevator. On the main floor of the building he turned toward the telephone booths. "What was the number of that little grocery store on the corner below the house that I asked you to get?" he asked of the boy, as they stopped before the desk of the operator.

The boy repeated it, and the blind man stepped into a booth and carefully closed the door behind him. In less than a minute he was out again.

"The car, Shrimp!" His voice was sharp, imperative. His nostrils quivered with nervous eagerness, a hectic flush was on the pale cheeks.

The boy caught the contagion. He knew that the blind man had picked up a thread in the tangle. His elbow touched the sleeve of Thornley Colton, guiding, by the touch of cloth against cloth, the sightless one through the throng of hurrying, jostling men in the main corridor and across the sidewalk to where the black car waited.

"Silver Sandals' house!" Colton ordered, and the car started the instant the boy's foot left the curb. Michael, too, knew that tone.

"Yuh ain't found Sydney?" The boy had kept that question bottled for blocks, but it had to come.

"I've located the thing I've been looking for. I think it will tell me where he is. If I am right—"

The words stopped with the grim compressing of the thin lips.

"What is it?" The boy asked eagerly.

"A crow! A talking crow!"

"The one that was in the picher?"

"Yes. The one the man who guided us told us about. The little Irish woman in the grocery store I asked to keep an eye out for anything unusual in the neighborhood told me over the 'phone that a crowd of boys were pestering a black bird in an alley. She told me the things the bird had been screaming." Again came the grim lines at the lips.

"Maybe they'll kill it, the darn kids!" gasped The Fee, and he leaned forward to speak to Michael. "More speed!" he demanded, with all the force he could put in his boyish treble. "Never mind the cops! Mister Colton's in a hurry!"

But there was no chance of the chauffeur obeying. They were already in the narrow streets of the Peck Slip section. Michael found it different driving this time. In the early hours the streets had been partially deserted. Now they swarmed with dirty, ragged children, and gaping men and women with their head bundles and pushcarts.

Around the corner came the shrill voices of children, the cries of men and women in a foreign tongue. Michael stopped the car before the small mob.

A boy's voice rose in a scream. Then came another voice, raucous, rasping:

"Poughkeepsie! Poughkeepsie! George Nelson! George Nelson! The greatest stunt New York ever saw. Pough-*kee*-psie!"

"Keep your horn going, and start slowly!" ordered Colton. He was standing in the tonneau, his blind eyes seemed to sweep the men, women, and children. The noise died as the crowd became aware of the newcomers. Men yelled warning. Women howled to their children. Such a fine car, and such a white-haired man could mean but one thing to them— the police!

Like magic, the crowd melted, darting into doorways, into alleys, behind pushcarts, till there was nothing but frightened eyes staring from a hundred hiding places.

"George Nelson! Age twenty-seven!" The sawlike voice came from a dark alley. "Under the noses of a hundred people! Poughkeepsie! Pough-*kee*-psie!"

"Get that crow, Shrimp! Get it! Hustle!" The voice was a whipcrack. The words of the bird seemed to have stirred something within him. His voice was commanding, unconsciously sharp. The boy ran to the mouth of the alley.

"Across the street to that little store!" Colton shot out, and the car swerved to the opposite curb. "Jump out and get a box to put the bird in! Give the woman a dollar! Hustle!"

Michael jumped from the car, and Colton settled back in the cushions. The spots on his cheeks seemed to glow now; his lean, cleft chin was set at an angle that boded ill for someone. He turned his head slightly as his super keen ears caught the beat of wings against the boy's arms as he struggled to grasp it, and the crow screeched its words:

"George Nelson! George Nelson! Age twenty-seven! Waiter! Pough-*kee*-psie!"

The boy came running back to the car, with the bird fighting vainly in his arms. Michael lumbered out of the little store with the box in his hand.

"Put it over the bird!" commanded Colton; his voice and manner like a live wire sending out its energy. "Police headquarters! Quick!"

The bang of the unmuffled exhaust roared, the car backed over the low curb as it swung around. Out of the Bowery, uptown at racing speed, regardless of traffic regulations or signaling police.

Before the big building that housed the central departments of the city police system the car stopped. Even before the wheels had ceased to turn, the blind man was on the sidewalk. He did not wait for the touch of the boy's sleeve to guide him here.

The doorman nodded to him, and got no answer. An unusual thing, for the blind man was noted for his courtesy. Straight to the office of the chief of detectives he went. A knock at the door, an invitation to enter, and Colton spoke before the chief had a chance to smile his greeting or put out his hand.

"I'd like to see that prisoner you've got on the Silver Sandals case!" The words fairly crackled command.

The chief jumped to obey—he had felt the touch of the live wire. Surprise had come to his face at the voice of the problemist, so different from the calm, even tones he had always heard before. But he did not question; he merely acted, just as bigger men than he had acted on that tone of command from the blind man.

"This way! Strange case!" jerkily commented the chief, as he led the way toward the cells. "Man's disguised with dyed hair, and all the color's gone from his face with drugs. Thought he was drunk first, but it's coke, I guess. Talks about the restaurant, and getting the man to the table, but we can't get a word about the actual killing."

Two detectives, lounging in a corner, straightened up as the chief approached.

"Shut up like a clam," growled one. "Can't get a word!"

"Here we are." The chief stopped before a cell, and glanced through the barred door at the man who lay huddled on the steel shelf that served for a bed. The prisoner did not even look up; his head was buried in his arms.

"Get on your feet!" commanded the chief. There was not a muscle movement of the man inside.

"Tell me your name!" Thornley Colton's words seemed to strike the man in the cell like a shock of a galvanic battery. His head lifted, a flash of expression came to the dull eyes for an instant; but the voice that answered was dead and mechanical:

"George Nelson. Waiter. Age—"

"That's enough!" Colton wheeled on the chief. "Release this man!" he ordered sharply. "He is my secretary, Sydney Thames!"

10

PREPARATIONS FOR MURDER

Another stone wall! Once more the path that had started straight had circled to its beginning. The discovery of Sydney Thames as the prisoner had thrown everything out of focus; made chaos of the carefully arranged puzzle pieces that had been put together in the mind of the blind man. He had expected an entirely different dénouement for his secretary's disappearance. He had expected a solution of the whole case in the finding of Sydney Thames. But the one ray of light had become darkness, black, impenetrable.

The strange words of the crow in its alley of refuge had told the blind man whom he would find at police headquarters. The apparently senseless reiteration of the waiter's name and age could only mean that the crow had heard the words repeated as they were taught to someone else. And that someone could only be his secretary. Drugs and hypnosis combined to explain the condition of the man the police captain had been so certain was the murderer.

The bird of ill omen had, however, apparently destroyed the basic theory Thornley Colton's intuitive reasoning had formed. Never before had the problemist known this strange faculty— made almost preterhuman by his blindness—to be wrong. In a hundred cases he had followed the mind processes of arch criminals to their logical conclusion, turning each corner at the proper time, counting accurately each footstep that led to the solution of the case. But here all paths seemed to be circles. The blind man was as much at sea as the keenest-eyed person in the world.

Was he all wrong? Was this a case for eyes? Was it a problem that required sight, instead of insight? This, Colton would not believe, because he refused to believe it. Perhaps it was egoism, but all masters have been egoistical, and Thornley Colton was a master. The thing he had built had come toppling down over his ears, but the foundation was there, firm, unshaken. The building must go on!

Once more the blind man sat before the desk in his darkened library. Upstairs, sleeping, was Sydney Thames. The blind man's sensational discovery at police headquarters had shaken the department from top to bottom. It aroused every detective in the city from the lethargy of easy-won success to furious effort. He had proved the identity of Sydney Thames when the police, supreme in their belief that they could not be wrong, had demanded it. And Sydney Thames, weak, dull-eyed, had gone home in the car. Now he was sleeping away the effects of the drugs and hypnosis that had made him a helpless tool to throw dust into the eyes of the police, and to build the stone wall that kept the blind man from touching the persons behind it.

On the desk before the blind man was a chessboard. His chin was in his hand, his head bent so that his sightless eyes under the folds of the alcohol-soaked bandages seemed studying each piece on the board. As time passed, there was no movement of the seated man. At his elbow the crystalless watch ticked off the minutes.

The blind man moved to touch the watch. It was eight o'clock; thirty-seven hours since he had slept. One fingertip touched a button of the row on the desk. The red-haired boy answered it on the run.

"Any new editions of the papers I haven't gotten, Shrimp?" he asked.

"Nope. On'y them I read to you. They ripped Silver Sandals' house apart, but they didn't find no thin'. Everybody's look in' for her an' the girl."

"Anything from the crow?"

"No, sir. It's just say in' Perkipsie over an' over, with that stuff about George Nelson. Can't make it say any thin' else."

"All right," the blind man nodded wearily. "Listen carefully, and write down everything it says, even if it's only part of a word or a letter."

"Yes, sir." The boy started for the door, and then turned. "I just tiptoed into Sydney's room. He's sleep in' fine."

"I can't do anything till sleep has weakened the effect of the drug," Colton said. "And, Shrimp," he halted the boy again. "I expect the district attorney in a few minutes. Bring him here, but don't mention the crow; I want to keep that to myself for a little time."

"Yes sir."

Again in the silent darkness Colton's head bent toward the board and its pieces. It was a strange game of chess Thornley Colton played. A black queen and king were pitted against a piece of broken wineglass with a spot of dried blood on its edge. Another black queen and a black pawn opposed a ragged black feather. Four small scraps of papyrus were held in check by a black bishop. It was the crime game the blind man was playing. Triumphant on the problemist's squares were a scrap of newspaper, the torn corner of a photograph, a crust of bread, and a silver dime. But there was no move of the pieces, for the blacks held Colton's "men" in check.

The electric front-door bell tinkled its alarm. Colton heard the door open, and Shrimp's polite, "This way, sir," and he snapped on the lights as the footfalls told him the district attorney and the boy were at the room entrance. Colton crossed the room to shake hands with the city official.

"What is it?" asked the blind man quickly, with his finger tip on the key-board of silence—the pulse of the wrist that told him the emotions of the heart. "You've heard from Bracken?" It wasn't a guess on the part of the blind man, but a certainty.

"Yes. A wireless. He is coming as fast as his engines can bring him. But he can't reach New York before tomorrow noon."

"Meanwhile the police are searching for his son," interposed the problemist.

"Yes. How did you know? The department has kept even a suspicion of such a thing from the papers."

"Sit down," invited the blind man. "If you don't object to the darkness, I'll snap off the lights; they make my eyes burn like fire, even through the cloth."

The district attorney sank lifelessly into a chair. His manner, his voice, told the blind man as plainly as eyes that the city official had aged years in the few hours since they had clasped hands in allegiance.

"How did you know young Bracken was suspected?" the district attorney repeated.

"Captain McMann is no fool," the blind man declared. "He's working like fury on this case. It means a whole lot to his bulldog nature. It's the only chance he ever had to beat me. No doubt he was in communication with Bracken the minute he saw the note of recommendation. And you know what would be the first thought of the father of a wild son."

"He's sent five imperative wireless demands to know how his son is implicated," the district attorney answered. "He is refusing to answer all other messages because he fears the newspapers."

"It's perfectly logical that he should want to know about his son. No doubt the messages to you were blunter than the answer to the police, but McMann only needed a hint, to connect the recommendation and the choosing of the Beaumonde with the son."

"But, my God, man!" the city official's voice was hoarse; "think of my position! He used my car! Why doesn't he come forward to explain?"

"Why?" echoed the blind man, his fingers touching the black king on the board.

"But he couldn't be guilty of murder!" The official's exclamation was vehement. "He's nothing but a young fool, a pawn of scoundrels."

"Wrong!" declared Colton solemnly. "He is one of the principals. He was the waiter at the restaurant."

"Bracken?" The district attorney refused to believe it.

"The testimony of the waiting captain that the waiter knew the dishes and silver but didn't know how to carry proved my original theory that the man was not a common waiter. Bracken would know them because he had used them all his life; but, of course, he wouldn't carry them like a waiter. And Bracken was the same type as my secretary, very dark. 'Phoning to a former friend told me that. The natural disguise would be dyed hair; opposites are always chosen. It was probably Sydney's visit to the house that gave the idea of throwing us off the trail by making him impersonate the waiter. That—and one other thing that occurred suddenly to change all plans."

"And that other thing?" broke in the district attorney.

"I don't know—yet. I think it's a crow."

"Is that what you expected the two women to carry away with them?" asked the district attorney suddenly. "You mean the crow that has been the mouthpiece of Silver Sandals for years."

"Yes, to both questions."

"Funny we didn't see any sign of it when we searched the house. But then there wasn't a thing but the clippings and the photograph." He broke off quickly. "That feather you found!"

Colton nodded. "From the crow. I am playing it here against a pawn and the queen. It should be against the king!" he decided suddenly. His hand changed the pieces. He snapped on the incandescents so that the official could see the chessboard with its strange "men." "Here is the crime. The queen is Silver Sandals. The pawn is the waiter who guided us. He stayed behind to find the crow. But you frightened him away. He is the real George Nelson, waiter, age twenty-seven!"

"How do you know that?"

"Because I'm blind. I've known it from the first. That's why I wanted you to locate him. I found out that he was a waiter a minute after he spoke to me. I touched his hand as he walked beside me to the house of Silver Sandals. He had the waiter's thumb, peculiarly developed by carrying heavy plates of food. But I realized that a man in his condition couldn't have been the waiter who had helped the man to the table. I recognized him only as a pawn. That's why I wanted to know if the man the police had arrested was he. When it wasn't, I thought they had just made one of their mistakes, until the words of the crow told me that another had been drilled to so often say the same thing that the mechanical brain of the talking bird had picked up the words."

"But why should he have pretended to be a guide?" the district attorney demanded. "Why should he be in rags, if he was a good enough serving man to have had a position on Bracken's yacht?"

"Why is my secretary sleeping, upstairs?" asked the blind man quietly.

"Hypnotism?"

"Yes. Superinduced by heavy drinking. He was gotten drunk so that his papers could be stolen. But he was too valuable a subject to let go. There was further use for him. He was kept under the influence of Silver Sandals because the waiter would naturally be the first person suspected by the police. And this waiter who had made his name and occupation so well known in the neighborhood that even the boys on the streets knew it was intended to be the blind to throw the police off the track—until my secretary became a better one. Oh, it was carefully planned; every step, every move."

"But I don't get it." Puzzlement brought slang in place of the official's usual careful diction. "The whole thing shows so many evidences of careful and elaborate planning, yet the results make a useless mess of unnecessary trouble."

"For instance?"

"The slashed wrists. Why, that alone almost precludes the possibility of murder, except for the marks of violence on the body. But there are so many easier and quicker ways of accomplishing the same result. And think of the evidence that must be left behind when the police locate the place where the murder was done. The blood and the marks on the body showed that the man must have struggled fearfully."

"The struggling was all done before the wrists were slashed. There is no doubt that he was drugged first."

"But, great Scott, man! If they could drug him, why couldn't they poison him in the first place?"

"And the natural next question," put in the blind man seriously: "Why didn't they leave him where he was murdered, instead of actually courting discovery by bringing him to a public restaurant?"

"I don't understand any of it!" The confession came almost in the tone of a curse. "The silver-steel frame! Think of the cold-bloodedness of fixing that to a dead body!"

Colton's fingers touched the dime on his chessboard. "That has already taken its place," he said. "Meaning," he added, "that I have already solved that part of the problem. The brace was not put on the dead body."

"But it was there."

"It was worn before the man was dead."

"You mean that the murderers forced the man who was to be killed to adjust it himself?" The district attorney could not keep the horror from his voice.

"No. I mean that he donned it without coercion. He put it on willingly."

"Why—why—" The interrogations came as gasps from the official.

"Certainly. Common sense and the evidence we have tell us that. The death notices, the photograph, the bottle of wine served at the table, the papyrus notes written by himself, the strange words of the ventriloquist woman—she was a ventriloquist despite the assertions of a thousand persons that she had been deaf and dumb for a quarter of a century. Even the method of getting him to the dining-room points to but one thing."

"The method of getting him to the restaurant?" That part of the blind man's statement made the district attorney forget everything else. That last sentence brought back to his mind the fact that no one seemed able to tell how the strange couple had gotten to the dining-room where they had been met by the waiter. "Do you know *how* they got to the dining-room?" he asked.

"Through the private dining-room that was built especially for the accommodation of Philip J. Bracken when he is in town, and which connects with his private suite by means of a private elevator."

"*Bracken's private suite!*" The words seemed to pull the district attorney from his chair by their very violence.

"Exactly," confirmed Colton. "Naturally you remember the talk it caused when the hotel was built ten years ago. Bracken's deep-rooted objection to newspaper publicity has kept it out of the public's mind ever since. Whenever he has to spend a few days on dry land he goes to his hotel and lives like a hermit. You know that."

"And the suite is forgotten from one year's end to the other." The district attorney was pacing the room before the desk. "I know it well, but I never even thought of it."

"Very few people have, up to the present," remarked Colton dryly. "For the simple reason that the seeing depend on eyes to make them remember. My brain instantly understood that possibility because it never forgets. But there were other things to be done first. That could not get away. The others could."

"And the suite has absolutely no connection with the upper halls." The official was turning the thing over in his mind as he walked the floor.

"When Bracken comes he brings his own servants, and the entrance to the dining-room is in the court beside the hotel!"

"But even Bracken had his gregarious moments," the blind man declared. "There is a door connecting the private dining-room with the big restaurant that is carefully concealed behind the palms near the lobby entrance."

"That has not been used for years!" put in the district attorney. "I know it. It is screwed shut. I remember when Bracken had it done. He had the—"

Colton cut in on the story: "It was used last night!"

"But someone would have seen the man and the woman coming out," protested the official.

"Not when everything had been carefully timed. The attention of everyone in the restaurant was centered on the new cabaret act. The two hat-check men were away. Although the restaurant entrance is into the lobby, it is arranged so that the lobby loungers cannot stare into the dining-room. The woman had to bring the dead man but a step through the door behind the palms, and the waiter was there to help her. It was but another step through the hiding palms to the door. The hour chosen was when only the tables in the center of the room had been filled and those near the entrance were empty. It was the work of an instant when all eyes were somewhere else. Eyes always are when the attention of the ears is attracted, and it was too far away for even my super keen ears to hear."

"The waiter—you mean young Bracken?"

That was the only thing that seemed to strike the district attorney for the moment. "Of course! Of course!" he answered his own question, hands working at his sides, face more haggard than ever as he paced the floor. "He could get the keys of the suite, he would know all about it. He is the only one who could do it." He stopped suddenly as another question popped to his mind: "But the police must have learned of that suite! Rooms in a hotel like the Beaumonde can't be hidden like secret chambers in a castle."

"No doubt," agreed Colton. "But police eyes probably saw the untouched screw heads in the door. They saw the marks of violence on the body that meant struggle. Their eyes told their brains that the murder could not have been committed in the hotel without raising an alarm."

"They are right!" The district attorney qualified it. "They *must* be right! If the murder was committed five hours before the body was discovered, it was committed in the daylight! The dead body would have had to be smuggled to the private dining-room, to the suite, and then back. That would be more trouble than taking it directly to the restaurant."

"Yes, if it was a dead body, but it wasn't. It was a living man!" Colton reached across the chessboard to pull the telephone toward him.

"You think he was forced to write the notes to the coroner and the police captain, and the death notices, and pose for the photograph, and adjust the brace in that suite before he was killed?" The words came impatiently.

"No. Those things were all done before he went to the private suite in the afternoon."

"Great Scott, man!" The district attorney gasped his incredulity. "You are saying that the man himself made all those elaborate preparations *to be murdered!*"

"Yes," Colton answered very quietly, as he lifted the telephone receiver from its hook. "That is exactly what he did."

11

CLEWS NOT FOR EYES

The problemist gave a number over the 'phone, but the dazed official did not even hear it. His mind was still trying to grasp the meaning of the amazing thing he had just heard. Then the voice of the blind man aroused him.

"Captain McMann? Good evening, captain. This is Colton. Any trace of the girl with the golden hair? No? Nor of the silver-sandaled woman? Nothing, eh? By the way, captain, do you know where the murder was committed? I thought not. The man was killed in the bathroom of Philip J. Bracken's private suite at the Beaumonde. That's true! Oh, you examined the suite thoroughly. Find anything? Probably not. But I'm going there in an hour or so, and I'm going to find something. Goodby!"

Colton's lips held a cynical smile as he snapped the receiver back on the hook and raised his head to face the district attorney. "The captain is working at high pressure," he observed. "He'll lose no time in getting to the Beaumonde. He's going to make sure that he doesn't miss a trick."

The district attorney shook his head in helpless bewilderment. "I don't know where I am," he confessed frankly. "Your statement that the man made all the plans to hide the guilt of his murderers is too much."

"That has been obvious from the very first." The first puff of smoke from a newly lighted cigarette ended the sentence. "Simply because the very elaborateness of the thing made it the only possibility. The timing of events alone proves that the thing was planned months in advance. According to the expert opinion of Brown, the making of the framework to support the body took years. And common sense would tell anyone that without the cooperation of the dead man there must have been slips. Remember that the final scene was timed to minutes!"

"More hypnosis!" the district attorney discovered suddenly. "The remarkable woman of the silver sandals; the one who hypnotized your secretary, and, you say, the missing waiter. Great Scott!" He mopped his forehead with his handkerchief. "Think of the diabolical ingenuity of compelling a man, by hypnotism, to prepare for his own murder months in advance!"

"A pretty theory," credited the blind man. "But false, or, rather, reversed."

"You mean—" hesitated the official,

"That the silver-sandaled woman and the girl were dominated absolutely by the will of the dead man!"

The watch beside the chessboard ticked off several seconds before the district attorney made reply. "That is the most incredible statement I ever heard!" he ejaculated, when he had carefully turned the blind man's statement over in his mind to see what lay under it.

"It is true, nevertheless."

"But it's unreasonable! It is practically an admission that the dead man forced three—"

"I said the woman and the girl were controlled by the dead man," interrupted Colton. "I did not mention Bracken."

"Two"—the correction came chokingly—"two persons drawn into a murder pact, with himself as the victim!"

Colton nodded. "Practically that," he admitted.

"I can't believe that sane persons would deliberately put themselves into the electric chair!" The district attorney was on his feet again, walking back and forth in characteristic lawyer fashion. "That is what it means. According to your statement, they are either murderers or accessories before and after the fact."

Thornley Colton merely shrugged his shoulders. "I expect Captain McMann to point out the murderer for me," he said simply.

"Captain McMann!" exclaimed the district attorney, making mental note of the blind man's evasion. "I thought you were fighting him."

"He is fighting me," corrected the blind man quietly. "But I am making him help me. They took away my eyes in this case"—a jerk of his head toward the ceiling told the other that it was Sydney Thames whom he meant. "They expected me to be helpless, and another pawn in the game. But they can't beat me!"

On the pale, masterful face was unalterable resolution. The lean, cleft chin was rigidly ominous. Under the skin of the cheeks the muscles played. The district attorney could imagine the eyes, beneath the folds of the alcohol-soaked bandages gleaming with the light of resolve. Despite himself, he shivered slightly. For the first time in his life he saw the white-haired man before him as a bloodhound; ruthless, unyielding. A blind bloodhound!

"Did you get any sleep last night?" asked the attorney suddenly.

A faint smile softened the lines around the tight-drawn lips. "You forget that but twenty hours or so have elapsed since the dead man was discovered. It was only last night, you know. Things have moved so quickly that it seems much longer." He touched the watch beside him. "Nine-twenty," he announced. "McMann should have been at the Beaumonde ten minutes ago."

"Are you going to let him go over the ground before you get a chance?" asked the surprised district attorney.

"He is my eyes tonight," the blind man said. "I am merely waiting for the link that has been missing. Ah!" The exclamation came as the telephone bell tinkled its signal. Colton took the receiver, and the official held his breath to hear the one-sided conversation.

"Yes?... Oh, good evening... He is?... What?... Yes... I'll be right there... Goodby!"

"Was that McMann?"

"No," answered the problemist, and the other thought he detected a note of disappointment in the voice. "It is Manager Carl. The police had visited the suite, and they are there again. He is furious! The murder is ruining business. He has something very important to tell me, he says. Come along?"

The affirmative came eagerly.

Colton put the watch in his pocket, his fingers brushed the chessboard, then his other hand swept the pieces and their opponents into a heap at the side of the board. "Four moves to checkmate," he murmured softly. Then, aloud: "We'll catch a taxi at the corner. I want Michael to get a little sleep."

He picked up his overcoat and light stick, replaced the bandages with his blue glasses, and, with a touch of his hand he led the district attorney through the dark hall to the front door. With his hand on the latch, he called out over his shoulder: "That's all tonight, Shrimp. Go to bed. Leave the notes on my desk."

From an upper room came the cheery voice of the boy: "All right, Mister Colton."

A blind bloodhound! How correct, yet how sinister the comparison. The blind man refused to take a minute's rest himself, but all connected with him must have their sleep. The civic official was trusting the man who had never seen light—who knew it only as a thing that tortured his tender eyeballs—to show him the ray in the darkness that enshrouded the strange case. And he knew the blind man would do it; just as Colton had led the man who could see through the darkness to the front door of the house. He knew that the man who had been blind at birth, whose one help had been taken from him by those he was fighting, would win!

They found a taxi at the corner, and a word from the district attorney put traffic regulations at naught.

The new atmosphere around the Beaumonde could be felt the minute they entered the big main entrance. The mantle of tragedy still hung heavy where only the care-free cloak of Broadway should have been. There was the usual crowd of loungers in the lobby, and Colton felt their curious stares. They were not guests, but others of the morbidly curious that infest crime scenes for days, like vultures seeking their scraps of carrion.

A page, evidently instructed to look out for the blind man, came up swiftly and whispered: "Mr Carl's office, sir."

A half-dozen alert-looking young men who had been standing by the desk fairly swooped down on them when they saw the district attorney. But with the experience of much practice he waved them aside smilingly. "I have no official connection with the case, boys," he declared. "I'm here merely as a friend of Mr Colton."

The blind man became the target for questions, then, but he refused to talk, and his manner caused even the persistent newspaper men to fall back and allow him to go on.

Thornley Colton opened the door of the private office as soon as he had knocked. The hotel manager's worried smile of greeting faded from his face as he saw the district attorney, and it went a shade paler. Colton closed the door tightly, and spoke. "It's all right, Mr Carl," he assured the other. "The district attorney knows of Bracken's connection with the case. In fact, the young man has already involved him!"

"You don't say—so!" gasped the manager, staring blankly. "Why"—there was shock of sudden discovery in his tone—"he's a villain!"

"Looks that way," Colton agreed seriously. Then: "McMann upstairs?"

"Yes!" blurted Carl wrathfully. "He and that iron-jawed detective of his are tearing the insides out of Bracken's suite, and he never allowed anyone to lay a hand on a stick of furniture. We'll have to work like the very devil to straighten it out before he gets back."

"Not much time before tomorrow noon," Colton admitted, finding a chair by the desk with a touch of his cane.

"Tomorrow noon!" echoed Carl blankly. "I haven't been able to locate him."

"He sent a wireless to the district attorney this afternoon," Colton explained, his fingers tapping idly on the piled papers that strewed the desk.

Carl darted a glance toward the district attorney, who nodded corroboration.

"Great Heaven!" The hotel manager's voice trembled. "That son of his!" He took a turn about the small office, and when he spoke again his voice was steady: "I've always loved that boy, Colton. And when he came to me and said that he'd straightened out and he'd met the right girl, I wanted to help him. He said that he'd been working for a year, and he wanted to know if he could have a spread for himself, the girl, and her mother in his father's private dining room. I knew it was going against his father, but here was a chance to help the boy along instead of giving him the kick his kind usually gets. I was away all yesterday afternoon, and my assistant promised to look after them. I didn't get back till late, and Norman had started away. Other things came up the minute I got here, and I never thought a thing about it until this morning, when McMann wanted to search the suite. Of course, I was nearly crazy, but when we got there I didn't see a crumb. The boy apparently hadn't arrived, and there was nothing to show that the suite had been occupied even when the two policemen went through it. Now they're at it again!"

"Almost exactly the same story he told me!" exclaimed the district attorney.

"When did he visit you, Mr Carl?" asked Colton.

"Day before yesterday."

"Ah, the same day he visited the district attorney; before he bleached his black hair and took his place in your dining-room."

"He was the waiter who helped the dead man!" The exclamatory sentence was a combination of pained surprise and certainty. "Of course! Who else could it be? My assistant has only been here about six months, and he wouldn't know the son of the owner even without the disguise. Philip hasn't been around in several years."

"No word of your assistant yet?" asked Colton casually.

The manager shook his head. "He was lucky enough to get away when he did," growled Carl. "The police are after him to answer a lot of their fool questions."

"Yes," murmured Colton dryly.

The tone caused the district attorney to open his lips for a question, but the blind man gave him no chance. "I guess McMann has had time to look over that suite," he said, as he rose. "Mind showing me the way up?"

"You don't expect to find more evidence of—Bracken's guilt?" The manager's tone was that of a man who hopes for everything and expects nothing.

"I expect to find something that the police are overlooking," the blind man replied, as he waited for a guiding hand.

The district attorney said nothing, but the look on his face expressed volumes; it was the look of a man utterly weary. He had been hoping against that the suspicion which each new tarn of the case was making stronger had been foolish. He had staked his all on the hope that Manager Carl would prove Bracken's innocence. But the boy had told the hotel man the same false story he had told the attorney; he had worked on the manager's sympathies in the same way as on his.

A hunted look came to the eyes of the manager as he opened the door of his office. The half dozen of the newspaper men hurried toward them; the loungers stared; the buzz of conversation came to their ears. Carl turned the reporters away with a snapped oath, and led his companions to a side entrance of the hotel. A nod to a doorman protected their rear, and they walked down the court beside the hotel where Carl fitted a key in the lock of a door and entered. When he had closed it behind them he breathed a great sigh of relief.

"Worse than leeches," commented Colton.

"Damn' sight!" choked the nerve-racked manager. "This way!"

They were in a small dining-room, and Colton stumbled over a chair.

"I beg your pardon," the district attorney said contritely, and with one hand on the blind man's arm he led him to the small elevator in the corner cleverly shielded by a screen. The elevator door slid closed behind them, and the car ascended noiselessly.

Even before it stopped they could hear the sounds of the two men inside the private suite, and when Carl sprang open the door, he shouted a wrathful exclamation. The rooms had been literally torn to pieces. Furniture had been pulled out, drawers overturned, and the carpet had been ripped from the floor. Captain McMann, red-faced, in his shirtsleeves, with perspiration beading his red face, stood in the center of the room. The square-jawed detective crawled from under a bed, swearing softly.

Thornley Colton stepped from the elevator. His thin cane located an overturned chair, and he stopped an inch or so from the overturned table.

"Thorough, at least," he observed, and his delicate nostrils quivered as he sniffed the close air of the tight-shut rooms. His finely chiseled lips wore the faintest of smiles as he realized the lengths the captain had gone when the blind man had telephoned his boast that he "would find something."

"Nothing here!" The captain spoke as though he would stake his life, reputation, and honor on it. "Never has been anything here!" he growled.

"No?" The short negative was almost a drawl. The problemist offered his cigarette case all around, and took one of the rolls. "Lucky you've got that habit of not smoking while on duty, captain," he said. "As soon as I light this cigarette the clinging smell of Egyptian incense in the rooms will be destroyed."

"What's that?" The captain sniffed the air with loud nasal gulps.

"Your sense of smell is not so keen as mine, captain." The match touched the cigarette end. "You are handicapped with keen eyes."

"Where'd the incense come from?" demanded Carl, with the snappishness the presence of the police always seemed to arouse.

"The man who was killed. There was just a faint trace of it that I detected when I touched him at the table. It was much stronger in the house of the clairvoyant. You smelled it there, attorney?"

The official nodded. "That establishes the fact that he was here."

"Incense ain't as rare as all that," declared the captain. "Lots of people burn it in their houses."

"True," nodded the blind man. "I said the *clinging* smell of incense. Anyone who has burned it knows that the odor does not hold. It is only in the aromatic smoke, and will not stay on clothes nor a room more than a few minutes. This is an incense odor; something that no common perfume has."

"You are trying to prove that the man lived here before he was murdered?" The captain was sarcastic.

"No. He merely came here to be murdered." The blind man turned to the square-jawed detective.

"Will you set that table upright?" he asked. His voice was sharp, the hectic flush was again on his cheeks. The detective jumped to obey without even thinking to look for orders from his captain.

"Thank you." Colton rested the slim stick against a chair. Slowly his finger tips moved over the polished top of the table. A forearm's length from the edge they lightly brushed the wood. An inch they moved slowly, two inches. He had examined a foot, slowly, painstakingly. The watching men became nervous as the minutes passed with no sound, no movement but the slowly sliding fingers. Suddenly the expression on the blind man's face changed. The fingers rested, then moved so slowly that the eyes could hardly see them move.

He looked up. "One thing you missed, captain," he said.

McMann's movement was a signal for the others. They crowded around the table, staring down where his fingers had stopped. But there was nothing, absolutely nothing, but the unmarred polish of the top.

"Keen eyes are not of much use there, are they?"

"Nothing there, that's why!" snapped the captain.

"A whole story, written out in English words!" Colton's fingers moved again. "If you have a very powerful glass you'll see the slight, almost invisible, indentations made by a heavy stylus that wrote a sentence. Here are the words, they may be of use: 'No human hand can unlock it. From out the dead dynasties.' There the writing stopped."

"Bunk!" growled the captain again. "Bunk!" he repeated.

"To anyone who doesn't know the capabilities of the blind, yes. But I can read Braille letters through a dozen thick handkerchiefs. Get a microscope, and you'll see the rough indentations."

"But what's it mean? There ain't nothin' to unlock!"

"Seems to me there's quite a bit to unlock," declared the blind man.

"I should say so!" gasped Carl, staring down at the table, with eyes narrowed in a vain effort to see what the blind man had said was there.

"Where's the bathroom?" Colton picked up his cane.

"Over there." There was no sarcasm in the voice of the police captain now. He couldn't keep it there nor on his face, though every ounce of his willpower strove to hold the mask. He felt, subconsciously, that the blind man would keep his boast; he knew that the senses of the man he was trying to beat would find something that his eyes, trained by years of experience, had missed. Already they had found one thing. Were there others?

"Lucid—to a blind man," remarked Colton. Then Carl took his arm to lead him to the bathroom door. The captain moved to where he could see everything the blind man did. Apparently he had not even noticed the presence of the district attorney, who should have had no connection with the case until the police had finished.

The problemist's feet felt the tiled floor, and he shook his arms free from the guiding hand. At the white porcelain tub he dropped to his knees, his fingers brushed the tiles under the tub. He straightened up, his hand held high above his head. The finger and thumb apparently grasped something; but they could see nothing from where they stood.

"Another clew your sharp eyes failed to find," announced the blind man quietly.

The district attorney was the first to move. The police captain had to jump to get ahead of him.

"A hair," Colton said. "A single hair."

They could see it now, glinting in the light from the one small window. It was long, of finely spun gold.

"The girl who sat at the next table!" The exclamation came from the mouth of the captain, and he bit his lips because he had been surprised into open admission.

"Right!" Colton dropped it carelessly in the tub. "In the shadow it was utterly impossible to see the hair, but my fingers, so sensitive that they could have located unerringly that same hair through several sheets of note paper, found it instantly. That's one of the feats of the blind that the average person doesn't believe until he sees it."

"But what does it mean?" gasped Carl. "Was the girl *here*?"

"The evidence seems to indicate that." Colton rose and carefully brushed his knees.

"Trying to tell us the old man lived in this suite and that the girl visited him without the hotel people getting wise?" asked the police captain.

"As I said before, the old man came here merely to be murdered." The blind man stood facing them, one hand in his trouser pocket, the fingers of the other twirling the thin cane.

"Nice, quiet little time, clubbing an old man half to death, and then cutting his wrists to finish it," observed the police captain shortly.

"You mean the marks on the body?"

"Plain enough, I guess," growled McMann.

"To a person with imagination, yes. That's your only fault, captain; the one thing that keeps you in a rut. You haven't imagination, any more than Doctor Brown had when he examined the body. The slashed wrists caused death, and, of course, there was no need of an autopsy, which would have proved that the man was drugged to unconsciousness before the wrists were slashed. There could be no sound because the murdered man took the drug unsuspiciously, and it acted at once."

"But the blood! Where is the blood?"

Colton's cane tapped the edge of the tub lightly. "A porcelain tub," he said. "That mark under the left arm, which your lack of imagination told you had been caused by the heavy club, was made when the body was jammed tightly against the round edge of this tub, as one hand on the shoulder held it in position and the other gripped the wrist to hold it over the drain. A simple turning of the hot-water tap, and there wasn't a bit of evidence. Simple, isn't it? — with a little imagination and without the handicap of eyes."

McMann swung around on the square-jawed detective. "Dust some of that fingerprint powder on the taps, Tom!" he ordered.

Tom, with the tip of his finger covered with a handkerchief, gingerly touched the hot-water tap, to raise it. A paper packet yielded some fine, white powder that dusted the polished tap, then was blown off. Everyone but the blind man stepped forward to stare; he merely stood back with his hands behind him.

"Not a sign!" grunted the detective.

"Forgot that Brown testified the murderer wore gloves so that he could beat Bertillon, didn't you?" suggested Colton quietly.

"Then the murdered man did, too," asserted the captain. "We haven't been asleep. We dusted that fingerprint powder round before."

"Eyes! Eyes again!" protested the blind man wearily. "Of course, there was nothing left to see! All a criminal has to fight is eyes. A simple cotton glove will defeat the most elaborate Bertillon bureau in the world. Naturally, the murdered man wore gloves. Do you suppose that detail would be overlooked, after months of preparation?"

"Theory!" snapped the captain. "All theory!"

"But you'll concede it pretty well borne out by fact—Don't turn off that hot water!" The sharp words caused the detective to straighten up suddenly.

Colton lowered the cane that had told him of the movement. From his pocket he took a handkerchief. He bent over swiftly, rubbed the cloth over the metal cross pieces in the tub outlet, and pulled his hand quickly from under the warm stream of water.

"See that! See that!" he jerked, holding out the handkerchief. "See the evidence of blood there! That proves it!"

On the handkerchief was just the faintest tinge of red.

"Great God!" The exclamation burst from Manager Carl.

"Are you *blind?*" the captain demanded explosively.

"This proves it!" Colton dropped the handkerchief into the tub and turned the tap. "If I wasn't blind I wouldn't have found that. But I know that every man who commits a crime works to destroy the evidence that eyes will see. The murderer in this case turned off the tap the minute the last sign of blood disappeared from the tub, and considered himself perfectly safe. But he didn't know that the sections of that drain guard that are in every bathtub would hold a few of the coagulated corpuscles which would soften again when the hot water ran. Eyes would never have seen them, because they would never think to look for them. A glass wouldn't have shown them because of their position. Perfectly safe, except for a blind man!"

His stick held before him, he walked from the bathroom. Mechanically the others followed. In the center of the littered room the problemist stopped. His head turned toward the door of the elevator as though his ears had caught some sudden suspicious sound. A tense expression came to his face, then faded.

"I think I've found all I came for," he said quietly.

"Three things I overlooked!" There was almost a choke in the captain's voice. Defeat came hard to the man who had staked his twenty years' experience against a blind man. The captain knew, now, that his vaunted abilities were nothing; he knew that he would be a second in the race he had started; that he had welcomed with such patent condescension.

"Four." The blind man recognized the note that had never been in the captain's voice before, and there was no gloating of triumph in his own. "Four," he repeated slowly. "I have found the object of the strange crime at last."

"The object?" The words seemed to come as an astonished chorus.

"Just that!" A pause, and the tense lines of listening came again to the problemist's face. He opened the hand that had been closed at his side since he rose from the bathroom floor and held it toward them, palm upward.

On it was a ragged black feather!

"A crow's feather," resumed the blind man evenly. "You didn't see it because you didn't know where to look. I got the crow while your men were at work searching the house of Silver Sandals, captain. It is at my home. You can have it tomorrow, with the compliments of the murderer. Goodby!"

12

A BRAIN FOR A BATTLE GROUND

It was a silent trio that descended in the private elevator. Colton had curtly ordered Carl to lead the way before the astounded captain of police and the gaping detective had had time to recover from the shock of the blind man's last statements. Nor did Colton speak until they had stepped from the elevator to the private dining-room.

"Where's the door that leads to the restaurant?" he asked abruptly, as he stood before the car, cane tapping his trouser leg.

Manager Carl shook himself as a dog shaking off cold water. "Great Heaven, Colton, but your work is startling!" he laughed jerkily.

An absent nod answered the compliment.

"A crow," muttered the district attorney. "And a feather."

"And a door screwed shut," reminded the blind man.

Carl, with a murmured apology for his delay, touched the blind man's elbow, and guided him to the door. Colton's fingers brushed the wood. The door had been screwed shut with heavy brass hinges. There were four of them above and below the door handles, fixing it closed so tightly that a battering-ram would have been needed to open it.

"I put those hinges on six months ago," Carl said. "They held the door tighter, and they looked a lot better than screws driven through the edge. When Bracken wants a thing done he wants it done well."

Colton's hand had gone to the other side of the door, and was feeling of the two original hinges.

"Ah! Opens from the inside," he said, with the satisfaction of one who has proved a theory.

"But the police examined those screws with a glass," put in the manager. "They haven't been moved in six months. The dust on the heads shows that absolutely."

"Quite right," admitted the blind man readily. "But see!"

A quick grasp of his fingers, a turn of his wrist, and the pin of the top hinge pulled out. A bending of his back, and the lower pin was in his fingers. The blind man stepped away. The door swung silently on the hinges that had been fixed to keep it shut!

"Good Lord!" The manager stared his bewilderment.

Colton paid no attention. He could hear the music of the orchestra as it jingled its lively air. A cabaret singer was earning her salary with one of the latest songs. The district attorney stepped to his side. He could see the shielding palms that hid the door. Through the thick branches he could see the sprinkling of early diners in the far end of the room.

"Those palms have been arranged differently!" Carl hissed it. "Look! A single turn, and there is an opening to the aisle that is hidden from the dining-room, and when the two hat-check boys were away from the door—"

There was no need of finishing. The district attorney saw the clever arrangement of the big plants.

"Bracken again!" The official gulped the words.

"It's hardly the duty of a waiter to move palms," Colton observed dryly.

"Certainly *not!*" ejaculated the manager, but there seemed no relief in his tone.

The blind man detected it instantly, and he shot out a sudden question:

"Where did that assistant manager go on his vacation? Winter seems a strange time for a man to go away."

"You don't think—" began Carl.

"It isn't what I think," cut off the blind man sharply, "it's what I want to know."

"He didn't tell me where he was going, and I wouldn't give the police any satisfaction," Carl said agitatedly. "He said something about going up to the North country, hunting. But his folks would probably know. They live in Poughkeepsie."

"Thank you." The blind man carefully closed the door and slipped the pins back into place. "If you'll take me to a taxi," he asked of the district attorney, "I'll go home and get a little rest. Tomorrow is going to be a strenuous day. You've got to locate that waiter from whom the Bracken recommendation was stolen, attorney. Call me the minute you've got him. I want him!"

They left Manager Carl at the private entrance in the court, staring after them. In the official's mind, as he held tight to the sightless man's elbow to lead him from the quiet court to Broadway, and across the crowded sidewalk to the curb, there were a dozen questions. This new character in the case—the assistant that had never even been suspected by him—seemed the one ray of long-sought light. But there was so much to explain. By all the possible twisting and turning the assistant manager could be nothing but an accomplice. The guilt seemed still to rest on the man who had borrowed the automobile, who had told the false story to Carl, the man who had acted as a waiter, so that he could help the dead man in his place at the table.

But Colton forestalled all queries, all talk.

"Nothing tonight," he declared. "Go home and get jour sleep. You'll need it tomorrow. Keep your men still on the trail of the missing waiter, and send a couple up to Poughkeepsie. Goodnight!"

A wave of his hand, the closing of the taxi door, and the district attorney was left on the curb alone. At the old-fashioned brownstone house where Colton had been born he ran up the wide steps as though weariness was a thing that never came to his well-kept body. But inside the door, his shoulders dropped a trifle, and he braced them back with a long, deep breath.

Forty hours without sleep, and the hardest part of the case to come! He was going to arouse Sydney Thames from the stupor of drugs and hypnotism. He needed him now. There must be eyes upon which he could depend for the final work on the case. He had worked without eyes, following each step to its stone wall; turning to begin all over again every time. Now he saw the straight path at last, and he had proved it straight. There was no chance of failure now. Those against whom he was pitted had but one course of action left. They would take it, because he had forced them to take it.

In the darkened library he poured himself a drink of brandy. Colton never drank; a glass of Célestins had been his limit of dissipation for years. The fire of the liquor coursed through his veins with its artificial stimulant. He knew that it was artificial, that it would demand its price in reaction, but the game demanded it, and Thornley Colton always played his games to the limit. There was no thought of self; every part of him was strained for one thing—the solution of a crime puzzle.

He swathed his eyes again in the cooling, soaked bandages, and made his way through the darkness to where Sydney Thames lay. The secretary was sleeping quietly, and his breathing was regular. Colton's finger on his pulse felt that the effect of the drug had worn off. It had taken but a touch, when he had found Thames at police headquarters, to detect the peculiar "bounding" pulse of morphia. But he knew that the hypnosis of the wonderful old woman with the remarkable eyes was still strong. He was going to try and combat it without the greatest aid to hypnotism—the peculiar eyes of the hypnotist.

He placed his hand on the hot forehead of Sydney. The man stirred uneasily, and a mumble came from his throat. The super keen ears of the blind man caught the word "Nelson," and he knew that even in the unconsciousness of sleep his secretary was repeating his lesson.

"Forget the eyes, Sydney Thames! Forget! Sydney Thames! Sydney Thames! Sydney Thames!"

All the wonderful will of the blind man was in the words. His whole face was drawn with the concentration of every ounce of strength he possessed that was in the tone of his voice. Once more Sydney Thames stirred; his voice, clearer, stronger, repeated the words:

"George Nelson, Waiter. Biggest stunt New York ever saw."

Behind the words Thornley Colton could see the woman, grim, terrible, commanding the drugged man. He could see the secretary fighting hopelessly against her, trying to make his morphia-weakened brain carry out the orders of the blind man.

"Thornley Colton! Don't you know Thornley Colton? This is Thornley Colton, Sydney! You are Sydney Thames! Sydney Thames!"

Over and over, in endless repetition, came the words. At times the voice of the blind man was soothing, crooning. Then the words came in hard-voiced command, sharply, coldly. The white hair that usually curled from the pink scalp straightened damply as the perspiration came from every pore. The coolness of the bandage was gone; the dead eyes under the folds burned with the searing flame hours' exposure to the light had caused.

"George Nel—son—twenty—age—seven—waiter."

The words came slowly, haltingly, as though the man on the bed were repeating a lesson he had not thoroughly learned.

Colton was winning! Winning! Sydney was forgetting the words that had been driven into his brain; the phrase that had been repeated so often that even the crow's mechanical brain had learned it, was being lost. In the mind of the semiconscious secretary, the will of the woman with the terrible eyes and the will of the blind man were waging battle. But Thornley Colton was winning!

A sudden chill shook the body of the man on the bed; his arm raised so that his hand could rub his forehead shakingly. Colton's fingertips, resting gently on Sydney's shoulder, felt the movement. His voice became tense, flintlike.

"*Sydney* Thames! Sydney *Thames!*"

For a minute the mumbled words that came could not be understood; then they came more plainly, but so slowly that there seemed spaces between the very letters:

"G-e-o-r-g-e—Nel—Thames. Thames—Syd—wai-ter—a-ge—Thames."

The blind man leaned closer. His hands clenched at his sides till the veins stood out in great, blue ridges. Now was the time, the instant for the thing to which he had been leading. Colton knew that the mind, in the process of hypnosis, takes its impression like a photographic plate. But it only remembers the stronger lights until they have been washed out by another and more powerful mind. At the instant of changing from the influence of the woman's mind to normal, Sydney would recollect things that the woman hypnotist had worked to make him forget. Little things, a word, a phrase, perhaps, but that was all the problemist needed.

Sydney's hands were moving slowly across his forehead; on his face showed the struggle that was going on in the brain of the body that was asleep.

"Another!" Thames muttered. "Another!" His voice strengthened, all the power in him went in the final hoarse whisper: "My God, another!"

"The girl said that!" Colton spoke sharply. "The girl said that!"

"The—girl—" Sydney Thames seemed vainly trying to remember something. "Yes—golden hair—something—wrong—hand—right."

"I know, Sydney, I know. She cut her right hand on a wineglass, Sydney."

"Yes—" The mumbling ceased. Sydney Thames lay still, but it was only to gain strength to speak again. "The crow!" It was almost a shout. "*She*—said that! The crow. Only—a feather! The crow knows! A feather, only a feather! Hurry, Ruth! A feather from Rameses. No time—a feather, girl!"

Colton's hands relaxed. A great sigh came through his tight-shut teeth.

"Sydney Thames! Sydney Thames!" The name, reiterated over and over, seemed to calm the man on the bed. His breathing came regularly again. Colton's face was almost touching the face of his secretary; he seemed to be peering into the closed eyes of Sydney Thames through the folds of the wet cloths that covered his own dead eyes. Once more Sydney Thames stirred. His eyes opened slowly.

"Thorn," he murmured weakly. "Thorn!"

Colton raised his head. "Go to sleep, Sydney." His voice was very gentle and the man on the bed closed his eyes like a little child.

The blind man arose. A fervent "Thank God!" crossed his lips; then the old lines of weariness came back. He touched the watch in his pocket. Midnight. The fight there in the dark bedroom had been going on for two hours! He tiptoed out of the room softly, down the stairs to the library. He took another drink of brandy, a stronger one this time, and he did not even feel the fire of it. His fingers found the empty chessboard. They felt loose sheets of paper. He picked them up and ran his fingers over the backs of them. They were the notes Shrimp had made of the crow's words.

Throughout the afternoon and evening the crow had repeated nothing but its one sentence: "Poughkeepsie! Poughkeepsie!

George Nelson! Waiter! Age twenty-seven!" There was not a letter, not a syllable but those words. Strange that the crow had such a small vocabulary. Why hadn't it picked up other phrases in its years of association with the woman? Was it the crow that had been the mouthpiece of the silent clairvoyant?

Colton's hand went to his breast pocket. His fingers felt a rough, folded paper. "No human hand can unlock it. From out the dead dynasties" was what the old man had written as he waited for death. That was—

The telephone bell tinkled. That drove everything else from his mind. With a single motion he pulled the instrument toward him and lifted the receiver from the hook.

"Hello!" he called.

Here was the thing he had been awaiting! The bit of evidence that he had forced others to put into his hands!

The voice that came over the wire was hoarse: "'Lo, Mr Colton. This is Beldon of the district attorney's staff. We've got the waiter! He's up here at the Twenty-seventh Precinct. Hustle up and get a line on him!"

"Right!" There was eagerness, triumph in the blind man's voice, and the snapping of the receiver on its hook came with the jamming down of the button that summoned his big black car. He grabbed his stick and coat and ran from the door. He jerked open the front door and rushed down the steps without even taking the trouble to see that it was closed tightly after him. The car swung around the corner out of the garage. The blind man ran into the street and jumped to the running board before the frightened Michael could stop the machine.

"The Twenty-seventh Precinct!" ordered Colton loudly. "Hustle!"

The car fairly leaped to its best speed. Colton swung nimbly into the tonneau. It raced uptown, and Colton, all the nervousness suddenly gone, leaned comfortably back on the cushions and let his whole weary body relax. He took off the bandage he had not waited to remove, and let the cool night air fan his burning eyes.

The car pulled up before the green-lighted precinct station. Colton spoke to the driver.

"How long did that take?" he wanted to know.

"Not more'n ten minutes, sorr," answered the chauffeur, with a touch of pride.

"All right! Back as fast as you can!"

Michael's face flashed his surprise before he turned, but he knew the blind man too well to question.

"Stop at the corner above the house!" ordered the problemist.

Back they raced. Colton jumped from the car as it slowed on the curb, whispered an order to Michael, and ran to the shadows of the houses along the sidewalk, and up the front steps of his own house. The front door was closed. He turned the lock silently and made his way soundlessly to the library. He listened a second at the doorway, then entered.

His nostrils had caught the faint odor of Egyptian incense, his ear had heard the sound of a sudden movement in the corner of the room. He closed the door behind him, and the lock snapped sharply. He heard a quick-drawn breath as the intruder realized that escape was cut off. Two steps took him to the desk and the light switch. One hand fumbled in the heap of chessmen beside the board. He turned to the corner where he knew was the intruder.

His hand was held out. On the palm glinted a piece of wineglass with a spot of blood on its edge.

"Pardon me," he said suavely. "Is this what you came for?"

His ears caught the fall of a collapsing body. He jumped to the corner. His hands felt the slight form clothed in man's rough clothes. One hand jerked away the cap, and his fingers felt the long, flowing hair it had concealed. He knew that it was hair of finely spun, burnished gold, and on his white face was a grim smile of satisfaction.

13

THE LURE OF THE FEATHER

As quickly as it came, the smile went, Colton bent over, his strong arms lifted the girl tenderly. He carried her to a couch at the other side of the room and laid her down. From the small bedroom next to the library, that he sometimes used, he brought a handkerchief soaked in cold water, and gently bathed her face and wrists and hands, feeling the adhesive-plaster bandage over the cut finger. The girl's eyes opened, she stared up at the blind man blankly for an instant. Then fright came.

The problemist seemed to know the moment the eyes opened. Perhaps there was some slight movement of the body; perhaps it was some subtle sixth sense he had been given to recompense the loss of sight. He spoke quietly as the girl returned to consciousness.

"Lie quiet," he commanded softly. "You can talk when you have rested a bit."

"The piece of wineglass I broke," she faltered. "You know?"

"Yes. My fingers felt the warm stickiness of the blood on it, and I have been holding it. I knew that when the time came it would prove your identity. I am blind, you know."

"Blind?" He could feel her gazing into his deep brown eyes that held no look of their deadness. He did not wear the disfiguring blue-smoked glasses now, and the eyes seemed to glow in the white, strong face.

"Your doubt is not surprising," he remarked dryly. "There are several hundred persons in New York who refuse to believe that I am blind. There are several hundred more who know me by sight, and who have talked to me for years, who do not suspect such a thing."

"So you are the man!" The faltering was gone from the voice; it had a sudden hardness that was wholly foreign to the girl Colton's secretary had described the night before in the restaurant. "You are the man who is trying to put us into prison!"

"Not us," he corrected, and his words were stern.

"Why did you come home so quickly?" she demanded.

"Because I knew that there would be someone here whom I wished to see," he answered frankly.

"You knew—"

"That someone wanted the crow badly enough to risk anything for its possession." He finished the sentence for her.

"And you pretended to rush away so that you could come back here and trap me?" she said scornfully.

"I didn't expect you," he said, very seriously. "I expected another. The movement you made as I entered the door told me that my visitor was a woman. You crouched in sudden fear. A man would have made a different sound as he moved to a position of defense. And the man I expected would not have carried the strange odor of that curious Egyptian perfume."

"He couldn't come! He hasn't—" She stopped as she realized what he had tricked her into saying.

"But he let you come!"

"I'm going!" she declared. "I'm going back!"

The hand that rested on her shoulder was so light that she had not even felt its touch until she started to move; then it held her with a gentle firmness there was no resisting.

"You are typically feminine," he said. "You don't realize the seriousness the penal code attaches to entrance with intent to steal."

"You're going to have me arrested?" she stammered.

He shook his head. "I'm going to listen to your story."

The blind man felt her whole body stiffen; his sharp ears heard the click of her firm white teeth as they snapped together. "I won't tell you a thing!"

"There are ten thousand police looking for you, to force you to talk," he asserted dispassionately.

If he expected to frighten her, he was mistaken. "I know it," she answered, and her sneer made the voice grating. "I wouldn't tell them a thing to implicate any one."

"You wouldn't have to!" the blind man said sternly. "You are one of the murderers of that man in the restaurant!"

He lifted his hand from her shoulder, but his words seemed to have driven all thought of movement from her. "You think I killed him!" In her tone and eyes and the hands working at her sides there was horror.

"In the eyes of the law you are a murderer!"

A moan came from her lips, and the sharp breaths sobbed through them. Suddenly she raised herself on her elbow and stared into his face.

"I—a murderer?" she cried. "*I*?"

A nod.

"That dead man was my father!" The words seemed to take all her strength, and her slight body fell back on the couch.

"I know it," Colton said slowly. "Your hands and the dead man's have the same hereditary formation. But I also know"—the sternness came back—"that anyone who deliberately plots and lays careful plans for the committing of a cold-blooded murder is as guilty, in the eyes of the law, as the person whose hand strikes the fatal blow!"

"He was not murdered!" she cried passionately. "They are all lies! Lies! The newspapers are filled with lies!"

"The slashed wrists?" questioned the blind man. "The unmistakable evidence of arteriotomy?"

"He commanded—it!" Again there was faltering.

"And you obeyed?"

"No! No! I did—not!"

"You merely sat at the table, where you could see that the commands had been carried out?" the blind man went on relentlessly.

"Yes—yes." The affirmatives came in a steadier voice; wonderfully steady. "That was my duty; my duty to my dead father!"

Colton rose from the couch and walked slowly across the room. At his desk he took out his cigarette case, pulled the tobacco from a cigarette end, and held it poised between his long, slim fingers.

He heard the groan of the couch springs as she suddenly sat up; but he made no move toward her. A strange girl, she baffled him continually. The things he had said to make her talk, to tell him things that he must know, had only made her stronger in her fight against him. Weak, for a moment, he recognized the strength that was now behind her words, even when her voice faltered. He must handle her differently.

"I want the crow!" she cried, coming back to the object of her visit with a doggedness that amazed him. Trapped, helpless, her liberty at stake, perhaps even her life, she was fighting for the thing that had brought her to the house in the night—a thief!

"Suppose I haven't it?" Colton seemed wholly engrossed with his cigarette.

"You must have it! You said you had it!" She was sitting on the edge of the couch; he could feel her eyes again.

"Admitted that I *said* I had it!" He put triumph and gloating in the words. "But consider the words as a trap to bring one of those I sought to my house. My blindness does not allow me to shadow, or follow, you know. I must be clever enough to bring those I want to me."

"A spider in its web!" she cried scornfully.

"Exactly!" He seemed pleased at the comparison.

"You must have it!" she averred. "You found a feather in the room at the hotel!"

"Did *you* hear me *say* that?" he asked significantly.

"No. I—"

"*Someone* who did told you," he finished.

"You found the feather!" she repeated, determined not to be tricked into further admission.

"Yes," he admitted. "I found it where you had dropped it. I also found a golden hair!"

The words brought the girl to her feet. "I wasn't there!"

"In the suite, you mean?"

"Where you found the feather," she parried.

"I found it where you had dropped it—at the home of your aunt. You tried to catch the bird, but something had frightened it, probably the drugging and hypnotizing of my secretary. You got a feather—*only a feather!*"

"Oh, don't! Don't!" There was pleading in her voice.

She was weakening.

"Sit down!" he commanded, and she obeyed him like a child. "You can see my secretary, helpless, can't you?" he resumed pitilessly. "Another! You knew that the waiter whose recommendations were stolen, who was hypnotized so that even his voice and manner and talk were those of the typical New Yorker your aunt has learned so well in her years of association, was the first one to make your game. You didn't expect *another!*"

He heard the springs of the couch creak as her hands gripped the edge. "You heard?" she whispered.

He shook his head. "My secretary told me. I had just finished the fight for his mind before you came in. From the snatches his brain retained I saw the whole picture; the grim room, with its dusty black hangings, the drug-dazed man, Silver Sandals, the flying crow. Then your escape, the bloodstains your hands left on the rail!"

"You are trying to frighten me!" she exclaimed, in sudden, vehement defiance. She was fighting again. "You are guessing. You found the feather in the hotel suite! I know it!"

"Certainly!" The admission was grave. "But the feather that brought you here I picked up from the chessboard on my desk before I went to the hotel tonight. I said that McMann did not find the feather, because he did not know where to look for it. Until the moment I showed it to him it was in my pocket. The whole purpose of it was to tell 'someone' that I had the crow. I knew 'someone' would try to get it. The finding of the hair was luck when I pretended to look for the feather. But I knew it would suggest to the mind of 'someone' the possibility of sending you here. How it got there I don't know."

"You know nothing!" she accused.

Colton lifted the cigarette to his lips. "May I smoke?" he asked. She nodded shortly. He still waited, and she almost snapped an affirmative. He lighted the cigarette carefully, slowly. There was a curious expression of respect on his face. Never before had he met a person who fought so long and so gamely. A half-dozen times he had trapped her; twice he had brought her to her knees. But she recovered each time, fighting gaspingly, but fighting, fighting every instant.

"You were frightened last night," he declared. "Something made you hurry from the house of Silver Sandals before you could catch the crow. But you left George Nelson behind. He, with his poor, befogged brain, was to bring Rameses." He paused, but there was no sound to tell him whether or not the mention of the crow's name had scored. "The district attorney frightened him away to some prepared rendezvous. And I got the crow, the one missing piece in the mosaic."

"So you have got it?" There was triumph in the cry, a peculiar sort of triumph.

"Yes." His voice was almost pitying as he went on: "The night of your father's death you saw the manager of the restaurant speak to me, didn't you? You didn't know who I was then, but when you saw me feel of the dead man's wrists sudden fright at the unconsidered possibility caused you to snap the wineglass. That located absolutely the second source of the incense odor which my keen nostrils detected on the clothes of the dead man. You saw me go back to my secretary. You knew that he was following you. In the Waldorf you and the 'someone' with you telephoned the alarm to Silver Sandals. You were waiting for him. Probably there was some trickery to impress him with the truth of a very strange thing; a thing that I have been working to prove despite the unexpected turns of the case. But Sydney showed that he did not believe, and that frightened Silver Sandals. She made him another pawn. My blindness, and mental visualization it has made necessary, enabled me to 'see' that when I found my secretary at police headquarters. That changed the whole game. It became a game for blood!"

"Blood!" she repeated, and again there was the peculiar note of triumph in her voice. "Do you know I have a pistol pointed straight at your heart?" she snapped.

His head inclined slowly. "You don't realize how keen my ears are," he said, with just the faintest of smiles. "I've been very interestedly listening for several seconds. The hammer snapped a thread in the pocket lining when it caught."

"Where is the crow?" she demanded. He heard her rise, take a step toward him, then another.

"My boy put him to bed," the blind man announced calmly. "All afternoon he had been listening to him and taking notes of the crow's words."

"Where are the notes?" Her voice was steady and hard. She was very close to him. He felt the muzzle of the pistol as she held it against his chest.

"Here they are." He picked them up from the desk behind him and held them tantalizingly before her for an instant before he held them high above her reach.

"Give them to me! At once!" The commands came almost hissingly.

The thin lips of the blind man tightened, even the blind eyes seemed to grow colder as they looked down at her face.

"You shall have them," he said grimly, "when I have talked to your husband, *Mrs Bracken!*"

14

A REVELATION

It seemed a long, long time that they stood, unmoving; the girl, her long hair sweeping the shoulders of the man's rough coat she wore; Thornley Colton, the notes held high over his head, his eyes apparently watching her face. Then the blind man dropped his cigarette into the tray behind him and raised his hand. The girl stood motionless as he gently unclasped her fingers from the pistol.

"I didn't think you'd use it," he said quietly, "or I'd have taken it when I felt the weight in your pocket as I lifted you."

He laid the pistol softly on the desk, and with one hand touching her elbow led her back to the couch. There was not even a murmured protest. The girl seemed stunned.

"A moment, please." He went into the next room and returned with a glass of water.

She drank it gratefully. "How did you know—that?" she asked, and pitiful defeat was in her voice.

"A little reasoning and a touch of your ring finger," he explained. "I know you took it off," he said, as she was about to say the words, "but the newly made circle in the flesh was unmistakable to fingers such as mine."

"He—won't come to any harm?" she asked pleadingly.

A REVELATION

"You are feminine, aren't you?" He was very gentle. "To faint at the sight of a piece of bloodstained wineglass, then to run any risk when only your own safety was at stake, and finally, to be terror-stricken with fear for a loved one. I didn't want to talk like that, girl, but I wanted you to realize the full seriousness of the thing. What I said regarding the murder is true. Listen, girl." His voice was wonderfully soft. "Your father was murdered!"

There was no passionate denial this time. "He died," she said, and her voice was as quiet as his own. "He died." She repeated it as though she was trying to convince a very dull person of a well-known fact. "I know it, because I have known all my life that my father was going to die at seven o'clock last night."

Only the words themselves were startling. The tone of the girl was strangely matter of fact. She seemed to be telling a thing of which there had never been a doubt; a thing as inevitable as the tides and the march of time. Yet she was speaking of her father's death—his murder!

"You have known the date of your father's death *all your life?*"

"Since I knew anything. Father knew it thirty years ago." To the blind man it seemed as though a child were speaking. And a few minutes before it had been a woman who fought like a tigress to escape from every trap he had laid.

"He knew it because it had been prophesied?" The way the blind man put it made a statement rather than a question. The strange, almost unbelievable theoretical foundation for the case that Thornley Colton's intuitive reasoning had formed was being proven correct. Half a dozen times it had been shaken; the stones above had come tumbling down, but the problemist had been right!

"Yes, a thousand years ago! Oh, I know you won't believe it!" she added. "But you didn't know my father—my wonderful, wonderful father!" Never before had Colton heard such adoration in the voice of a human being. "People who didn't understand him said that he was queer; the ignorant called him crazy. But he was the most profound student of Egyptology in the world. He knew the old dynasties as you know the steps of your house. He lived in them, I think. To him the world was very young, the pyramids were building, the first Pharaohs were mighty powers. Perhaps you have heard of him. He was John Neilton."

"Neilton!" Colton's wonderful memory came to his aid. "Thirty years ago he was conceded to be the greatest Egyptologist and Archaeologist in the world!"

"Yes." Pride was in her voice. "Then he found the thing he had been searching for all his life—the Saiseogyus Stone of the Cycles of Life. Do you believe in reincarnation?"

"I have thought of it," Colton answered seriously.

"Father proved it!" Again the girl's tone was that of one who states an incontrovertible fact. "He figured his own 'lives' back to the First Dynasty. He knew when this cycle would end. I have known all my life, for he taught me that death is but a transition."

Colton understood, then, the girl's strange lack of emotion when speaking of her father's death. From the cradle she had been taught that dying was only a passing to a higher plane of existence. False or true, it was as deeply ingrained as man's belief in God, that is learned at his mother's knee. A curious girl, who had led a curious life with the father she adored, and who had been taught to believe as he believed. It had only been the blind man's talk of murder that had unnerved her.

She was speaking again. "My aunt and he were fellow students for years; she is older, much older, and she was his guide and philosopher."

"You mean Silver Sandals?" put in the blind man.

"Yes; his sister. But father was very different. The thing he had discovered would have made him the greatest of all men; for it was the long-sought secret of the universe. He knew it was too great a thing to be given into the hands of an ignorant world. My aunt loved fame and adulation."

"She was Sarah Neilton, who deciphered the Rosetta stone?" exclaimed Colton.

The girl nodded. "That was the beginning of the estrangement between my father and my aunt. There was something of the charlatan in her nature, I think. The translation was proved to be wrong, you know. She thought it easier to deceive, and hurry a deciphering before the world, than to spend the years necessary for correct results. My father married, then, and my aunt went away, angry, swearing that she would never enter the house again. Perhaps it was jealousy of my mother; but she never entered the house, though mother died when I was born.

"There was a terrible scene when Aunt Sarah went away. Father accused her of going to tell the world the great thing of which she had learned parts by watching him. But she was a strange woman, terrible sometimes. She swore that she would never speak another word as long as he lived." She paused.

In his mind's eye, Colton could see the old, old woman going silent through the years, knowing nothing but the one grim promise she had made in a moment of anger. Mad, perhaps. Only such a woman could have carried out the scene in the Beaumonde restaurant.

"My aunt frightened me sometimes, when I went to visit her," the girl went on. "She had become a clairvoyant, because it would hurt my father, I think. In the years she built up a wonderful clientele, learning from one person the things she told another. With her fund of knowledge she could do things that were wonderful to the ignorant. In the later years I always had to visit her heavily veiled, because she had a 'control' that looked like me. There was another of father. Golden Locks and The Prophet, she called them, and they were her grim revenge on my father. She never spoke. Never till last night did I hear her utter a word; but last night I realized that she had not been able to live without deceit."

"Ventriloquism," put in the blind man, as she stopped again, in her mind, apparently, the picture of the night before that she could not forget.

"You knew!"

Colton nodded silently. Another proof that his lack of eyes had enabled him to learn instantly the thing no one else had suspected for a quarter of a century. He had known that the woman was not deaf and dumb the minute the dead man's lips had apparently uttered the words in the restaurant. Yet the police had tried a hundred times to trap the old woman into admission that she could hear and talk.

"Then the date for father's passing came near. It was hard to lose him—hard!" She could not keep the tremor from her voice this time. "But it had to be. In the fifth cycle father was in the Court of Talasephes, who ruled Lower Egypt before the first pyramid was built. It was he who first wore sandals of silver. My aunt took the name he had borne. For her it was only an advertisement. He changed his name from Neilton to Sladnas. It was the only acknowledgment he ever made, until the passing date drew near, of her existence. She had taken the name he bore; he reversed it. You know of the old Egyptian belief of Death being present at the feast?"

"Yes."

"In the later years father was annoyed by the people who refused to understand. They gibed at him when he appeared in the garden of our big, old house, where we lived with two Egyptian servants."

"In Poughkeepsie?"

She looked up suddenly. "The crow?" she asked.

"Yes."

"It was a bird father trained. It was part of his plan, and it should never say but one thing—that one word. But I am getting ahead. Father thought people were too worldly; they did not respect old age; they did not realize, with the life and gayety, that they, too, would pass. I think at last it became an obsession, mono—" She stammered over the word, and there was a pitiful break in her voice.

"Monomania," suggested the blind man. "I understand." He did understand the thoughts of the strange old recluse, and of the daughter to whom he was a king who could do no wrong.

"For years he planned, for he understood that the years had changed. He must plot and plan to carry out his scheme. He asked my aunt to help; you can't realize what that cost, but it proves the lengths to which he would go to do as he intended. It is in the blood, I think."

Even in his blindness, Colton could see the square, resolute, little chin of the girl beside him, that his hands had touched when he had bathed her face with the reviving cold water. Yes, it was in the blood. She had proved it when she had fought clear of his traps and pitfalls; she was proving it now by telling him the story with which she intended to set at rest suspicion against one she loved.

"He built the silver frame, perfected it. Built another. He wanted the biggest, brightest, gayest restaurant for his purpose. The difficulty of carrying out his plan seemed insurmountable then. But his theory was proved again!" Her voice took a new tone of quiet, wonderful reverence. "I guess God sent the one person. He came to our door, hungry. We fed him. He worked in the garden, and father, who spoke or thought of almost no one but me, loved him at once. He took an interest in father's work. They were chums. Father learned his name, and who he was when he asked permission to marry me. We, too, had become chums, and more."

"Bracken?" asked the blind man, very quietly.

"Philip Bracken, junior," she answered. "I think he tried to dissuade father from his strange idea, but we were firm."

"We?"

"It was my father's wish," she said simply. "In the years, as I grew, it had become part of my life; this doing of the one great thing my father wanted. Philip set about making the plans to help, then. There was the suite; the one method of having father get to the table. Philip went to see his father, and he showed Mr Bracken that the wildness was gone. Philip went on one of his father's voyages. There he induced the waiter to leave. Then I began to realize the deceit that would be necessary, and I was frightened a little. Six months ago Philip arranged for the help we would need inside the hotel."

"How?" interrupted Colton.

"I don't understand it exactly." For the first time since she had begun to tell the story the words came hesitantly. "He secured the position of assistant manager of the hotel for a man named Norman. He had lived around Poughkeepsie, and he used to visit father until—" She veered hurriedly. "I never liked him, but he arranged everything without even arousing the suspicions of Mr Carl.

"Father and Philip went to the suite in the afternoon. It was hard to say goodby; it is always hard when a person goes on a long journey, and you will not see them again for a long, long time." There was just a suspicion of tremble in her voice, but the wonderful attitude toward death that had been instilled into her mind from the cradle steadied it immediately. "There he waited for the hour that had been named."

"There was no doubt that it would come?" put in the blind man, his voice low. Something inside him forced that question to the problemist's lips when he did not want to speak—to interrupt. It seemed incredible almost, that this girl, who was young and beautiful, by all the standards of the seeing world, should have such strange, unwavering faith in the greatest of all mysteries. Was it a great loyalty to the ideas of her father? Was it, too, a monomania? No, not that last. The word was too suggestive to the blind man, whose mental visualization of the girl beside him was more complete than even eyes would have made possible, for that mental picture saw under the ivory skin, behind the wide hazel eyes, and under the hair of burnished gold. It was not monomania as the world knows monomania. It was a religion, almost—a sacred belief that had been put into the girl's heart and mind by the father she loved. A strange belief, perhaps, but a strange man of strange blood had given the world this girl.

"There was no doubt!" She repeated it firmly, and in her tone seemed a bit of wonder that there could be thoughts of doubt. "Philip was with him, as the plans had been made, until the end came. It was then the three slashes on the wrist were made—symbolic of the three Egypts of the ancients: Upper and Lower Egypt and the Egypt of the hereafter.

"Silver Sandals, my aunt, and I entered the private dining-room by way of the court, without being seen. I watched my opportunity through the palms, and went to the table Philip had ready. Aunt closed the door behind me. Father had asked me to promise that I would be present at this last scene. I made the promise when Philip and I were married. I did not see father then; he was in the suite upstairs. My aunt brought him down. The frame worked perfectly; there could be no hitch in that. Philip was at the palms. Norman closed the door, for he had not gone at six, as Carl supposed, but had stayed hidden until the last part of his work. Philip and my aunt carried out their part without trouble. I thought the waiting captain would upset the carefully arranged plan at first. He tried to, but my aunt and Philip prevented him.

"Then you came into the case. You were right. I didn't know you when Mr Carl spoke. But there was something in your face, or manner, as you touched the wrist, that frightened me. I broke the glass and cut my finger. Then you spoke to your secretary. I knew that he followed me. Philip was waiting at the Waldorf, for he had not overlooked even the slight possibility of my being drawn into the case, and he had taken every means to keep me out. He telephoned my aunt to be ready. Then he went to the car Philip had borrowed from his father's friend, the district attorney, so that he would be interested in the case, and be in a position to help us instead of working against us, as he might otherwise have done."

Colton nodded his understanding of the cleverness that had involved the official so that he must work for instead of against. Bracken had been the brains of the whole thing, working and plotting to see that there was no possibility of the plan going wrong in a detail. Only one thing could have made him take such risks, and Colton knew what that one thing was.

"Father intended that the truth should be known the day after his death. He did everything he could to protect us. He sent the notes, with the bottle of wine. He knew that it could be easily proved that he had written them. The notes to the police and the coroner were Philip's idea. Father sent the death notices. He posed for the photograph in the robes he always wore at home. They seemed, to us, the things that would convince any one that there had been no foul play.

"But the sudden following of your secretary frightened us. I think my aunt began to realize then just what the thing she had done meant: the coming of the police, of which she had always had a horror. They had persecuted her continuously because she refused to pay money to the powers for protection. She thought that by making your secretary think that the man he had seen dead in the restaurant was talking to him, and telling him the object of the strange scene he had witnessed, that he would convince you of the truth. But he refused to believe. It was one time Silver Sandals' trickery failed to deceive. The man who impersonated my uncle was the waiter who had been living at the home of my aunt. He wore the disguise that the 'controls' she had had worn. And he also wore the first silver frame my father made. There was only one thing she could do when your secretary came. She had to force him to become an ally until the thing was cleared. I hated it!" the girl said tensely. "The poor waiter had been forced to help us, and here was another!" A shudder shook her body. "She tried to put the morphia needle into his arm, but he fought so that it went into his side. Then the fight she had to make him do as she willed! Of course, it seemed to be the crow that was talking to him, and he tried to get it, scaring it half to death. Philip, grown impatient with waiting, because he did not dare come to the house, telephoned that the district attorney's car must be taken back. "We had to hurry. We tried to get the crow. It was then I heard my aunt speak for the first time in my life—that is, directly. She was half crazy when the bird that had been trained to perch on her arm and do its other little tricks refused to come to her. She commanded me to catch it. I attempted it, but failed, only once getting near enough to pull a feather from its tail. We couldn't wait; we didn't dare. Philip had told us that your car had gone, and he thought you might come with your chauffeur and the police.

"My aunt ordered the waiter, who was under her control, to take your secretary to the cafe where he was found, and then to return and bring the clippings from the papers, and catch the crow. But he failed. We left the other things that were to be found, hoping against hope that you would understand. Everything else of my aunt's she had destroyed days before, because she never intended to come back. But the papers next day frightened us more. The police had called it murder! Everybody called it murder! You were trying to pin the crime on us! Thousands were watching and searching! We could only hide!"

Exhaustion weakened her voice. She stopped. Without speaking, Colton fetched her another glass of water, waiting patiently for her to finish. Nor did he speak as his hand took the empty glass from her fingers.

"You don't believe me!" she cried. "You think—"

"I believe you implicitly," he said, his tone quietly convincing. The story she had told him was the true story—as she believed it. But there was the crux of the whole thing. As she believed it! The plans of years, worked out with infinite care for detail, figured to each last possibility, tested so that they could not go awry, had gone wrong in one detail—death had not come as the old man had expected. Someone had taken advantage of the carefully laid plans. Someone had murdered him, killed him in cold blood; because every move that had been made was a move to protect the guilty and convict the innocent.

"Of what value is the crow?" asked Colton, for he knew that there lay the secret of the one loose screw.

He could feel her eyes still searching his face, trying to peer under the mask and behind the words of assurance he had spoken. He knew that she was thinking of the statement he had made that her father had been murdered.

"One million dollars." She answered hesitantly, almost tremulously, as if a new fear was coming into her mind.

"Explain that!" Colton spoke almost sharply. Here was the missing link, and it was bigger than even the blind man had expected. One million dollars! Incentive enough for murder!

"Rameses holds the secret of my father's fortune," she continued hastily, for the tone of the blind man had made her want to explain away the fear that had been so evident in her former statement. "I have told you that father was a strange man; that he lived in the dead centuries. He was rich, for his father had been rich."

Colton nodded understandingly. "His fortune enabled him to fit out the expeditions that made him famous for his archaeological discoveries at the age of thirty-three."

"Yes. He would have nothing to do with the modern things of life, like banks. Every cent of his money was in rubies; the blood stones of the age cycles. They were hidden only he knew where. It was known that he had an immense quantity of jewels, and I have known of many attempts at robbery, but none ever succeeded. My father said that his sister should get them when he died, and she was to leave them to me. You know I was never anything but a child in his eyes. But he left them in a strange way, a way that showed he had never forgotten the cause of the estrangement. When he died he had a cryptogram. The crow he gave my aunt ten days ago had the key. It was trained never to speak when on her arm, or to learn another word. Father knew how to do that. He said that there should be one thing she should do without deceit and trickery. She must solve it! For hours she listened to the crow repeating its endless repetition, but she got no farther. Her own crow that she had used died."

"She got the cryptogram?"

"No. He did—not have it!"

"But he had the key?" asked Colton quickly.

"There was nothing. His pockets were absolutely empty. He had forgotten the one big thing of all. That is why we were all so excited. He had left it behind, at our home in Poughkeepsie. And we did not dare go near to find it."

"He had it in the suite!" Colton's statement was almost brutally positive. The unfinished words his seeing finger tips had read on the table had been written on the cryptogram itself to show the keen mind of Silver Sandals the key! Colton knew that! "Where is your husband?" he demanded.

"I don't know." The words came chokingly, presaging the utter breaking of nerves that had been strong for so long. "He went to Poughkeepsie last night when he had returned the district attorney's car. We have not heard from him!"

15

FACE TO FACE

Bracken again! Each drawing of the net caught him tighter in the meshes of the strange crime. The murderer of John Neilton, who had lived for thirty years under the name of Sladnas Revlis because his sister had taken the name of Silver Sandals, had played for a big stake. The old man himself had made possible the necessary months of preparation for his own murder. Colton knew that the murderers had been forced to prepare the various details as carefully as the old man himself. The plans of the man who was to die had worked out too smoothly, too well, for them to have been merely *his* plans. There had been more than cooperation—there had been leading!

Bracken had won the confidence of the strange old man. He had won the heart and the hand of the girl. To him had been left the perfecting of the plans. According to the girl, he had been with her father until the time came for him to go on duty in the dining room of the hotel. And he had disappeared at the first opportunity! Ostensibly he had gone to Poughkeepsie to get the cryptogram the girl thought he had neglected to bring. Apparently she believed in Philip Bracken with the same unalterable faith she had given to her father. Had he betrayed that faith, thrown aside the girl who loved him, because she had been merely a tool to get the million dollar's worth of jewels her strange father had secreted?

Across the room a slit of gray showed between the heavy curtain and the window edge. Another dawn was greeting the sleepless blind man in his library. The blind man detected the different "feel" of the light at once. He snapped off the electric at the desk and raised the curtains, to fill the room with the sickly light of the new day. A chill seemed to shake the body of the girl on the couch, but the blind man paid no attention. At the desk he bathed his eyes and forehead with alcohol, and adjusted the tortoise-rimmed, smoked-glass spectacles.

A touch of a button on his desk was answered by a sleepy-eyed servant.

"Coffee, John," the blind man ordered. The servant bowed and withdrew. He showed no surprise at the presence of the girl. All Colton's household knew he was working on a case, and anything strange that might happen in the house was only part of it.

"I'm going!" The girl jumped from the couch. Colton slowly turned and walked to where she stood. His hand on her shoulder once more gently forced her back.

"A little coffee will straighten your overwrought nerves," he said.

"You think—that something went wrong—that Philip is guilty of—you said murder!" She stammered the disconnected sentences, and his hand on her shoulder felt her trembling. He knew how her thoughts had been working in the silence he had forced after she had told him the thing he wanted to know—the confession of Bracken's absence that she had withheld so long.

He did not answer her question. When he spoke, it was merely a soft-voiced command to rest.

"You are going out!" she suddenly accused.

"As soon as I have taken a bit of black coffee," he nodded.

"I won't stay!" Once more there was fear in her voice, and he knew it was fear for the safety of the man she had so trusted.

"You will." His voice was quiet. "I am going to call up a girl to stay with you. She is a great friend of Sydney. They are to be married," He went to the desk and took the telephone. "Until she comes, John will stand outside the door. I hate to do this, girl"—the softness was in his voice again—"but you refuse to trust me fully. You have fought me for three hours. You have given way only as far as you wished. I know better than to ask you anything further, for I can see your mind at work. It's the kind of a mind that made your aunt keep silence for years because she had sworn not to speak; the kind that made your father carry out his scheme despite all obstacles he knew would be in the way. You are the only woman that ever made me confess defeat. I shall have to go my own way to help you, and God knows you need more help than you realize, girl!"

"Where are you going?" she demanded, refusing, toward the last, even to listen.

"I am going to see your aunt." Colton moved the chessboard so that the servant could put down the tray, with its cups of coffee, got the telephone number he wanted, and asked Sydney Thames' fiancée if she would help him.

"You will never find her!" declared the girl beside him triumphantly; but under the triumph the blind man knew there was a trace of fear. She did fear him! The look on his face that had caused her nervous fingers to break the wineglass in the restaurant, when she had seen him touch the wrist of her dead father, was there now. "You can't find her!" she repeated, but she was trying to convince herself rather than him.

"I will find her," he said, "and when I do I will show her something that will end the case." The hand that did not hold the coffee cup made a gesture over the chessboard. "Last night there were four moves to checkmate. The visit to the hotel and your visit here were two. The game will end at noon today."

He set down the empty coffee cup, picked up his hat, stick, and gloves. At the door he turned. "You may sleep, if you wish, until Miss Nelson comes. No one will disturb you. This door is very thick, so thick that even sound won't go through it. John will be outside. The windows are locked securely. *Auf wiedersehen*"

He closed the door behind him, turned the key in the lock. Then he ran lightly up the stairs to his own room, took the receiver from the hook of the extension 'phone, and listened. He was not a minute too soon. Came the click of the receiver in the library downstairs, then the girl's voice:

"Sixteen-twelve, Bell, quickly!"

She was trying to warn her aunt! Colton did not replace the receiver on the hook. He set it gently on the table and tiptoed from the room so that there would be no possibility of her hearing a sound over the wire. The plan had worked! She had followed the lead he had so cleverly worked out. His telephoning to Nadine Nelson had put the idea into her mind, as he had intended it should. His impressing her with the fact that he could not fail; his talk of the soundproof door had made her clutch at the one straw. It was a straw, for Colton had cut the outside wires with his knife, concealed in the palm of his hand, when he had finished talking over the 'phone.

He had located the hiding place of the aunt in the only way possible. All that was necessary now was a call to the telephone "information," and the big car. Colton ran upstairs and looked into Sydney's room. His secretary was sleeping peacefully, quietly. In a few hours he would be the normal eyes of the blind man once more. The problemist knew that there was no need of a guard outside the heavy door of the library, so he left the key with John, and gave him his instructions.

Colton walked around the corner to the private garage, and found Michael filling the big car's gasoline tanks.

"Anyone watching for the girl to come out, Michael?" asked Colton as he stood in the doorway.

"Yes, sorr. A stout felley in black clo'es. But his face looked like a sport."

"Norman, probably," declared the blind man. "I thought perhaps he'd be the one looking for the girl to come with the crow. That's why I asked you to keep an eye out. How long did he wait?"

"More'n two hours, sorr. An' he seemed mighty scared when he passed here, sorr. I was watchin' t'rough a crack in the windey shade."

"Beginning to close in on them," the blind man said grimly, "and they realize it."

"Seemed a bit queer, beggin' yer pardon, not to bother him, sorr," the Irish chauffeur said, a bit dubiously.

"This isn't a case for the blind, Michael." Colton smiled a bit queerly. "Eyes are solving this puzzle. First it was the eyes of Sydney. Then your eyes, that located the house of Silver Sandals. The eyes of the district attorney, the eyes of the police, and the eyes of all the others that have been connected with the case have helped clear up the ends since Sydney was taken away from me. The eyes of the girl and the eyes of the man who was watching will make the finish easy for me, I think. Eyes can only see the obvious, and the actions of men and women are governed mainly by eyes."

"There's few people believe your eyes don't see," remarked Michael sagely.

"I know of one who won't," Colton said dryly. Then: "Did you see how the girl came?"

"Big Fairfield car, sorr. Driv it herself. It's 'round the corner."

"Jove, but she's game!" Colton ejaculated admiringly. "The gamest woman I ever met!" he repeated. Then he finished softly: "But foolish—very, very foolish!"

"She is, sorr, to be tryin' to beat you, sorr." Michael shook his head wisely.

"See anyone else around?"

"No, sorr."

"Sure?"

Michael scratched his head. "Well, a drunk fell down in front of the garrige a few minutes back."

"You went out to pick him up?"

"I helped him, sorr. He was in bad shape."

"Thickset, square jaw?" Colton asked sharply.

The chauffeur stammered "Yes, sorr."

"Thought McMann was too blamed humble!" Colton jumped into the big car. "Watching to get a line on the thing that's too much for him! Piker!"

"If I'd knowed!" belched the Irishman, furious at the thought of anyone trying to beat Colton.

"Never mind," cut in the blind man. "The nearest telephone. Quick!"

Three minutes later the problemist was in an all-night drugstore 'phone booth. A minute of palaver, and Colton had the address the girl had tried to get. It was a house on the Boston Road, just below Yonkers, and the telephone was under the name of Bracken!

So that was the hiding place they had chosen. One of the retreats of the publicity-hating hotel owner. No doubt the son had secured the key to that, too, and made it the rendezvous where the woman of the silver sandals and the girl might hide safely. And it was one of the Bracken cars the girl had used. There was no doubt of that; nor was there much doubt of the fact that she had driven her aunt to the place when they had left the small car to be taken back to the district attorney's garage. It had been clever work, borrowing the official's car to involve him, and then returning it at a time that would prove he had nothing to do with the escape of the two women. But the case was nearing its end now, and it would be a grim end for someone. For the first time in his life Thornley Colton put the criminal ahead of the crime puzzle. A man who would try to put murder at the door of a girl like the one who was locked in Colton's library!

"Speed!" ordered the blind man, and he got it. There were few persons abroad at dawn, and the wary Michael knew how to dodge and avoid the police. Up above Van Cortlandt Park the car started to eat up the miles. Colton straightened in the cushions, his whole face drawn with the concentration of listening.

"Lose that car trailing us!" he yelled at the driver; then he spoke to himself: "Sometimes McMann shows evidence of a brain. He's picked up that Fairfield car the girl left. Bulldog!" Colton was angry. The bungling captain could spoil the whole plan by doing the wrong thing at the right time. "Sure that man who was watching for the girl got away?" he yelled again.

"Yes, sorr!" Michael screamed back. "There was no one around when he went. I know that!"

"Thank the Lord!" murmured Colton fervently. "It's taken him these hours to figure that watching me is his only chance."

The blind man leaned back in the cushions, every tired muscle of his aching body relaxed; his burning eyes soothingly cooled by the wind that rushed past them at cyclone speed. If Michael's work had been good before, it became wonderful now. The big car jumped ahead, every wheel seeming to leave the ground for feet at a time. Careening until there seemed no possibility of it ever staying upright, it took the first turn. The frightful jolting told the blind man that they were on some little-used crossroad. Another turn, worse this time, into some bylane. As rough as a newly plowed field, this new course shook and rattled the big car till it seemed impossible for mechanical endurance to stand it longer. For an hour, in, out, twisting, turning, through lanes, over crossroads, the Irishman drove the car with the daring of his race and the instinct for direction that is in the make-up of all good automobile drivers. The blind man was in the air as often, and as long, as he was on the seat.

Every part of him was a steady, sharp pain. But when he felt the smoothness of the main road under the tires they had lost the following car. Michael shouted the news.

"Don't let up!" Colton shouted. He knew the bulldog nature of the captain too well for any chance-taking. The blind man must have an opportunity to play his third move alone. Alone! There was a certain grim humor in that word. The players in the game he was trying to solve had sought to cripple him by forcing him to work alone. Now all the resourcefulness of his chauffeur had been needed to keep his lone hand when he needed it.

From his pocket the blind man took a folded paper. He opened it, and his finger tips felt the roughness of papyrus. It was the first chance he had had to study this thing for which everyone was looking; that had been stolen, then stolen again. In the speeding car, Colton's fingers went over and over the surface, feeling each line, visualizing the whole, until it was as clearly in his mind as it would have been before the eyes of a person who could see.

The cryptogram! The million-dollar cryptogram that had caused the murder of the strange old man who had believed so utterly in his own solution of the one great secret. It had cost him his life; it had put into danger the lives of three others whom he loved; and it was in Colton's hands! He had stolen it. He had forced the hands of the guilty ones by holding the crow as bait. They had not suspected that he held the cryptogram as well as the key. He had given them no chance to suspect that. Not even the girl knew!

"That must be the house, sorr!" Michael's voice waked him from the study of the curious papyrus cryptogram.

"Deserted, isn't it?" Colton asked.

"All closed an' boarded, sorr."

"Drive up to the front door."

"Lettin' thim know yer comin'?" gasped Michael, turning his head in surprise.

"Not much chance of a blind man crawling up through the shrubbery to discover whether or not any one's around," Colton remarked dryly. "I guess someone will see me."

The big house, shuttered and boarded, was set far back from the road, completely hidden by giant pines. It was such a place as the solitude-loving Philip Bracken would have chosen, and it was just the kind of place for anyone who wanted to hide.

"Take the car around back," ordered Colton, as he alighted under the porte-cochere. "You'll find the garage where the Fairfield was stored. Wait, but don't come near the house. Keep out of sight."

"Yes, sorr." Michael obeyed without even a dubious shake of his head. He knew the blind man.

The problemist's lips pursed in a soft whistle, the slim stick twirled idly in his long fingers, but in the idle swings there was method. Each move told the blind man where he was and where he was going. He stopped directly in front of the big door. His hand found the bell without a false movement. His keen ears caught the ring of it in the depths of the house. He waited. No answer. Another ring. There was no impatience. Thornley Colton jabbed the button easily. A short ring. Silence again, except for the soft whistle. The pursed lips straightened in a smile that flitted instantly. Soft footsteps had sounded at the other side of the door, and Colton continued his musical effort.

The door opened silently, the blind man's cane followed its movement.

"Good morning!" Colton doffed his hat politely, and the whistling stopped only for the two words. There was no answer, no sound. But as the door had opened Colton had heard the swish of a skirt. He knew that before him stood the old woman of the restaurant—Silver Sandals, the silent. He knew that she had determined to play her part as she had played it for twenty-five years—the part that the police of New York had never made her betray. She was deaf and dumb, because her will was steel. He was blind.

"Interesting." Colton got the word in between two bars of one of the latest musical atrocities.

The woman's strange eyes narrowed, her wrinkled face was drawn in a black scowl; but there was no other movement of her body. The blind man knew the scowl had come the minute it appeared.

"The whistling annoys you?" he murmured contritely. Then, as the scowl became darker with anger, "I thought perhaps it would. Very grating on the sensitive ears of a woman."

16

THE CRYPTOGRAM

Thornley Colton lowered the thin cane that had been resting lightly against the open door, and entered, with a murmured apology for passing in front of the woman. The door closed silently behind him. The woman did not move. He knew that she was staring at him with her strange eyes; for his highly attuned nerves could feel a stare more poignantly than the normal person feels one upon him when his back is turned.

"I'm really blind," he assured smoothly. "But it's a curious anatomical truth that a person can't scowl in anger without a slight clenching of the fingers. Yours were gripped on the door. My cane touched it. The slight movement told me. Simple, isn't it?"

She turned her back to him and walked down the hall. The blind man's ears caught the faint footfalls, and the sound of them told him that the woman still wore the silver sandals. He followed her slowly, turning when she turned. The woman made a gesture toward a chair. He bowed his thanks and seated himself. His slim cane had been touching her dress hem so lightly that she never even suspected it.

She stood before him. Once more he could feel the eyes, and even in his blindness he was aware of the dominant, compelling will of the strange old creature. It was minutes before there was a movement or a word to break the strange tableau. The blind man in the chair of the big room, in the great, empty house. The woman standing over him, trying to force his will to become her will, just as she had forced others so many times. But Thornley Colton's lips smiled up at her, even the brown eyes behind the smoked glasses seemed to twinkle with enjoyment of the unique situation.

"In case you didn't hear before," he said, very quietly, "I'll assure you again that my eyes are perfectly useless. They can't even help you gain control of my mind. You see"—there was polite mockery in the words—"I have considered my lack of sight an asset for years. A valuable ally most of the time."

She turned away, and her very footfalls told the angry bafflement that contorted her wrinkled face. He heard the rustle of a sheet of paper, the scratch of a pen. He held out his hand as she came toward him, and took the paper. His fingers touched the back and he read the words:

"I understand the lip language. I know what you have said."

"Quite remarkable." Colton was really impressed. "I consider that quite a feat," he went on, "because I was careful to form only every other word with my lips. What you 'saw' me say was: In you hear I'll you that eyes perfectly they even you control. A ally of time! And you got the sense of what I said from that? *Quite* remarkable!"

There was not even the queer throat sound of anger that Sydney Thames had heard when he stood before the woman on the steps of the old house in the Peck Slip section. There was not a movement to show that she had heard. She stood before him, her eyes on his face, waiting patiently. Then she took the paper he held out, and wrote again. With a slight smile he received the writing, and his fingers told him once more the words:

"Why don't you answer?"

Colton had not moved his lips at all!

The blind man realized that again he was pitted against the dogged will that characterized the strange family. Silver Sandals had fought against betrayal for a quarter of a century. She realized the handicap her silence put on the blind man, and she was playing it to the limit. She could see every move he made; hear every word he said. He could depend only on his ears, and she was determined to make them useless.

"I said," Colton enunciated the words with slow distinctness, "that your ability to see things that are not to be seen should be a valuable aid in deciphering the cryptogram that caused the murder of your brother."

She snatched the paper from his hand to write:

"What do you know about my brother's murder?"

He could feel the trembling of her hand as he took the paper, but even in her agitation she did not forget her purpose.

"So you know it was murder?" he asked accusingly.

She took the paper again, and the trembling had ceased. The instant loss of control was over.

"What do you know of the cryptogram?" she wrote.

"I have it in my pocket"—he moved his hand upward, under his coat; he could hear the sharp catch of her breath; he knew that she was leaning forward, hand outstretched—"where it will stay," he finished, and he held his hand over the pocket. "You do not need it," he added, with just a touch of sarcasm.

She reached for the paper to write. He held it away. "It is filled," he told her.

Silver Sandals crossed the room to where she had gotten the other sheet. Her back was toward him. He spoke:

"Eyes like yours do not need to *see* the cryptogram." There was not a move to tell that she had heard. "I know it by heart. There is no need of any one seeing it!" His hand lowered; there came the soft ripping sound of tearing paper as fingers worked.

The woman whirled on him in fury.

"Now we can talk!" he said simply.

The tearing paper had betrayed her into forgetting. It had done what police tricks had failed to do for years. She could not keep the pose now, for the blind man had made it impossible.

"Only the unnecessary notes you insisted on writing," he explained, holding out the scraps of paper so that she could see. "The police methods have been crude. One can pretend to not hear a falling house, or any big noise. But slight, significant sound—" There was no need of completing the sentence.

"Where did you get the cryptogram?" He heard her voice for the first time. It was husky with the huskiness of disuse. It sounded deep in her throat, because years of "throwing" it as a ventriloquist had changed its pitch. But behind it, despite the unnatural

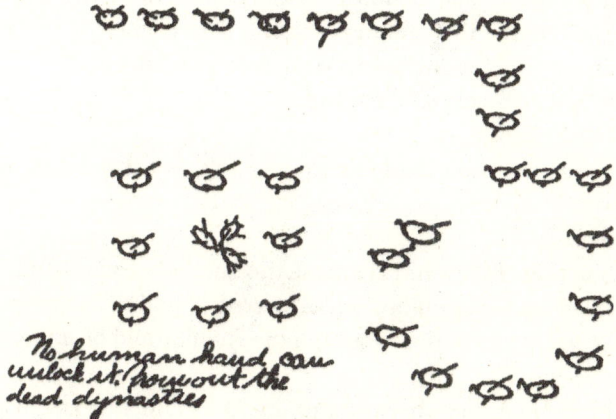

THE CRYPTOGRAM

tone, was the strength that was behind the coal-black eyes that glowed with the unquenchable fire of the will.

"I stole it." There was no hesitancy in the blind man's confession.

"Where is the crow?"

"The same place it was when you let the girl go for it!" The blind man's voice was stern.

"My niece has been—" The harsh tones quavered. She was a woman, after all. The years of her hard, unyielding life had only left a veneer of their passing. Underneath was the softness she had betrayed that minute in the restaurant when her lips had touched the forehead of her dead brother.

"She is not under arrest—yet," Colton said. "She is at my home."

"Let me have the cryptogram!" she demanded harshly. There was no hint of softness nor break now.

"Is that more important than the girl?" The sudden change in the woman made Colton's voice as hard as her own.

"She needs that money—now!" There was a sinister significance in the words that Colton detected at once.

"Where is Bracken?" he asked.

"I don't know."

"It was he who called her up and told her that I had the crow?"

"No."

"She thought it was?" He made the question a command.

"I told her it was Philip," she answered. "I told her he wanted her to get the crow from your house. There would be a ruse to get you away."

"Philip must have been in the city. Why didn't he go?" The blind man was impatient.

"He was afraid!" There was curious contempt in her voice.

"Philip Bracken killed John Neilton, and you know it!" The problemist made the accusation unqualified, tensely, dramatically.

Silver Sandals did not answer at once. The silence, following the exclamation, seemed doubly oppressive. He heard the light swish of her dress as she half-turned toward him, then the sound of her silver sandals on the carpet. She stopped in front of him; again he felt the stare of her eyes in the instant before she spoke.

"No," she said, and the harsh voice seemed very quiet. "I killed my brother!"

There was no emotion in the tone, no feeling. It was just the voice that had been softened to make it more impressive. It was not a confession. It was an incontrovertible statement.

Colton's answer, too, was quiet, and it seemed queerly incongruous. His hand took from his pocket the papyrus sheet and held it toward her.

"Here is the cryptogram. You have earned it."

She took it eagerly, spread it out on the table his cane had felt when he took his seat. He knew what her eyes were seeing the same strange puzzle that his fingers had visualized in his brain. The legacy of the man who had been murdered. A piece of paper worth a million dollars, that he had intended to be solved by the woman who had just confessed murdering him! Another queer kink in the case that had been a mass of kinks.

Colton, in the eye of his mind, saw the papyrus with its roughly drawn characters; the strange will of a strange man. The silver-sandaled woman, who had lived all her life as a charlatan, must be honest now. She must solve the riddle. The blind problemist had always been interested in cryptograms. He knew their hundred forms, but never had he seen one like that which the woman studied on the table. It appeared to conform to no rule of cryptography, but seemed merely a disorganized design of freakish-looking character.

The woman apparently forgot everything in her absorption in the papyrus sheet. There was no sound but her regular breathing, which the super keen ears of the blind man caught subconsciously. He could picture her staring at the thing her brother had left behind him. He could picture her coal-black eyes glinting and glowing with determination not to let the dead man beat her. Apparently all thought of the murder had gone from her mind. All thought of the consequences had vanished with the sight of the hieroglyphic-covered papyrus. Nothing existed in her world but that one thing.

Colton let his body relax a bit in the chair. His hand pushed the tortoise-rimmed glasses up on his high, white forehead, and one hand covered his eyes, that were beginning to feel again the pain that had been alleviated by the cold air. He shot a question suddenly:

"Tell me how you committed that murder!"

No answer. No movement to tell that the woman had heard.

"Want help on that cryptogram?" His tone was casual, but it commanded instant attention.

"What do you know of it?" she asked, and it was more than a question; it was a plea.

"Merely the significance of the significant," he answered. "There are thirty-three crows pictured. Figure where you have the number thirty-three before. It is thirty-three years since John Neilton discovered the Saiseogyus Stone of the Cycles of Life. You were at the Beaumonde's table thirty-three minutes."

"He told me to leave him then," she said, and for the first time there was a note of interest in her voice. "I had a wrist watch. It seemed only another part of his plan of passing."

"Thirty-three seems a number of peculiar significance." Colton paid no attention to her calling death a "plan of passing." "There were thirty-three joints in the silver-steel frame."

She looked up from the papyrus. "The cycle that ended with my brother's death was his thirty-third since he was Silver Sandals. Of the twenty thousand Egyptian deities, the crow ranks thirty-third. The crow!" she exclaimed.

"Has nothing but its word," Colton said. "Poughkeepsie."

"I've listened to it for hours." Again her head bent in concentration on the queer figures that the blind man had known were crows the minute his fingers had felt them.

Once more the problemist heard the raucous voice of the bird. Poughkeepsie! Poughkeepsie! There was the key. Colton straightened his relaxed body at the sudden association of ideas. The key! He remembered then the town name as the crow had screeched it. Pough-*cee*-psie was what it had said. But where was the key in that, and how was it to be used? There was no starting point in the queer design, no end. The Poe method of counting letters was useless. There was no mathematical beginning but the number thirty-three. What significance had that? The words on the bottom of the cryptogram, the words that had never been finished, came back to him. "No human hand can unlock it. From out the dead dynasties—" No human hand could unlock it because the crow was the key. The crow was the key. That was it! But where did the key fit in the strange assortment of figures? From out the dead dynasties? The crow had been named Rameses. The old man had believed implicitly that it was a reincarnation of a Pharaoh.

So the blind man's mind worked. Keener, ten times, at solving puzzles than the average mind, because his lack of sight had made all life a puzzle that must be solved, even to the steps he took, Colton's brain could make nothing of the cryptogram that old man had left to be solved by the woman who had confessed to his murder.

Suddenly the problemist forgot the cryptogram and the motionless woman at the table. His ears had caught a sound in the empty house. His acute hearing strained to the utmost, he listened. Someone was stealthily making his way along the dark halls. McMann? Had the police picked up the trail again? Were they going to spoil it before Colton had gotten the thing for which he had come? He knew McMann would find the place; there was too much bull-dog in the police officer ever to give up because he had been lost by the big car and the daring Michael. But Colton wanted to beat him to just one thing. The listener was outside the room door now.

"Why did you murder your brother?" Colton shot the question.

The old woman did not even raise her head. "Because he deserved it! Because—"

The crash of the flung-open door shook the big house. A voice came to the blind man's ears:

"So you did do it! You did! You killed the father of that girl! You—"

Colton's smooth voice cut in: "Sit down, Bracken! I've been waiting for you!"

The problemist heard the man whirl to face him. "Who are you? Colton, eh? The blind man! You got here first, did you?"

"I've been waiting some time." Thornley Colton spoke patiently.

"Where's Ruth?" Again Colton heard the man whirl as he turned toward the woman, but the blind man answered the question:

"Your wife is at my house."

"Your house?"

"Yes. Sit down, as I told you. Silver Sandals is working on the cryptogram that means the girl's fortune."

The blind man's ears heard the sharp intake of breath.

"Where did you get it?"

Again the question was addressed to the silent woman. Again Colton answered:

"I gave it to her. She must have time to solve it. The girl's future is on that papyrus."

"Her future." All the snarl, the wrath was gone from the man's voice. Colton could picture him, staring at the woman, who gave no sign of his existence; whose whole mind was fixed on the thing before her. Again Silver Sandals was deaf and dumb to the world. Colton, who appeared to be watching so intently, was blind. The man who stood in the center of the room in the big, empty house was the one Colton had accused of murder.

"She said that she killed him?" he asked. "She said that?" The second repetition was a hard-voiced demand.

"She has confessed," Colton assured him.

"The confession is a lie!" Bracken almost shouted the words. "A lie, understand!" he leaned forward so that the very words seemed to strike the blind man in the face. "I killed Neilton!"

"I know it." Colton nodded solemnly.

"Yes, I killed him!" The husband of the girl who was locked in the room at Thornley Colton's house was walking back and forth before the blind man like a caged tiger. "The girl never had a chance. She was his slave. She wouldn't leave him to his fool books and theories. He gave me the opportunity. It was simple. Now she's free!"

"Is she?" Colton demanded, his voice curiously quiet. "Doesn't the million dollars that the solving of the cryptogram means go to her? I found evidence that pointed to her presence in the suite—a hair on the floor!"

"She wasn't near the suite!" Bracken's voice fairly trembled with fear, and in it, too, the problemist detected the shock of surprise. That was a possibility Bracken had not suspected. "That's a lie, and you know it!" The blind man's knees felt the touch of Bracken's knees, so close was he. The hot breath of the man struck his face. "You know that I am the only one who could have killed him! I was with him! I knew his plans!"

Colton did not answer. He leaned far back in the chair. His face, with the tortoise-rimmed glasses pushed high on his forehead, was raised, the brown eyes appeared to be reading the innermost thoughts of the man who stood over him. He could feel the tremble in Bracken's knees. He could hear the steady breathing of the woman. He knew that she had not betrayed, by move of a muscle, that she had heard. He knew that her head was still bent in study over the papyrus figures.

"Why don't you arrest me?" demanded Bracken hoarsely. "Take me away!"

"I'm not a policeman," Colton answered smoothly. He had lowered his head so that the man standing over him could not see the new lines that came around the brown eyes; lines that the strain of listening to some far-off sound had brought.

"You're worse than a policeman!" The tone was bitter. "You've spoiled the whole game from the start with your infernal—"

"Spoiling the games of murderers is a sort of hobby with me," Colton interrupted. "Isn't it, Silver Sandals?"

"Don't bother her!" Bracken fairly snarled the command. "Call your police. The 'phone's in the next room!"

"Unnecessary." Colton waved his hand. "In a moment you'll hear the police at the front door. A Fairfield sixty, with Captain McMann, is coming up the long driveway to the house."

"I'll go out to meet them!" Bracken turned to the silent woman, glanced at her a minute, but did not speak to interrupt her work. He took a step toward the door.

Colton's hand shot out to grasp his arm. "We'll wait here!" he said sharply. "The police are on the porch."

They could hear the heavy footsteps now. Then the insistent clang at the front door.

The woman rose, and Colton spoke quickly: "The front door is unlocked. I slipped the catch in the instant you turned your back to lead the way to this room."

He heard her resume her seat. His hand, gripped on Bracken's arm, felt a trembling shake his body. They heard the front door open, then slam shut. Came the heavy footsteps of running men. The door was pushed open. Police Captain McMann stood in the doorway.

"Got them both!" he shouted in triumph. Then to Colton: "Thought you'd lost me with your slick work! Thought I'd given up! But Jimmy McMann never gives up!"

"He never admits defeat, either," the blind man declared shortly.

"You bet he don't!" McMann gloated. "I'll get a confession out of them!" he swore.

"Late, as usual, captain." Colton's voice was very dry. "Both have already confessed to the murder of that man you found at the Beaumonde." The old compelling manner came back; the dominant ring of voice that Captain McMann had heard so many times before characterized the blind man's next sentence. "But if you arrest them, I'll make you the laughing-stock of New York City!"

17

CONFESSIONS

Tense, strained silence followed the words of the blind man; the shock of them seemed to stun, overwhelm. The first statement had struck the police captain squarely between the eyes. The swift change of tone and of attitude, coming so close on its heels, completed the effect. Only the woman at the table was unmoved. The entrance of the police captain had not caused her even to lift her head or to change a line in the age-wrinkled face. Not even the eyes had moved from their fixed stare at the papyrus.

It required a Newfoundland shake of the burly captain's body to throw off the shock the blind man's words had caused. Then bluster, the refuge of the defeated, came.

"Trying to scare me, eh?" he sneered. "Snap the cuffs on Bracken, Tom!"

The square-jawed detective who had been a background for Captain McMann ever since the case had begun, took a step forward.

"Go ahead," Colton's voice was quietly ominous; arrest him, and by the Lord Harry, I'll see that you lose every cent you have on a false-arrest suit"

"He confessed, didn't he?" The snappishness of bluster was still evident, but there was anxiety, too, that only Colton's threat could have brought. A suit for false arrest meant something, even to bulldog Captain McMann. He was getting old, and a false-arrest suit is the Nemesis of a policeman who has money—especially with men like the son of Millionaire Bracken and Thornley Colton.

"Yes," the blind man answered evenly. "He killed him!"

"For God's sake take me to jail then!" Bracken stepped toward the detective with outstretched hands. "I killed him! I'll confess as soon as you get me to police headquarters!"

"False arrest on *that!*" Gloating triumph was in the captain's manner. "Slip on the bracelets, Tom!"

The two sharp clicks sounded in the silence of the room. "I guess that's bad! *Bad!*" The detective spoke, and for the first time in the case, and proved that he was human, and that human emotions were behind the hard-looking face with the square chin.

"Better arrest Silver Sandals, too," remarked Colton quietly. "She confessed, too."

"That's a lie!" Once more the snarl was in Bracken's voice. "I did it! I did it alone! Take me away!"

"Your hurry is suspicious." The way Colton said it made it a gentle hint.

Captain McMann took it up. He strode over to the table where the silent woman sat. He glared across the table at her. She did not move.

"What did you have to do with that murder?" he demanded. "No lies! Come on!"

Not a quiver of an eyelash told that the woman had heard. There were twenty-five years of stolid-faced posing behind her. Her eyes were on her pad at her elbow. The ink-dipped stylus wrote queer combinations of figures, of designs.

"I'm guilty, I tell you! I did it! *Alone!*" Bracken screamed the words in rage, his face pale with fury and fright.

Only the detective, who kept within touch of his elbow, paid any attention to him. Captain McMann glared across the table at Silver Sandals. Thornley Colton appeared merely as a disinterested spectator who was bored.

"You're under arrest for the murder of that man!" snapped the captain.

"John Neilton was his name," put in the blind man casually.

"How'd you know that?" McMann spun around as he asked the question. Colton waved a hand toward the woman.

"His sister," he explained.

Only for a second was the police officer taken off his mental feet by this new evidence of the blind man's getting ahead of him. His pugnacious obstinacy wouldn't let him swerve from his path longer than that. His hands gripped the table edge as he leaned across toward the woman.

"You killed your brother!" The accusation came like the vicious snap of a whip.

"Third-degree methods aren't very effective on a deaf-and-dumb person," observed Colton dryly. "Let me try." He walked to the table, and leaned over to wave his cane so that the shadow would fall across the woman's eyes. She looked up, with never a shade of expression in her cold, black eyes.

"You killed John Neilton," he said quietly.

The captain watched her eyes or the blind man's lips. He watched her as she pulled the pad nearer, without haste, without outward indication of any inner emotion. She tore the top figure-covered sheet off. She wrote slowly, and as slowly extended the paper toward the blind man. Captain McMann grabbed it.

"Easy!" He gloated. "Easy!"

On the paper the woman had written:

"I killed John Neilton!"

Bracken broke away from the detective. He saw the words on the paper before the captain had a chance to conceal them.

For some reason they seemed to take all the strength from him for the moment, before he braced himself to furious outburst.

"What did you do that for?" he demanded in fury, hands clenched on the table edge as wide apart as the chain of the handcuffs would allow. "Great God! Don't you know what it means? It means jail! It means that you'll be shut up in a cell, where you can't—" He stopped, fairly gulping the words back.

"The girl doesn't need help!" Colton put in the apparently irrelevant words sharply.

"Keep her name out!" snarled Bracken, and Colton heard the detective jerk him roughly back.

"Where's the girl?" demanded Captain McMann. "What was her part?"

"So you don't know everything?" There was the faintest trace of sarcastic surprise in Colton's voice. The unintelligible growl of the captain was apparently the encouragement he sought to go on. "The answer to your first question is: She is safe from badgering and fool police work. The answer to your second question may surprise you: She killed John Neilton!"

The blind man's words made of Bracken an unleased, rabid animal. He broke again from the detective, sprang across the room, straight at the blind man, mouthing his oaths of fury. McMann yelled his warning. The woman jumped to her feet. Colton did not move a muscle until Bracken reached him, manacled hands upraised for a crushing blow. Then the problemist's hand shot up, grasped the chain of the steel cuffs, pulled the arms down, and held them rigid as the infuriated man twisted and writhed.

"I thought you'd be easier to handle that way," Thornley Colton said smoothly. "That's why I let them handcuff you."

"Damn you!" shrieked Bracken.

The detective took him then, and snapped a nipper on his wrist, so that he could not move without breaking his arm.

"Jam him down in a chair, and sit on him!" ordered Captain McMann. Then he spoke to Colton. "What did the girl have to do with it?" he demanded again.

"I told you she killed him. He was her father." Colton was as unruffled as a summer sea. He could hear the struggle of Bracken trying to get at him. He heard the sharp breathing of the woman.

"Bunk!" McMann snapped. "Man's job, with the help of a woman like that!" He nodded his head toward Silver Sandals. "Girl ain't the kind, even if she wanted to. Tryin' to kid me by saying *three* people killed him."

"He killed himself." The blind man's voice was almost gentle. In sharp contrast came the imperative question he shot at Bracken: "You know that?"

"I killed him," the answer came, sullenly and doggedly.

McMann snorted. "'Nuff fool stuff!" he growled. "No suicide! It was murder!"

"The nastiest I've ever encountered!" The sharp note was still in the blind man's voice. There was a new tenseness of muscles that showed even under the well-cut clothes. The faint flush was on his pale cheeks. "It was murder!"

"And I've got the murderer!" McMann positively chuckled.

"You haven't! You don't even suspect him! You never would suspect him!" The sentences crackled from the lips of the problemist.

McMann had no sarcastic rejoinder, no sneering expletive. He had heard that tone before. It backed him up against the wall like a strong fist. He knew the blind man, after all, and in the instant he realized that he had been led on and on, after warnings.

"You said Bracken killed him," he declared, and the weakening showed plainly in the way he spoke.

"I did!" Colton pulled the tortoise-rimmed glasses over his eyes and found a chair with his cane. "He did kill him. So did Silver Sandals. So did Ruth Neilton! And he killed himself!"

"What d'ye mean?" The backing down of the blustering police captain was almost ludicrous.

"They all killed him, because they made possible his murder! Everyone of them worked to help the real murderer! Everyone of them would be adjudged guilty on the evidence of eyes! That's what I've been working to overcome. The murderer is as safe as the President of the United States himself. Arrest him, and these two persons and the girl would be found guilty by any jury in the land. But I'll get him!"

There was a passion in the voice of the blind man that the captain had never heard before. It was a new side that the police officer had never fully realized. For the first time he saw Thornley Colton as the district attorney had seen him—a bloodhound, a blind bloodhound. All bluster, all thoughts of bluster left McMann's mind. Once before he had accepted defeat momentarily, but the conceit of a score of years' experience had made him fight on. He had had to beat the blind man, and he hadn't cared how he did it. But now there would be no recovery. It was the end.

He turned to the detective. "Take 'em off, Tom," he said, and his voice was that of a man who is very tired. He spoke to Colton then, and the words came slowly: "You're in charge of this case! Give your orders, and I'll go to hell, if you say so!"

The blind man understood what that confession cost. It was an acknowledgment of defeat from a man who had never acknowledged defeat before; from a man who had fought honestly or crookedly to make his own game win, because the game he played was his life's game, all he knew, or wanted to know. And he was putting himself under the orders of a blind man at whom he had sneered—treated with contempt at every opportunity! The police captain was a man when the showdown came.

"You'll make the arrest, captain," Colton said. There was no need for more.

Bracken seemed to wake from his daze. The snapping of the steel bracelets and the nipper he had not even noticed. He had sat, staring, stunned, at the blind man, till he made that last statement. He jumped from the chair.

"You don't mean it!" he cried, and there was terrible pleading in the voice, that was broken and strained. "You know who killed him?"

Colton merely nodded. Silver Sandals had risen, and was holding toward him one of the sheets from the pad. To the last she was keeping her pose before the police. Not even this could startle her for a minute into forgetting. The blind man read what she had written, and crumpled the paper into a ball with his fingers.

"Yes." He nodded, and he was careful that she could see his lips move. "He will be in Poughkeepsie. I'm going to call the district attorney on the 'phone. He should be in at the death!"

The last sentence seemed to strike Captain McMann as suggestive. He opened his lips to speak, closed them again, and silently watched the problemist leave the room in search of the telephone.

18

THE SUMMONS

The Fee, wild-eyed with excitement, burst into Sydney Thames' room.

"Wake up, Sydney!" he cried. "Mister Colton's cleaned up the Silver Sandals thing, an' he wants yuh to see the finish."

The eyes of the secretary opened sleepily, stared at the boy blankly a minute, then he leaped from the bed.

"Silver Sandals!" Thames repeated, trying to stir the memory that was not yet awake. Then events came back to him with a rush. "How did I get *here*?" he demanded dazedly. "Where is the woman? The crow? The girl? The murdered man I spoke to?"

"Mister Colton's got the woman. The crow's locked in the front room here. The girl's downstairs, an' I don't know nothin' 'bout the last," rattled the boy.

"What time is it?" Thames asked. "What day? I felt the eyes, then saw a silver flash. I was stabbed, I guess."

"I'll tell yuh about it while yer gettin' dressed."

As Sydney got into his clothes, The Fee rattled off the events so fast that the words tumbled over each other. It was difficult, at times, to follow the boy's story, so fast did he chatter; but when Thames got to his collar and tie he knew everything that had happened while he had been out of the world.

"So the district attorney has been taking my place?" mused the blind man's secretary. "That seems strange."

"He met us down to Silver Sandals' house, an' him an' Mister Colton's been goin' 'round together ever since."

"You say he's coming here?"

"That's what the—gee whiz!" The boy whistled. "I fergot to show yuh the telegram." He dug into his pocket and extended the yellow paper.

"Telegram?" questioned Thames.

"He couldn't telephone." A grin spread over the boy's face. "He cut the outside wires so's the girl downstairs couldn't use it to talk anywheres 'cept to the extension upstairs."

"You say Nadine is with her?" Thames asked the question eagerly, his somber face lighting up at the mention of the wonderful girl that had come into his life.

"She came more'n three hours ago. Mister Colton told John he wasn't to wake yuh."

Thames saw that his tie was in just the proper careless knot, brushed an invisible spot from his coat collar, and took a step toward the door.

"Ain't yuh gonna read the telegram?" grinned The Fee.

The apple cheeks of Thames went several shades darker as he unfolded the telegram that he had forgotten completely. The words so surprised him that he read them aloud unconsciously:

Follow orders of district attorney unquestioningly. Bring girl, crow, and crow's feather to place D. A. will know. I have Silver Sandals and Bracken. Case cleared, but think will need eyes.

Thames read the thing again. Why should he follow the orders of the district attorney? Why didn't Colton issue his orders direct? Where was the place the district attorney knew? And why did he need Sydney Thames' eyes? The district attorney wasn't blind.

"How long ago did this come?" If Colton had telephoned the district attorney direct from wherever he was the official should have beaten the telegram.

"Five minutes," The Fee answered, and the grin was still on his face. "Yuh got time to see N'dine 'fore he comes."

The sensitive Sydney strode from the room, straight-backed, scowling. The Fee made a horrible grimace, and followed. Sydney wanted to run down the stairs, but the thoughts of the grinning boy behind him made his steps draggingly slow. In the hall below they met John with a tray.

"The girls just had a bite, sir," he informed Sydney. Thames cursed the minute of delay that caused, but he nodded smilingly. He took a step toward the door when the ring of the front bell halted him.

"I'll go!" exclaimed The Fee, and he darted past to answer.

It was the district attorney, and suppressed excitement was in his manner and voice. "Hustle along!" he commanded, and it was only the smile that took the sharpness from the words. "The waiter has been found!"

Sydney instantly bristled at the idea of taking orders from anyone but the problemist. A sharp answer was on the tip of his tongue; then the words of the telegram flashed back to his mind. Unquestioningly, the blind man had said. Unquestioningly!

Sydney glanced longingly at the closed door, then took the coat and hat the boy had taken from the hall tree.

"Coming along, Shrimp?" he asked as he started toward the door.

"No, sir," the boy answered soberly. "I got a telegram, too. Mister Colton wants me to count the feathers in Rameses' tail."

"What?" scowled Sydney.

"Hustle!" exclaimed the district attorney, with what Sydney thought was unnecessary sharpness.

But he obeyed unquestioningly.

"Know who the waiter is?" asked the district attorney as the car started across the city.

"Shrimp told me of the guide," Thames answered a bit shortly. The district attorney searched Thames' face intently for an instant, then he seemed to understand the shortness of Sydney's reply.

"Got me up in the air, too," he said. "Colton had me on the wire. Told me to hurry over and get you. Made me call off the detectives I sent to Poughkeepsie, and he issued orders through Captain McMann, as representing the New York police department, that any guard over the old man's house at Poughkeepsie should be instantly withdrawn. I don't understand it. Colton said that he had Bracken and Silver Sandals, and that both had confessed. Why doesn't he bring them down to the city? And why does he want me to look for a feather?"

"A feather?" put in Sydney, the instructions of the telegram and The Fee's words coming back.

"Yes; I'd just got the 'phone message about Nelson, the waiter, when he called. Wanted me to see if there was a feather on the body."

"Body?"

"Yes. We've been trying to locate the waiter ever since yesterday morning after the murder was committed. We couldn't find him because he was in the river."

Sydney nodded. His mind was trying to piece together the ends Shrimp had told him. The Fee's eyes and ears had been wide open, as usual, and he knew things that neither the blind man nor the district attorney had suspected he knew. The boy had followed every move of the case, and Sydney had a pretty thorough knowledge of all its twists and quirks. There were things he did not know, many things, but he made no attempt to question the district attorney. That official seemed strangely silent, and Sydney wondered.

The car was bowling along East Twenty-sixth Street. It stopped before the grim-looking morgue building that was part of the grimmer-looking Bellevue group. The district attorney was important enough to get ready admission and courtesy; the morgue-keeper himself was on the job, ready and willing to do anything he could for so great a personage.

"Plain floater," was his casual comment, grunted around a badly chewed cigar, as the body of "George Nelson, waiter, age twenty-seven," was pulled out on its slab. He pulled back the sheet. "Drunk," grunted the morgue-keeper again. "Fell in. Picked him up around Peck Slip. In the water about twenty hours."

The district attorney nodded. The pseudo guide had evidently wandered into a saloon when he had run away from the blind man, had a few drinks, and had fallen into the water. He took a closer look at the bloated face.

"Jove! Now I remember him!" he exclaimed. "He was a hotel waiter that was to be a big witness at one of the gambling trials last winter. He disappeared. No doubt he got a job on Bracken's yacht. Of course he felt the lure of old New York, and he snapped at the chance to work in the Beaumonde. Even in a state of hypnosis my appearance shocked him into remembering. He thought I was after him."

"That Beaumonde case?" put in the morgue-keeper with real interest.

A short nod answered. "Anything in the pockets?" he wanted to know.

"Funny thing!" A jerk of the keeper's thumb ordered an attendant to shove the body back into place, and he led them to the "rag room," where the clothes of bodies found in the river are kept for the identifiers of bodies. An envelope yielded a rusty key, a few coins. Then a grunt of satisfaction from the custodian of the morgue. He held out a silver feather! "In his inside pocket," he explained. "Musta stole it. Pretty thing, ain't it?"

The district attorney took it. It was a beautiful piece of work. A perfect feather of burnished silver, the size of a crow's feather.

"That's what I want!" The district attorney put out his hand, and the morgue-keeper gave it up without question.

"You're all right," he grinned. Election wasn't far away.

"Thanks." The district attorney turned on his heel, and hurried out. Thames followed him silently. He was merely background, and he resented it a bit. "A stop at the Beaumonde next," the official said as they were again in the automobile.

Silence marked the trip. The district attorney was too greatly preoccupied to talk. Sydney Thames was too busy with his own thoughts to listen. In the hotel lobby a small group of newspaper men hurried forward. The official waved them aside. "Nothing doing!" he snapped out, at variance with his usual smile.

"Can I see Manager Carl?" he asked the clerk.

"Can't be disturbed!" The man at the desk was plainly following an explicit order.

"I've got to see him!"

The tone made the clerk wilt a bit, but not much.

"Can't do it," he declared. "My job means something to me."

"Where is he?"

"In his room, and it's worth any hotel job in New York to wake him—wait a minute!" He reached in the mail box. "Here's a 'phone message that came an hour or so ago."

The district attorney read it, whistled, and passed it to Thames, who read:

> Never mind Carl. Have you cleaned up Wall Street end? Sydney knows rest.

The clerk put in a word of explanation. "Mr Colton tried to get Carl, but we had orders not to disturb him for the president himself. He left that message for you."

"All right." Again Sydney found himself following the silent official. The district attorney seemed more than puzzled; he was perturbed. Something was wrong! The hypersensitive Sydney felt it. The attitude of the district attorney was unnatural, strained.

"What does Colton want at the house?" the district attorney asked.

"The girl, the crow, and a feather," Sydney answered.

"The girl! What girl?" demanded the official jerkily.

"The one who sat at the table next to the dead man." Sydney had learned that from the boy.

"Jove! Did he locate her?" The district attorney turned to stare.

Thames shrugged his shoulders. "She is at the house. How she got there I don't know."

"Funny he told me nothing of it," mused the district attorney. His voice became harsh with impatience. "But what the devil is this crow-feather part of the case? I don't understand it."

"Colton does!" Thames snapped it. The blind man knew what he was doing. The fact that anyone could imply that he didn't was enough to arouse Sydney's ire always.

There was no further talk. They reached the brownstone house. It was Sydney who led the way this time. It was the district attorney who followed at his heels. John opened the door. Sydney hurried past him. He wasn't going to miss the chance of seeing Nadine. A knock. An invitation to enter, and Thames stopped short on the threshold.

Before the desk stood the two girls. Behind them stood The Fee. Perched on the telephone was a big, black crow; the crow he had last seen on the grinning skull in the room of velvet while the woman with the age-old face and the terrible eyes had advanced toward him. As he took the first step in the direction of the desk the crow flapped its wings, stretched its neck, and screamed:

"Poughkeepsie! Pough-*kee*-psie!"

Some kink in the bird's brain seemed to straighten as he took another step. It flew from its perch and wildly circled the room, screeching:

"George Nelson! Waiter! Age twenty-seven!"

"You've frightened it again!" The words came from the lips of the girl with the burnished gold hair who stood beside Nadine Nelson. The great hazel eyes stared at him. She was dressed in a simple blue-tailored dress that brought out the soft lines of her slim, girlish figure. Thames didn't know that it was one of Nadine's dresses that she had sent for the minute she had seen the clothes the other girl wore. He just saw it as a pretty setting for the girl with the face of a young Greek goddess and the square little chin. And this was the girl who was connected with the murder of the man in the restaurant!

Nadine slipped her arm from about the other girl's waist. "Are you ready to go?" she asked eagerly. "Are you ready to take us to Mr Colton?"

"Gee! I hope so!" the irrepressible Shrimp broke in. "I fixed the wires, an' Mister Colton's been talkin' to us. He wants yuh and the distri't attorney to hurry. He knows where the murderer is an' he wants yuh to help get him."

"He knows where he is?" The district attorney spoke for the first time since he had entered the house. The words were accompanied by an eager, nervous glance toward the telephone that puzzled Sydney Thames mightily.

19

ASSASSIN

Speed laws ceased to exist. Traffic regulations meant nothing. Policemen scowled ferociously, took a step forward with upraised hand, then stepped back suddenly as the hand dropped to salute. The district attorney of New York was on official business. The attorney was on the front seat beside the driver. In the roomy tonneau of the big car were Nadine and Ruth Neilton, Sydney Thames, and the eager-eyed Shrimp with a perforated box clutched tightly between his knees.

With each swaying and jolting of the big car the crow's muffled protests came; sometimes in the metallic "Caw-caw!" of its species, at others with disjointed parts of the words it had been taught. Sydney Thames' mind was a whirl of unanswered questions. He had lost all recollection of things with the cry of the golden-haired girl ringing in his ears. He had regained it again with the problemist's message. As is peculiar to hypnosis he remembered nothing of the blind man's fight for his mind nor of the things he had remembered subconsciously.

There had been no chance for questions at the house. The district attorney, with the strange nervousness that seemed so queer to the blind man's secretary, had bustled them into the big car he had brought before there was a chance for anything; Thames, obeying the orders of Thornley Colton, had followed the instructions of the attorney unquestioningly. But what was it all about?

What significance had the crow? The boy had told him of the notes and listening to the conversation for hours. But that was all he knew. What had a silver feather to do with the case? Why silver? Then he remembered that every thing connected with the strange old man in the restaurant and also the old woman had been of silver. The silver sandals, the weird silver designs on the black velvet at the house. The silver girdle. Even the framework that had been responsible for the automaton-like movement of the man who had entered the restaurant and the man to whom Sydney had afterward spoken was of silver.

Weird, uncanny, the case seemed to have no connection with the present-day, practical world. It seemed to belong to the past, dead centuries when the Borgias made Death the guest of honor at the elaborate feasts of Rome. The old, old woman. The man. The crow. Surely such things did not belong to busy New York. Back to Sydney Thames' mind came the message Colton had telephoned to the district attorney at the Beaumonde: Have you cleaned up the Wall Street end? The Wall Street end? Somehow that seemed an anachronism in this case of crows and crows' feathers and deaf-and-dumb clairvoyants. That was a sordid, "practical" side of the murder that had never been in evidence before. How had the old man been connected with the street of frantic money-changers? As Sydney remembered him, there at the restaurant table with one hand loosely grasping a wineglass, there had been no suggestion of modern things. The woman with the wonderful eyes? It seemed impossible to associate her with Wall Street. The girl with the hair of burnished gold! He eyed her covertly. Her eyelids were drooping over her big hazel eyes. Nadine's arm was around her waist with its comforting, gentle pressure.

Sydney knew that in the hours she had been with the girl Nadine had impressed her with some of her own great faith in the blind man who solved crime puzzles. No, a girl like that could not commit murder. The new twist the blind man's message had brought made the murder a man's crime; and the crime of a man who needed money. Wall Street seldom meant anything else.

The district attorney turned in his seat so that he could speak to them.

"Did you ever see this before?" he asked, and he stretched out his hand to show them the silver feather.

The girl's eyes opened; blankness was in them a moment; then a startled look of understanding came. "Father made it. Rameses used to hide it in play."

"Did he ever say anything to you about it?" It seemed to Sydney that the district attorney was particularly persistent.

The girl shook her head slowly; then sudden recollection came. "Once he said that only a feather stood between me and the fortune. Only a feather!" she repeated. The curious glance she shot at Sydney caused him to wonder. She saw that he had no recollection of ever hearing the words before. "He must have said the same thing to my aunt," she declared. "She—" The girl broke off the sentence and changed it to a question: "Where did you get it?"

"Thames will tell you." The district attorney appeared to have lost all interest.

The girl glanced questioningly at Sydney, and he twitched uncomfortably on the seat. Why had the official left this to him? Why had he shifted the minute the girl had mentioned fortune?

"The waiter had it," the secretary blurted.

"Where is he?" she asked quickly. "He was to have met me on the road yesterday morning with the crow. He never came."

"He is dead, at the morgue," Sydney told her quietly.

"Dead!" The word seemed to choke her. "He wasn't— killed?" Her voice broke piteously on the last word.

"He was not murdered," Sydney answered solemnly the question she could not put. "The district attorney had been looking for him a year. He had been drinking heavily, and he probably fell into the water trying to hide."

"Thank God he was not another!" she murmured. Nadine's arm drew her back comfortingly. She added a word of explanation. "We never understood his drinking. After the first time, when his papers were stolen, Silver Sandals ordered him not to drink. It was the only thing she seemed unable to control."

"Don't talk of it, please," was the gentle command of Nadine, and the girl obeyed.

The car raced along past the scattered houses.

"There's where my aunt is!" cried the girl suddenly, but the car shot past the stone gates of the big house set far back in the trees.

"Colton is going to meet us on the outskirts of Poughkeepsie!" shouted the district attorney over his shoulder.

On the car sped. Fast as it went Sydney's mind was working faster. They were speeding toward the end of the strange case. But what was the end? What was awaiting them in Poughkeepsie? Was anything awaiting there? He turned his head a bit so that he could see the district attorney in the front seat. The official's shoulders were hunched, his fingers were playing nervously on his knees. Was Colton waiting for someone who was coming? Times before Sydney had known the blind man to arrange the denouement of a case at a certain scene that would bring the confession necessary to convict the guilty. Was he doing the same here? He knew that every bit of evidence pointed toward Silver Sandals, the girl, and the waiter who had been at the restaurant. Thames, from what he had learned, was positive this was the Bracken to whom Colton had referred. Colton evidently knew that they were not guilty, but he realized that some part must be played that would convince *others* that they were innocent. The problemist never finished a case without proving it beforehand.

"There they are!" It was the district attorney who discovered the big black car with Michael at the wheel. The automobile was drawn up at the road side. Behind it was a runabout with a rumble seat in which Sydney recognized one of Colton's pet enemies—Police Captain McMann.

Sydney saw the blind man jump from the car, turn to the captain, and speak. The policeman and the man who was with him jumped from the car. Thames was surprised that the blind man and McMann seemed on the best of terms. Before the big car stopped Colton was issuing orders in the curt, sharp way that came when every part of him was working at high pressure.

"Get out, Sydney. You and Shrimp. Bring the crow." The district attorney started a question. The blind man cut in sharply: "I've been issuing orders under your name and that of the police department. Your men were ordered to leave Poughkeepsie. The Poughkeepsie police were notified that the murderer had been arrested and was on his way to New York. They had connected the old man who lived in the house and the one who was murdered in the Beaumonde. Naturally they'd see the connection. There's no one at the house now but two Egyptian servants. I tried to talk to one, but I couldn't make her understand. We're going in this car that luckily was in the garage at Bracken's house. Give us ten minutes and follow."

"How about me?" The district attorney got his question in this time.

"You stay here with McMann," Colton said sharply. "He's put the case in my hands! Do what he says! I've got to look over the ground first *alone!*"

"I've got the feather," put in the district attorney, who had been glancing nervously at Bracken, who seemed to avoid his eyes. "It was—"

"Don't need it yet!" cut in Colton. "Hold it! Hustle, Shrimp! Take the rumble seat."

Sydney jumped from the car. In the other car he saw the old woman with the coal-black eyes. But the terrible look that had been in them was gone now. They seemed soft, kindly. The whole wrinkled face seemed to have mellowed. The thousand lines that crossed and crisscrossed it had lost their harshness, their coldness. Her eyes were on the girl; in them was the look of hunger insatiable. Beside her on the seat was the man Sydney had last seen in the restaurant; but now the black was beginning to show in the hair that had been straw-colored with bleach. His eyes, too, were all on the girl. But there was no move. Everyone was completely under the domination of the blind man.

"Hurry, Sydney!" Colton snapped out the order with the impatience that was part of him at times like this.

"Who's goin' to drive?" McMann asked the question surprisedly as Thames took the other seat.

"I am. I've driven cars before!" Colton threw in the clutch, backed the car to the road with never a false swerve around the other car that his ears had located unerringly when it stopped. "Ten minutes!" he shouted back at them, and the dust cloud his speed raised hid him from their sight.

"House with high wall. Egyptian-scarabed gate," jerked Colton. "Use your eyes. Describe everyone you see near it. Know the turns. Bracken made me see the road."

It seemed but a minute to Sydney that they took in reaching the gates. Even before he spoke the blind man had slowed down the machine.

"Lotus," explained Colton. "Bracken said there was a lot of it. Gate open?"

"Yes! No one around!" Sydney, too, had caught the contagion. He also was talking in exclamations.

"Expect someone!" snapped Colton as he drove the car slowly through the big gate. "Watch hand of first person you see. Anyone! I want a 'V' veined back. Nudge me if it is."

Up the great, winding roadway with its high-arched trees the car crawled. Sydney could see the extensive grounds, well laid out with winding paths, fringed with trees, some of them curious-looking trees that had no place in America. At the left of the house was a miniature pyramid, a roughly hewn sphinx. Before them stretched a large artificial patch of yellow sand. Everywhere was the influence of Egypt.

The house, closed, deserted, looked sinister in the dark shadows of the overhanging pines. At the porch steps two winged lions guarded the silence and gloom. A fitting climax for the case that had begun in the brilliantly lighted Beaumonde, where life and gayety had reigned before the coming of the dead man!

Before the wide steps the car stopped at a touch of Sydney's fingers on the blind man's arm.

"Hand!" whispered Colton tensely.

Sydney glanced around in surprise. No one was in sight. Then he saw that the front door was opening slowly, and, to his normal ears, silently. In the semi-darkness of the hall he saw who had opened it. A woman, but a strangely dressed woman. Robes hung so low that they concealed her feet. A curious cap covered her head. A veil that hung under her eyes concealed every part of her face. From the figure of the woman, whose looseness and fat the hanging robes could not hide, Sydney thought her old. One of the Egyptian servants! The woman made no sound, and Sydney thought again of the silent door opened by the silent woman at the grim-looking house in the Peck Slip district. He tried to see her hand, but the darkness of the hall prevented him. Colton had ordered him to see the hand, and there would be no move until he did.

For a minute the tableau remained unchanged. Then the irrepressible Shrimp broke the spell.

"Gee, Mister Colton, dere's a hoochy-koochy woman from Coney!"

Sydney thought he saw a sudden change of expression in the eyes. Then the woman stepped to the threshold of the door and waved a hand in a command to enter. The veins on the back of her hand did not form a "V." They crossed diagonally, over the fat, big hand that looked so like the hand of a man.

"Take the crow, Sydney!" ordered Colton as he jumped down. "Stay where you are, Shrimp!" The boy made a grimace at being left out, but he did not demur audibly. Sydney took the box that contained the bird, and followed the blind man up the steps.

Colton walked with maddening slowness. But Sydney saw the red spots on his white cheeks over the cheek-bones; he saw the grim, ominous set of the chin, the tenseness of the thin lips. He had seen those signs before. He knew they meant the steel-spring tightness of muscles held in leash by the brain back of the dead eyes.

Without turning his head toward the woman who stood holding the door open the blind man walked past her. Sydney followed. The door closed behind them. The woman took a step forward with surprising agility. Her hand fumbled in the folds of her dress. Colton's shoulder almost knocked Sydney down as the blind man leaped past him. The blind man's weight sent the woman crashing against the wall. A blue-steel pistol clattered to the floor.

"I want you, Norman!" the blind man's voice rang out in the empty house. "Quiet! Take the handcuffs from my pocket, Sydney!"

Thames obeyed mechanically. The veil had been torn from the face, and Sydney recognized the man from having seen him around the Beaumonde.

"Cuff him to the newel post of the stairs!" ordered Colton sharply. Together they dragged the panting, cursing man to the heavy post.

So this was the murderer!

"No!" Colton seemed to read Sydney's very thoughts. "This is only the tool!" He spoke to the raging man. "Where is he?" he demanded. "Where's the brains of the devilish thing?"

He shook him as a terrier might shake a rat.

"Find him!" snarled Norman sullenly.

"I will!" Colton's cane guided him around a heavy settee that lay on its side. Sydney noticed that the whole hall was disordered and pulled apart as though vandals had been at work.

"Use your eyes!" Colton shot out the words. "How many steps to that back door? Keep at my heel and count every turn!"

"Five!" Sydney answered without an instant of hesitation. For ten years he had practised judging distance with his eyes and reckoning steps for the blind man.

Colton ran. Sydney followed. A turn.

"Three!" Sydney shouted the word in time. Colton swung around. He had dropped his cane in the hall. In his hand was a pistol.

"Door!"

Colton flung it open. Sydney caught the flash of a robe in the dense grove of young pines at the edge of the yellow sand.

"Fourteen! Left!"

The blind man dashed in pursuit of the robe flash that he could not see. He ran with all the speed in him ahead in the darkness that had been his always. The sun was shining brightly overhead, but to the blind man it was midnight. He was running with a pistol in his hand to get a murderer! And the only eyes he knew were two paces behind him, guiding the wonderful body that God had made guideless. Panting,

Sydney put the last ounce of strength in his legs to gain the pace necessary to see ahead.

"Five! Right!" he hissed. The chase went on. Their footsteps on the soft bed of pine needles were almost noiseless. Sydney knew that even Colton's wonderful ears could not follow the footfalls of the man in the robes, who was twisting and turning in the narrow paths between the pines whose branches swept the ground.

"Four! Left! Right! Left!" The guiding words fairly ran together so fast did Sydney say them.

"Never mind! Drop back!" ordered the blind man suddenly. "Hear him panting!"

Sydney would not think of letting the blind man go alone, but he could not help himself. Colton seemed to have become the sudden possessor of wings. He leaped out of sight around a clump of pines. Sydney kept doggedly after. He could hear nothing; see nothing in the thick trees. But ahead of him was a murderer, and he was a blind man!

Suddenly Colton's voice rang out: "I'll fire!"

Came a growled, animal-like curse that ended in a sudden, choked-off scream. The fall of a heavy body. Sydney Thames rounded the last tree, and stopped dead in his tracks.

On the ground was a silent figure. The robes had been torn and the trousers showed beneath them. The veil that had covered the face was beside the path. Colton was leaning over the man. He spoke, without looking up:

"Flung the pistol at the sound of his panting. Caught him in back of the head."

He turned the unconscious man over. "The man who murdered John Neilton," said the problemist quietly.

Sydney Thames could not choke back a cry of stupefaction. *The man on the ground was Manager Carl, of the Beaumonde!*

20

CARL'S STORY

Two persons in the great, vaulted room that had been the study of the strange old man whose life it had cost to prove his theory that he had discovered the Great Mystery, were calm and cool. The others had not yet recovered from the shock caused by the denouement when the cars had come to see the blind man guarding the former manager of the Hotel Beaumonde. One of the two cool persons was Thornley Colton. The other was Manager Carl!

"You've got me right," he said, with only a bit of sullenness in his voice. "I did it. I'd have got by with it, too, if I hadn't been damn' fool enough to try and play safe by getting you in."

"You are the only man who has ever deceived me by tone inflection," declared the blind man, and in his tone was the compliment the clever criminal always gets from his detectors.

"Thanks, but you see I had several months to practice in it. I figured that that short-tempered attitude because the police were spoiling my business was the only one to use."

"Tell us how you pulled it!" Police Captain McMann blurted the exclamation, and for the first time since he had seen the murderer the look of almost doglike admiration he had been giving the blind man changed.

"Miss Neilton—" put in Colton sharply.

"I want to hear it all! All!" put in the girl, who sat, white-lipped, with tightly clenched hands, by the side of Silver Sandals. The old woman had her arm around the waist of her niece. One withered old hand held the plump white hand of Ruth. She murmured a low-toned, endearing encouragement, and no one seemed to notice the fact that she talked.

"That's what gave me the first idea." Carl jerked his thumb viciously toward the huddled-up figure of Norman, who was handcuffed to the wrist of the square-jawed detective. "I used to know him when he was a real hotel manager and not quite as crooked as Doyers Street. About six months ago he came and told me he wanted a position as assistant manager. I was going to kick him out, but he told me why he wanted it. He told me of the old man and his—idea. I thought he was kidding. I didn't think there were people like that. But I found that what he said was true. He knew that the old man had money, a million at least, somewhere here. He knew how it was going when he died, too. Been around here a lot, I guess."

He paused to glance inquiringly around. Colton nodded.

Carl continued: "Somehow Norman knew how in the hole I was. He knew that Wall Street had been getting me strong. Bracken was off on his yacht all the time, and I was the whole works around the hotel. In the last year or so I knew it couldn't go on. The boy was taming down, and I knew it wouldn't be very long before he took a hand in the Beaumonde. And I was a couple of hundred thousand into Bracken.

"This was an absolutely safe way to get it back with a lot more. I gave Norman the job, and never let anyone suspect that we were working together. You never knew that?" he asked of Bracken.

"No." The negative came hoarsely. "I offered him five thousand dollars to do his part. He knew the father of my wife. He knew there was nothing but the whim of a strange old man to be respected. I thought he had secured the position on his merits."

"You haven't been around New York much," declared Carl dryly. "Well, Norman knew the whole stunt. We knew the day the old man had figured he was going to die. We knew the minute he wanted to be led into the dining-room. I don't suppose there ever was a murder that was figured out like that. Six months ago I fixed the door to have everything ready. I got the new cabaret act that would make people sit up and take notice and forget everything else that was going on at the minute the old man and the woman were to get into the dining-room. I let two of the waiting captains go, through Norman, of course, so that the one would be too busy to keep near the table all the time. Of course Bracken thought Norman had fixed it for his part. But I did that, too. I was grinning almost when he came to plead for the private dining-room, but I solemnly let him have it.

"The old man came in the afternoon with Bracken. Norman slid them up to the suite without any one getting wise. Bracken left him right away, and Norman told the old man that he'd better wear gloves so that his hands wouldn't get dusty from the unused furniture. He put 'em on without a question. We didn't want any finger prints around. We'd had months to figure that end of it, too. I had it fixed so that I could watch him in the room. We knew that he had the paper with the hiding place of his money or jewels on, because Norman knew that the woman was to get it before she took him to the dining-room.

"He took it out and started to study it. That was the signal for Norman to enter and ask him if he wouldn't like a drink. It was a grim sort of thing, that old man sitting calmly before the table waiting for death that he'd figured was coming at seven o'clock, just because a lot of figures he had gotten from some old stone said so. He'd been sitting there, for hours, without a move. When the time came nearer I suppose he wanted to see that everything was right.

"He took the water and thanked Norman, who was already beginning to show the yellow. There was a good stiff jolt of chloral in it, and if the old man had been at all wise he'd have seen that Norman was shaking like a leaf. I watched him. He took a sip of the water, then suddenly decided that he wanted to write another few words on the funny-looking sheet he had. He took a pen from his pocket, a sort of a fountain stylus, and started to write. Then the chloral got him.

"Norman wanted to steal the thing and get away. But I knew what that meant. It wouldn't be two hours before they got wise. The thing had to be carried out the way he had intended. That made it *safe!* They couldn't come back because they'd made every plan themselves! The next part wasn't very nice. Norman crawled like a whipped dog. But there was a bunch of money in it for me, and on the other side was the jail that waited when Bracken discovered how I'd run his hotel. Bracken wasn't the kind of a man that'd let up.

"Norman knew about the slashes. The woman was supposed to make them when she came up to take him downstairs. I made 'em, and the killing was done just the way you said!" He jerked his head toward the problemist. "We left him there at the tub, so that when the woman came she'd think he did it himself. I knew her well enough, from people that have been to her and also from the story Norman told me; I knew that she wouldn't think it a bit strange that the old man had taken things into his own hands. She didn't either. Her whole mind was on playing the game the way she had promised. And she did it. But a fool play of mine spoiled it. I thought you'd ball the thing up with your blindness, and *that's* what *got* me. Your blindness! I was laughing at you, up my sleeves, until last night when you came to the hotel.

"The thing that we thought was going to get the money for us was a puzzle for fair. We couldn't get the key because we didn't know what it was. I figured on it—I used to be a wonder with puzzles—but could make neither head nor tail of the thing. Then Norman, who was scouting around under cover, found out that a crow was the thing we needed.

"Norman had been taking the waiter that came off Bracken's yacht out every day and getting him full of whisky so that he'd talk. Silver Sandals had him pretty well, but we got a lot of things from him.

"Then you came up and found the words on that table. I began to realize what I was up against then. You found the hair. D'ye know the old man had folded that up in the cryptogram, and it must have fallen out when I took it from his pocket there by the tub? When you found that I didn't know what was going to happen, but I knew it was up to me to get that money quick. Then you found the crow's feather, and said the crow was at your house. I figured the best play in the world to get it. We'd gotten from the waiter where the girl and Silver Sandals were. I called up. The girl wanted to know if it was Phil. I told her yes and gave her the idea for stealing the crow. They were up in the air, too, about the cryptogram. I sent Norman to lay for her. Well"—he laughed grimly—"it was all a game to lead me on, wasn't it? And then I lost the cryptogram."

"I stole it from your pocket," the blind man put in seriously.

"*You* stole it?" Carl jumped in amazement, and McMann pulled him back.

"Yes. Another thing my blindness enabled me to do. As I said before, your voice deceived me utterly. Your pulse was absolutely normal when you shook my hand. I can understand this because there was no excitement such as a sudden crime would have caused. You had prepared for months, and you thought that nothing could go wrong. I didn't connect you with the case at all, first. My blindness told me the true facts of the thing; that it was the curious idea of a curious man. I didn't think it was murder. It was only with the disappearance and finding of Sydney that I realized something was behind it all besides the mere carrying out of a dead man's wish.

"I supposed Norman had been paid to do his part. Then various things pointed inevitably to the fact that even he must have had your cooperation. Yesterday afternoon I spent several hours in my library, figuring out the case. Some of the time was with the telephone to Wall Street friends. Then I found out how deeply you were in the hole. I realized that you were desperate. But I knew that there wasn't a thing to prove your guilt. You could laugh at me while the three persons who had done nothing but carry out the wishes of John Neilton went to prison or the chair. They had all plotted and planned to make possible your murder of Neilton.

"The only thing to do was make you convict yourself. I knew the crow had some mighty-important part. The finding of the feather that the girl had dropped in the house of Silver Sandals when she was excited over getting away proved that there had been a desperate attempt to catch the crow. When the time came I took it to let you know that I had the crow and to make you send someone after it. At the hotel I found the words on the table."

"That told you I had the cryptogram!" put in Carl.

"No." The blind man shook his head. "You told me that."

"I?"

"Yes. You have just said that you tried to figure the thing out. You did that on the desk of your office. It was littered with papers. You didn't bother to push them back, and my wonderfully sensitive fingertips felt the indentations your pencil had made through the paper on which you had written to the loose papers underneath it. My fingers were feeling them as I sat at your desk before we went to the suite upstairs. Of course you had destroyed the paper, but that made no difference to my blindness. It was simple, then, for fingers such as mine to search your pockets at the time I asked you to lead me. I let you know that I was very anxious to have the district attorney locate the missing waiter so that you would have the thing you needed to get me from the house. I pretended to listen in the suite to see if you would try to direct suspicion against Norman, who,

I knew, must have been your pal. You did, very cleverly. Then I waited for the girl. Her story proved the correctness of my theory and told me the thing I could get in no other way—the hiding place of Silver Sandals.

"I understood then that both Silver Sandals and Bracken had come to know that Neilton had been murdered. They kept it from the girl. But Bracken had an idea Norman was guilty, and he was trying to find him. Both realized how their hands were tied, and they were powerless because no jury in the land would believe their story. I knew that Bracken must come to the hiding place early this morning because he would want to report and to see the girl. He couldn't have stayed away longer."

"Then I heard Silver Sandals confess!" Bracken exclaimed.

"Yes." The faintest suspicion of smile hovered over Colton's thin lips. "I intended that to bring you into the room. She thought that you had committed the murder!"

"She thought—" Colton could hear the sudden movement that told him of Bracken's turning to stare at the silent woman whose arm was around the waist of the girl.

"You were supposed to have been with Neilton. Even your wife thought that. Silver Sandals loved Ruth as much as you do. She was willing to sacrifice herself to save you for Ruth."

"I wasn't in the suite except to take him up," said Bracken. "He wouldn't let me stay. But I couldn't go back to the old house. I was afraid to do anything that might get the police on the trail of Ruth. I never"—he hesitated a second, then plunged bravely on—"I never believed that death would come. I expected father would be back at the house when I got through my work. Then when Ruth came—" He shuddered. The thing was uncanny, dreadful.

"Then you confessed," reminded the blind man gently.

"Your object was obvious," interrupted the blind man. "Your love for your wife controlled you, too. You wanted to give Silver Sandals time to solve the cryptogram that meant so much. You were willing to go to jail so that she might carry out the wishes of Ruth Neilton's father. I've said once before that only the girl and the woman were dominated by the dead man; you were dominated by love; love for the girl who believed as her father believed."

"And now"—Carl coolly crossed his legs to be more comfortable—"I hope you have the time of your young lives solving the damn' thing. We tore up the whole place and couldn't get a thing. The fool police left and made it easy for us. But the Egyptian disguises were the safe play, and I thought I was playing safe all through. You'll find the two servants in Cairo, by this time. They never stopped running when the cops came. We had to lay around for an hour or so before we could get in."

"Yes," Colton nodded grimly. "I had them called off to give you your chance. That's why I was so careful to tell you that Bracken would be home today. I knew you'd be desperate to get the thing before he arrived. I knew that when I stole the cryptogram the only thing you could do was to come here and try to find it without. I forced your hand at every turn of the game. But your slipping away from the hotel after calling from your room that you weren't to be disturbed was a master stroke. You could have slipped in again, and every employee of the hotel would have sworn that you never left it. Their jobs depended on it."

"What a fool!" murmured Carl, and there was a bit of awe in his voice. "What a fool!" He touched the back of his head tenderly. "Pity I couldn't have got a jolt like that before," he smiled grimly; then he glanced toward the huddled, twitching Norman, and a disgusted look came to his face. "I'm glad you got him, too."

"What did he have to do with the death of Nelson?" asked Colton sharply.

Norman raised his head. "I didn't have nothing to do with it!" he screamed. "He said he couldn't find the crow, and I left him in a saloon on the water front."

"He's right," growled Carl. "He wouldn't have the nerve to push him in."

"The waiter had the one missing link," Colton said quietly. He reached out his hand toward where the district attorney was sitting. "The feather?" he asked. Silently the attorney extended it. "I think this will find the rubies," the blind man declared.

21

NO HUMAN HAND

Each person in the room leaned forward to see the thing the problemist held in his hand. Even Sydney Thames, who had seen the silver feather before, looked at it with new interest that the blind man's words had brought. Was this simple thing of silver the cause of the murder of the man at the hotel and the death of the waiter whose body had been found in the river? On the faces of those around the big circular room, with its littered papers and torn-up rugs that Norman and Carl had pulled up in their frantic search for the rubies, was depicted the whole gamut of human emotions. Silver Sandals' eyes were on the face of the blind man, trying to read the thoughts behind the words he had spoken. In the eyes of Ruth Neilton was only sorrow. There was no interest in the thing that meant so much to her. She seemed only to see the death and the suffering it had caused. Bracken stared frankly his amazement. The district attorney's face held the same puzzled look that had been there ever since he had visited the morgue. On Carl's face was disgust, and he was looking at the slouched figure of Norman with death in his eyes. Norman looked down at the floor. McMann and the square-jawed detective leaned back comfortably, with their eyes on their prisoners. Their case was ended. The Fee grinned frankly at the effect of the blind man's words, and shifted the perforated box a bit between his knees.

"The cryptogram was as strange as John Neilton himself." The blind man's voice was very low, but the words came clearly. "I puzzled for hours, trying to find a solution by all the known rules of cryptography. It was not until I entered this house that the answer came. That, too, because of my blindness. John Neilton knew that Silver Sandals could solve any puzzle by the short cuts and turns she had learned in the years of working over hieroglyphic fragments. So he made the crow the key. She had the crow. She was supposed to have the cryptogram. But there was the silver feather that he never spoke of. He mentioned it once to the girl. Once he told Silver Sandals the same thing: Only a feather stands between you and the rubies. She had never seen the silver feather. What he intended to do with it so that she would find it when she was clever enough to remember I don't know. But in some way the waiter who was at the house got hold of it. Probably he took it only for its intrinsic value and because it appealed to him. The words of Silver Sandals that Sydney told me when I was bringing him from the hypnotic state were instantly suggestive. Only a feather! Only a feather! She remembered then. While we were waiting she told me the facts. She thought it was a feather of the crow that was meant. Then Miss Neilton dropped the feather in her haste to get away. I found it."

"The solution! What is the solution?" Silver Sandals was standing. Her husky voice made of the words exclamations rather than questions. She seemed to tower over the seated girl like a great black specter in her satin gown that she had worn in the restaurant. She had forgotten everything else in her eagerness to find the solution that the dead man had left her as his legacy. Sydney Thames realized, as did Thornley Colton, that it wasn't the rubies nor the fortune they represented that the woman wanted; it was merely the answer to the puzzle that she had been unable to solve.

"As is the case when a really clever person tries to work an unsolvable puzzle, John Neilton made it simplicity itself. It isn't a cryptogram at all. It's a map!"

"A map?" Silver Sandals took the papyrus sheet, with its strange figures, from the bosom of her dress. She laid it on the table in the center of the room. Colton, too, was on his feet, walking slowly around the room, touching the circular walls with his hollow, slim stick.

"I said before that my blindness figured the thing. I haven't proved it, but I'm certain. My lack of sight has made step-counting automatic and unconscious. I can't help it. I knew every line of the cryptogram because blindness has made the development of my memory an absolute necessity. The minute I walked down the hall in the house here when I had brought back Carl a peculiar thing struck me. There were just as many steps from the front door to a door that led through a short passage as there were crows pictured on the top straight line of the papyrus; eight. I turned to my right. Three steps, and there was another door. A turn to the left two steps, and I was in this room. It is circular. You have known that for years, yet because your eyes had accepted it as a common thing, you would not get the significance as I would, because I have always been compelled to figure my steps and the shape of things. From the door, nine steps around the circumference of the room."

Breathlessly they watched him count off the paces. Then an exclamation of disappointment rose. He was standing at a window. Sydney stood up with the others. The window overlooked the grove of pines. Outside of it a giant maple kept all the sunlight from the room.

"Nothing there!" The words came from Bracken disappointedly.

"Wait!" The command came sharply from the blind man's lips. He flung open the window. "Sit down, all of you!" he ordered. They obeyed meekly. On the window-sill he put the silver feather. Then he stepped back.

"Release the crow, Shrimp."

Colton resumed his own seat. The boy lifted the cover of the box. With a screeched "Caw, caw!" the crow fluttered out. It circled the room slowly. It perched on the green glass shade of the heavy light that was suspended over the table by a silver tube from a raised design of Egyptian scarabs that made a circle in bas-relief as large as the globe itself. They hardly dared breathe as the crow walked around the heavy glass shade, his head cocking from side to side as he regarded them with his wise eyes.

"Poughkeepsie!" it suddenly screamed. "Pough-*kee*-psie!"

It seemed to see the shining silver then. It swooped down, picked it up, and was out of the window.

"Crows are the greatest thieves in the world," Colton said slowly. "They'll steal anything that has a bit of shine, no matter what it is, and hide it in some place they have picked out. That's why the feather was made of silver."

"He's takin' it up in the tree!" The Fee was the only one who had not been impressed into silence and immovability by the weirdness of the thing.

"Goodby feather," laughed Carl jerkily. "It's—Great Lord!"

His exclamation was only part of the startled chorus. The whole heavy shaded light and the design of scarabs had swung downward. Where the heavy raised ceiling decoration had been was a square of silver! On it was painted crows!

"The square design!" cried Bracken.

In the center were pictured, with startling vividness, the under sides of three crows, with their heads together. And to complete the effect, six tiny legs of silver cord dangled.

"Don't move!" Colton's command came in a sibilant whisper. They waited for the last weird move in the whole weird game. Silent they sat around the vaulted room and stared upward at the curious thing in the ceiling that had been covered with the heavy design. The light on its straight silver tube swayed back and forth from the center of the hinged door that had opened.

Like a black shadow the crow flew in through the window. Once more they watched it, not daring to move, lest they disturb it. But the bird paid no attention. It flew ceiling ward. Its bill picked at a dangling leg, pulled it, then darted to another. To Sydney's mind, as he watched, came the picture of the crow as he had seen it in the velvet-hung hall in the old house when its bill had pulled the cord that had opened the curtains to the room where he had lost all recollection of things. From one cord leg to another the crow darted, apparently without rhyme or reason jerking one at one side and then a leg connected with another bird before it flew back. With a sudden scream it flew downward to perch on the table. The square of silver swung slowly downward. Resting on two bars was a heavy box.

"The rubies," Colton said. "The crow was the key that unlocked them. If you will look in the tree you will probably find a clever crossing of fine wires in the hiding place of the crow. The simple dropping of the metal feather on them closed the electric circuit that opened the first door. Clever, yes, but a man who could build the supporting frame that brought John Neilton into the Beaumonde Restaurant was clever enough to do anything." His voice became very solemn. "Anything but to solve the Higher Mystery," he said softly.

Once more Thornley Colton was in the darkened library of the old, brownstone house. Once more his burning eyes were swathed in bandages. In the darkness sat the district attorney and Sydney Thames. It was several hours after the scene at the house in Poughkeepsie. Carl, still cool, was in a cell at police headquarters. Norman was in another. On the streets newsboys were yelling the damp extras with Police Captain McMann's name spread in great type over the first pages. At Poughkeepsie Silver Sandals, the girl, and Bracken were beginning the new life that had opened before them. In an upper room of the

Colton house Shrimp was petting Rameses. It had been given him by the old woman, and was the only fee that had come for the long hours of work and risk and pain.

"There is one thing that puzzled me," declared the district attorney slowly. "How did Bracken get out of the dining-room at the Beaumonde?"

The darkness hid Colton's smile. "He walked out," he said. "It was the simplest thing in the world. He was in a dress suit. He sauntered leisurely into the lobby when he saw that the captain's eyes were not on him after he had apparently hurried away to carry out an order of the girl. He presented a hat check that he had arranged for, got his hat, and sauntered out. Then he got the car he had left near by, and was all ready for the girl."

Sydney put in a question: "But I remember that the eyes of the old man were very bright. I noticed them."

"Silver Sandals told me of that, while we were waiting for the time to come for the dénouement. It was a chemical he had discovered that was used by the ancient Egyptians for their mummies. He had also found another secret, in his years of research, that the old embalmers used. It prevents stiffness of dead joints. The incense odor was another secret, just as was the making of papyrus for all his writing. He wouldn't have so modern a thing as paper."

Silence for a few minutes, then the district attorney put another question: "The woman found the body, with the slashed wrists, beside the tub?"

"Yes, but, as Carl said, she merely thought that her brother had taken the thing into his own hands. It didn't seem strange at all to her. She was a curious woman, strange as the old man himself. And you must remember that there was nothing else she could do. She did not dare mention the fact of it being suicide, because that would mean the police, and explanations of the things they had done. I think that was the real cause of the nervousness that she never let the girl suspect.

"Reading of the coroner's inquest and the police surgeon's testimony showed her that it was murder. But still she dared do nothing. She thought that only Bracken could be guilty. I accused him of the murder to draw her out. Naturally she thought that he had stolen the cryptogram map. But she figured he had only done that to see that it was the girl who got the rubies. She told me those things at the Bracken house. Of course young Bracken was nearly crazy. He was trying to locate Norman as the only one who could be guilty. Then, when he heard the woman as I intended he should, he thought that she had killed her brother because of the long-nursed scheme of revenge."

"Thank God it all came out right!" There was fervent thankfulness in the official's exclamation. "This morning my nerves were raw. I realized what a slip meant to me. Now I'm clear. McMann will see that it doesn't come out. Election's only a little way off."

Once more the darkness hid the smile that curved the thin lips of the blind man. "Isn't it very true," he said quietly, "that we can't go backward? The old man thought he was living in the centuries that were dead and gone. He died as the old Egyptians died. Yet modernism thrust its way in. Wall Street, money, speculation, caused his murder, though he knew nothing of them. You have been worrying over election, ballots, and newspapers. But time halts for no man, nor can it be pushed back a second!" He rose from the desk and dipped the bandages in the solution of boracic acid he had been using since his return to relieve the burning of hours. "Sleep is the only thing that is worrying me. It is only about thirty-seven hours since John Neilton sat at his table; but events have come swiftly. I'm tired, very tired, and my eyes haven't had sleep for fifty hours. I was up early day before yesterday. For eyes that are dead and useless, they cause a lot of trouble—a lot of trouble!" he finished, with grim emphasis.

A fan of Sherlock Holmes?
Then meet Solar Pons

The original fan fiction from the great August Derleth—the Sherlock Holmes of Praed Street.

"the best substitutes for Sherlock Holmes known."
– Vincent Starrett

"an excellent series of adventures in detection in their own right." – *The Chicago Tribune*

For more details and a full list of titles:
visit https://www.hachetteindia.com/home/yellowbacks